NANA'S
ARK

NANA'S
ARK

Michael Borich

THOMAS NELSON PUBLISHERS
Nashville • Camden • New York

Published in Nashville, Tennessee by Thomas Nelson, Inc. and distributed in Canada by Lawson Falle, Ltd., Cambridge, Ontario.

Printed in the United States of America.

Library of Congress Cataloging in Publication Data

Borich, Michael, 1949–
  Nana's ark.

  I. Title.
PS3552.0753N3 1984   813″.54   83–13256
ISBN 0-8407-5855-3

NANA'S
ARK

1

I glanced at my left arm to see what time it was, only to discover that in my hurry, I'd forgotten my watch. Still dazed, I wiped steam off the car window and peered across the gray fields toward our east stand of pines, where the sun soon would be coming up.

I shivered as much from an interior chill as from the coolness of the bleak April morning. The car coughed and then died as it coasted down the hill toward the one-lane bridge at the bottom. I started it again as it rolled across the bridge, all the while noticing how black and swollen the river was. *Too much rain,* I thought, but I didn't dwell on the weather. My thoughts were still spinning from the phone call that had awakened me no more than ten minutes earlier.

Ludy had sounded so far away, as if he were talking to me from the bottom of an old cistern. And I hadn't understood at first why he didn't want me to call his father. He had repeated something over and over, and then I realized he was calling from the Cedar Falls police station. "You've got to come get me," he pleaded. Now, as I stopped at the highway intersection, waiting for a semi to thunder past, I felt an oppressiveness sweep over me like the dark water I had crossed a mile back. I was nervous and scared for Ludy, and sad for David and Sheri, and just sick to my stomach and so tight inside that I wanted to cry. But I knew I couldn't. The engine throbbed regularly, and heat from the dashboard was clearing the window.

I came to the S-curve on the outskirts of town and realized I couldn't remember any of the past seven miles—except the river, which was always mysterious and inexpressibly frightening to me.

A man was unloading a bread truck at the supermarket. Farther down the street, the orange light from the Dairy Sweet was still on, more garish than usual in the early dawn. A paperboy on a bike pulled up next to me at the stoplight. He stared ahead emotionless, then rapped on the window.

"Light's green! You gonna sit through this one, too?"

I glanced up at the light just as it turned orange, and then I stomped on the accelerator. The signal changed as I crossed the intersection, but there was no traffic either way.

I couldn't understand what had happened to Ludy. Why the joyrides, the drinking with his friends, most of them older? I wanted desperately to grasp why. Why, Ludy? What was driving you to run from your parents, from me, from everyone who loved you? What inside you was so alien to all of us? What was pushing you imperceptibly away from our lives? "We don't want to lose you," I heard myself repeating. But I felt he had

7

slipped—dear God, I didn't want to say it—had slipped away from his parents already. Why else would he call me, an old lady he saw once a month, if that?

I drove past the police station, unaware I had done so until I looked to my left and saw the train depot and then the post office across the street. I went around the block and saw a black and white squad car two blocks farther on. The adjoining lot was empty...no, there was a cab driver, smoking in his car and reading a newspaper. I parked in the middle of the lot and turned off the ignition. It was a damp morning, the sky still overcast. I knew there would be no sunrise, at least not for me to see. I tried to think of a reason not to go in. I didn't want to look Ludy in the face. I didn't want his explanation. I didn't want to know why his father wasn't here, and why I was.

Crickets, I realized. No. Cicadas. They sounded like hearts gone rampant in the heavy oaks. All throat. I didn't know where those strange pictures in my head were coming from. I closed my eyes and saw squirming hearts beating, whining on the nearby branches. *I've got to get Ludy,* a part of me said. I felt fragmented, almost like I was barely holding the various parts of myself together—expecting any minute for the disembodied whirrs to draw my heart up among the shadowy limbs.

A policeman came out of the building with a helmet under his arm and a nightstick in his hand. He wore no gun, which for some reason pleased me. I didn't want him to have a gun. Especially not with Ludy somewhere inside, waiting for me. *I wonder if he's as scared as I am,* I thought as I struggled from the car. I wondered if he had slept, or if he had been mistreated, and most of all I wondered what I would say to him.

An enormous wall clock in the hallway ticked ten to seven, nearly the time I usually got up. I tried to take a deep breath, but my chest was constricted. Wrapping my arms around myself, I shivered again.

I wasn't expecting to see a woman behind the desk, especially a slim, dark-haired one in a man's uniform with a gun at her hip.

"Can I help you?" She sat at her desk, filling out papers, and did not look up. I stood watching. "Yes?" She finally looked up. "May I help you?"

"I'm here for my grandson," I said faintly, aware that those were the first words I had spoken that morning.

"And your grandson is?"

"Ludy...Ludy Morgan," I stammered, eyeing her gun. "He's..." I looked back at her face quickly, realizing I had spoken to her gun. "He's here because he called me just a while ago, and I'm not his parent, but he called and said to come get him and I don't even know why..." I broke off, shivering. This time I couldn't stop shaking, not until she offered me a cup of coffee. "No...I...."

"It's okay," she said firmly. "I'll get you a cup." She went into an adjoining room where I could see her pour the coffee.

I had never been in the new station before. It was modern and reminded me of a business office about to open for the day. An older man in a brown suit strode behind me and down the hall. He turned under an arrow marked *Examiner* and vanished down another hall.

"Be careful; it's really steamy!" The officer handed me a Styrofoam cup. The warmth felt good in my hands. She turned momentarily, listening to a police radio in the next room; static mingled with the faint music that came through invisible speakers in the ceiling. The coffee was too hot to sip, so I continued to blow on it.

"Ludy was brought in about 3:00 A.M." She looked directly into my eyes with a familiarity that surprised me. "Since he is so young," she continued with deliberate emphasis, "we called his father." She paused and shuffled a handful of papers.

"Yes, that's my son David. He and Sheri and Ludy's older sister T.J...." I stopped, embarrassed that I was interrupting her.

"His father refused to pick him up."

"Well, yes, that's like David not to come down in the middle of the night. He said the next time Ludy was in trouble he would let him sit and brood for a while."

"Mrs. Morgan." She sighed and stared past me to where a janitor was emptying a wastebasket in the corridor. "Mrs. Morgan, Ludy's father refused to pick him up at all." She leaned against the counter. "We can insist that parents come down for their children, especially when they are as young as Ludy." The word *young* seemed to jump out at me.

"He's just fourteen," I said.

"Mrs. Morgan, we called you because Ludy's father isn't coming to get him, and since you are the next closest relative..."

"What's he done?" I interrupted.

"It's not serious. Just a curfew violation. We could have called you sooner, but Ludy insisted you shouldn't be awakened until later."

"He always has been thoughtful." I tried to smile. "Unfortunately more like his mother than his father."

She watched me speak. I could see the weariness around her eyes. She glanced over at the clock. It was seven. I realized it was time for her to go home.

"I'll go get him." She came around the counter and went down the hall where the man in the brown suit had gone, but she turned in the opposite direction. I sipped my coffee. It was still too hot, and it needed sweetening.

I tried to sort out what David must have been thinking; it was not like Sheri to let him abandon Ludy, and if Leroy were here he would have known what to do...but I was tired. I felt as if I had been up all night. The terror at being awakened by the phone had embedded itself inside me.

Dear God, I wanted to pray, but the internal numbness seemed too vast, like a pre-dawn tundra where, coming out of the shadows far away and so small, was Ludy.

I was surprised at how easily I slid my arm around his shoulder. He didn't resist or draw back as he usually did. His eyes were red, and his brown hair tousled and damp. He didn't acknowledge me but continued to stare, eyes glazed, at the wall beyond my left shoulder.

"Are there some papers for me to sign?" I asked the policewoman.

"No, nothing." I thought I detected tenderness in her voice. "You're free to leave. We've already talked with Ludy. Isn't that right, Ludy?"

He nodded glumly, his eyes still staring toward the wall.

"Well, thank you for the coffee." I handed her the cup and turned away. I felt Ludy stiffen and ease out from under my arm. He loped off ahead of me and was in the car before he said anything.

"Sorry if I woke you up." I fumbled in my purse for the keys, but I had left them in the ignition.

"You should have called me sooner. I don't like you to spend all night in jail. Something could have happened. Why, there's all kinds of people in..." He sighed, as if admonishing my naivete.

"I'm hungry," he moaned.

"I'd better get you home." He shook his head as I started the car.

"I can't go home yet."

"Why not? Your mother must be—"

He shrugged. "Let's go to your house, Nana."

"Well, all right." I wasn't sure I wanted to deal with any problems this morning. "We can call your parents from my house while I fix you breakfast."

He leaned back and closed his eyes. I noticed how large his hands were on his lap, almost too large for the rest of him. *But he's growing again,* I thought. It astonished me how much he had changed in the past year.

The morning traffic was zipping past us now, and I found it hard to concentrate on my driving. I wanted to ask Ludy what his father had said to him, but he was almost asleep. I had the uncomfortable feeling that whatever had triggered David's response was partly my fault. Had I shown favoritism to his older brother Glenn? Perhaps if I had tried a little harder to...to what? I couldn't think straight. I had just missed the county blacktop I should have turned on. It was two more miles to the gravel cutoff. A red pickup, anxious to pull around, honked steadily. Ludy sat up, leaned out the window, and shouted, "Aw, stick it!"

As he glared over his shoulder, I noticed the blue veins on his neck, the thick tendons flexing. The transformation frightened me. Something inside me recognized the anger that was evident in his face, but I couldn't understand what brought it on.

I turned off at our road. Dust rose behind the car and obscured the pickup, which was turning into a farmlane.

"Who's that idiot think he is?" Ludy spat out the window. His legs stiffened against the floorboards. He stared out at a fine mist which was thinning and lifting across the recently furrowed fields.

"Ludy?" He didn't look at me. His neck cords tightened, almost as if someone were stretching them. "What did you do?"

"Nuthin'!"

"You must have done something to spend the night in jail." We slowed down as a tractor and grain wagon jounced ahead of us.

"Why don't you get a radio in this car?" He started slapping his thigh.

I dismissed a desire to question him now and watched the tractor ahead of us. A girl, eleven or twelve, was driving it. She'd look back occasionally and smile at us. Ludy stared out across the fields.

I tried to rehearse what I would say if David answered the phone. Sheri was more open, less complicated. I knew that David loved his children—there was no doubt about that. But he had so many tangles inside him that I couldn't understand. If only Leroy were here; he could handle the situation. Why was David more like me, and Glenn like his father? And Ludy? *I don't know anything!* I wanted to cry out. Tired and upset and anxious for this day to be over, I didn't know why anybody did anything. *And who,* I wanted to say, *can I talk to?*

"The orchard needs cleaning," I murmured as we turned into the lane. Heavy winds during the winter and a rainy spring had left fallen branches rotting under the dozen trees that bordered our property on the west.

"What's that?" Ludy asked absently.

"Molly had a new litter of kittens," I said, easing the car into the garage.

"That was three months ago!" Ludy pulled at the door handle.

"Has it been that long?" I knew it had. Time in the last ten months had seemed to stand still and then leapfrog with an irregularity I couldn't control. And the farm sagged with a weariness that was visible everywhere. The barnyard smelled of decay; the iron pump handle hadn't been cranked in months; cobwebs overran the house, and the few chickens that scuttled around the back coop went days without feed. The fence would need new paint this year. Fortunately, Glenn would drive the twelve miles over from his own farm and plant the bean field; the corn field would fallow this year.

Ludy was ricocheting stones off the ancient windmill, trying to get the blade to turn.

"It's too rusted." I struggled up the back stoop. "Come on in. I've got some fresh eggs." Ludy threw at one of the wild cats that was edging along the barn. It snarled, leaped into the air, and ran off behind the woodlot.

As I came into the kitchen, I heard my alarm ringing in the bedroom. Suddenly tired, I went upstairs to switch it off. It was strange to see my bed unmade and my dressing gown strewn over a chair. The alarm had been ringing for nearly an hour. I sat on the edge of the bed and looked around the room. Pictures, letters, crocheted doilies, throw pillows, a bowling plaque, an abstract watercolor, Leroy's handmade secretary. Over thirty years of possessions, so lifeless and dreary I wanted to throw everything out. I wished a fire would engulf the house so I wouldn't have to bother getting rid of anything. I didn't have the energy to fight. Whatever there was in that room seemed faraway to me. I didn't know what to do. I closed my eyes and waited for something to carry my thoughts off so I wouldn't need to think at all.

"How 'bout those eggs?" Ludy called. "I'm starved!"

After five rings I thought no one was home. And then Sheri's sleepy voice was on the other end of the phone.

"Sheri? This is Nana." I tried to sound cheerful.

"Nana?"

"Ludy is here with me, so don't worry." There was a long silence. "I just picked him up, and now I'm giving him breakfast."

"Thanks, Mom. I just called the police station, and they told me you had." I waited for her to continue, but she was silent.

"He's fine, Sheri. He told me he wasn't in serious trouble. They talked with him and let him go."

"I know," she sniffled.

"Is David there?" I tried to speak with authority, but my speech was raspy and slurred. My right eye began to twitch. I tried to sip a cup of coffee as Sheri related that neither she nor David had slept much, and that David was driving T.J. in to school.

"Why is he so stubborn? Ludy's just a little boy."

I heard Ludy stop eating in the kitchen.

"I don't know, Mom. Who can understand David? He blew up. He jumped out of bed like a madman. You know he worries about those kids like crazy, even more so now that they're in high school."

The back door opened, then slammed. I tried to listen to Sheri, but I felt faint and my eyes ached.

"He waited around home until eight o'clock just to make sure that you had picked up Ludy. He was ready to go himself. I know he regrets what he said, but you're right, Mom, he's so rock-headed stubborn." She sounded more upset as she kept talking and trying to catch her breath.

I stared out the front window. The fields beyond the road were chocolate brown, and in the distance a thin slat of blue was opening above the trees. Sheri was explaining how Ludy and David didn't really talk to each other any more, just yelled, when I recognized the green Plymouth turning up toward the house.

"Sheri, I've got to go now," I broke in. "David's here."

"Okay." She sighed, then hung up.

I didn't go out back right away. I knew that David would probably want to talk with Ludy alone, so I puttered around the kitchen, put a slice of bread in the toaster, and poured another cup of coffee. Finally, I ambled to the door. I expected to find Ludy and his father talking, but only David sat on the steps, staring into his hands.

"David?" My voice sounded strained. He didn't move when I put my hand on his shoulder to steady myself and came down next to him. "Where's Ludy?"

He looked up, startled. "I thought here with you?"

"Well, he was. I just gave him breakfast. He left half of it on his plate."

He gazed across the barnyard to the pasture. "He doesn't want to see me, then. I don't blame him."

"Oh, no, he probably went for a walk in the timbers. I think he said he was going when I was on the phone with Sheri." David stared at me but didn't speak. Finally, after picking at a blister on his palm, he began "You know, Mom..."

I didn't want to be there. I wanted to be alone very much just then. So many other mornings I had watched from where I stood, as David, much younger, a boy even, sat where he was now, and laced up his muddy work boots. He had become too serious. I looked away so I wouldn't have to watch the pain wrinkle up his face.

"Mom, I hurt inside so much because of that kid. You know what I mean?" He shook his head. A chicken hawk slow looped a couple hundred feet above the silo. "You must have felt the same way about me and Glenn. You and Dad must have made mistakes too, didn't you?"

I wanted to watch that hawk; in fact, I felt I wanted to be up with him making lazy scrawls against the morning sky. He looked so calm and detached, as if he had all the time to soar up there and look down and circle and watch.

"Of course we did! I can't count all the sleepless nights . . ."

"But dammit, what can I do?" He stood up impatiently. "Mom, sometimes I'm afraid I'm gonna kill that kid. I want to put my fist through a wall. You just don't know. . ." He ran his hand through his hair and then raked his cheeks.

"I know. Really I do. But David, you know deep down that he's a good kid. He is. You know that."

He put his hands in his pockets and looked around the yard. "Mom . . . Mom, you want me to come and help out here?" The tone of his voice had changed; he sounded tired. "I know I haven't been much help since Dad died." He walked forward a few paces to survey the house. "Everything needs paint. Look at those eaves. They're barely hanging on, Mom. The fence has to be fixed."

"Glenn comes over twice a week." I knew I was unconvincing. Molly, my half-wild cat, had wandered around the chicken coop trailing two kittens. The kittens jumped her from behind, wrestling her over, and began to suck her worn nipples. The kittens were nearly as large as their mother.

"Maybe he's in the barn," David said to himself. I followed him across to the barn door, which hung askew. Ludy was not in the barn. A nest of wrens stirred uneasily as we crossed into the shadowy dampness. The scents of rotting hay, dust, and old engine oil were nearly overpowering. I realized I hadn't been out here since last August. "That old boat. What are you going to do with it, Mom?"

He walked over and wiped a palmful of dust off the green fiberglass hull of a huge sailboat that sat propped and unfinished across ten milking stalls. Trying to laugh, he gurgled deep in his throat and said, "How long did Dad work on that? A couple of years, wasn't it? You think he really would have gone anywhere in it?"

14

"He said we would." I marveled at what my husband's hands had built. It was too bad I had not seen his full vision; at least I would have enjoyed the neighbors' faces when he really did launch it and sail away. But not in the middle of Iowa.

"Would you really have sailed around the world when he retired, or was this just a hobby for him?" He climbed around to the back side. "There's sure a lot of work in this, but it's got to go. How about the tractor and combine?" I followed him through a narrow doorway into the tool shop and on to the equipment shed.

"Glenn thinks he can get it running."

"It's ancient, Mom. Like everything else around here." He started to pull himself up to the seat and then glanced over his shoulder at me. "I didn't mean everything."

My face was flushed. Old memories rushed back over me as he fiddled with the knobs. The air was so musty and close that my head spun. I leaned against the lid of an old cream separator and brushed my hair off my forehead.

"Hey, Mom?" David smiled, oddly transformed as he tested the steering wheel. "Why don't we get Ludy to work on this! He's good with motors, and it will give him something to do. Sure, he'll do it for you; I know he will."

He was pleased with his idea. The gear shift broke off in his hand as he yanked it sideways. "Oh, brother. I've got to get home," he said glumly. "Maybe we should junk it all," he suggested as he climbed stiffly off the tractor. "You think so, Mom? Maybe we should get you a house in town. Haul out this old stuff and that crazy boat and fix the place up enough ..."

"No!" I said it louder than I had intended. He sighed and nodded. I stood in the doorway of the barn as he trudged to his car. Even though he was only thirty-eight, he suddenly looked too old. Once, I remembered, it had been so easy to cry.

2

As I expected, Ludy had been watching from the timbers until he saw his father drive away. He sauntered back up to me innocently, stopping every few feet to pick up a stone to heave at the windmill.

"Just missed your father."

"Oh yeah?" He attempted to be coy, but his eyes shifted awkwardly away.

"He came for you."

"What for?" He refused to look at me.

"He was worried about you."

"Doubt it."

I tried to change my tactics. "Ludy, you're old enough to be addressed like an adult." He rubbed the back of his neck. I wasn't sure what I wanted to say, but I felt I had to keep pecking away at his resistance. "I want you to know that you're not the only one who makes mistakes. Your father feels bad about last night."

"Doubt it." He swallowed hard.

"He and your mother both need you." My voice cracked. I was finding it difficult to hide whatever it was that tightened my throat. "They love you."

"I don't need 'em!" He threw hard at the rusted blades. A rock pinged and sent sparks off.

"It's hard to forgive people, especially when you hurt inside."

"I don't need 'em," he yelled as he threw wildly into the air. He saw the hawk that coasted above the yard and threw at it, even though the rock fell far short.

"But Ludy, all you've got is your family . . . and T.J. and listen, Ludy, will you just stop and listen for a minute . . . "

He snorted and shook his head, his face contorted in anger as he backed away. "Just . . . just . . . shut up, Nana!" He turned and ran toward the road. I heard him crying.

"I'll drive you to school," I called. It was a stupid thing to say. He didn't hear me anyway, or pretended not to. By the time I went inside and returned with the car keys, he had disappeared. There was no sense going after him. He would probably follow the river back into Janesville. There was a bridle path that followed the Greenbelt for three miles, and when he came to the riding stables, he would cross the railroad trestle and be at the edge of town. It was a half-hour walk that he made occasionally when he came out to scavenge the orchard or fish in one of the ponds.

I hobbled back into the kitchen. My legs and lower back ached. I still hadn't gotten winter out of my bones. The coffee was cold, so I brewed a new pot. As I sat at the table and traced my finger through grains of sugar on the worn Formica, I tried to reconstruct the morning's events. I wasn't used to dealing with life on such a direct level. The water began to percolate. It was a comforting sound, like rain dripping from the eave spouts at night. It happened without ceremony, or was a ceremony unto itself. It was soothing. I wanted to lie back and forget and just listen.

But I couldn't relax. For how many years had I longed to be by myself, to have time to do what I wanted to do—to read, sew, visit people when I wanted to, even travel—and now all I could think about was, *What shall I do next? How can I fill this hour with something?* Funny, how there was always work to do and never any spare time, how I would bustle from sunup to late at night, and always at the back of my mind was the idea that someday my time would be *my* time. And now, I'd give it all away for a nickel. A wooden one at that.

I got up to make a piece of toast. The bread was green with mold. I tried to scrape it off, but the bread tasted yeasty.

"Oh, God," I whined aloud. My voice sounded unfamiliar. *Let's not play any games today,* I said silently. *Let's not make any excuses, let's not feel sorry or mopey, let's clean up this place, let's. . . let's. . .* Why, why, I wondered, was I talking as if there were someone answering. Was I inventing conversations? Who was I including? "Oh, God," I breathed quietly. I gazed out the kitchen window.

Ev Hipman, the neighbor whose house was just visible through the poplars, was disking his field. A reddish glint spun through the stubbled earth. He had on his familiar faded Harvester cap; even though he was too far away, I could visualize the furrowed cheeks and forehead. What a loyal neighbor he had been, and a good friend of Leroy's. All the years they bowled together, every Thursday, and they never improved.

With stoic regularity, he would come by to help load cattle going to market; he would drive over after wind storms to see if the place had survived and if he could lend a hand; he would ask about the boys, would offer to fix a stubborn piece of machinery, and would always, no matter what the weather, arrive at six-fifteen sharp on Thursday evenings, his hair wetted back and his red cheeks always chapped. Invariably, Leroy would greet him with the same mischievous smile, point to Ev's hair, and chuckle, "Why don't you rub some of that grease on your ball for luck." Then Ev would wink at me.

I surveyed the kitchen. The room was disgustingly familiar. Like the bedroom, everything was old and tacky. There was nothing new; the green wallpaper was yellowed; it curled up from the door frames. The wall clock, a painted millpond scene, was spotted with grease. The stove was crusted black. The refrigerator sagged in the corner. A ripped and spotted curtain covered the pantry, and I knew some of the jars on the shelves, jars I had stuffed with tomatoes and cucumbers and beets, were possibly ten years old. They would never be eaten. It was difficult to tell what color the tile floor had originally been. There was the burned spot where someone had knocked the iron over. I wanted to hate everything that I saw in the room, but I felt only tired and unable to muster any emotion whatever.

It had been easy not to dwell on the past when I kept busy. But what use was keeping busy when there was nothing to do?

"Somebody's got to invent us a thirty-hour day," Leroy used to moan.

I sat down at the table and stared at my coffee, the rising steam warm on my face.

"I'm fifty-eight years old," I whispered to my wavering reflection. "I've got two hundred and forty acres of the best land in the country. I've got buildings that house machinery, animals, corn, beans, and grains. I've got a pump that draws up the cleanest, coldest water I've ever tasted. I've got this house. I've got a car that needs new tires and an exhaust system. I've got two sons, two daughters-in-law, five grandchildren, and friends I see regularly. If that's not enough to keep me busy..." I didn't know where my conversation was going. Had I already come to the perimeters of my life?

"What more is there?" I asked myself. "What more do I want?" I poured a dash of milk into my coffee. The reflection vanished into a murky brown. I wasn't going to think about being alone. I had enough to do. "Sure," I mumbled. "Sure, lots of things to do."

I couldn't resist looking at the clock. Ludy was probably home. But then, he wouldn't go right home. I thought of calling Sheri back, since I had hung up so abruptly. No. I rubbed my arms. My skin was dry and puffy. I wanted to begin something, find a reason to get up and move out of my introspection. I knew I could successfully avoid looking back at the clock to see how far the hands had moved, if I could just think of something to do. Something I wanted to do.

Maybe I would call Glenn and Evelyn. I could drive into town and pick up some groceries. Nobody that I could think of was in the hospital. The ground was too muddy to walk about. Besides, my lower back was nagging again. I would lie on the sofa with the heating pad tucked under me and try to watch television. The mailman would be by shortly. I might walk out to the road and meet him, invite him in for coffee. Was it against regulations to do that? I didn't know. I sipped from my cup. The coffee had turned cold. Out of the corner of my eye, the clock's hands imperceptibly moved.

I heard a car pull into the driveway, stop under the red oak, and then a car door open and slam. I struggled to my feet and went to the back door. I recognized Pastor Bill Shaffer's coconut-brown sedan, but Pastor had gone around to the front door. He rapped twice. I hurried to the front, smoothing down my hair. It needed to be washed. Bill was smiling genially on the porch. His prematurely white hair seemed even whiter than usual, and his eyebrows almost blond. With my eyes closed I could have recognized that cheerful voice.

"Well, Dorothy Morgan. You're looking splendid on this lovely spring morning." He reached out and took my hand. I felt lumpy and unmade. There was a stale taste in my mouth, so I held my lips together when I spoke.

"Oh, Pastor, you've chosen the wrong day for a visit."

His eyes widened. Even when he was serious, an unmistakable twinkle lit the corners of those gray-blue eyes.

"Whatever's the matter? I didn't drag you out of bed early, did I?"

I met his eyes and couldn't help but smile. There was an infectious gaiety about him. *All pastors should be like him,* I thought. I had seen Pastor Bill every Sunday for nearly ten years, and never had I known him to be anything but full of zest. I envied him.

"Oh, Pastor." My shoulders slumped; I felt old and tired, and reluctant to face anyone who was so enthusiastic about anything at all.

"Now, Dorothy, try as you might, you're not going to make yourself less pretty than you are." I drew back a half step into the doorway shadow. I wasn't prepared for his persistence. "And even if you weren't expecting me, you wouldn't let me go back to a cold, empty church without a cup of coffee, would you? Besides, I've something to ask."

I stepped away from the door and nodded, attempting to smooth out the wrinkles in my housedress as he entered. Detecting an odor about my person, I was sure I'd worn the dress for at least four or five days in a row.

"And now tell me," he said as he settled into the brown rocker, "what's the matter with today?"

I was conscious of the intensity in his eyes as he waited for me to explain. My hands suddenly felt awkward dangling at my side. I tried to remember how long since I had washed my hair. He watched me with patient interest.

"I..." I felt too vulnerable standing in front of him. I needed to sit down, or find something to put in my hands. "Let me get you some coffee." I stared down at the floor and realized I was averting my eyes, that I couldn't look at him.

He sensed my distress. "That would be fine, Dorothy. Can I help you?"

"No, no, I've got some brewing." I knew the coffee was cold. "I'll be just a minute. You sit and I'll ... I'll be right back. Cream and sugar?" I asked over my shoulder as I went into the kitchen.

"Thank you, yes." His melodious speech—tinged slightly from his seminary days in Scotland—often sent me staring off dumbly into space, captivated by his words. He enriched ordinary words, and sometimes in church I would close my eyes and be swayed by that voice. I knew he was almost as old as myself, maybe older, but that abundant vitality made him seem so youthful.

Like most women in my church, I was charmed by his intelligence. He never spoke condescendingly, but always made me think things that surprised even me. And he was sensitive. His soothing voice made me feel like he understood everything about me. I had never really known how unique Pastor was until Leroy died.

The morning I rushed to the hospital and was told about the heart attack, Pastor Bill arrived and took my hand in the waiting room and looked at me with tear-filled eyes. He knew Leroy was gone. As he slowly spoke the words I already expected, I was puzzled that he should be so moved. At the time, I resented his emotion, because I was unable to cry as freely as he.

Just a year earlier his wife had been killed in an accident with a speeding semi. Bill's two married daughters came for the funeral, and as I went through the receiving line at the funeral home, I had felt awkward, almost embarrassed at their grief. It wasn't right for me to have felt that way, but as Pastor sat with me in the hospital waiting for Leroy's body to be taken from the emergency room, I felt a bond grow between us. His eyes spoke to me, and they were comfort enough.

Then every couple months after, he would drive out to the farm and fill me with regret that I wasn't able to be as cheerful, as resilient as he.

As I carried the serving tray with china cups and saucers into the living room, I realized that Pastor's presence had changed me considerably. In just the few minutes since he had come, I felt like I was rising out of myself. I managed an unforced smile as I handed him a cup.

"You've left me sitting lonely and wondering about your reluctance to my visit for almost five minutes," he said. I sat across from on the sofa. He was not very successful in holding back his smile.

"I'm sorry, Pastor." I settled back. "It's been one of those days when I should have stayed in bed."

"Didn't see a groundhog's shadow, did you?"

"No," I said and smiled again. He was drawing me out of a familiar, sticky murk. I wanted to say something impulsive and girlish.

"Aha!" He stroked his chin. "I'll bet it's your birthday?"

I shook my head. "Actually, Ludy has been in some trouble."

"No. What kind?"

I told him about the early morning phone call, and about David's refusing to pick up Ludy. Pastor Bill leaned forward, his head tilted slightly as he listened. I recounted David's coming to look for Ludy to apologize, and then Ludy's running off alone. I wasn't sure I should continue, but I needed to unburden my thoughts, so I told about the strain that had developed in my son's family. I was concerned, but I had the funny sensation that I was an Alice who had tumbled into a rabbit hole. The farther I fell, the less afraid I became, as if the bottom were no more real than the words I was speaking. I felt devoid of emotion again. I wanted to feel fear and sorrow, but I was falling inside.

Pastor crossed his legs and sat back when I finished. "Hmmm." He wrinkled his eyebrows.

"I don't know what to do, Pastor."

"Hmmm," he mused down into his coffee. "Well, I don't know. What do you think?"

I hadn't expected that. I wanted answers from him. I wanted to get out of the way of something I couldn't understand. But then, I was ambivalent too, as if I knew the answers all along, but somehow was unable to define what I felt.

"I . . . I think somebody should sit down and talk with them."

"I agree," he quickly responded.

"Then you'll visit them?"

"No."

I knew something was coming. The coldness of the tundra rose in my stomach.

"You will!" he said.

Not, "you should," or maybe "you ought to," but "You will!" It was too definite. I spoke uncomfortably to the floor again.

"I want to help, but I don't think I can." Yet I knew he was right. I was not even surprised. I sensed all along he would shake my stick-house of self-pity. It was for that reason I didn't want to let him in. I looked up. He was appraising me.

"You've got a special family, Dorothy. You're a special woman." My face flushed. Something inside me wanted to deny the feelings Pastor Bill awakened, but I was responding to his gentleness. He kept on speaking softly, his voice penetrating. I looked out the window past him as he spoke. The sun had burned the haze. The sky now was crystalline through the oak branches. A hummingbird bumped the window.

I couldn't concentrate on what he was saying. His presence was warmth enough. I wanted to do something frivolous again. I felt giddy, as if my head were revolving about the room. I watched his mouth, the moist upturn of his lip. He was speaking through me, lifting me like I was a feather. I didn't know what was happening, but the energy kept flowing from him, and it washed over me until I wanted to jump up and dance him around the room.

Then he was on his feet and I was nodding, yes, yes, with a silly grin on my face, and he was going out the door, a scent of cloves, of new hay, the sun like warm butter on the grass and a breeze that ruffled my dress against my legs.

"Oh, Pastor?" I thought of something.

He paused as he bent to get in his car. "What is it?"

"When you first came . . ."

He nodded, his eyes translucent.

". . . you wanted to ask me something?"

An indelible smile flowed across his entire face.

"You already answered it." He sat down behind the steering wheel and started the engine. I bent in the passenger window, puzzled.

"I did?"

"Sheri called me this morning." He winked. "You already answered my question. Have a beautiful day, Dorothy."

I watched him back out the drive. The air was not as warm as I thought. I was chilled. The wind picked up and clouds were charging across the sky. And inside, the ground fell away from under me again.

3

I awoke screaming.

Something appeared to be in the room with me. I was certain that a wing or a hand had brushed lightly over my face. I switched on the light next to my bed. The wind was fluttering a loose windowpane, and just visible beyond the red oak was the moon, cold and implacable. But the room was empty. I sat up in bed and listened intently to my shallow breathing. My closet door was open part-way; the clothes hung dark and formless. Old newspapers were strewn about the room. I peered at the clock, and even though I could see the luminous dial clearly, my mind would not focus on the meaning of the numbers. It was 2:20.

A shapeless fear made me draw the covers around my chin. I tried to reconstruct what I had been dreaming. For the past several months, the dreams had become increasingly vivid, and this wasn't the first time I had awakened unexpectedly with a vague sensation of fear. The room was quiet. Only the wind stirred, trying to enter. *What had it been,* I thought to myself, *that was troubling me?*

I remembered a room, very much like something I recalled from childhood. I used to spend summers visiting my grandparents in Missouri on their subsistence farm outside of Joplin. There had been a root cellar that was built into a small hill behind the house. The cellar had no windows, but the door boards were broken off in places, and thin beams of light illuminated the wall shelves stacked with preserve jars and label-less cans and cider bottles filmed with dust.

When the days would get unbearably hot, I would sneak barefoot into the root cellar and squish the cool, moist dirt between my toes. I was only seven or eight at the time. The cellar was rank with rotting vegetables and spiders; I remember spiders would sometimes drop silently onto my shoulders as they webbed the various jars.

But the room in my dream was empty—there were no jars on the wall; there were no spiders; no mice scurrying in the dirt. Still I felt strangely alarmed that I was waiting for someone to enter the room. And I was frightened. I felt like a little girl, but I remembered looking down at my hands, and they were wrinkled and caked with mud; there was dirt under my fingernails, as if I had been digging at the walls or the floor. Then I remembered hearing a sound that appeared to come from just behind me and slightly above my head. I turned and reached out wildly, but there was nothing.

I was sure someone was in the room with me. I tried to hold my breath to see if I could hear anything, but I was too frightened. I rushed against the wall, scrambling to find the door. As I frantically searched, I felt something brush over me. By then, I was sitting up in bed staring around the room where I had spent each night of the last thirty-two years.

I wanted to get up, but the air was cold. I did reach out of bed to close the closet door, and then slid back down under the covers. But I couldn't relax. I tried to syncopate my breathing with the relentless ticking of the clock, until I became short of breath. I tried to remember what day it was, or what day it was becoming.

The moon through the oak tree, I realized, was not the moon at all, but the yard light, which I had left on. I always left it on all night. From the bathroom next door, I could hear the pipes ticking, and the drip, drip of the faucet.

I took a deep breath and exhaled. *What did my dreams mean?* I wondered. If I could have remained awake and followed my dream along the darkened corridors it had taken me, would it have meant anything? There was an ache in my hipbone, deep down. I tried to rub it, but the center of my bone felt frozen. Had I locked the back door? I reached over and switched on the table light.

The sudden brightness of the room only confirmed my fear. The hallway seemed even darker. I swung my feet onto the floor, trying to feel for my slippers. I could only find one. I wriggled my foot into it, hopped across the cold floorboards, and picked up my robe from where it was flung across a chair. When I had tightened the sash, I knelt down to look under the bed. My other slipper was not there. I looked in the closet: a tangle of dirty clothes lay in the center. A dozen odd shoes, some nearly twenty years old, were tossed haphazardly about the floor. I was upset to find one of Leroy's old dress shoes mixed in with mine. All his other clothes had long ago been boxed and given away, and as I held the lone reminder of his wardrobe which had once filled half the closet, I wanted to throw the shoe out the window.

I don't know why I felt so strongly that I had to get rid of the shoe, but when I went over to the window and tried to unfasten the latch, I realized that the storm windows were still on. I would have to dismantle the entire window. At a loss, I dropped the shoe into an overflowing wastebasket. My slipper, however, was not to be found.

In the yard below, the only movement was the tree shadows flickering across the lawn. I watched the yard light swing in the wind. It was too early in the year for nightbugs, although I thought I heard frogs out in the pasture.

On impulse, I crossed the hall to David's old room, reached my hand in to where I knew the switch would be, and flipped on the light. I knew what would be in the room, but had forgotten how it would all appear. My shadow on the floor made me look scrunched and deformed. The walls were violet—the color we had let David choose when he was a teenager. He had painted the room himself; drops of paint were evident on the wood stripping.

David had also put in his own shelves. Dozens of dusty books were stacked irregularly along the wall, and peacock feathers—at least twenty of them—were tacked above the shelves so that the immediate impression was a swirl of color and numerous black eyes amid the design of feathers. His old mattress and frame were upended against one wall, and against another wall was a paint-speckled easel. From the doorway, a hand appeared to be detached and frozen to one leg of the easel. As I came closer, I saw that the hand was a large wolfspider, which backed up at my approach and then scurried off into a stack of magazines.

From David's window, much smaller than mine, I could see only the roof of the tool shed and a dim reflection of the yard light. I suddenly felt faint. There was a catch in my side, and my slipperless foot was cold. I went into the bathroom and sat on the toilet cover. The faucet dripped, I thought, in precision with the clock. I took an aspirin bottle from the medicine cabinet, shook out two tablets, changed my mind, and dropped one back into the bottle. It was almost empty. I stared into it, trying to pick out among the six tablets, the one I had just returned. Would it feel rejected? It was a silly thought. I wondered what the pain in my side might be. It was too high for appendicitis. I was certain it wasn't my heart.

I tried to recall what I had eaten for dinner, but couldn't. Most of the time anymore, I paid no attention to what I ate. The food may have been bland, or too hot, or even uncooked, but ten minutes after I had eaten, I couldn't have told anyone what it had been. I tried to picture what the food looked like as it went down my throat. I wanted to peel back the skin and watch the organs spring into action, the tunnels the food dropped through, and the fluids which were put into operation. Lately, I had worried that my colon and intestines, intricate nests of coils and tubes, had become clogged. I went for days, possibly weeks, without the least desire to relieve myself.

And all the while I lost weight; my sides sunk in, as if the food inexplicably evaporated. I remembered a story a friend had told about someone's daughter-in-law eating and eating voraciously and continuing to lose weight. Finally the doctor diagnosed tapeworms. I massaged my side and tried to dismiss the thought of worms twisted in a snarl. In the flowerbeds at night, the kids used to pull slimy curls of worms that were mating. *Is that how worms reproduce?* I didn't know.

I was disturbed that my thoughts were running off in uncontrollable directions. I wanted to go back to bed. I went into my room, left my robe on, and climbed under the covers. The wind came from the west; miles and miles of open prairies and lonely distances through the night had brought it to batter against my house. *Who cares,* I said to myself. *Who cares?*

I stretched back on the pillow. *Leave the light on,* I thought. I closed my eyes and tossed fitfully for hours, imagining huge, hairy hands dropping out of trees, and somewhere in the distance, the wind moaning like a telephone. And then I jarred awake and did hear the telephone ringing downstairs.

I jumped out of bed, amazed at how quickly I could hurry downstairs. Just as I reached the phone, it stopped ringing. I picked up the receiver and, in my ear, the empty hum of the line left me guessing, *Who have I missed?* The hum was final and irrevocable. I hated it.

A half-full coffee cup sat on the kitchen counter. I grabbed it and threw it across the room. The cup shattered against the wall, pieces scattering everywhere. A brown trickle dripped down the plaster. Now fully awake, I was startled at my sudden action. I had felt no surge of anger, no satisfaction. The fury came from somewhere inside me I didn't recognize. I hadn't been a violent person; at least, I was sure that destroying the cup had little to do with the telephone, or the cup itself, or even the general dishevelment of the house. I felt no remorse, either. It was just an old cup, stained beyond any washing. The coffee in it may have been a day, perhaps two days old.

I stared out the window. The glass was watermarked and smudged. I wondered what it would be like to put my fist through it. I didn't care about cutting my hand, but it would have been too much trouble to repair the window.

Out in the south field I saw our battered tractor turning in wide circles. My breath caught in my chest for an instant because, from the angle of the morning sun, it looked like Leroy driving.

The driver hunched forward, his right arm constantly shifting gears. His head would swivel periodically to watch the ground behind him, and at each pass the tractor swung so the driver's face was visible. He looked over to the house. I realized it was Glenn.

More and more he was beginning to look like his father—lanky, with a brown thatch of hair that constantly flopped onto his forehead. His chin was solid and pointed, and from where I stood, it was the only part of his face not shadowed by his workcap. I hadn't known he was coming to work the field; or if he had told me, I hadn't remembered.

The clock whirred softly; it was nearly eleven. I walked to the back door and saw Glenn's pickup parked next to the barn. How long had he been here? I should have heard him come, especially when he started up the tractor. An acrid smell was nearly overpowering on the closed porch. Four plastic garbage bags were stacked under my plant table. I propped open the door with a brick to let in the crisp air. In my robe and nightgown, barefoot on the cold cement of the steps, I felt unwashed and as stale as the garbage that had sat untended for weeks.

A car came up the driveway. I rushed back into the kitchen and glanced through the window. It was Evelyn. She parked next to the pick-up, and without waiting for her to get out of the car, I hobbled upstairs to get dressed. As I pawed through my drawer for clean underwear and for a brassiere that wasn't frayed or torn, as were most of them, I called to Evelyn. "Be down in a minute!"

"Okay, Mom. I just got here." Her voice, as usual, sounded enthusiastic, and I doubted if I had ever heard or seen her harried. Even in raising three boys, all of them teenagers now except for Jay, she always seemed to possess a wealth of patience and energy.

The snarls were so stubborn as I attempted to brush my hair, that I just patted the springs of hair down where I could. I didn't feel like scrubbing my teeth, even though they were gummy and yellow, but I took a dab of toothpaste on my finger and wiped it off on my tongue. As I came down into the kitchen, Evelyn, her back to me, was at the sink washing dishes.

"You don't have to do those, Evelyn."

"No bother." She didn't turn around. I came over next to her and managed a smile.

"I was just straightening upstairs."

"Uh huh." She looked at me solemnly. "It's a pretty big job, isn't it?"

"Not at all." I hadn't meant to sound defensive. I took up a dish towel and dried the cups in the sink. "It's really no trouble with everyone gone. You know what it's like to have children that always ... well, you know what it's like."

"I know," she nodded sympathetically. I sensed a sadness about her.

"Why don't I close the porch door? It's getting chilly in here."

Her eyes squinched up in a smile. "I wondered what you were doing with it open."

I went out and kicked the brick away from the door. Glenn was farther down the fence line. He had plowed almost half the field.

"Well, I haven't gotten around to putting on the screens yet. Some of the storms are even nailed shut," I said as I came back into the kitchen. "Want some coffee?"

"Oh, I was making some fresh," she said. "It's probably ready now; you want a cup?"

I thought about the cup I had broken earlier. Some of the pieces were visible under the table and along the wall where the largest chunks had fallen. A long streak of coffee had dried on the wall. I didn't say anything about it. When she finished with the dishes, she wiped her hands, took a small bottle from her purse, and sat next to me at the table, rubbing on a lotion that smelled faintly of roses.

"Have you talked to Sheri about yesterday?"

"No." Her eyes widened. "What's happened now?"

"Surely you know about Ludy?"

"You mean down at the station in Cedar Falls?"

"Then you did talk to her."

"That was on Monday, Mom." She pursed her lips. I tried to calculate what today was, but a mild panic had risen inside me. *What was today?* I wondered what was happening to me.

"That's right, Monday, and today is . . ." I didn't know.

She frowned. "Wednesday, Mom. Today is Wednesday."

"Sure, Wednesday." I tried to laugh, but only a weak grunt slipped out. "I guess everything upset me more than I thought." I smiled, but she could tell I was troubled. She leaned forward, her mouth slightly open, watching my eyes shift around the room.

"Sheri's really sick about what happened, too," she said with deliberate emphasis.

"I know. It all seems so unnecessary. He's really such a good kid."

"Maybe some of that rebelliousness needs to be skimmed off."

"Do you think so?" I was surprised by what she said.

"I didn't mean it like that, Mom, but you know how Ludy is."

I waited for her to finish.

"And of course, David sometimes . . . well, you know, Mom."

I didn't know what she meant, but I was anxious to keep talking to fill up the silences. Even Evelyn, who normally talked nonstop, had become subdued.

"I talked to both of them yesterday, no, Monday. That's right. Sheri probably told you that I went down to pick Ludy up."

"Poor T.J."

"Why? Did something—"

"No, it's just the kids at the high school. Jerry came home and said everybody was teasing—no, not teasing, but more like, poking T.J. about it. It is funny, though. From the way Jerry talked, everybody thinks Ludy is some kind of hero."

"What for?"

"Being in jail, I guess."

"What does Glenn think?"

"He told the boys at dinner that he'd bust their heads if they did anything like that." She grinned. "Sounds like him, doesn't it?"

I swirled the coffee in my cup. "I don't know. I just don't know what's going to happen."

She placed her hand across mine and frowned. "I know you're upset, Mom. And I think it will help if you do talk to David and Ludy." I looked up at her. "You *are* going to talk to them, aren't you? Sheri mentioned it."

"Yes, if . . ." I felt unprepared. "I'm not quite sure what to say, but both my sons went through a troublesome phase and . . . he really is a good boy . . ." My thoughts trailed off into nothingness. I wasn't sure where my mind had gone, but I was conscious of Evelyn sipping her coffee nonchalantly and watching me. The silence had become comfortable. We must have sat for ten minutes without talking when the tractor roared into the yard and brought me out of my daze.

We walked out to the back porch, Evelyn still drinking her coffee. Glenn was sweating when he came up, even though the air was cool. He wiped his forehead with his sleeve and smiled as he climbed the steps. I stepped away from the door.

"Well, there you are!" He spoke too loudly, almost like he was addressing someone hard of hearing.

"You're an early one, aren't you?" I pretended to scold him.

"And how about you sleeping all day? Why, I pounded at the back door for ten minutes this morning and couldn't rouse you." He winked at Evelyn.

"You must have tapped like a mouse." *Why hadn't I heard him?*

He led me by the arm into the kitchen. "I got the old tractor running, Mom."

"I see that. I'm surprised."

"Me too. Even after it sat all winter. I should have drained the engine block. Why didn't you think of that for me, Evelyn?" He grinned.

"That's because you never consult me." She wagged her finger at him. "Anything falls apart at home," she turned to me, "guess who usually fixes it?"

Glenn feigned surprise. "That so? Could have used you early this morning then."

She squinted at him. "Watch yourself!"

"Ummm, coffee smells good," he said, picking up the pot. "Naw." He changed his mind. "Let's go get some lunch at the café in Janesville."

I instinctively stiffened. "You go without me. I couldn't be ready."

"We'll wait for you," he said firmly.

I looked at Evelyn, who glanced at Glenn and then back at me. "Actually, Mom, I came over to invite you to lunch with us. I should have mentioned it when I came in."

"No, really," I began, searching their faces. "I don't feel much up to going out."

"We'd like you to, Mom," Glenn insisted. "We've got something we want to talk over." They were both serious. I knew something was coming that I wanted to avoid, but they stood silent, expecting me to do whatever I needed to.

"All right," I said finally. "I'll be just a minute."

They remained quiet as I went to gather up my purse and a compact. I suspected that what they wanted to talk about had nothing to do with Ludy or David. It was obvious they were concerned about me. Did they think I was losing control of the house and the farm and myself? I was sure that was it. They had both spoken to me like I was an invalid or a child. I could hear a broom sweeping up broken glass in the kitchen.

When I walked by the water-spotted and dirty bathroom mirror, I turned away from my reflection, wanting to push my hand through the glass, deep into my face.

It was an uncomfortably quiet ride to the café. We drove along Janesville's main street, past the old-fashioned post office, two taverns, the hardware store, the feed and grain elevator, the library and fire department which shared the same building, and farther on, the new supermarket and the bowling alley.

Just a half block off Main, I could see the community school all five of my grandchildren attended, and where my own sons, years ago, had played football and basketball and had helped build the new annex and cafeteria. Now they were supporting the school through an expensive school bond. As we parked in front of the café, I glanced at the Presbyterian Church down the street and Pastor Bill's car in the drive.

Since it was almost noon, the café was busy with farmers who regularly showed up in town around mid-morning, had lunch at the café, and later straggled over to one of the taverns. I didn't know how they managed to run their farms, but I expected their operations weren't too successful. Besides, it was still too early for planting, although most of the field preparation was done.

We squeezed into a corner booth, which was too small. I scanned the menu but found it hard to concentrate on food. After the three of us ordered hot beef sandwiches, I finally blurted out what had been bothering me.

"Don't try to talk me into selling the farm."

Glenn and Evelyn glanced at each other knowingly. I sensed a family conspiracy. Glenn looked out the window, turned back to his ice water which he stirred with a spoon, and spoke softly.

"Momma, we don't want you to sell the farm." I was puzzled. He paused, intent on his ice. "But we would like you to move in with us."

"What for? I can't just leave my—"

"That's not what we mean, Mom," Evelyn interrupted. Her voice was lulling as she continued. "You see . . .we, Glenn and I thought you might like to come stay with us for a while."

I started to protest. "Oh, not right now," she said. "But how about next fall when it turns cold again? Glenn is refinishing the basement into a small apartment, and it would be just perfect for you, wouldn't it, Glenn?"

"That's right, Mom. The kids would love to have you."

"You've talked to them about my moving in?" I asked, alarmed.

Glenn looked out the window again. "You know how they feel about you. It's just that . . ." He rubbed his hands together.

"It's because we worry about you by yourself," Evelyn said.

"There's nothing wrong with me."

"We know that, but, well, the winter is hard enough to manage, and you're kind of isolated out there." She stopped and looked to Glenn for help. He didn't respond.

"And who's going to take care of the place?" I wanted to know.

"Well," Glenn sucked in his cheeks, "David and I can handle the land, and some of the equipment is old and doesn't get used enough to keep. You haven't got any livestock. You should be able to rent the house out for six months or so. We aren't asking you to give everything up and move in full time. But Mom, you've got to realize that . . .well . . ."

"That what? I'm old? You think I need somebody to take care of me?" I was growing visibly angry, I could tell. "And when do I go to the nursing home? When you get tired of me?'' My voice quivered. ''For over thirty years I've had only one home, and nobody is going to yank it away from me.''

Glenn looked around the café, embarrassed. ''Momma, please. We want you to keep the farm for as long as you live. I hope to God it's for fifty more years. But we just . . .'' He looked at Evelyn, helpless.

''We worry about you, Mom. There was broken glass all over your kitchen floor this morning. You could have been hurt.''

''I was going to clean it up.'' My hands were shaking; I put them under the table so no one would notice.

''I'm not saying you can't take care of yourself. We love you.'' There was tenderness in her voice. ''We don't want you to be alone. It's a big old house.''

I stared sullenly at the table. ''Did you flip a coin with David and Sheri to see who would take me?''

''Don't be like that,'' Evelyn said.

Our food arrived. The waitress, an overweight girl about twenty, went back for our coffee. Glenn leaned across the table toward me.

''Just think about what we said, Mom. You don't have to decide now at all. We've always got room for you.''

I wanted to say that I did love them, and I did appreciate what was in their thoughts. I could even picture myself living with them. I could have a garden out back, and flowers, and I did enjoy spending time with Evelyn; we frequently used to go shopping together.

The three boys were spritely children, and I did want to tell Glenn and Evelyn how important they all were to me. But I just nodded and poked at my food and watched the farmers guffaw and hitch up their pants and spit on the sidewalk before they entered Red's Inn.

On the way home from Janesville we stopped at Glenn and Evelyn's farm. The buildings were clean and well kept, the animals healthy; even the stray cats looked more content and well fed than mine. I knew the whole family worked hard to be productive; in that way, Glenn was every inch his father. Each of the boys had his chores: eggs to gather, bales to bring down from the loft, and repairs all the time. Even Jay, the eleven-year-old, could drive a tractor. I often saw him jouncing along with a hay rick behind one of their tractors.

I liked the energy I felt when I visited their place. It was infectious, and I almost wanted to say yes then, about spending the winter. But Evelyn came out of the house and handed me a book entitled *God Will See You Through,* and I was immediately resentful.

"What's this?" I demanded.

"Just a book that came to me in the mail." I tried to hand it back, but she pushed it at me again. "It's really very good, Mom. I thought you might enjoy it."

"Why?" I asked suspiciously. I turned it over and recognized the author's picture on the back as a popular evangelist I had seen on television.

"It just perked up my life when I read it."

I wanted to say something, to tell her that I didn't need it, but my mind went blank again, and it was almost as if I couldn't think in words. I felt that vague terror inside me, which, more and more, was disturbing my sleep. *Maybe it's the house,* I thought. *Maybe it is too big and empty.* What did happen when someone became senile? I remembered an elderly neighbor who always drooled when I visited her. She would call me the name of her daughter and coo to me in German. No, I was too young to be senile.

I tucked the book into my purse. I might look at it when there was nothing on TV, I decided. At least it would please Evelyn for me to take it. Glenn came out of his workshop with an oil can wrapped in a greasy rag and put the can into the trunk of the car.

They drove me home, Glenn analyzing the contour and condition of each field we drove by. I stared off to the line of trees where I knew the river was high and muddy. Each spring during flood season, it was defiant and fearsome. That pleased me, though I didn't know why.

4

It began to drizzle as I drove along the gravel roads that took me the back way into town. I wanted to avoid the highway because it was shortly after five, and commuters would be rushing home. Besides, I liked the solitude of the country, and the ominous sky was majestic and fierce against the open fields. I tried to rehearse what I would say during dinner at David and Sheri's. I wasn't expecting to make my plea for harmony so soon, but when I had telephoned Sheri early in the afternoon, she insisted that tonight everyone would be home, and that I should come.

The more I turned over my involvement in patching the strain between Ludy and David, the more incapable I felt of saying anything. I was certain to mumble something that would make the family nod patronizingly for a meddlesome old woman. But this was Sheri's idea, and Pastor Bill had approved it. I knew I would have done anything Pastor requested of me.

I flicked on the defrost, but the cold air had already fogged the windows beyond repair. I drove slowly, anticipating a cattle truck or a car going too fast for the slippery roads, but I drove past no one, and soon the bowling alley sign flashed just ahead.

T.J. was staring morosely out the front door as I drove into the driveway. She came out on the porch in the light rain, and I saw she was shivering.

"Hurry inside, you!" I chided.

"I love the rain." Droplets clung to her hair and sparkled in the fading light. "It makes me want to run barefoot through all the puddles."

"You've been seeing too much Gene Kelly," I said as I came onto the porch next to her.

"Who's he?" she asked, puzzled. I started to explain but stopped myself.

"You needed to have been there."

"Oh." She looked at me askance, shrugged, then tilted her head back, mouth open, and tried to catch drops which slid off the awnings. I went in. Sheri bustled about in the kitchen. Music blared from Ludy's room, so I knew he was home.

"Brrr. Feels almost like snow." I took off my wet shoes.

"Hi, Mom." She was washing lettuce for a salad. "David should be home from work anytime."

"I thought he worked until three."

"Well, he does, but the company is putting in a new process operator, so he's been staying late all week."

"Uh huh. He'll be tired then." I didn't know why I had made such an obvious statement.

She turned off the water from the faucet. "I'm sorry. What was that?"

"Nothing. Just thinking aloud, I guess."

"Oh." She nodded, a thin smile pulling the corners of her mouth.

"You should come see the farm."

"Why's that?" She began slicing tomatoes.

"Glenn's got the fields plowed the last couple days."

"That's great! David will be glad to hear that because he was going out this weekend to see if he could get the tractor running."

"It's running. Is there anything I can do?"

"No, just relax. Everything is done."

T.J. came into the kitchen and shook her hair. "Don't act like a dog," her mother scolded.

"It's good for my hair," T.J. said. "Makes it soft."

"That's what we always used to do," I said. "Every rain, we'd let the cistern and rain barrel fill up, and then whenever we wanted soft water, there it was."

She sat down at the table beside me, her eyes wide.

"Did you ever use the well water?"

"Too cold," I grimaced.

"Sometimes I use an egg on my hair."

Sheri turned away from the sink, her hands dripping. "I used vinegar when I was a girl."

"Yuk! Didn't it smell?" T.J. asked.

"Well, you rinse it out. It made my hair so soft." She pushed her hair back away from her face with the back of her wrist.

"Yuk!" T.J. repeated.

The stereo music from Ludy's room became louder. T.J. thumped an imaginary drum set on the table top.

"I can't even hear myself think," Sheri said. She went down the hall to the bedrooms, wiping her hands on a dish towel. I heard her knock on the door and ask Ludy to turn the noise down. Abruptly the music stopped. The door opened, and Ludy grunted a sarcastic "What was that?"

"Please turn it down," she asked gently.

"Oh? What for?"

"I doubt very much if you are hard of hearing."

I watched T.J.'s face tilt back, her eyes closed. Her head swayed to an interior music. Ludy's door slammed as Sheri came back into the kitchen and glanced at the clock.

"He should be here soon. Want some coffee, Mom?"

"No, I'm fine." I tried to rehearse sentences that would sound authoritative and loving, but I knew it would be difficult to broach the subject when the family sat down to dinner. I wanted very much to be home. It was no problem to speak with Ludy alone, or David. I felt confident one to one. But I didn't want to be a family counselor, especially since the family was mine.

Maybe everything will just smooth out in time, I tried to convince myself. *Ludy is at a difficult age—fourteen always brings out the worst, but . . .*

"Here he is now," said Sheri. Car headlights swept past the kitchen window.

T.J. got up drowsily and began to set the table as Sheri took a casserole from the oven. When David came in, I could tell by his drooping head that he was exhausted.

"Hello, Mom." He looked down at me and managed a smile. "I would have been home sooner," he turned to Sheri, "but there was an accident at the Illinois Central crossing, and only one lane of traffic open."

"Somebody hit a train?" T.J. gasped.

"No, just two cars that hooked fenders. No one hurt. The roads are real slick."

"Well, we're all ready to eat if you want to wash up," Sheri told David.

He groaned. "Oh, man, have I got time for a beer?"

"We've been waiting for you."

"All right, I'll have one with dinner." He went into the bathroom. I felt in the way with T.J. setting the table and Sheri placing dishes in front of me, so I began to get up.

"No, that's okay, Mom, just stay where you are."

"Let me move," I protested. I was sitting in the chair that David usually occupied. "Doesn't David sit here?"

"You can sit there, Nana," T.J. said. "I do lots of times."

David came back from the bathroom and knocked on Ludy's door. "Dinner's ready," he said.

Ludy said hello to me when he sat down at the table but ignored everyone else. I couldn't understand what was bothering him. David blessed the food. Everyone must have been hungry, since nobody said much.

"How's school?" I asked T.J.

She waved her fork in the air, and with a mouthful of food, said, "So-so. Only one more year."

"She made the honor roll last semester," Sheri added.

"Gonna slip this semester, though," T.J. said.

David sipped his beer. "How come?"

"I don't know. Just bored, I guess."

I looked across at Ludy, who was disinterested. Suddenly I knew how to ease the conversation toward him. "School will be out soon, won't it, Ludy?"

He didn't look up at me. "Twenty-seven more days."

"The spring prom is next week," T.J. said. "I wish somebody neat would hurry up and ask me."

"She's already been asked twice," Sheri said.

"Yes, I know, but I made it clear at school that I'm waiting for someone special to ask me, only HE hasn't gotten around to deciding yet if HE wants to go."

I was amused each time she emphasized "he." We continued eating in silence. David watched Ludy, then he handed him a napkin and took another swallow of beer.

"Have you got any plans for this summer?" I directed the question to T.J. She looked at her mother, and then at her father.

"Could detassel corn again, but I've got my application in at the supermarket. They might need somebody. A couple of really cute carry-out guys work there."

"How about you, Ludy?" I knew what to say, but I wanted his attention.

"Nope."

"No, what?" Sheri reprimanded.

"Don't know what I'm gonna do." He laid down his fork.

"Your father and I were talking," everyone looked at me, "and we thought you might be interested in doing some work around the farm." I began speaking rapidly, trying to get all the words out. "I was going to place an ad for someone anyway, and there's lots that has to be done, and I doubt if I could handle everything myself this summer."

I looked directly at him. "And your father says that you are mechanical and could tinker around with the mower and the conveyor, and help me clean out some of the junk. I'm willing to pay you two dollars an hour—"

"Mom, that's not—" David interrupted.

I cut him off. "I would pay anyone I hired the same. It's worth it to me just to get things shipshape around home. What do you think, Ludy? I'd like to have you help me."

I felt confident about what I had said. Ludy stared down at his plate as we waited for him to speak. Sheri appeared to be pleased with my gesture. I felt that I was skirting the real issue, but I was glad everyone was allowing Ludy to make his own decision. David pushed his chair away from the table and leaned back.

"Well," Ludy said hesitantly. "I guess that would be okay."

"That's great! In fact, you don't have to wait until summer. I've got work that needs to be done now. If you want, you could start after school and on weekends, and I'll pay you just the same and then on through the summer."

"That's an excellent idea," Sheri said. "You could ride your bicycle out to the farm and back."

"Tire's flat," Ludy smirked.

"We can get you a new one."

Ludy looked at me solemnly. "Two dollars an hour?" I nodded. "For as many hours as I work?" He scratched his head. "I could buy that motorcycle that Denny Davis wants to sell, then."

"No motorcycle," David said, shaking his head.

Ludy looked to his mother. "Why not?"

"Maybe when you're older."

"It's my money."

"No motorcycle," David said. "And that's the last I want to hear about it."

We sat silent, aware of the new tension. Ludy stared at me, a puzzled half smile on his face. "But if it's my money, I can spend it the way I want."

"You don't even have a driver's license," T.J. said.

He ignored her remark. "He only wants a hundred and fifty dollars for it," Ludy calculated on his fingers.

"You heard what we said, Ludy," Sheri said patiently.

He stared straight ahead. "I'm gonna buy it," he emphasized.

"No motorcycle!" David exploded, startling all of us. He was barely controlling his anger. I remembered how, as a boy, he would calmly hold back his emotions, and then unexpectedly and furiously shout and swing wildly at the wall or at his brother, or smash something on the floor. I thought of the coffee cup that I had hurled against the wall yesterday.

Ludy got up and stepped back from the table, his eyes teary. "If it's my money, I'll buy what I want." He spun quickly and went toward his room.

"Not as long as you're living here!" David shouted after him.

"Go to hell," Ludy mumbled, slamming his door.

David jumped up from the table and rushed to Ludy's door. I sat stunned. I could see him unbuckling his belt, a response he had inherited from Leroy. He attempted to open the door, but Ludy had locked it.

"Open the dang door!" David pounded.

"David?" Sheri called to him weakly. There was no answer from inside Ludy's room. David had his belt in his hand. T.J. watched fascinated, only too aware of what would happen.

"Open it!" David thundered.

Loud stereo music began coming from the room, easily drowning out David's voice. He hammered louder. Finally in frustration, he began forcing the door with his shoulder.

"David?" Sheri attempted to stand up, but David was throwing his full weight against the door, ignoring her pleas.

The door began to splinter on its frame, as it tore partially loose from its hinges. Ludy, aware of his father's anger, had turned off the music.

"Open it!" David demanded again.

Ludy opened the door, whimpering, and implored his father not to hit him. I wanted to do something, but I sat frozen. I had the impulse to stop David, but I knew it was no longer possible for me to mediate what was inevitable. We could hear the snap of leather, and I hoped that David wasn't hitting Ludy on the face. Sheri and T.J. sank down, almost visibly, into themselves. Ludy was crying now, imploring, "No, no, don't hit me. I'm sorry," but David didn't stop until he had swung seven or eight times.

When David came back into the kitchen, we were busy clearing the table. I could hear Ludy sobbing. Was it my place to say something? I felt torn and bruised, and I wanted to go put my arms around Ludy like when I used to comfort David. More than ever, I saw the hurt child in Ludy, and the diffused anger on David's face. I wanted so much to understand the turbulent love that I knew existed between my son and his son.

As I drove home, I felt brittle and weary. I had failed everyone. The sky was clearing. Through the rain-spattered windshield I could see stars appearing indistinctly. And if I had been able, I would have cried for Ludy and myself and for everything innocent and wounded.

5

Periodically, I experienced a renewed interest in work around the house. One morning I was in Glenn's old bedroom where we had stored boxes of pictures, the boys' yearbooks, steamer trunks of clothes, toys, and assorted knickknacks I had forgotten about.

I sat on the floor in the dim light from the dust-encrusted window and pawed through the boxes, surprising myself with the discovery of long-neglected treasures. I even found a slim portfolio of my wedding pictures—pictures I thought had disappeared years ago. Leroy looked gawky and stiff in his suit; it wasn't often he would oblige to wear such clothes.

Under a box of old clippings about the boys' football days, I came upon a packet of correspondence between my mother and father, when my father was a young lieutenant stationed in France. He wrote movingly about the war and the poverty written on the landscape, as he described it; I was enthralled with the tender, lyrical nostalgia he felt for his home and family and my mother. Much of the ink was faded, and the paper yellowed and crumbly, but the sentiments moved me nearly to tears. I couldn't ever remember reading the letters before, and had either of my parents been alive, I would have felt odd, like an eavesdropper, reading those cherished vestiges.

Some mornings I would walk out into the pasture and watch Ev's Herefords cropping the meadow grass. The cows chewed comically and stared at me with their saucer brown eyes. I wanted to walk along the creek that ran into the river, but the ground was too mushy yet.

If I followed the gravel road that ran in front of the farm for a half-mile to the west, I would come to the west fork of the Cedar River. An old suspension bridge hung over the water, and each time a car crossed the bridge, the wooden cross ties clacked, and the whole bridge swayed as if it would topple from its pylons.

But it was quiet in the mornings, and as I watched driftwood spin lazily in the current and vanish around the river bend, I imagined floating across the vast prairies, gradually sliding along under other bridges and over small rock dams as the river imperceptibly widened until it reached the Mississippi two hundred miles west. And then I felt dwarfed by the immensity I remembered about that river; but still, I knew once on the Mississippi, the Gulf of Mexico and then the oceans were inevitable weeks and weeks away, and I envied and hated the wood that rolled in the eddying trough under my feet.

Other days, when the sky was overcast, or even brilliant with a buttery sun, I stayed in bed late, then dragged downstairs to drink stale, over-

43

warmed coffee and lie on the sofa watching soap operas about people I neither knew nor cared about. Often, I drowsed until early evening, the heating pad therapeutically tucked under my lower back, and then wandered into the kitchen, stared at the cans in the cupboards, and finally trudged up to bed.

I still slept fitfully; I would drop to one level below consciousness and prowl through barely illuminated corridors looking for something or some object I couldn't recall, but with a sense that once I stumbled upon it, I would recognize it—whatever "it" was. Another recurring dream was that I seemed late to an appointment, but all I could do was stare at my hands as they dissolved into a spongy dough at the end of my arms. I knew I had to be somewhere, but I was too fascinated by my disintegrating hands to move. But most often, I tossed uncomfortably and stared at the clock and blinked at the yard light, all the while listening for any noise that might be an intruder among my catalogue of familiar noises.

Even when someone stopped by, my family or a friend, I felt as if we were talking from opposite ends of a tunnel with only a small light bulb hung somewhere between us. My hair hung limp, my breath seemed foul no matter how often I brushed at my teeth, and my clothes stayed wrinkled and damp.

A couple of weeks after the disastrous dinner at David and Sheri's, Ludy started coming by. He wouldn't knock on the door to tell me he had come, but I would hear him start up the mower to cut weeds or the chain saw to trim branches. One Saturday morning he was hammering new shingles on the barn roof at six o'clock. I didn't disturb him at first. I let him work uninterruptedly, and when he was done with something, he vanished until I saw him again a couple of days later.

It was nearly the first of June, and summer had settled in with its fanfare of mosquitoes and grasshoppers, an eavesful of sparrows, and nights that were muggy beyond endurance. I'd gone into the barn to investigate what further improvements had appeared around the farm, when I noticed muddy footprints on the fiberglass of Leroy's enormous unfinished sailboat. I stood on a wooden crate and peered over the side. Ludy was curled into a torn sleeping bag, snoring lightly. He must have heard me lean against the boat, because he opened one eye.

"Hey, Nana," he said, groggy.

"What on earth...?"

"Oh." He sat up, a sheepish look on his face. "Sometimes I take a nap here."

"What for?"

"I don't know." He tried to focus on me. "It's quiet and comfortable, I guess."

"I could fix you a bed in the house."

"Naw. I like it here. It's almost like being on a ship."

"It is a ship," I said quickly, although I knew it was far from finished—just a hull and an open cabin tucked into the empty, inner part of the boat.

"Oh, you know," he smiled. "Like a treehouse is really a fort."

"I see." I had caught him off guard. It was good to see him relaxed and smiling. "Do you want anything to eat?"

He sat up. "Yeah. What time is it?"

"About noon, I think. Didn't you have school today?"

He scratched his nose, half hiding a sly smile. "Naw, this is just test week, and I didn't have nothing."

"Didn't have anything," I corrected him.

His dark eyes glimmered. "Yeah. Didn't have anything."

"How about some peanut butter?"

He appraised me. I felt closer to him than I had felt in a long time. "Got any jelly?"

"Grape jelly! Homemade grape."

"Yeah?" He stretched. "My favorite."

"I know." He stared at me quizzically, then stood up in the boat.

"I like this boat." He paused. "How come Grandpa didn't finish it?"

"He would have if he hadn't died. He'd work on it off and on in his spare time. It took him nearly two years to do just this."

Ludy ran his hand along the hull. "It's good work. What was he gonna do with it?"

"Sail it, I suppose."

"Really?"

"That's what he said, although there's no water big enough around here, and he didn't know how to sail anyway."

"Wow! That's great." He shook his head and swung his legs over the side.

"Of course the neighbors thought he had flipped out."

"I bet."

"Ev said he was like Noah getting ready for the next flood."

"Hmmmm." He walked thoughtfully around the boat, inspecting the smooth and seamless texture of the fiberglass.

"How about that peanut butter now?"

"Yeah, okay. Nice boat, really nice." He followed me into the house. I stuffed him with two thick peanut butter sandwiches and milk with heaping tablespoonfuls of chocolate powder. I asked how many hours he thought he had worked. He pondered for a minute, his tongue working away at the peanut butter.

"Twenty-two and a half hours," he said.

"I'd like to pay you now." He didn't say anything as I went into the living room closet for my purse. When I came back into the kitchen, Ludy was biting into a shiny Winesap.

"Let me see, at two dollars an hour..."

"Forty-five," he said between bites.

I counted out two twenties, four ones, and a handful of change which came to eighty-seven cents. "I'll have to owe you thirteen cents."

He grinned when I handed him the money. "This lunch," he munched, "is worth more than thirteen cents."

I reached over and tousled his hair. He smiled, blushing.

He began appearing more regularly after that, and he usually came to the door when he arrived, or knocked before he left to tell me what he had accomplished. Sometimes I tagged along after him, reluctant to get in his way as he repaired the fence around the garden, or put a new pane of glass in the porch window, or oiled the machinery. Sometimes Glenn or one of Glenn's two older sons, Jerry or Jason, would come by to start up the tractor or just nose around, but Ludy only chatted with them for a minute before going back to work.

I noticed that when Ludy wasn't around, I started to mope and my sore hip acted up again, and I paid more attention to how lousy I could make myself feel. Every Friday or Saturday afternoon I drove into Janesville for groceries. If I happened to see any of my friends at the supermarket, I hurried to the next aisle and busied myself reading labels until they went past. I didn't want to act like a recluse, but I realized they found me equally difficult to talk to. They predictably asked how I was, if I was getting along, chided me for not calling them, prided me for my bravery in carrying on alone, and they never, *never* stood too close or looked at me too directly, as if a nameless contagion might pass from me to them. It was something about death and the loneliness of being near a death, that frightened them, I was sure. Only the courageous patted me on the shoulder, to brush their hands unconsciously when we turned away.

As I sat alone, staring out at the luminescent fields at night, I thought of Pastor Bill. He was the only one I wanted to see.

46

On Sundays, sitting in the last pew, I closed my eyes as his slightly Scottish brogue conjured visions of green, stone-walled fields and cobbled streets winding narrowly through thatched villages. And Bill would drive a donkey cart overflowing with hay, and I, perched precariously as the cart swung from side to side on the road, would be laughing and pointing at birds and ancient trees and rocky paths that went up hills into mist. And the sea would thunder in the distance.

Everyone swarmed around him as they left church, so I always lingered until last. Then he would take my hand and hold it longer than he held anyone else's, his blue eyes sparkling as he laughed and asked how I was and did I know he prayed for me every night and sometimes every morning and before meals. Then I would laugh and nod all the way to the car, still warm and happy inside.

But it was hardest in the evenings. Just to look out the windows during the day was enough to keep my mind occupied. The corn shoots were coming up, trucks kicked up funnels of dust as they drove by, the mailman stopped sometimes. Ludy would industriously hammer and dig and repair and paint; the cats would fight, would drag plump mice onto the porch and drop them at my feet. If I wasn't actually busy, I could at least be distracted. But in the evenings, the night brought me close to myself, and there was no one I could merge my presence into; there was no activity that would transport me beyond the frail walls of the house, where every board that creaked, every cricket that buzzed under the furniture, proclaimed that I was desperately and unrelentingly alone and lonely.

6 I was surprised that Pastor Bill answered his own telephone when I called; usually, Mrs. Hill, the parsonage housekeeper since Mrs. Shaffer died, assumed the small duties around the church, including secretary to Pastor Bill. But Pastor said she had the week off to visit her sister in Kansas, and yes, he was managing fine, and would I like to come by for dinner on Thursday night?

I offered to cook, but he reminded me that his chili was notorious in the area, and if I would come prepared to throw my doubts about his culinary ability to the winds, he would amaze and entertain with folk songs, tales, and witty observations about life. I stuttered a hesitant yes, and before I knew what I had agreed to, I was holding the empty drone of the telephone to my ear.

My reluctance was not that I didn't want to go—I did. But I was unaccustomed to being entertained by men in their homes, even if the host was my pastor. The more I thought about the intended visit, the more skitterish I became. I had called to tell him of the encouraging changes I saw in Ludy, but now I felt like a young girl accepting her first date.

During the next two days I even attempted to call him back and cancel, but once the line was busy, twice there was no answer, and the fourth time I called, I hung up after the phone rang once. I wanted to see him; there was an irresistible attraction about him, and after all, I told myself, we were friends and he was my pastor; it would be nothing like a date.

As I prepared to go out Thursday evening, I again began to doubt my ability to carry on. No amount of powdering or primping would make me feel ready. My hair was uneven and thinning on the crown; my dresses felt baggy. I thought surely I was coming down with the flu. Even the car wouldn't start. But Ev happened to be chasing a heifer through the pasture, and when he heard the grinding motor, he came over, fiddled under the hood, cleaned the battery connections, and started the car on his first attempt.

All the way into town, a nagging thought kept rising to my consciousness—I couldn't force it out. I wanted to tell Bill how sick and tired I was of being lonely, of nodding pleasantly and telling friends I wasn't strong like they thought; I didn't want sympathies any longer. It wasn't me, but Leroy who had died. Yes, I was breathing, I was alive, and I wanted very much to be treated like a normal woman whose life continued even though her husband's had ended. I knew Bill would understand, and perhaps, I hoped, he would not give me consolation but joy—the joy that was so pervasive in the air around him.

I parked in front of the parsonage and sat in the car for a long while. He must have heard me drive up, for soon he came out the front door yodeling "My Bonnie Lies Over the Ocean," and flashed me a radiant smile. He took my hand as I came up the porch steps and led me into the book-lined living room. He pointed to the fireplace.

"I would have fired up something for atmosphere, but who wants to eat chili on a warm June night in front of the fire?"

I laughed. "It is warm, isn't it?"

"Warm?" He threw back his head and roared. "The ice cubes I just took from the freezer melted before I could get them into the pitcher of tea. If you don't mind watered-down orange pekoe . . ."

"Not at all. Can I help with anything?"

"No, no. Just have a seat and tell me what's new." He ushered me to the couch, and then he sat in an easy chair across the coffee table from me.

"Well," I began, "I haven't told you that Ludy is working on the farm nearly every day."

"That's splendid, Dorothy."

"And I'm paying him two dollars an hour so he can learn to manage his own finances."

"Yes?" There was genuine interest in his voice.

"There have been so many necessary improvements I just wasn't able to do by myself. You can't imagine how pleased I am to see new paint, and gates back on their hinges, and screens up, and I've even repainted my kitchen a sunshine yellow."

"Is that right?" He leaned back and crossed his legs. "I could tell there was something different about you tonight. You're more cheerful than I've seen you in a while, and is that a new dress?"

"Oh, no. It's one I made myself years ago."

"It's becoming, as my mother would say, though I never understood if she meant *becoming* or *begoing*." I smiled. He stood up. "Let me see if my chili has burned a hole in the pan yet. Excuse me."

After he left, I looked around the room. The light was on in his little office, which was just off the main entryway. The clutter of books and papers was probably off-limits to Mrs. Hill, I surmised, since the rest of the living room was ordered and tidy. I tried to take a deep breath, but all I could do was yawn. There was a fluttering inside of me I couldn't identify. I didn't think I was nervous; no, Bill was too easy to be with for me to feel nervous. It seemed to be an expectant feeling, as if, as if—I didn't know what I felt. I stared at my hands. They were dry and wrinkled, red at the knuckles and *ugly*, I thought, *so ugly*. They were bony and reminded me of two dead birds perched on my lap. I wanted to hide them under the cushions. I closed my eyes and listened to the bangs and clinks coming from the kitchen.

He was a remarkable man. He seemed out of place amidst the slow-talking, red-faced and rough farmers of the Midwest. He was spontaneous and unpredictable. There was nothing I detested more than the crude, boisterous gatherings at the bowling alley, or Farm Bureau picnics, or the smelly and sloppy old men crowding the county fair midway.

He came back smiling. "I'd invite you to eat in the kitchen, but the steam is so dense, we wouldn't see each other. Would you mind greatly if we ate in the living room?"

"Not at all," I said, leaning forward.

"No inconvenience then?"

"It's fine with me."

"Very well then, let me offer you the Spanish version of Bill's special stew, my standard company dish. Depending on how much hot sauce I dump in, it can be either stew or chili, though I don't know what in the least is chilly about it."

I started to get up. "Let me help . . ."

"No, no, no." He motioned me back down. "Please. You're my guest. It's rare indeed when I invite attractive women to dine alone with me. Usually Mrs. Hill is hovering like a vulture, although she insists I go about like she isn't there. She's a lovely woman and I appreciate her dearly, but she is impossible to ignore."

I smiled understandingly. In her sixties, Mrs. Hill was a large woman, almost two hundred pounds. "I'll be just a moment." He went back into the kitchen and soon returned with a large tray.

"As you see, the tea is no longer orange but a watered-down rust. I apologize."

"It looks fine." He handed me a steamy bowl of chili.

"I was exceedingly economical with the Tabasco sauce, given the temperature and humidity. During the winter I indulge myself."

I tasted the chili. It was slightly burnt, and the taste of pepper was distinct. "Ummmm. It's very good." Had he served cold oatmeal, I'm sure I would have said the same.

"Well," he tasted it, "you've got to admit, it has a unique taste." I laughed, swallowed the wrong way, and began choking. Bill sprang across the room and thumped me on the back.

"I'm all right. I'm all right," I nodded hoarsely. He handed me my tea.

"You're sure now? I haven't had a casualty yet from my cooking."

51

I took a drink of the tea and cleared my throat. My face was flushed. "Oh! The chili is fine, it's my throat that swallowed wrong."

He sat back down, relieved. "I thought for a minute you'd gotten the whole tablespoon of cumin."

For the rest of the meal Bill did the talking. Always animated when he told a story, he related his adventures when he first arrived in Des Moines from four years of study and two years of pastoring in Scotland. At one point, he strode across the room and pulled down a framed picture of his college rugby team. As a young man of twenty, he sat scowling fiercely, his cheeks ruddy under curly, blond hair.

I thought I would laugh uncontrollably again as he reenacted his ordination, when his senior pastor tripped over his robes and tumbled onto two young candidates for the ministry who were kneeling solemnly. But the paperboy rang the doorbell, and as Bill excused himself to hunt out a dollar's change, I dabbed away tears of laughter, sat back relaxed, and drank my tepid tea.

Bill returned, sat across from me smiling, and asked if I wanted more chili.

"No, I'm stuffed to the gills."

"That's a fine expression. 'Stuffed to the gills.' How about 'stuffed to the withers'? Or 'stuffed to the maw'? We do have a funny way of sending information, don't we, this language that's supposed to convey messages. Have you got any more messages?"

"Well," I stared at him trying to think of something clever. "Well, just that I've broken a sweat."

"Broken a sweat! Yes. Perspiring. And how would one mend a sweat?" He sank into the chair, his face aglow from the heat. "It is exceptionally warm, isn't it?"

"And I think the chili raised my body temperature ten degrees."

"I should have prepared something else." He looked down at his watch and sighed deeply. "You've got time for a visit, haven't you?" I nodded. "Good. Tell me then, how are you getting along yourself?"

"Just fine," I heard myself say.

"Jiminy," he said abruptly. "Would you care for some cider? It's quite good. . ." He winked and went into the kitchen before I could reply. When he returned, he handed me a tall, cool glass, nearly full with a pungent, amber liquid.

"It's very good," I said, toasting him.

"Yes," he answered in mock earnestness. " 'To warm your wee cockles,' as the Irish would say."

"What are cockles, anyway?"

52

He sprawled back in his chair, laughing. The cider was quite filling, but unlike the chili, it was mild and soothing. I watched Bill look out the living room window. Dusk was brilliant in the western sky; pillars of light serrated the horizon. I felt no inclination to jump up and leave with an excuse. I didn't care if I moved from the chair for a long time.

"Now, Dorothy, you were telling me how you're getting along."

I tilted my head back against the cushion and closed my eyes. "I told you about Ludy, and the improvements, and...I don't know...what else?"

"Yourself." He paused for a long time. "What's happening inside of you?"

My body tensed as a bolt of terror shot through me. "Like what?" I knew what he meant, but a defensive mechanism had taken over again.

"Are you seeing people?"

"Of course," I said guardedly.

He stroked his cheek, and watched me shift my legs. "Well-intentioned friends are always so anxious for you to get back in circulation, aren't they? My daughters wanted me to remarry less than a year after—"

"Why didn't you?"

"I did." A sly grin lifted the corners of his mouth. "I married the church. It seemed impossible to ever rebuild my life with another person, so I rededicated my energy to the church. Still, there are times..."

I waited for him to continue, but he seemed in no hurry. I felt the silence in the air around me, as if tiny, invisible wings were fluttering patiently between us.

"I think I know..." I stopped.

He raised his eyebrows, waiting for me to continue. The wings seemed to enter my throat; I became aware of my faint exhalations. He sipped his drink.

"I guess I...I don't know." I stared hard into the glass. Delicate particles floated up to the dome of yellow bubbles which clung to the cider's surface. I swirled the liquid and breathed in its bouquet. *Over-ripe apples in autumn,* I thought.

"Do you carry a burden of Leroy's death?"

"Not at all," I replied quickly.

"Many people do keep a great deal of guilt for inexplicable reasons."

"I feel numb sometimes."

"Yes, that's quite natural."

"And sometimes I want to cry, or to empty out my...my...I don't know, frustration, I guess. It's not that I don't miss him, I do. But..." I took a deep breath and let it out raggedly.

"Have you talked with anyone about your feelings?"

"No. There's been no reason to. I'm all right, and now that I'm busy again . . . it's just that sometimes . . ."

"What?"

"Oh, Pastor, I don't know. How can I explain it, if I don't even understand it myself?"

He smiled. I sipped again and felt a stillness settling over me. The words, the correct ones, seemed to elude me.

"You see, sometimes I think it's all fine, that I'm over it. I can get along by myself. And then I think, what does it mean to live with someone for over forty years? What does Leroy mean to me now? I ate thousands of meals with him, I sweated in the field beside him, I slept with him, held his head when he was sick, brought two children into the world with him and moved in the same space until I should have become part of him. That's what the wedding vows said—that we two should become one. And now, even less than a year since he died, I can't even remember his face. Occasionally, a scent or an object will bring his impression back to me, but any more, all my memories of him are just . . . foggy."

"It's not something we recover from overnight."

"I know that. When I'm busy, I'm fine. But I'm sick of inventing little tasks just to keep busy. I don't want sympathy from anyone."

The fist in my throat began dissolving. "Some mornings I just don't want to get out of bed. I don't want to do anything but go back to sleep, but I can't sleep and I can't get up and I don't want to see anybody, and I want to have my friends visit me, but when they come I just want them to leave. I won't talk to them, they stare out the window uncomfortably, and the pity in their eyes just makes me sick until I wish I could smash something, and when they're gone . . . oh, God . . . I don't know." Tears blurred my vision, and I felt a constriction in my chest. "I can't even cry," I croaked.

He began speaking softly, his voice like the sound of water from a distance. At first, I couldn't hear what he was saying.

" . . . and we're such frail stems, aren't we? And the wind sounds like weeping when you lie in bed at night, and the trees have a way of speaking, too. Oh, it's so easy to give up on life . . . yes, I see the elderly in the hospitals with that glazed, faraway look in their eyes just like they're listening for somebody only they can hear, to call their name, and then they'll rise and go sometimes gently and sometimes with such bitterness in their faces that it makes me want to turn away and cry; but they don't realize how much they have inside of them that's valuable, how much they can give to others. Do you understand what I'm saying?''

I stared at him, uncomprehending.

''You see, Dorothy, you've got many who love you dearly, and now that you're by yourself you've got to reach out for others even more.''

''It's so hard. I just can't.''

''Have you asked God to help you?''

I could hear the clock ticking on the wall. Bill placed his glass on the floor next to his chair.

''Do you ever pray, Dorothy?''

''Is this where the sermon comes?'' I said sarcastically, regretting what I had said as soon as the words were out.

He sighed. ''No, no sermon.''

''I didn't mean . . .''

''That's all right. I want you to know, and you don't have to believe me now, that even though you haven't found your strength again, it's close, very close. What is it that awakens a cocoon after three months of slumber into a butterfly? That mysterious force is the will to live, the will to shake off the deadness. And it's going to happen to you—it's happening to you right now. No sermon. Would you like some more cider?''

''Uhhh . . . no. No, thank you.'' I focused my thoughts on him. He made everything seem lucid, as if I could simply reach out my hand and touch whatever he said.

''You do have to stretch out your arm in the dark and wait until you feel another warm, groping hand.'' He sat on the edge of his chair and offered me his hand, palm up. I drew back. His face was radiant and peaceful, his eyes sadly colorless in the dim light. His hand was still outstretched. I felt my right hand rise hesitantly and reach toward Bill's. An overpowering surge of warmth swept over me, and before I knew it, I was shaking and crying unabashedly. Still holding my hand, he came and sat on the sofa next to me, his other arm around my shoulder. I leaned against his chest.

Finally, I controlled my sobs and whispered, ''Just hold me, please hold me.''

''Yes, Dorothy. God has His hand on you, even now.''

I sat up, rigid. I didn't want to withdraw from Bill's warmth, but I felt he was lying to me, thrusting God at me, when what I needed was his own flesh-and-blood arm close around me.

''You've got to know that God does work through His ministers on earth.''

''I'm not interested in that.'' I sat on the edge of the couch, rocking

55

back and forth in my arms. "I just don't know."

"Don't misunderstand me," Bill said. "I care about you very much. Even if I weren't your pastor, you would still be special to me."

I tried to focus my thoughts, but a rush of feelings made it impossible for me to do anything but hold myself and stare at the carpet. Bill continued speaking.

"And you're right that a large part of you has died, but you've not forgotten Leroy. Not really. I do wish I could grab ahold of all your sadness and just yank it out. I would, you know."

I turned to look at him. His hand stroked my hair, which felt sticky and limp on my face. I was exhausted, and I just wanted to wrap myself into his arms and close my eyes. He tried to make me smile, but I could only close my eyes halfway and concentrate on his hand glazing the nape of my neck. I felt like a kitten about to purr.

"Come on now, where's a smile?" His hand stopped and tightened lightly; he could have shaken my whole body with his hand if he had wanted to. I attempted a smile.

"That's better."

"You probably think I'm a sad old woman."

"Of course not. You've been through a difficult year, and as I said, your life is about to change in a most amazing way. I know it, and I'm never wrong." He reconsidered. "Well ..."

"I wish." I stopped myself.

"Very well. I grant you three wishes."

"No. I was just thinking, that I wish I had known you when you were younger."

He chuckled. "I was never young, Dorothy. Youth was a luxury forbidden in my family." His face remained serious. "My parents were exceedingly strict and only allowed us children to be young on holidays." I was certain he was fibbing. I narrowed my eyes and squinted at him.

"You think I'm gullible?"

Unable to contain his laughter, he slapped me on the back affectionately and hugged me to him. I was surprised that he wasn't perspiring; the room was warm and stuffy. He smelled of peppercorns and sweet onion. We were both silent. I could again hear the wall clock over Bill's regular breathing. He stood up, uncomfortable.

"Can you believe it's dark already?" He went to the window and stood looking out, his back to me. "What an enormous moon. And bright yellow, just like a saucer of fresh cream." He put both hands into his pockets. "It looks good enough to drink, you know." He continued to stare quietly out the window.

I hadn't noticed before how broad and erect his shoulders were. His back appeared muscular, almost too strong for his thin legs. Even though he was no more than a dozen paces across the room from me, I felt I was watching from a great distance, as if the space between us was vaguely unapproachable in the dim light.

"I'd better be going." He made no indication that he had heard me. I stood up. "Thank you for dinner, Bill." He turned slowly. I detected a wistfulness in his unfocused eyes. He came forward and took my hand.

"I'm sorry again about the chili."

"It was fine."

He looked past my shoulder and then down at his own hands. I shivered. The night bugs and crickets and tree frogs had begun their racket out beyond the window. A large moth thumped twice against the screen.

"Well," he brightened. "God bless you, young lady."

I opened my mouth to speak, but my tongue was thick and dry. I nodded and let him lead me to the door.

"I want you to keep me abreast of Ludy's progress and be sure to see that he comes to church also. I haven't seen him come with his family in a while. And . . . and, thanks for coming," he added gently. I felt like he almost wanted to say more, but he didn't.

"Good night, Pastor." My voice was weak. I walked to the car, my heels clicking on the sidewalk. He stood on the dark porch as I drove away, the front door open behind him. The church cast a huge shadow over the road. I shivered again and wondered if I might be coming down sick. I drove for two blocks before I realized that I'd forgotten to turn my headlights on. A car went past me in the opposite direction honking as I pulled on the headlight switch.

Three semi-trailer trucks roared past me as I cautiously approached the highway intersection. I decided to go straight across and follow the river home. The gravel roads would be quiet. The moon, just to my left and visible over the treetops, was indeed large. As I drove slowly, I tried to remember Bill's voice. Now that I was alone again in the dark car, I felt an oppressive weariness settle over me. I glanced nervously into the back seat to see that no one had hidden in the car. I wondered if I had said something wrong before Bill went to the window. He seemed subdued. I knew what feelings he evoked in me. I wanted to press his hand between mine and tell him that he was warm and sensitive and I needed that in my life, in me. Had I frightened him?

I peered out the window to see where I was. The moon had gone behind a cloud; the intensity of the headlights weakened. I turned on the dome light inside the car to get rid of my nervousness and felt suddenly hollow, with an emptiness even the light couldn't help. Was I breaking apart inside? I remembered a rose bush that had grown out by the front gate that froze unexpectedly one September. When I went to snip a stem in the morning, the entire flower shattered to pieces in my hand. The day before the petals had been soft and vibrant.

I came to the Illinois Central crossing and stopped the car. It was difficult to see both directions because of the weeds growing around the signal poles. I rolled down my window. The moist air, alive with bugs, smelled of young corn and beans and alfalfa pushing up in nearby fields. It was a sweet scent I never tired of.

I looked down the road behind me. Had I expected to see someone following me? My eyes ached; periodically for the past couple of years I had been bothered by vision problems, especially at night.

"Is anyone," I asked myself aloud, "thinking about me now? Am I like those flashes of stars, traveling alone through miles and miles of space from a dead planet to an unknown destination?" I smiled, pleased with the poetry of what I had said.

I could barely see the road through the windshield, so as I drove forward again, I left the window down. The ditch blurred past. Gravel jumped up from the tires and hit the underside of the car.

"I can't believe how boring I am," I said. "I didn't say a single intelligent thing tonight. Who wants to talk about washing and baking bread and my oven that needs cleaning and the new drapes? That's all I know about, isn't it? Sometimes I even have to think twice to remember who the President is. I'm sure I don't know the state senators." *What had I accomplished in fifty-eight years?* I wondered. I hadn't even been out of Iowa in over two decades. I'd never been to New York or Washington or Florida or New Orleans or anywhere really.

The road ahead was like a dark wall which kept receding at an even distance from the car. How long would it take for someone to realize my absence if the road abruptly dropped off into space? I wanted to close my eyes and sleep. I wanted to shut out the jumble of images that were flashing by the open window. I was tired.

Something rushed in front of the car from my right. I couldn't tell if it was an animal or a bird, or if my eyes were playing tricks, but I jerked the wheel sharply to the left. The car began a slow spin which didn't alarm me since I had driven on ice often enough to know not to panic—just ride the momentum until I felt the wheels grip again. The gravel sounded like a flock of birds leaping out of bushes, and I briefly saw the moon spinning in the dark, and the ditch weeds, as the tail end of the car dropped off the road, and then I turned free and somersaulted forward, my knees thrusting my head back and back until the car stopped rolling over and was still on its side in the silent field. "And now," I murmured drowsily, "let me sleep."

7

I didn't know how long I had been unconscious, but I felt groggy and sick to my stomach. A mosquito was biting my cheek, and I couldn't lift my arm to swat at it. My arm was twisted under my hips. The entire car tilted at a forty-degree angle, leaning against the ditch slope. I heard a whippoorwill calling from somewhere behind me. I wanted to sit up, but I could only lie cramped, not entirely uncomfortable, listening.

It was difficult to tell how much time had passed before a car came along the road. From my position, I couldn't see the other car, but I heard it barrel past, slow, turn around and come back. It stopped just behind me, and I heard a couple of voices.

"Look at that," one said.

And then a female, "I wonder if anyone was hurt?"

"Help," I groaned. There was absolute silence, and then a young man's face was peering in the front window at me.

"There's someone still in it," he called to his companion. "A woman!"

"Is she hurt?" the female called back.

"Are you hurt?" he asked me.

"No. I tried to sit up, but my arm seems to be caught . . ." It was difficult to speak. He stared wide-eyed.

"I'll go call the highway patrol real quick. You just stay here and don't move, so the car doesn't topple over backwards." I heard him scramble up the ditch, say something to the girl, and then roar off down the road. It became very quiet again, and then the girl's face was at the window, staring in at me.

"I must look ridiculous." I tried to smile, but I could see the girl was frightened.

"Do you hurt much?" She looked about T.J.'s age; her blond hair was close-cropped, and she appeared tanned and athletic.

"No, not at all. I'm just kind of stiff, and I think my arm has fallen asleep."

"You've got a cut on your forehead."

I gingerly touched my forehead with my free hand. There was a small cut but very little blood.

"How'd you go off the road?" she asked.

I tried to think back. Even though I'd lost track of how long I had been in the ditch, when I tried to remember the accident, it struck me ludicrously, as though I had been at home in front of the television, watching the entire event unfold. I told the girl about something running in front of the car startling me, and then the graceful spin of the car, the sudden jolt at stopping after the roll, and then how relaxed and comfortable I felt until I heard her drive by.

"I didn't want to stop and come back," she began. "But Donny insisted. He's my boyfriend. We just got engaged, and I work at the bank in Cedar Falls. You know, the one across from the courthouse? I'm just a teller, but I want to go to college and major in finance."

I closed my eyes, wanting to listen to the night sounds again, but she continued.

"He said he wanted to see the wreck. And I told him I didn't want to 'cause there might be blood all over the seats. My girlfriend's father was killed in a car accident last fall. He ran into a dump truck out near Parkersburg. It wasn't his fault, but that didn't help much. Her family got a lot of insurance money though, and she bought a new Mustang. Hey, is that your foot there?" She pointed into the dark interior of the car.

I tried to wiggle my toes, but my feet felt remarkably far away from the rest of my body.

"Gee, I guess it is. You kinda got tangled through the steering wheel there." She panted excitedly. "We didn't think anybody was in the car. Somebody oughta be coming real soon." She peered down the road. "You okay?" she asked, trembling slightly.

"I'm okay. I just feel embarrassed." It was difficult to find a satisfactory position, because I could not turn my body. I watched the girl, surprised at how lucid my thoughts were.

After the girl babbled on for a couple more minutes, I heard a siren wail in the distance. I couldn't see the police car or the ambulance arrive, but I could see the sweep of the revolving red lights. The girl vanished in a rush of bodies and voices, which sounded calm and rehearsed as if my car upended in the ditch was no more unusual than any other accident on any other night.

A bald-headed officer and two ambulance attendants pried the door open. I expected to see white garbed medics, but both attendants wore blue jeans, and one had on an unbuttoned, western leather vest. They efficiently lifted me from the car, and I was soon strapped to the portable bed, wheeled into the ambulance, and speeding down the road. I wondered what would become of my car.

From the direction we headed, it was evident we were going to the city hospital in Cedar Falls. Even though we drove fast, I could hear the attendants between wails of the siren talking about motorcycles and the local racetrack and stock cars, and then they agreed to go for dinner after this run, but argued about where they should go. It seemed incongruous that they ignored my presence, but we were soon at the hospital, and the fluorescent ceiling slid past, along with faces that bobbed above me. *He needs a shave,* I thought, as the emergency room doctor bent down to examine me. He quietly asked my name and said, "Just relax, Dorothy. You don't appear to be seriously injured, but we're going ahead with some tests to make certain."

I thought about my family, and I wanted to ask the doctor or nurse to tell them not to worry about me. I could picture them being upset when the hospital called. The doctor thumped my chest and squeezed my legs firmly, his warm hands all the time moving over my skin. *Funny,* I thought, *how a man I've known for five minutes should be exploring my body so intimately, so methodically.* And then he bent close to my face, his dark eyes bloodshot, and spoke slowly. "You're going to be fine. We'd like to keep you here overnight." He said something to the nurse, and she returned shortly with a syringe which she waved past my eyes.

"To help you sleep."

And then I felt the pinprick in my arm. I glanced down, but I couldn't see the needle. It felt hot as she withdrew it. I tried to trace the injection as it moved along my arm. An immediate flush washed over me as waves bore me up and off under a dazzling tropical sun. *Toucans,* I thought, *and honeysuckle and a beach, wide and immaculate and deserted.* The sand was gritty, warm, as warm as the water that trickled around my toes. I sat in the shallow surf, watching brightly colored birds swoop low over the jade water. A milky foam swirled against my legs and lifted them. I leaned back, buoyant. "The tide is coming in," I said. "It's coming from thousands of miles, and the moon, invisible up beyond the blue, is drawing the tide in and out, and I feel it, the water inside me rising, rocking my warm ribcage like a boat sliding down the incline of the beach toward the deep, deep sea."

When I awoke, Glenn and Evelyn were standing beside the bed. My head spun, and I looked down at a cast that covered my right arm. I tried but was unable to lift it.

"Mom, Mom," Evelyn cooed persistently. I reached up with my left hand and rubbed my eyes. Gradually, I could see their faces clearly: Glenn's tense and furrowed, Evelyn's intent on forming the words she kept repeating.

"Mom? Are you back?"

"Whew," I groaned. "I was fine until they gave me that shot."

"How are you feeling?"

"A little woozy." I started to sit up. Glenn held me back against the pillows.

"No, no, just stay there, Momma. Doctor says you've got a mild concussion and shouldn't move for a day or so."

I frowned and pointed at my wrapped arm. "What's this?"

"A sprained wrist. Not too bad," Glenn said.

"You both look so serious."

Evelyn smiled at that. "Just worried. What happened, anyway?" she asked.

"Something ran in front of me, and I swerved, but the car skidded on loose gravel. Then I don't know what."

"You rolled over," Glenn said. "You should have seen the car."

"Is it bad?" I was more worried about repairing the car than my own injuries.

"Surprisingly, no. A door needs to be replaced and the top has a dent to be pounded out, but it'll run again."

I nodded and closed my eyes. "I was in paradise. You should have felt the warm sand," I sighed.

"What's that, Mom?" Evelyn took my left hand.

"Nothing," I whispered, "nothing at all."

And then I was back on the beach staring up at the green tangle of vines which hung over the sand. A magnificent parrot was watching me; his head tilted to the right and then to the left. His short, hooked bill was orange, and purple plumage cascaded along his back and blended into a violet bib. He looked like a waiter in an elegant restaurant blinking at me. He ducked his head under a wing, scratching, and he turned sideways again and croaked in an unmistakable voice, "Dorothy, Dorothy, Dorothy." I opened my eyes, amazed. Dr. Whit, our family physician for thirty years, was calling me awake.

"Dr. Whit?" I sounded sleepy and faraway.

"I've been trying for twenty minutes to rouse you," he said gruffly.

I smiled. "Where's Glenn and Evelyn?"

"Probably home enjoying dinner," he said as he took my pulse. "Just what I should be doing."

"What time is it?" My eyes still felt heavy and my right eyelid twitched uncontrollably.

"Twenty to seven," he said, glancing down at his watch.

"I can't believe I've been here a whole day." My neck was stiff. I tried to roll my head from side to side.

He jabbed a tongue depressor into my mouth. "Open up. Wider, please." My jaws ached. I felt that every part of my body needed a good lubrication. I wanted to unscrew my head and shake it out to clear it of the buzzing, which sounded to me as if a swarm of wasps had settled in.

"Tomorrow," he said, snapping his medical bag shut.

"What's tomorrow?" I asked, alarmed.

"Home. You can go home."

"I don't have to stay here?"

"Not unless the food's better here. Get plenty of rest, no heavy work, take aspirin for the slight headaches you'll have for a couple of days, and come see me next week. Got that?"

I saluted him weakly, familiar with his brusque manner. He turned and limped out of the room. Though he was in his sixties, he was still regarded as one of the best general practitioners in the area. I tried to remember all the stitches, measles, cuts, and stomachaches I had bothered him with, but it was difficult to separate David's face from Glenn's and then Leroy's and Ludy's and Jay's and Jerry's and Jason's and Pastor Bill's, and then T.J. was staring in the car window at me saying "Yuk! Yuk!" screwing up her face until it melted in the dazzling moonlight.

I awoke again sometime during the night. My head was clear. The door was ajar and a soft glow from the corridor dimly illuminated the room: the radiator under the window, a blue vinyl chair, a metal utility table on wheels, the folding wall in front of the bathroom fixtures, an arrangement of pink tea roses on the bedside table to my left—everything seemed incredibly visible.

I stared at the roses just beginning to droop on their thin stems; I could see the delicate patterns interlacing the petals. I had an uncanny feeling that my eyes were able to see through objects, as if the essence of the roses, the table, the gauzy curtains in front of the window were penetrable for the first time. My whole body seemed to have evaporated so that nothing remained but my eyes, aglow in the dark, conscious of so much at once.

I was certain that if I concentrated, I could see through the wall into the next room: an elderly man would be snoring on his back, a clear tube strapped to his arm where it entered the artery. His covers would be kicked off carelessly, and his feet, grossly white and obscene, would dangle past the metal bars at the end of the bed. In the room beyond him, a woman was curled tightly, clawing at her stomach and moaning softly. In room after room, I could see the sick and injured and dying strain for sleep under the scrutinizing eyes of the starched nurses who swooped from room to room like storks or pelicans on their bony legs. I knew if I commanded, my eyes would detach from their sockets and ascend, and all the walls would be transparent like glass, or water, or air in the rooms of the gasping patients.

I lay for some time listening for the slightest movement in the corridor. The window was closed, but cool air ruffled the curtain bottoms and rose along the wall to my right. It smelled metallic, and I wondered how many pipes and vents it had traveled from the hospital depths before arriving in my room.

My stomach growled. I hadn't eaten since I left Pastor Bill's. I tried to recall the drive home and the accident.

What had dashed in front of my headlights? It was a dark blur, wasn't it? I tried to convince myself that the spin had been unavoidable, that I was fortunate not to be seriously injured. Something rose in my subconsciousness and spiraled through the murky depths. Up and up and up and up through currents and ultramarine rivers, past exotic fish and minute, breathing organisms, it came toward me. I knew that as soon as it caught the light, I would recognize what was captive in its tiny sphere. Was it my face? I had been thinking of the road disappearing into space, I remembered. I was driving with the window down, breathing the night smells. Up ahead, farther than the lights could shine, a chasm had opened in the road. Water was flowing upward, from the center of earth, pouring up toward the moon from the tunnels that interconnected beneath the surface pipes which carried the cool air under the entire hospital; and rising toward me, inescapably, was what?

Had I swerved off into the ditch because I was sick of myself and my life? *Suicide* seemed like a funny word. Something stronger than me had jerked the wheel, had pulled me toward the dark rush of the weeds, like the moon irresistibly drew me off the hot sand into the cool green sea. I wanted to laugh and shout that no one jumped into the churning waters on his own; it was the swift, fragrant stream of energy just a step beyond the headlights that carried everything up into space, cool and green and resolutely peaceful.

I had often thought of driving straight into a tree that happened to attract my attention. I could see the impact, the car fold in against the stunned wood, and myself catapulted through the shattered glass. But I would shudder and dismiss the thought as crazy. But I wasn't crazy, and I wasn't senile. I was lonely and weary, and I wanted something that Pastor Bill stirred inside of me. I didn't want to say I loved him; that was an impossible thought. But I could feel the blood flowing through my arms and legs, my lungs pumping, my skin prickling under his hand. No, it wasn't him exactly. I knew that.

I didn't want to think anymore. I just wanted to lie quietly and let the cool air wash over my face. Maybe Leroy had anchored me. Now, the stability of the farm, my family, who I was, crumbled through my fingers. I didn't want to go home, and I didn't want to spend another night in that hospital room. I tossed restlessly, certain that hospital beds were not made for sleep. I wanted the sun to come up. I wanted to cry. Try as I could, the beach and jungle and the parrot would not come back. A nurse squeaked by. Down the hall, someone coughed, then gagged. I wanted to pull the walls down on top of me like Samson. I wanted to cry myself to sleep. *I don't know what I want,* I thought. *I don't know anything anymore.* And it was true.

8 Late the next afternoon Sheri and T.J. came to take me home. I'd been watching anxiously out the window all day as children bicycled past the hospital on their way to the city park. Both Sheri and T.J. were cheerful, and as they came to my bedside, I could feel their energy, their zest for life. It was a feeling I wanted very much inside of me. Sheri had picked me up a new dress on the way over. I was surprised at her thoughtfulness. I didn't know what had happened to my dress I had worn the night of the accident, but the new cotton print was a vivid sherbet orange. I liked its clean smell. I couldn't remember when I had bought myself a new dress.

"Nana," T.J. said to me in the car. "Nana, we were awful worried about you. When the Highway Patrol called and told us where your car was, we drove out to see it get towed into town. I couldn't believe that you had rolled over a couple of times and weren't ..."

"Killed?" I finished her sentence. "Well, somebody must have been watching over me."

"Dad spent all night at the hospital. Me and Ludy had to stay home," she added dejectedly. "But we came by after breakfast."

"Did you?"

"Yeah, but you were still sleeping."

"You almost did sleep around the clock," Sheri said.

"I feel like Rip Van Winkle."

T.J. picked at her sunburnt legs, which were peeling. "Doesn't that hurt?" I asked.

"Naw, not anymore. The first night it sure did. I had to take a bath in milk, and then I couldn't sleep with covers. But now it's just dead skin." She stripped off a large section. "I'm an old snake, huh, Mom. Shed my skin every summer."

"Yuk," I grimaced. Sheri looked at me and chuckled. "What's Ludy been doing?"

"Oh, he said he was going out to your place early this morning. I haven't seen him all day; he's probably tinkering with something."

"He called about lunchtime, Mom," T.J. added. "He said he had a surprise for Nana—real mysterious, and he wanted to know when we were bringing her home."

"Something for me?" I wondered aloud.

"He probably bought you a present. He's been putting all the money you pay him in the bank, you know."

T.J. snorted. "I told him he could go in with me to buy a car, and then

I could drive him around once in a while, but he said who wants to ride around with his sister?''

As we slowed to drive through Janesville, I noticed how everything in town had changed. The maples and elms and oaks were magnificently lush, the lawns trimmed, new paint and siding adorned many of the houses that I had remembered as being run-down, and children, toys, bicycles, wagons, and stray dogs sprawled under hedges and homemade forts and in the porch shade of late afternoon.

"It is summer," I breathed deeply. "It's really slipped by me. I don't even remember spring."

"There wasn't much spring this year," Sheri said.

"Personally," T.J. gawked at her freckles in the rearview mirror, "I wouldn't mind if we had summer all year."

"You'll have to move to California for that," Sheri said.

T.J. blinked at her mother. "I plan to. When I graduate from college, me and Amy are going to get an apartment on the beach."

"Sure," Sheri smiled. "So was I."

"We are, though. Just wait and see."

"I've never even been to California," I sighed.

T. J. tossed her head back like a debutante. "Oh. You may come and visit me." I looked out across the fields which stretched to the horizon beyond town. *Why not?* I thought. I had money in the bank from insurance and now social security and our savings. I could go anywhere I wanted to, couldn't I?

"Everything is up and growing this summer, isn't it?" Sheri pointed out the window. "Look at that corn. I've never seen it so tall this early. Must be the hot weather."

"Now I do feel like I've been sleeping twenty years," I said. "I haven't paid attention to any of the planting this year. Leroy used to make me check the almanac every morning to see what time the sun rose and set, and if the growing cycle would be short or long, and we always had to watch for signs."

T.J. popped her gum. "What kind of signs?"

"Oh, you know. Just signs."

"Like the sky?"

"Yes, the sky, how early the trees budded, when the robins returned, how much rain we got in the cistern, the grasshoppers, bee activity—simple things like that."

"What for?"

"Wisdom," Sheri said.

"Oh, I guess wisdom. Those were just things we always did. Kind of our old-fashioned ways of measuring things. Watch the signs, he always said."

We crossed the river. An old man and a small boy, perhaps seven or eight years old, were fishing from the bank. I caught just a glimpse of their red and white bobbers in midstream.

"Goll-lee, look at that!" T.J. sat up in her seat. Ahead on my right, I could see the east side of the house. It had been painted a glorious bright yellow. As we turned into the driveway, it was obvious that the entire house had been painted in the last two days.

I wasn't sure how to react. The house, with fresh paint and trim, looked better than it had in years. That was unquestionable. But deep inside of me, I felt betrayed. Ludy's improvements around the house were one thing. I had supervised his work and even suggested new jobs when he ran out of ideas. But the drastic change of paint—I didn't know. I felt like cold water had been thrown in my face to awaken me.

"The house looks positively gorgeous," Sheri said, climbing out of the car. "The white and brown trim makes it look almost quaint."

I leaned against the car weakly and surveyed it. "Did he tell you about this?"

"No." Sheri threw her arms up into the air. "None of us knew. Did you, T.J.?"

She shook her head incredulously. "Nope. I can't believe he did it all himself. I didn't see any paint on his hands last night. He must have worked solid for two days."

Just then Ludy came strolling sheepishly from the barn. He had both hands in his pockets, and his head wagged from side to side like a horse's.

"That's some surprise," Sheri said.

He looked at me, half-smiling. I realized that I was staring dumbfounded, and I probably appeared angry or glum.

"I, uh," I cleared my throat. "I think it's just ..." I could feel the tears cloud my eyes. I tried to blink them back. Ludy looked down at the ground, embarrassed. "It's wonderful, Ludy. It really is. You deserve a raise." He grinned and kicked at the ground, tracing a circle with his foot.

"Well, I just found these old cans of paint out in the shed." He glanced up at me. "I hoped you'd like it."

I wiped my eyes with the back of my hand. "I do. I really do."

"Can we come in and help you fix some dinner, Mom?" Sheri asked.

"No. I had a big lunch at the hospital. I'm just going to have a cup of coffee and sit in my wicker chair out on the lawn, and stare at the house.''

They all laughed. "You're sure we can't help now?''

"No," I insisted. "You better get on home and tend to David. He's probably wondering where you are.''

They piled into the car, Sheri agreeing to let Ludy drive. As they backed out toward the road, I could see T.J. kibitzing in the backseat. Whorls of dust dissipated behind them until they vanished in the distance. It was nearly twilight. The branches above me quivered slightly, and the moon, like a faint skull, was coming up in the east as the sun settled through the pines in the west.

The almost golden transformation of the house made it look magical. For as long as we had lived in it, it had been white; never a pristine, snowy white, but a worn, grayish white that seemed to expose the sag of every beam and stud. But now—now, even though it was a startling change, I felt uncomfortable. I thought of those old women I saw in church with too much rouge and pasty makeup who were sadder for trying to disguise what they really were. I knew what was in the house. I didn't think the old spirits of the place could be driven out with new paint.

As I painfully wheezed up the back steps, I dreaded the dark interiors that could never be painted over, the lumpy furniture that needed to be burned, and the dusty air which forever smelled of liniment and garlic and fried fish and of someone old, who would never be anything but old.

"Why don't I take a bath?" I suggested to myself.

No, I don't have the energy to get off the sofa and draw it.

"But I'll feel better. I'll feel clean and relaxed.''

Too much trouble!

"I could lie back in the warm water and let my thoughts drift. It would be good for my sore wrist.''

I can't get up from the sofa. My body is sunk into the cushions, and my muscles won't respond. I'm certain they won't respond.

"Oh, do it, go on. Get up. Just slide one leg off the edge to the floor.''

No, it's impossible.

"Ridiculous. Just move a single finger and . . .''

Overcome with lethargy, I stared at the dark ceiling. The internal debate continued for some time. There was a third part of me that was immobile and detached, as if I could at once be sitting between the will to be active, to rise and move about, and the desire to let myself drop through the sofa and floor and cellar into oblivion. Finally, I sat up on my elbow. I had left the lights off in the living room. It must have been two or three in the morning.

I wasn't hungry, but out of habit, I tottered into the kitchen. I reached for the light switch but stopped, fearing the light would sear my eyes. I opened the refrigerator and stood in a sickly glow from the small bulb, scanning the bottles and plastic bowls and foil covered cans and deciding on a rubbery carrot from the vegetable drawer. *What am I doing*, I thought, *standing in a dark kitchen, holding a carrot that is more jello than vegetable, at three in the morning in a wrinkled housedress with a stale taste in my mouth? I'm not even hungry, am I?*

I found a paring knife stained with grape jelly. As I scraped, the brownish skin of the carrot slowly turned moist orange. I peered out the window. The yard light was aswarm with bugs. I scraped and scraped and looked down at the carrot. It had shrunk considerably. I stroked again, aware that the blade had slid the length of my thumb. I felt nothing. I scraped my thumb again. *I should feel something, at least a blunt pain or discomfort,* I thought. Fascinated, I opened a raw wound, a half inch long. My hand wasn't asleep; I didn't feel the pinpricks of blood rushing back. No, it was as if my hand didn't belong to the arm it was attached to. I could will that hand to move, but I experienced no pain in it—nothing. I scraped it a couple more times, sure that the five, six, seven layers of tissue came off with each stroke, as a trickle of blood seeped along my thumb.

I extended my arm over the sink, watching the vivid drops slide off. *What is happening to me?* I screamed inside. Bemused, I held my hand up. The thumb vaguely resembled a carrot, a carrot with a bloody gash. I held the thumb in my other palm and moved slowly across the kitchen to the dark stairs. I thought there were bandages in the bathroom. I should wash and wrap the thumb. As I climbed the stairs, I wondered if I would have felt anything had I lopped the entire thumb off.

In the bathroom, I ran cold water over my hand. For a long time I leaned my forehead against the mirror, staring down at the water and blood which ran down the drain. I wanted to be frightened, but all I could muster was weariness; no emotion, no pain, just a heavy, dull nausea.

After the bleeding appeared to have stopped, I went into my bedroom and sat on the edge of the bed, staring out at the fields. Leroy had always said "Snap out of it!" whenever I was depressed. Usually, I could just busy myself into forgetfulness—at least there was always so much work to do, that I didn't have time to dwell on my personal troubles. In fact, I rarely had time for reflection. "You can't pamper yourself with a family to worry about," he had chided me. He was right. But now, busyness didn't fulfill my inner aches, and since I had no family to lavish my attentions on, I could only worry about myself. I didn't want to meddle in my children's lives; they had their own problems, and I was determined not to be a burden on them. I was afraid that I loved Pastor Bill in an impossible way; I had to avoid him so my feelings wouldn't become more confused.

I looked over my property from the second story window, unable to see farther than the yard light and dim moon allowed. In sudden desperation I clutched my raw scraped thumb to my chest. *What is happening to me?* I wanted to shout. If I could no longer feel pain, I could no longer feel anything. I had no desire except to sleep and be left alone and not to worry about the house or the farm or anybody at all.

Everything was too complicated. How I hated Leroy for dying. Everything he had taken care of so well was dumped on me, and now I was suffocating under it. I wanted to scream, but there was nothing inside I could dredge up. It was too difficult to be angry. *It would be much easier just to lift the window and fall forward. I'm not afraid. The knife hadn't hurt me. I'm beyond pain.*

Suddenly, I felt calm and untroubled. *Everyone's problems would be simplified if I just went away.* The logic of oblivion was inescapable; I wanted only peace. No more fighting; simply a drop down on the warm earth through the window, a foot, two feet in front of me. I had fought against the idea for the past few months, but now, as I admitted what I had hidden, everything inside of me fell quiet. There was nothing to be afraid of. Having to struggle out of bed each morning was fear. Trying to seem interested in people was fear. Deciding what to wear, what to eat, and grappling with the thousands of daily questions was fear. Hooks, hooks were constantly catching on my skin and pulling for attention.

I thought of the enormous wolf spider still under the magazines, no doubt, in the next room, and the web it had laced from one end of the room to the window and back to the door. I never went in the room anymore because I knew it would tangle me beyond hope; I was already tangled by all the threads my life had woven. It was impossible to do anything but fall out the window. I had to extricate myself. My family would think I was clumsy as usual, had tumbled forward accidently against the old window, and "Isn't it really the best thing for her since she's old and alone and stubborn and dead inside? And now we can go on with our lives," they would say.

It was a peaceful night. There was a placid moon, and the stars were infinite in the quiet sky. I stood against the window glass. I could see far into the ground, as I had seen through the walls of the hospital. The earth was inexpressibly deep. My fall through the air would last two or three seconds, but as I looked down, I knew I would go on falling through the black loam and oceans and oceans of rock and sediment and boiling liquids and gases and then, since there was no bottom to the earth, I would come out in space which would be black and inimitable and peaceful.

I could not feel my body at all. My eyes were going out from me, and I saw the long descent and knew the house, the room, something in the very air around me was gently easing me forward. I watched my hands touch the rusty metal sash. My fingers wrapped around the window catch and lifted.

The window was immobile. I stared hard at my hands. I ordered my arms to raise the sheet of glass in the ancient pine wood frame. And then I knew: the upstairs windows were still nailed shut. I tried to deny the realization that months ago last winter, I foolishly nailed all the windows shut, fearing a burglar, when in actuality, an unconscious part of me had foreseen this night when I would struggle unsuccessfully to hurl myself onto the ground below.

I tugged stupidly at the window. I pounded the frame with my fists and spat on the glass and then slumped to my knees and fell limply on the floor. My head banged against the bed frame. Tears of frustration and anger and hate, tears I had refused for months, suddenly exploded over my face. I bit down hard on my hand. Nothing could hold back the tremors that rushed over me. "Oh God, oh God, oh God!" I cried, thumping my head again and again against the dusty floor. I wanted to reach inside and tear all my organs out. I would have shredded my arms and hands and legs with my teeth, but I couldn't stop crying and rolling from side to side, moaning and aching in every part of me.

I caught my breath and sat up quickly. From deep inside me, I felt someone had spoken distinctly and ordered me up off the floor. I looked around the room, suddenly calmed; everything was in its familiar place. The dresser, piled with dirty clothes and cologne bottles and hairbrushes, stood in the corner. My unmade bed was still in the middle of the room with its small night table and the antique lamp, the shade tilted awry.

I felt I should be quiet. I sat on the floor listening to my irregular gulps. My arms tingled. An incredible warmth seemed to wrap me in silence. And then, an unmistakable sensation, soothing and tender, drew me into silence and peace. I lifted myself onto the bed.

An overwhelming feeling to write down my thoughts swept over me. I picked up a writing tablet from the table next to the bed and the words began to flow out, faster than I could write them down:

"If you will but throw yourself into My arms, I will catch you. I will catch you with My love, and you shall know peace, only the peace that I can give, that I choose to give. You have been searching a long time in the dark, but sit and listen and know that I am about you. Give Me your hand, and I will lead you and protect you and give you comfort and repose. There is nothing you can do for yourself that I will not bless, if you will only listen."

I lay on the bed, calmer than I had been in a long time, than I could ever remember. Each word etched itself into my mind. I placed the tablet back on the table, next to the book Evelyn had given me, *God Will See You Through.* As I glanced at the title, I knew that God had spoken to me. I stared at the words and repeated them to myself again and again. I knew what the words meant; they resonated inside of me, but I was unable to think beyond them. I spoke them quietly like a prayer.

For years, going to church had been a ritual, a weekly visit to the home of an immense and unapproachable Being who was never home. The minister, so human and visible, was my tenuous link with something I never cared to understand. I had never prayed. There was no time to when Leroy had died. It was too quick.

I had promised to live a righteous life if the boys would recover from chicken pox and flu and pneumonia. But I had never made a prayer.

As I repeated the words, tasting each syllable, I knew God was speaking to me, and I couldn't refuse Him.

Minutes ago, I had wrestled with a window frame, and only two slivers of steel had kept me from plunging uncomprehendingly beyond despair. My warm, moist hands folded together. "Oh God, dear God," I prayed. "I know You are here with me." My tongue bunched up in my throat. I didn't know what to say, but I wanted to keep emptying out what stirred from somewhere miles and years inside of me. "Dear God, I'm so disgusting. I'm so vile and ugly and unworthy, I can't live anymore like this. Oh God, just take all of me if You want me. I don't know what to do. I can't think straight, I can't even pray." I stopped and looked at the words on the title page again. And then, I began to cry.

I cried for most of the night, but as the tears kept coming and the sobs shook me from every fiber, I cried knowing that each outburst, each harsh word or hurtful thought, each hidden frustration and denied pleasure or desire I had tucked away day after day for years was now washing out of me, and it was so good and necessary to cry. I felt clean, thinking of snow, pristine and delicate drifting out of the night sky, and even though the sheets were damp and my housedress soaked, I felt like snow, untrampled and untouched by anyone.

I prayed again for God to forgive me and to remake me, and I remembered a little prayer to Jesus I had learned as a child which I repeated until the words were meaningless. I laughed inwardly, realizing that the more I cried, the better I felt. I was sure the entire room shook with joy, and when the sun came up across the green fields and the darker green trees on the east horizon, I knew, without any doubts, that this morning even the sun rejoiced, and it came up for me. I owned it. I started crying all over again when I noticed that the yard light had burned out. *God's yard light,* I thought, *will be my light.* Exhausted, but at peace with myself, I closed my eyes and slept.

I awoke mid-afternoon, still clutching the book in my hand. I reread the title page to convince myself I had not dreamed the visit of God in my room. "Oh, thank You, dear heavenly Father," I said as I looked out on the brilliant day. It was a new day, I was certain of that.

I went into the bathroom and let the water in the bathtub run until it nearly overflowed. And then I sank beneath the water and soaked for a long while, amazed and thankful. I had never felt so clean; I even felt energetic. I wanted to call someone and just say, "Aren't you happy? Dear God, isn't this a beautiful day!"

After the bath, I went back, put on a dress I hadn't worn in over a year, and lay on the bed paging through the book.

Each page seemed to speak directly to me. I didn't understand everything I read, but I couldn't help but feel that God had placed that book in my hands for me to read. It was His hand reaching out to me, and I accepted it.Much of the book was quotations from the Bible, and as I read them, trying to understand their meaning, I thought of all the times in my life I had picked up our family Bible. Not often. And when I had picked it up, more than likely I was writing a birth or death or wedding in the flyleaf under all the dates recording our lives. Never had I read for inspiration or consolation or guidance. It was difficult to contain my surprise and awe at the statements Jesus said about life and truth and God's kingdom. I wanted to smash something through the same window I had been ready to jump out of and proclaim my happiness to the marigolds and oaks and stray farm cats in the yard below.

And as I thought of Leroy, I felt no anxiety. I knew God had drawn him up from the cemetery, and he was in God's hands now. I wanted to throw my arms around everyone I could think of and hug them until their eyes popped and they gasped for breath. I sighed and thought about the past year. As I flipped each page of memories, I shook my head, unable to realize why I had been a woman of stone, unable to see or hear or touch the beauty of my life and the goodness of those I loved, of those who loved me.

I looked around the room. Every object was comfortable and remarkable, and I didn't hate anything anymore. I was at peace. I lay relaxed, trying to distinguish the different birds flitting about the trees. In the distance I could hear the whine of a motor, which drew closer and then turned into the drive. I looked out the window. On a small, shiny motorcycle, Ludy had arrived.

9

For the next couple of days I experienced a vigor and excitement I hadn't felt in years. I woke up praising God, I read the Bible at intervals throughout the day, and I went to bed singing psalms and hymns half-remembered but not forgotten. I'm sure I startled Ludy one morning when I charged out of the house as I saw him approach on his small motorcycle. I literally danced across the farmyard toward him and tried to whirl him about, all the while beaming like a demented but earnest dervish. He stiffened and drew back, but I pulled him in circles until we both roared with laughter.

"What's got into you?" he asked tentatively.

"I can't explain how truly good I feel, and how everything is so wonderful," I trumpeted.

"But why?"

"Oh, Ludy, do you pray to God?"

He shrugged. "Sure, I guess so. Why?"

"Because God gave me my life back, and now I'm going to use it. I'm not going to lie down and die—no sir, not me. Why, I'm only fifty-eight years old. I've got a long ways to go to reach a hundred yet, maybe even two hundred."

"Hmmmm." He stroked his chin mockingly. "I don't understand what's happened, but I'm glad you're happy."

I squeezed his hand. "Me too, Ludy, me too. Now show me how to ride your bike there."

He looked askance. "Really?"

"Really. Teach me how to start it." I lifted my leg over the seat and straddled the motorbike. Ludy shook his head, but he showed me how to jump start the kick peddle. Within five minutes I was zigzagging around the house, between the barn and corncrib, while Ludy whooped and shouted. Ev drove past on the way to his farm, his head hanging out the window and his mouth agape in disbelief. I waved to him as if my riding a motorcycle was nothing out of the ordinary. I even startled a couple of chickens, which had unavoidably fluttered down from their perch as I zipped past. They screeched, flurried their wings, and hustled back into the coop.

As I jerked to a stop, nearly out of breath, Ludy threw his hands up. "Now I've seen everything. Mom won't believe this."

"I'm not sure I do. How come you're the only one to visit me since I've been home?"

"Aw, I don't know. Everybody's busy, you know."

"It looks like I'll have to go see them."

"On the motorcycle?" he asked wide-eyed.

"No, not on the motorcycle. Say Ludy," I looked at him seriously, "I thought your father insisted you couldn't buy one."

"Well, yeah." He looked away. "But I just . . ."

"They don't know, do they?"

"No, not exactly."

"You keep it at someone's house?"

"Well, yeah."

"And then just ride it out here and back, huh?"

"You aren't going to tell them, are you?"

"I'm not going to lie about it."

He hung his head. "It's my money." Then he brightened. "Hey, you can say it's yours. Yeah, then I can come out and ride it. And you can ride around whenever you want. That'd be okay with me. Huh, what do you think?"

I adjusted the rearview mirror; my reflected face looked distorted. "I don't know. I'll have to think about it. Your father . . ." I stopped, remembering the night David had exploded at dinner over the motorcycle. David's anger had been over more than just a motorcycle, though; I didn't want that to happen again. "Well, we'll see."

"You mean I can drive it out here then?"

"Your parents will know sooner or later."

"It's okay then?"

"For now," I assented. "But we can't hide it from them."

"All right!"

I shook my head, exasperated with his tenacity. "Now, what kind of work do we have planned for today?" I followed Ludy as he wheeled his bike into the barn.

"I was gonna touch up the trim on the eaves," he said. "It's too high for you to help."

"That's fine. I'll clean the house from attic to cellar and wall to wall. I think I've got dust on top of the dust. Maybe when you're finished, you can bring a hammer in and help me take the storms off the upper windows. I want the inside to shine like the outside."

"You like the paint job then?"

"It looks drenched in sunshine."

"It's kinda bright." He smiled.

"The heavens declare the glory of God, and the firmament proclaims his handiwork," I said, surprised at my recall.

"What's that?"

"A psalm I was reading before breakfast—Psalm 19, I think."

"Oh." Unimpressed, he picked up his can of trim, shouldered the ladder, and strode off toward the far side of the house.

I didn't know how or where to begin with the house, but I felt so energetic that my indecision didn't matter. Just a few days before, I would have slumped into the couch and stared blindly at the television, too numb to even fix fresh coffee. I carried the kitchen table and chairs out into the sun and stacked them on the sidewalk. Within an hour I had swept, mopped, and waxed the kitchen tile. As the floor dried, I went around the house to check on Ludy. He leaned precariously from the top rung of the ladder and swiped at the rain gutter with his brush.

"Oh, Ludy, be careful!"

He turned slowly, dripping paint. "This side is easy. You should have seen me balance the ladder on the porch steps."

I shaded my eyes against the sun. "You just be careful," I grumbled. He nodded and turned back to the house. I went in the front door, got out my old upright, and vacuumed the living room, dining room, and Leroy's old office, which I had converted into a sewing and storage room. Flocks of dust trailed me wherever I went, so I rolled up a couple of throw rugs to take out and beat in the front yard.

Marveling at the changes inside me, I paused occasionally to shake my head and chuckle. Songs came constantly to my mind, sometimes softly, sometimes breaking into peals of operatic revelry. Finally, about noon I reviewed the rooms under attack. They were satisfactory. I knew as the layers of dirt and webs and clutter were driven out of the house, so too, the layers of inactivity and frustration and despair had vanished from inside me.

"This is the day the Lord has made," I chanted. "This is the day, this is the day . . ."

I carried a plate of cold meat sandwiches outside. Ludy was not on the ladder. I went into the barn, suspecting he would be polishing the chrome on his motorcycle. Instead, he was sitting on the hull of the boat, his feet dangling lazily.

"Hungry?"

He took two sandwiches, looking at me puzzled. "I still can't figure out what Grandpa was going to do with this."

"Travel, I guess."

"Were you gonna go, too, Nana?"

I bit into half a sandwich. "I don't know. I never thought seriously about it. It would have been fun, but . . ."

"What?"

"Well, I don't know how to sail."

"You could learn."

"I don't really like the water."

"Oh." He nodded understandingly.

"And I get seasick."

"Is that all?" He smiled.

"He had so many crazy plans."

"Like what?" he munched.

"Well," I added between bites, "we were going to sail down the Mississippi River and then into the Gulf of Mexico, you know, around Florida, and then out into the ocean and then . . . anywhere in the world, I guess."

"Wow. Really?" He leaned forward, amazed.

"I haven't thought much about it in the past year, but gee, I don't know if I would have gone. It seemed so . . . crazy."

"You should, though. You could go to South America and then to Africa and Europe and the South Seas and . . ."

"Wait a minute," I interrupted. "You just don't jump in the boat and go. It's not like a treehouse where you can pretend and everything turns out like you dream it. Sure, he finished the frame, but he didn't complete the cabin and this and that, and it's far from being seaworthy. I'll probably advertise it in the paper and have someone haul it away."

"It's not finished," he protested.

"I don't want it sitting here taking up room another year."

"Let me work on it," he said.

I appraised him as he stopped chewing and gazed at me seriously. "It's a lot of work."

"I know. But I'd like to finish it. I could work on it in my spare time, after the chores, and you wouldn't have to pay me anything for fixing it up. I'd just like to." He ran his hand along the hull. It was a remarkable achievement for one man; there probably wasn't anything Leroy couldn't have done had he decided to.

"Okay, if you want." I tried to frown at him. "See what a bad influence you are on me. Besides being a motorcycle Nana, you've got me interested in that boat again. Let me go make some iced tea."

"I'll have milk," he replied, taking the last sandwich as I turned toward the house. "Nana?"

"Another sandwich?"

"No. I was just thinking . . . maybe when we finish the boat, we could . . ."

I shook my head slowly. "I get seasick."

"But you can get over that."

"It's unrealistic."

"You don't want to stay here forever."

"This is my home."

"I know. You can come back, though." He slapped the side of the boat. "This can be your second home, and you could sail anywhere you wanted to."

"I don't know . . ."

"I'll go with you."

I sighed, exasperated again. "You finish the boat, and we'll discuss it later." As I walked to the house, I thought about Ludy's wild scheme. *It's just too ridiculous,* I told myself, but I vowed to mull it over later. As buoyant and overflowing with God's graces as I was, nothing seemed too farfetched.

The phone rang that evening, and it was Pastor Bill. He sounded tired and distant. I wondered if my attitude toward him had changed markedly, or if he was revealing a side I hadn't seen before, but I felt less unsettled talking to him than I had in the past.

"I take full responsibility," he said.

"For what?"

"My bad chili and the conversation I subjected you to."

"Nonsense."

"And I kept you too late."

"Now don't blame yourself. I was distracted, and something ran in front of the car. It's nobody's fault."

"I do feel guilty about not coming to see you in the hospital, though. I went down one morning, and they said you had gone home the preceding day. I'm sorry for missing you."

"I hope you're on your knees asking my forgiveness," I snickered.

He paused and then laughed uproariously. "You've become feisty. I like that."

"I feel good, too."

"I'm glad." He paused again, then sighed. "I've been praying for you. You don't mind my saying that, do you?"

An easy warmth, as if the sun had just come out from behind bleak clouds, swept over me. I felt almost maternal toward Pastor when I spoke again. "You're a good man. I know you have been praying, and God has touched me." Tears came to my eyes. "You can't imagine, Pastor, just how strong and clean I feel deep down inside. I wish I could explain . . ." I spoke haltingly. "I can't really understand what's happening to me . . . but . . . I just . . . thank God for you and . . . and my family . . ." I turned my head and wiped my eyes and sniffled. Bill waited for me to speak again. "I never knew how happy and at peace I could be. God is so good."

"God is good," he repeated.

"Well," I bubbled. "There I go from feisty to . . ." I couldn't find the word. I wiped my eyes with the back of my hand.

"You are happy, aren't you?"

"I don't hurt anymore. Do you know what I mean?"

"I think so," he murmured.

"It's like God just scoured me and . . . I can't explain it. I just feel good."

"We all need some renovation from time to time, don't we?"

"I guess so. It's funny, though . . ."

"What's that?"

"Well, when I came home from the hospital, Ludy had repainted the house a canary yellow and . . ." I couldn't piece the logic together. The events were clear in my mind, and I sensed a thread connecting everything. I was certain God was using all the things about me to work for His benefit, but something vital eluded me. ". . . well, I don't know, it just helped." He didn't respond immediately.

"I understand."

"I'm not really explaining myself very well."

"No, I understand," he said softly. I sensed that he did. "Listen," his tone changed. "I've got someone knocking at the front door. Let me stop out sometime in the next week . . ."

"I'd like that. Maybe I could invite you for dinner?"

"Don't go to the trouble."

"No trouble. I've got an excellent recipe for chili," I teased.

"You are a heartless woman," he laughed. "Okay, I'll call you back in a few days on that. I've got to run now. God bless you, Dorothy."

"God bless you, too, Pastor Bill." I meant the words, feeling them reverberate inside me. There was a click, and Bill was gone, but I held the receiver against my face as if it were a warm hand—Pastor Bill's hand? Leroy's huge, chapped hand? It was both their hands, I felt, and also the compassionate hand of Jesus that had drawn the fever from the little girl's forehead, the hand that had returned to innocence the agonized brow of Mary Magdalene, the hand that stroked lepers and the blind and the paralytic and now was smoothing the wrinkles and scars and pain from my tear-streaked face.

"God is *so* good," I whispered.

10

"Nana," Ludy said to me the next morning as we carried boxes outside from the upstairs bedrooms and attic. "Nana, I'm going to need some money."

I thought immediately that he was planning to buy a car. "Now don't try to finagle for a car."

"No." He stacked his box on top of mine at the foot of the back steps. "We need some supplies." I brushed an unruly strand of hair back from my eyes.

"For what?"

"Well, you know, for the boat."

I sank to the bottom porch step, my aching legs stretched in front of me. *What has my consent triggered inside of Ludy?* I wondered. "What kind of supplies?"

"Oh, just some things."

"What things?"

He took a crumpled list out of his back pocket. "I just figured up some things we'll need right away."

I scanned the list and recognized some obvious construction items: wood screws, plywood, caulking, shelf lumber; but many of the items were unfamiliar to me. "What's this?" I pointed at one of his scrawls.

"Ummm." He scratched his nose. "That has to do with the rigging."

"And how about this?"

"Cleats? Those fasten the lines to the boat."

I leaned back on my elbows, amazed. "Since when did you learn about boats?"

"Well," he beamed. "I stopped at the library on the way home yesterday."

"Ludy! You went to the library? This is June. Your mother says she can't even force you to go during the school year."

"Well, yeah, I know," he smiled sheepishly. "But I just wanted to pick up some books on sailing and boats and boatmaking."

"You really plan to finish that boat, don't you?"

He pulled off his sweaty tee shirt. Because he was so skinny, he looked much younger than fourteen. The sun was at his back as he sat down on the sidewalk. "It should only take a month or so. We can probably have it in the water by late July."

"Where? The river? What makes you think it will even float?"

"It will."

"Maybe I was wrong giving you permission—"

He squinted at me. "It's a good frame, watertight. I've just got to finish the cabin, and we can order a specially made sail and mast from Dubuque. I called a marina there this morning . . .''

"Whoooooo," I exhaled. "You're really serious about all this."

"Nana," he pulled a handful of grass. "I really want to work on that boat. I know I can fix it."

I didn't doubt his capabilities. I stared at Ludy thoughtfully. He was good with motors, and he had a natural skill with wood. Even when he was nine he was building birdhouses and race carts and a coffee table with his father's tools. I didn't want to admit that my reluctance had nothing to do with Ludy; ever since he had suggested the idea to me, maybe even when Leroy had concocted the whole insane plan, I had suppressed the urge to agree that maybe it was all possible, maybe I did want to go. *People do crazy things like that all the time.*

As hard as I tried, though, I couldn't see a fifty-eight-year-old, clumsy, slightly overweight woman who hated water, sailing off to Bora Bora with her impulsive grandson. It was an improbable, irrational idea, and I couldn't deny that it frightened me. I thought of old Noah, toiling away in his backyard, wondering what God had called him to. Was God calling me? No, no, I shrugged off the thought. Ludy was scratching his name on the sidewalk with a pebble.

"How much will it cost?"

He tossed his head to one side and smiled. "Not much."

"And how much is that? Oh, go to the hardware store in Janesville and bring me an estimate. If you insist on completing this boat, you can use our old farm account there for what you need. But don't expect me to go on that thing with you!"

"Okay!"

"And I'm not going to pay you for working on it either, so long as—"

A truck coming up the drive interrupted me. Glenn and two of his sons had arrived to cart off the junk I was tossing out. Evelyn had been startled when I phoned my request for help that morning. Why, she had asked, did I want to get rid of my keepsakes? She was silent as I patiently explained that the only essentials I cared about were the people I loved, and would she mind telling that to Glenn also, and the sooner he came the better. I also thanked her for the book she had given me some months earlier. That probably tipped her off to the changes inside me, and the new confidence and authority in my voice. She was a perceptive woman, and God had come to me through her.

I surprised Jay and Jerry by hugging both of them.

Glenn watched curiously. "You're looking fit, Mom!"

"Never been better. Never!"

He looked from me to Ludy and then to the house.

"My word, what . . ."

"Ludy did it," I said. "Looks almost new, doesn't it?"

He stared at the house. "You did a good job, Ludy."

"You don't think it's too bright then, Uncle Glenn?"

"Pretty neat," said Jerry.

"Yep," I smiled. "And wait until you see the inside."

Glenn looked at me, his lips slightly parted.

"It's a great feeling to throw out that old stuff," I said, motioning toward the stack of boxes on the sidewalk. "Can't figure out why I kept most of it for so long. Maybe you should go through it and see if you want anything."

Jerry and Jay ran off after two stray cats that were yowling and prancing sideways at each other. Ludy and I followed Glenn over to the boxes, where he began to rummage idly.

"Oh, Mom, you don't want to get rid of this," he said, holding up a plaque from the Lions Club inscribed for Leroy.

"Why shouldn't I?"

"It's for twenty-five years of service. Dad was especially proud of it."

"I'm not keeping it. You can have it if you want. Nobody ever gave me a plaque for service, did they?"

"And here's my stamp collection," he said excitedly.

"The pages are all faded."

"Look at this, a 1912 commemorative!" He held a torn page in front of Ludy.

"Uh huh, very nice," Ludy said politely. "Should I put these boxes in your pickup now?"

"Look at these Roosevelt stamps. I bet they're worth something." He turned toward me. "Mom, as long as those rooms are empty, why don't you just keep all this?"

"I'm not a storage business, Glenn. I don't want it around anymore, so take it home and put it in your attic if you wish."

He probed his ear with his index finger and inspected me thoughtfully. "Are you getting ready to sell the house?"

"No, of course not. I told you before, it's my home. I simply want to clean out anything that sits in corners gathering dust."

"But don't these have any memories for you?"

I bit my lower lip and stared past Glenn to Jay and Jerry, who were tossing a kitten onto the compost pile.

"Every object in those boxes, the old letters and scrapbooks, and report cards and stamp collections and momentos do mean a lot to me." I sighed, as Ludy stooped to gather a box in his arms. We watched him lug it off toward the pickup. "But it's all the past."

"So what?"

"Do I have to explain?"

He closed the stamp album and brushed the dust from its cover and looked at his gray fingertips. "Okay, Momma." He flexed his hand and then made a fist. "But I'll take it home in case you change your mind."

"It's up to you."

Ludy hefted the box onto the truck bed. "Want me to back the truck up to the boxes?" he called.

Glenn appraised the stack of boxes. "Yeah, that'd be okay. Keys are in the ignition."

Ludy snapped his fingers and slid into the cab. I guided him across the lawn as he inched the truck back. "That's good!"

I wandered out toward the barn, and Jay and Jerry raced ahead of me to the hay loft. *They scampered up that rickety ladder like a couple of kittens themselves,* I thought.

"You coming up?" Jay shouted.

"Not me. Don't you two walk out on the rafters. They aren't sturdy like they used to be."

"Can we jump on the bales?"

"What for?"

" 'Cause it's fun."

"They're awful dusty."

"We don't care."

"But your mother will."

"What if we have to escape?" Jerry asked.

"Escape from what?"

"Oh, you know, monsters!"

"Yeah, like vampires and stuff," Jay added.

"I don't allow them in my barn."

They gazed down dejectedly. "What fun is there, then?" Jerry asked, peering down for an answer.

"Pirates!" I snarled.

"Yeah!" They jumped up and disappeared squealing. I heard them scurry between the stacked bales. Ludy's motorcycle was propped along the far wall next to the boat. I went over to it and touched the chrome, leaving fingermarks. *Wouldn't Glenn faint,* I mused, *if I were to come tearing out of the barn on the motorcycle? He really would think something was wrong with me.*

I felt an urge to pray. *Dear God,* I pleaded silently, *please help me know that I'm doing the right things. I don't know from one day to the next if I'm following Your will. In the past, I haven't exactly sought Your direction, but I am now.* I paused, wondering if I had spoken my doubts acceptably. Why should I bother God with my petty problems? And yet, I was certain He understood all of the unsaid yearnings inside of me. *And thank You for my family,* I added.

"Whose motorbike?" Glenn startled me.

"Oh, it's . . ." I stood in front of it feeling oddly embarrassed. "It's Ludy's."

"Oh yeah? When did he get that?"

"Just recently. I sort of bought it for him . . . well, I mean, he bought it for himself with the money I pay him for working."

"Uh huh. That's good you're taking the time with him, Mom, since he's been in trouble and all." He took a cigar out of his pocket and bit the end off. "He did a heck of a job on the house."

"He's a good worker."

"Kids up there?" I nodded. "Jerry? You two come down now, we're gonna go," he called.

"Okay, in a minute," they yelled.

He shook his head, his mouth puckered around the cigar. "Always in a minute." I watched him light up.

"That's a smelly one!"

He smiled, held it up to the light filtering through the roof beams and examined it carefully.

"Havana. Best tobacco in the world." He puffed it, then gestured, "How about that boat, Momma? We could probably hoist it on a trailer and haul it away." I turned and traced the contours of it. Ludy's interest had gotten me to look seriously at the symmetry, the painstaking construction of the parts, the correct names of which I didn't even know yet.

"No," I yawned. "No, we're going to do some work on it."

"Who is?"

"Well, Ludy and I are going to touch it up some."

"Oh, Momma, just get rid of it." He pointed with his cigar. "We can back right under it there and knock the braces out."

"No, we're just going to tinker around with it for a while."

"Suit yourself." He called up into the loft. "Hey, you guys! I'm going home now."

"Wait for us!" Jay backed down the ladder. Jerry, more recklessly, hung from a cross beam and dropped about four feet to the ground. "Hey! Race you to the truck!" They sprang out the door and sprinted across the yard. Though Ludy was only slightly older, there was a self-assurance he possessed that his cousins lacked. He was intense and complex in a way that fascinated me. More importantly, I was pleased with the changes so evident in him the past couple of weeks. He stood bemused, his hand casually resting on his hip as Glenn and I approached the truck. Jay and Jerry were bent over, huffing.

"Think I got ya," panted Jerry.

"Don't think so."

"Who was it, Ludy?" Red-faced and sweaty, both boys looked up at Ludy.

"Got me," he shrugged. "Probably a tie."

Jay punched Jerry in the arm, then leaped into the back of the truck.

"Thanks for your help," Glenn told them sarcastically. "Glad I brought you two along. Thanks, Ludy," he winked.

Ludy nodded. "No trouble."

As Glenn lifted a leg into the cab, he added, "Well, Momma, you know where this stuff will be if you want it."

"No thanks!"

"Okay. Call if you need anything."

"Ludy," I said while we watched Glenn drive off, kicking up dust swirls. "Do you know how to sail?"

"Well, no," he grinned. "But I've got a friend who has a boat, and this weekend . . ."

I held up my hand. "All right, all right. Let's go have some fresh lemonade and talk more about this boat."

"Got any cookies?"

I smiled demurely. "Maybe. Maybe we can hunt up a couple." He bowed and swept his arm gallantly for me to lead the way.

One of the chapters in the book Evelyn had given me discussed the importance of daily Bible reading. Each morning, as soon as I awoke, I reached over to my bedside table and took up the old, green-leathered family Bible. I began with a psalm, reading them in order, and then I read from the Gospels, skipping around as I felt God led me. The Old Testament seemed too forbiddingly historical for my tastes; I hadn't yet discovered a systematic approach for studying Scriptures.

Again in the evenings I reviewed the day's events, and then with the Bible propped against my knees, I pored over the words until I nodded drowsily and drifted off. One verse in particular, the night after I had cleaned and carted off the boxes of mementos, seemed to rise up in boldface to dispel any hesitations I might have retained toward the house cleaning. The twelfth chapter of Hebrews begins with the verse, "Let us lay aside every encumbrance," and continued, "let us run with endurance the race that is set before us." As I read those words, a burden lifted from me, as distinctly as if a balloon inflated with helium had carried up and away any oppression. And the excitement of running a race set before me was too real to deny. Even though I was unable to articulate what impending course was mapped out, I eagerly searched for more clues, more verses to illuminate the rising excitement.

Something is going to happen soon, I know it, I know it, I said to myself. I not only felt new and remade, but I was sure this new me was so incredibly different from the timid, boring, and frightened Dorothy of the past, that soon my friends would no longer recognize me. I sat up long past midnight, but when sleep came, it was deep and peaceful and dreamless.

Two days later I had driven to the supermarket for groceries when, as I wheeled my cart among the aisles, I encountered an old friend I hadn't seen for some time. She and her husband, friends of ours for too many years to recall, had divorced shortly after Leroy's funeral. The last I saw them together was at the services, both of them sullen and crisp with each other, though the significance of their behavior meant nothing until I saw the notice in the newspaper a few weeks later. A mutual friend phoned and said, as I had expected, that another woman was involved.

"Betty?" I was surprised at the sadness in my voice. "I heard you moved to Minneapolis."

She managed a smile. "Well, I did spend the winter there, but you know, it's hard pulling up roots."

"Were you working?"

"For a while as a secretary. But don't believe what people say. There's nothing glamorous about starting over at fifty."

"So you're back here now?"

"Not because I want to be," she said bitterly.

"I'm sorry things aren't going well."

"Oh, well, what can you expect."

"And how about . . ."

"Donald? That worthless bum. Yeah, he moved in with what's-her-name for a couple of months, and then he was going with a nurse, and now one of our old neighbors told me he's taken up with a college girl. Can you believe that? A college girl. What do you think that does to me?

Just be glad that your husband died before he had the chance to cheat on you."

Fortunately, God cushioned her remarks. A month earlier I would have been devastated by what she had said. "I'm very, very sorry for you," I touched her arm. "You really don't deserve all that."

She winced. "I deserve everything that's happened. You know, when I think about how I just let him push me around for so long, and I smiled and nodded and kept silent like a good little momma, that's all he wanted me for—to take care of him. Yeah, I'm so sick of him, I'd spit in his face."

"What about Betsy?"

"Oh, she's out in California someplace. I don't know. She never writes, which is fine with me. She chose to side with her father, and you know, she actually accused me of not understanding him. That's fine with me. That's her decision."

I found it difficult to look directly at her, but not so much because her hair appeared greasy and her makeup was uneven. She had put on weight, and her shapeless clothes hung sloppily. But something else about her troubled me, something not visible but definitely uncomfortable. Her eyes jerked about me but seemed not to focus. Her mouth had become small and cruel.

"What about you? Seeing anybody?"

"I'm not sure I know—"

"Dating anyone," she interrupted. "You know, looking around to get married again."

I shook my head.

"Yeah, you and Leroy always had a better marriage. Your kids probably even love you, huh?"

"I'm content."

She stared past me impatiently. "Maybe you were right to stay put this year. I sure didn't get anything out of moving. And don't let anybody tell you men are any different in Minneapolis," she snorted.

"Are you staying here for a while?"

She licked her lips. "Maybe. No place I want to go. I don't know, though. I'm not going to let him rub my nose in anything—you can bet on that."

I glanced at the contents in her cart—two six-packs of beer, a frozen pizza, potato chips, a box of sugar-coated cereal, a small tin of instant coffee. An overwhelming sadness swept through me. She reminded me of what I had been; perhaps not as angry, but just as bitter and pitiable.

"You look real good," she said quickly.

I impulsively wanted to say that I *felt* good, that I was happy because I had surrendered my pain and frustrations to God. I wanted to put my arm around her shoulder, hoping she would weep as I had, emptying herself of the darkness, the grotesque hatred I saw in her eyes. And I could comfort her. I could tell her plainly and simply about how God had rebuilt me, and how he could do the same for her.

"I don't know, maybe I'll go south. I hear Atlanta's a good city. It's gotta be warmer than Minneapolis."

I felt a surge of energy. My chest suddenly seemed to have risen into my mouth, and my heart beat fast.

"That creep doesn't send me money anymore, though. How am I supposed to get anywhere, huh? How's that for justice, huh?"

I couldn't think of the words to begin. Verse after verse was flowing past, tangled and fragmentary. If only I had the book Evelyn had given me, I could have slipped it into her purse.

"We're holding up traffic."

Two women with carts were waiting behind me. A small boy wailed in the closest cart and tore at a box of crackers. I moved past Betty. "Can you come for dinner some evening?"

"What for? Cry on each other's shoulders?"

I had a final urge to ask if she had a Bible, but as I looked at the two carts attempting to thread their way between us, I kept silent, wondering what the two women would think. Betty called back, "Let's get together for a drink sometime, huh?" She turned and headed toward the checkout.

I watched her, speechless and disappointed in myself. I had drawn back in revulsion, but, I told myself, I could still have been like her had not God taken my hand when I reached out for Him. *Why*, I thought dejectedly, *hadn't I blurted out a word, a single word, which might have changed her as remarkably as I had been changed?* I still had much to learn.

11

I sat on the porch in my wicker rocker breathing deeply the smells of cut grass from the lawn and the pungent alfalfa. From the house, I could see Ev's tractor swing in wide loops in the early morning sun, baling the green-gold stalks that fell under his whirring blades. It was the first crop of summer, and I knew that he would be out in the corn slicing off brown tassels and in his bean field cultivating, in anticipation of an abundant harvest.

I closed my eyes contentedly and breathed the cool aromas as I rocked, listening to the rocker creak on a loose porch board. A whippoorwill called to my left, and from farther away I heard the answering melody of its mate. I could pick out the whine of a motorcycle in the distance, and by the time Ludy arrived, I was standing beside the mailbox, smiling and batting at the dust that trailed him.

He lifted his goggles up on his forehead. "Boy, I can hardly breathe."

"I can see why," I coughed.

The engine's chug and ping reminded me vaguely of a popcorn wagon that used to sit on Main Street. On muggy summer evenings my mother would pile a half dozen children, dogs, and cats onto our flatbed pickup, and we'd sing all the way to the popcorn wagon. I even kidded Ludy about his "popcorn wagon," but he just smiled impishly and shook his head. I followed him around to the backyard as he went to park his bike. He had acquired the habit of toweling off any dust before he parked it in the barn, and when I caught up to him, he was already wiping the smudged chrome.

"I almost forgot." He paused and looked up at me. "I picked up something on the way out this morning." *Oh no*, I thought—*more additions to our boat construction bill.* We had recently passed the three-hundred-dollar mark, and the boat was still far from complete.

"You see," he continued. "I was just turning off the county blacktop when I saw this huge old crow sitting on something in the road. Well, he squawked and flapped off to a fence post, and I saw that a mother coon had gotten run over." He turned back to polishing the grillwork.

"Uh huh, so what's the point?" I asked.

"Oh yeah, the point." He glanced at me mischievously. "Well, it must have happened last night, because there was blood and guts and all that stuff on the pavement."

"Skip the details."

"Aw, Nana, it was just a coon." He saw I was unimpressed. "But like I said, it was a mother coon and she had two kits."

"All of them killed?" I grimaced.

"No." He reached into the saddlepack over the back fender and brought out a handful of fur. A tiny, shivering raccoon, possibly ten weeks old, yipped like a kitten as it tried to run up Ludy's arm. "There was another kit too, both of them in the ditch crying, but he got away in the weeds. This one was so scared he just hunkered down."

I took the baby raccoon from him and held it to my shoulder. It clung frightened, its needle-like claws raking at my skin. "It sure has some sharp claws," I said.

"I know, look at this." Ludy stretched out his arm which was laced with pencil-thin scratches. "I wish I could have caught the other one. It'd be a lot easier to raise them together."

"You're going to keep it?"

"I thought I might."

"Don't you want to let him go? He'd be a lot of work."

"I don't mind." He took the kit back and curled the fur ball into the crook of his arm. "He's a little young to fend for himself."

Ludy stroked and rocked the raccoon, cooing to it. The raccoon calmed down, its moist, wide eyes blinking at us, expectant and intelligent. Burrs were tangled in the dark bandit mask. Ludy pinched them out between his fingers.

"He can't weigh over five pounds."

"Let me get him some milk." I rushed up the back steps, amazed at my concern for a raccoon. I often saw them around the farm but usually ignored their activities.

"Why don't you warm it?" Ludy called in after me. I tried to surmise what baby raccoons might eat in addition to milk. I knew from gardening that they have almost no preference among fresh vegetables, so I dug a stalk of new celery out of the refrigerator. On impulse, I tore a slice of bread in half and sopped it in the milk. I had no sooner put the dish in front of the raccoon when he lunged at it and noisily devoured the contents. Finding the stalk a bit more unwieldy, he rolled on his back, grasped the stalk in his paws and nibbled away at one end.

"Where you going to keep him?" I asked Ludy.

"I thought maybe in one of the old rabbit cages."

"The ones out by the sheep pens?"

He nodded.

"You'll need to fix the hinges on the door; they're all broken off."

"No problem." He stooped down to pick up the raccoon and remaining celery. "Hungry little guy, weren't you?"

"You sure you want to keep him?"

"Yeah, why not? They make good pets, and besides, they usually run away after a year."

"You take care of him, then."

"I said I would." Ludy scratched him under the chin, and the raccoon purred like a kitten. "Pretty soon you'll take care of yourself, won't you?" He put the raccoon down in the grass, and we watched to see what he would do. He looked around curiously, his nose twitching, then he plumped up his back, hopped forward, and crouched down again. His tail seemed too large for the rest of him.

"Your father had a pet skunk for one summer," I told Ludy.

He looked at me, surprised. "He did?"

"It was a smart little fellow, too, always came from the barn when David whistled. Your father built him a snug little burrow up in a hay bale, and as regular as clockwork, Stinky—that's what we called him —would show up for his morning and evening feeding. I think we even had Molly, our sheepdog, then. Everybody got along with Stinky."

"Was it fixed?"

"You mean the perfumer? No, but we never did have a problem."

"Dad really had a pet skunk?" He looked at me, mystified.

"Yes. Ask him about Stinky sometime."

"He's never said anything about it."

The raccoon charged the back steps, cautiously peered up over the bottom one, grabbed a paper sack of cherry tomatoes I had been meaning to wash, and dragged it off under an evergreen.

"He looks like a little hobo with his pack." Using his nose and deft paws, he had stuck his head into the sack. We could hear him chewing.

"Raccoons can be little scamps, always into garbage. I don't think a raccoon-proof garbage can will ever be invented." His tail flapped on the ground. "What are you going to call him?"

Ludy stared off into the distance. "Oh, I don't know. How about Tramp? No, that's a dog's name. How about Hobo? Yeah, he sorta reminds me of a hobo. Hey, Hobo." The raccoon pulled his head out from the sack, startled.

"I guess it's Hobo then!" I said.

I sat down on the ground to watch Hobo frisk around the lawn, wrestle with my foot, and pounce on imaginary enemies as Ludy went to repair Hobo's new home. I tried to distract him with one hand that imitated a giant spider while trapping him from behind with the other, but his vision was too good. He would pivot quickly and box my hand just before I grabbed him, and then roll on his side, hiss ferociously, and kick at my other hand. Suddenly, he would lie perfectly still on his back, cover his eyes with his paws, and peek out at me. After about ten minutes, Ludy came dragging an old wooden cage and stand across the barnyard.

"You're puffing," I teased.

"It's heavy and the bottom is nearly rotted out. But it should be a good enough home until he's trained to stay around here."

"Say," I remembered. "I've got an old dog leash and chain in the house somewhere. You could tie him up while you work and then cage him at night."

"That's a great idea." Ludy picked up Hobo and thrust him inside the cage. Hobo sniffed each corner, examined the floor carefully, then rattled the wire walls when Ludy shut the door.

"It won't take him long to figure that out," I said, pointing to the latch. Hobo scratched at the door and whimpered.

"Okay, okay," Ludy lifted him out. "You'll like it better when I put some sticks and papers and rags inside so you can snuggle down and hide. Won't that be a good idea?" Ludy asked as he dangled Hobo in front of his face. Hobo studied him carefully. Ludy held him closer, watching for a reaction. Faster than Ludy could draw back, Hobo extended a back paw and kicked Ludy's nose.

"He'll get used to you," I laughed. "Let me go get that collar." I remembered seeing it in a kitchen drawer during the house cleaning. When I returned, I was not surprised to see Hobo sitting on Ludy's shoulder, obviously having reconciled any differences. We went out to the barn, Ludy to finish the paneling of the cabin, me to hand tools and hold wood in place, and Hobo, our new compatriot, to rummage among the nail sacks and scold the pigeons, who looked down nervously from the rafters.

The cabin was progressing well, with all but one wall completed. Ludy had drawn sketches of each angle, showing where the bunks would fold down, where the cabinets and shelves would hold our provisions and emergency equipment, where the small stove and refrigerator would be fastened in. It would be a compact arrangement, but as Ludy assured me, everything necessary for a sustained voyage would be conveniently stashed in living quarters smaller than my bathroom.

At lunchtime, I went in to fix peanut butter and jelly sandwiches and a pitcher of iced lemonade. Ludy set Hobo on the lawn, where the two of them scampered and wrestled in the shade. When Ludy put a half sandwich down in front of the frisky raccoon, he scrunched out flat on his belly, his coal tip of a nose twitching furiously.

"Maybe he doesn't like peanut butter," Ludy said.

"Don't bet on it," I replied. "I think he's just stalking it." And sure enough, he crept forward slowly until his nose touched the crust of bread, then he sprang into the air, flipping over the sandwich, and gamboled sideways around it.

"He's acting like a little hunter, huh?"

"I think that's instinctual, Ludy."

"Boy, I'm gonna have to learn more about raccoons."

I winked at him. "The library has some good books on raccoons."

Ludy paused in mid-bite and tore a hunk off his sandwich. "That's funny, isn't it, Nana, that all winter I never opened a schoolbook, and now this summer, I'm probably the library's best customer. Hey, look! I think he does like peanut butter!"

Hobo sat back on his haunches and stared at us as he nibbled. Before long a gooey smear of peanut butter spread from his nose across the white ruff around his mouth and clung to the long whiskers which flicked contentedly.

"You're going to have to teach him some manners," I scolded.

"Should I insist upon a cloth napkin?"

"That's not a bad idea," I said in my best Emily Post voice. "Raccoon etiquette must begin at a young age."

"By all means," he added snootily. "Your wine, sir." He placed a glass of lemonade in front of Hobo. Hobo stood up against the glass and peeped over the rim, and the unbalanced glass toppled over. Hobo jumped back but still took a good dousing. He shook his little body and then began licking his paws and smoothing his fur.

"That is really cute," Ludy said. "Don't they sometimes wash off their food, too?"

"Uh huh," I nodded.

Just then one of the friendlier stray kittens galloped from around the house to investigate the new addition. Hobo and the kitten were about the same size, and as the kitten stopped a foot away and hissed, Hobo reached out a tentative paw. They sniffed each other. Hobo's ears flared back slightly, and the kitten's tail thumped the ground. It was the kitten's turn to tap Hobo on the head, and after a cursory examination that satisfied both kit and kitten, they soon were chasing each other in circles.

"If only people could get along that well," Ludy said, munching his second sandwich.

"I've always said we could learn a lot from watching animals. Except chickens. They have got to be the dumbest animals I've ever seen. You just watch, though, and see how smart that raccoon is."

"Maybe I'll teach him some tricks."

"They have very nimble fingers, and they're good climbers, and I think they even know how to swim."

"I sure can't see why anybody would want to kill them," Ludy frowned.

"Ummm," I agreed, my mouth full of lemonade. "They're God's little bandits." Ludy looked away, kicked off his tennis shoes, and flexed his toes.

"You're not gonna start talking about God again, are you?"

"What's wrong with that?"

"Aw, I don't know."

"Do you ever think of God, Ludy?"

"Why should I?"

"Because He should be part of your life."

"I go to church." As an afterthought, he added, "Once in a while."

I wasn't sure how to continue. I didn't want to say anything that might scare Ludy off. I knew how easy it was to say the wrong thing and have Ludy clam up for days—I had seen that side of him often enough. But again, I felt such an urge to share the happiness I was experiencing, that I wanted to sound him out more to understand where God was in his life.

"God is more than church. Have you ever read the Bible?"

"Naw, too old-fashioned. I can't understand all those 'thee's' and 'thou's.' Besides, it's boring."

"I'm sorry you feel that way." I searched for the right approach. "You shouldn't wait until something drastic happens in your life to speak with Him." He stared at me disinterestedly. "You know, you don't even have to pray. Just talk to Him. Tell Him what's on your mind."

"Why should He care what's on my mind?"

"He just does. You're special to Him, and even though you deny it, He does watch over you."

"Naw, that's kiddy stuff and for old ladies." He lay back on the grass and shut his eyes.

"I'm an old lady."

He opened one eye, blinked at me, and shook his head.

"Ludy, for a long time I felt deserted inside. Nobody lived in here." I tapped my chest. "In fact, I was ready to end my life one night, but I cried out that I was tired of being empty and lonely, just like my house, and don't laugh or think I'm crazy—but God heard me, and He came down right inside and cleaned the whole place up, swept it clean, slapped on new paint just like you did to my house, and I was new. My property value has gone up, and I couldn't be happier."

He stared up at me. I knew he was turning over what I had said. I watched the kitten run up to a low branch, then Hobo dashed up the other side of the tree. They took turns being pursued and pursuer. After about five minutes Ludy pulled his shoes back on.

"I'm glad you're happy," he said.

I tried to analyze his face for further clues as he stood up, but he gazed impassively at the sky. A black wall of thunderheads was sweeping slowly from the west. I knew, though, that I had left a kernel of thought for Ludy to ponder. We had drawn together the past month, partially from our mutual solitudes; but also, I suspected, for other reasons not entirely clear to me yet.

The excitement of the boat and our wild plans of sailing off to unknown destinations fired both of our imaginations. I tingled inside. A vast plan was unfolding before us, and Ludy and I were just taking the first, unsteady baby steps. I knew that.

"Looks like it's coming in pretty fast."

"We haven't had a good storm this summer, have we?" I said as I stood up.

"I think I'll buzz on in to town so I can order our mast and sails. Is that okay with you?"

"How much?" I groaned.

"I don't know yet." He stretched. "I'll call you on the phone. You want to see the dimensions I figured?"

"No, they won't mean anything to me. Just let me know how much my bank account is going to suffer before you place an order, all right?"

"Sure." He grinned. "You want the best, don't you?"

"Let's go for the second best if they're cheaper." I laughed and pointed to the tree. Hobo and his new accomplice sat side by side, washing each other's ears.

Ludy ran off toward the barn and came back pushing his motorcycle. He jump started it and drove up on the lawn next to me. Both kit and kitten cowered in the tree.

"Hey, are you busy Saturday morning?" he shouted over the engine.

"Not that I know of. Why?"

"We're going sailing." He gave me a thumbs up and skidded away. His goggles made him look like a grasshopper. I didn't think the playmates would be out of the tree for awhile, so I carried the sandwich tray and lemonade pitcher into the kitchen.

When I came out a few minutes later, Hobo was gone, but the kitten was rolling in the driveway dust. I walked around the house, then out to the barn, poked my head in the chicken house door, and even ambled out to the road, thinking the raccoon had trailed after Ludy. When I came to the back porch, the screen door was banging in the wind. As I expected, the ingenious Hobo had let himself inside and was prowling the kitchen cupboards, sniffing each container.

"Oh no, don't get over eager," I chided him as I took him out to his cage. He wasn't pleased by the confinement, but after I padded his cell with old rags, a carpet remnant, and newspapers, he settled down to arrange his own furniture. He pawed and tore paper and bunched rags for at least an hour, and when the storm hit, I bustled into the house. I came out after the rain slowed to intermittent spatters to find Hobo snug and snoring, oblivious to any rain or thunder.

That evening, though, I jumped out of bed, startled by a plaintive cry. As I hurried downstairs I thought of the raccoon, away from its mother for the first night. Hobo was indeed wailing like a forlorn, abandoned infant. I put a bowl of milk in his cage, which settled him down a little, but remembering numerous litters of kittens and Molly when she was a pup, I decided on an age-old remedy.

I wrapped a wind-up clock in a soft towel and placed it under the papers. Unable to locate a hot water bottle, I carried out my heating pad, connected it to two extension cords which just reached the porch outlet, then set it to low heat. I didn't hear a peep from him the rest of the night.

In a couple of days, he wouldn't need the maternal substitutes. By then, he would have learned to unlatch his cage door, scramble onto the porch, and curl up in the sleeve on an old coat he had dragged down off a nail. So long as I didn't have to sleep with him, that was fine. Our most prolonged disagreement, however, was over who would control the kitchen. For stubbornness, he had the mule beat by a long shot.

12

"A tech dingy," Ludy explained, "works on the same principle as our boat, except ours is three times larger."

"And when did you become an expert on sailing?" I asked.

"Since yesterday, when I had my first lesson," Ludy grunted as he shoved the eleven-foot sailboat bow first into the murky water. He glanced up, his head tilted to the screams of swimmers and sunbathers that echoed the tree-lined shore. The four-acre lake drew its water from the adjoining Cedar River on the north edge of Waterloo, and even though a foul scum was evident, at least forty people had trooped out to the park that Saturday morning.

"Who would want to swim in this filthy water?"

He glared at me, hands on his hips. "I suppose people who want to swim."

"Well, they should use the swimming pool."

"Nana . . ." He began to say something but stopped and shook his head. He recovered the life jackets he had tossed onto the sand and slipped one on, lacing it tightly up the front. He nodded towards the other. "That one is yours."

"I think I'll just watch you."

"No," he said, exasperated. "You've got to learn how to do this. It's really very easy to sail, and we might as well practice here."

"I would rather wait for the big boat."

"Like I said," he reminded me. "The principle of wind is the same no matter what the size of the boat. It's fun, it really is." He scrambled into the front of the boat and fiddled with a knot at the base of the mast.

"You sure your friend trusts you with his boat? I'd hate to have anything happen to it."

"What could happen?" Ludy sighed. "Look, it's a beautiful clear morning, temperature seventy-eight degrees, wind twelve miles from the west, barometric pressure falling slightly . . ."

"So you're a weatherman too?" I teased.

"Nana, would you please take this seriously!"

"I'm just trying to hide the fact that my knees are clanging together and my hands won't stay steady enough to get this cord in the hole here." I fumbled with my life jacket.

"There's no reason to be nervous."

"There is if you can't swim!"

"Don't worry, we can stand up knee-deep anywhere in this lake."

"You mean we're going to tip over?" I tried to hide my alarm.

"Capsize," Ludy corrected me.

"That sounds even worse."

"No, we won't. Let me help you tie that." He splashed over and laced my jacket until it was snug. "The first thing to remember is that sailing is a matter of wind and vectors."

"Vectors? That sounds pretty complicated. What are vectors?"

"I'm not sure exactly, but the way Linda explained it to me—and she's only been sailing a year—is that if you can tell which direction the wind is coming from, then by figuring the angle you are going, you use the tiller and the sail to adjust your speed."

"Oh, that sounds easy enough," I said a bit sarcastically.

"It is when you get out on the water." He waded over to the boat. I tested the water with my left foot; it was tepid and slimy. A gang of teenagers ran along the beach behind us, then veered sharply toward the water and dove headfirst. A younger girl trailed them with an air mattress. Halfway between the teenagers and the sandy, roped-off area where most of the swimmers were, a German shepherd nipped after a small dog that was retrieving floating sticks.

"What's that in your hand, Ludy?"

He held up a pole attached to the sail. "This is called a gaff. It fastens on right here."

"And what's that rope for?"

"Ropes on a boat, Nana, are called lines. And this one raises and lowers the sail. Don't ask me why, but this line," he held it up, "is also called a sheet. And down here is the boom."

"And that swings from side to side, doesn't it?"

"That's right."

"I've never been in a boat before."

He stared incredulously. "Never? Not even a rowboat?"

"No, never had reason to."

He pulled the line attached to the mast and the sail rose slowly, fluttering against Ludy until he tightened and tied off the line at the bottom. Then he turned and squatted as he fit the tiller at the back of the boat.

"The rudder, you probably know," he said quickly, "steers the boat underwater, and we guide it with the tiller, which I'm adjusting like this, and the extension here is the hiking stick."

"Hiking stick?" I repeated.

He stopped and looked up at me. "We've got to use the right names."

"Aye, aye, Captain," I saluted. Across the lake, two boys were swinging a girl between them. On the third swing she sailed free and plopped into the water.

106

"Okay, we're all ready," Ludy said.

Blithely I marched forward into the lake, aware of Ludy's interest at my apparent change of attitude. The water was mild and comfortable, even though a gritty film floated on the surface.

"Where should I sit?" I steadied the boat.

"Just step over the gunwale in the middle there, and I'll balance the other side."

With an "Oof," I was over the gunwale and into the boat. "Ready to heave-ho, sir!"

"Okay, I'm turning about." He guided the bow around until we faced out toward the lake. "Please hold the mainsheet until I shove off." I took the line, feeling a persistent tug of wind against the sail. Ludy hoisted himself into the boat, and we glided noiselessly away from shore. I tried to follow the bottom of the lake, but the water was so cloudy, I could barely arrange the fragments of my reflected face.

"The wind is perfect today." He tightened the sail. "It's usually best that the sail doesn't luff like it is now. See how it's fluttering? Well, we're in irons, which means the wind is coming straight at us and the boat isn't going anywhere."

"How long do I have to kneel cramped?" I moaned.

"You can sit up now. Look!" He pointed at the sail. "We're coming into the wind. Feel it? Okay, here we go."

I was fascinated by how the boat imperceptibly gained momentum, my eyes shifting from the impression of wind against the sail to Ludy's animated face. I expected to hear the boat move, but the ridge of water we cut rippled silently behind us, and the wails from the swimmers seemed to disappear. We could have been skimming across ice. I reached down to cup a handful of water, amazed at the speed with which we were propelled. The wind just stirred my hair; on the beach I hardly noticed it. But now, trying to gauge our velocity by a tree I picked out a hundred yards to my left, I knew the wind we captured momentarily on the small canvas sail was under our power—at least until we swung suddenly to our right and came to an abrupt stop.

"In irons again," Ludy said. I glanced over my shoulder at him. He sat on the back side of the boat, the line that ran through a pulley and two swivel blocks that controlled the sail wrapped around his right hand, and his fingers clenched around the tiller. He watched the sail intently. "It just takes some practice. See those little ropes tied up there?"

"You mean the red ones?" I responded.

"Uh huh. Those are the telltales, and they show the direction of wind. The thing to remember is that we can't sail straight into the wind, so keep an eye on the telltales to adjust the sail and the tiller."

"You mean I'm going to navigate?"

"Why not?"

"I'll probably tip us over."

"No, it's almost impossible to capsize this boat. Here, you may as well switch places with me since we aren't moving."

Holding onto the narrow side deck, I managed to crawl to where Ludy sat. He handed me the mainsheet first, motioning for me to wrap it around my hand, and then he placed my other hand on the hiking stick.

"Keep in mind," he emphasized, "that when you pull the tiller toward you, the stern will also come toward you."

"And what if I want to go left?"

"Left? You mean port?"

I shrugged.

"Port is left, starboard is right, and the wind comes from windward and it goes to leeward. So just play around with the tiller until it feels right."

"What about the sail?" I wondered if I would be able to use both hands at the same time and still remember that port was right and starboard left, or was it the other way around?

"You're doing fine. Let a little more slack in your line."

"Mainsheet," I corrected him. He smiled and nodded.

"You've got it now, Nana!"

"I can feel it! I can feel it!" I shouted. "Look, the wind is picking up again." With a slight whoosh, the sail puckered and then filled suddenly. Instead of bobbing, we shot off at an angle away from the beach.

"Ease off a bit, ease off."

"How?"

"Just let the sail slacken more, or you can turn the tiller slowly."

I let a foot of rope slide through my hand until the sail flapped like clean wash on a backyard clothesline.

"Tighten it some," Ludy instructed.

A gust of wind shook the sail. The boat swung forty degrees, lifted slightly, and gradually gained momentum as the sails billowed. The boat began to tilt up on its right side.

"Ease off a little," Ludy coached as he leaned backwards out over the water.

"What are you doing?" I said, alarmed at the precariousness of his position.

"I'm okay, just balancing us out, that's all."

I tried to calculate what would happen if I pushed the tiller away from me. Ludy had said the stern would move in the direction the tiller moved, and as I pushed it firmly, the stern did pivot. I experimented with other basic maneuvers, each time assessing what the boat did, and what I needed to do in correcting something that Ludy frowned at. After a half hour of zigzagging from shore to shore, I was able to steer toward any mark that Ludy pointed at and increase or slow our speed as I wished.

"This is fun," I grinned.

"Told you so," he added.

"You want to be captain for a while?"

"Sure!" He clambered under the boom and crawled toward me.

"Don't rock it!" I scolded, but he just smiled and rocked the boat even more.

"Be serious, Ludy, or we'll both be swimming to shore."

"Thought you said this was fun?"

I handed him the mainsheet and felt my way forward until I could comfortably sit under the boom. I squinted against the brightness of water. *Maybe I'll learn to swim,* I told myself. *Maybe I'll even learn to like water.* I wanted to know more about vectors and wind and the nautical terms familiar to sailors. Ludy kept up a nonstop dialogue with himself as he steered toward imaginary targets.

"Watch out for that sub dead ahead," he roared in mock frenzy. "Here comes Nessie from Loch Ness," he screamed. "We're being torpedoed, we're being torpedoed!"

I leaned back against the side, trying to concentrate on the remarkable blue of the sky and the clouds that scudded overhead like whitecaps. At times as when he was teaching me, Ludy seemed entirely in command, all business; but now, giving free rein to his imagination, the fourteen-year-old boy struggling out of childhood was all too visible.

"They're flying the Jolly Roger, matey," he winked.

Unabashed, I shouted back, "Prepare to attack!"

"Aye, aye, mate!"

"Shiver me timbers, they're firing on us." He winced as he took a slug to the chest and fell backwards, tumbling out of the boat.

"Ludy!" I grabbed the tiller, startled, but his laughing face sputtered out of the water behind the boat. He slapped the water with both hands and told me to take the boat in; he would swim for shore. Confidently, I swung the boat around. As I glided past him swimming lazily on his back, I called, "Watch out for sharks. I see a fin circling you."

He pulled up abruptly and stared at me as I went past.

"Piranhas ahead," I said in wild-eyed fear. He thrashed like he was being eaten alive.

"Nana," he yelled. "I'll get you for this!" He swam madly after the boat, but the distance between us increased until he gave up and went again to his easy backstroke. Meanwhile, I concentrated on the exact spot we had launched from. As I took aim, I realized a young couple necking on the beach had sat up and were watching me head straight for them. The landing was perfect, even though I had never landed a boat before. About ten yards from shore I let the sail go slack, and the boat coasted in. I jumped out, splashed around to the bow, then dragged the front end as far up on the sand as I could. The young boy and his girlfriend came over to help lug the boat farther forward so it wouldn't drift back into the water.

"That looks like great fun," the boy said. "I bet it's hard, huh?"

"No, not really," I answered smugly. "Not when you know what you're doing."

"I'd like to try it sometime," the girl broke in.

"The thing to remember," I said, brushing sand from my ankles, "is that sailing is all a matter of vectors and wind."

"Sounds too difficult for me," the girl said as she adjusted her bikini top.

"Been sailing long?" the boy asked.

"No, not long."

"That sure is a nifty little boat."

Impressed with my ability, I couldn't stop bragging. "You should see the boat I've got at home."

"Yeah, what kind?" The girl leaned against her friend, his arm draped casually across her bony shoulders.

"Oh, it's much bigger." I made an expansive gesture with my arms.

"A yacht?"

"Well, it's a magnificent sailboat, over thirty feet long. My grandson, swimming there, and I are building it ourselves."

"No kidding?"

I was intrigued by the amazement on her face. I had never spoken of the boat to anyone before, especially with such affection.

"You're not going to sail it here, are you?" the boy said. There was a large gap between his two front teeth and his eyes crinkled up when he smiled. As I studied his face I thought of Hobo. There was something about the boy that reminded me of a raccoon.

"Oh no!" They waited for me to explain. I briefly thought of letting the matter rest there, but their eager expressions made me continue.

"No, the lake here is too small for that boat. No, we're going to sail down the Mississippi to the Gulf of Mexico and then probably around the world. I don't know—maybe by way of South America first."

"Wow, really?" The girl arched her head forward when she spoke.

"Oh man, oh man, that's a super idea," the boy added. "Just super!"

"We've got lots of work to do so we can get the boat seaworthy by the first of August."

"Wow, I can't believe that," the girl said. She looked at the boy, shook her head, and repeated, "Wow!"

"Wish I was going with you," the boy said, watching Ludy straggle onto the beach, still pretending to swim.

"Uh, uh, water!" Ludy groaned as he collapsed onto his face. I laughed and reeled my finger near my ear to show them that he was crazy. They grinned and nodded as Ludy panted again, "Water! Water!"

"Well, have a great trip around the world," the boy said as he scooped up the girl's legs and carried her off down the beach Tarzan-style.

"Let me know if you have room for one more," she called over her shoulder.

Ludy sat up and watched them. "What'd they want?"

"They wanted to sign aboard." I sat down in the sand next to him and began tracing the outline of our barn-locked ship.

"Oh? We could have used the girl."

I glanced up at him.

"I mean, to swab the deck, you know," he said, embarrassed.

"Sure, sure," I teased.

"Well, you know."

"Uh huh." I threw my head back and laughed.

He tossed a handful of sand at me, then raced into the water, disappearing under the surface with a cry of "Banzai!"

As Ludy drove back to the farm, I stared pensively out the window. He had struggled almost singlehandedly to tote the dingy onto the trailer, and as I watched the trailer sway behind the car in the rearview mirror, I realized what little help I was. Invariably I had called Leroy to change a worn tire or to replace a frayed wall cord. Even after he was gone, I depended on David or Glenn for hauling trash or unloading sacks of garden fertilizer. As a farm wife I had done my share of baking and household chores, but so many areas of my life had been taken care of by my men. It seemed that someone always stepped in, having decided that I should not be allowed to tinker with motors or sit around the bowl-

111

ing alley one night a week, or even spit in front of someone if I had a mind to.

And I resented Ludy's grunts of disapproval in wrestling the boat on the trailer, even though he was justifiably annoyed. I wasn't pulling my share. I didn't need to be relegated to only "feminine" activities. I was capable of hammering, of using a skill saw, even of getting my hands in engine grease. I resolved to learn men's work instead of just watching and to cross those boundaries that kept me from doing what I knew I could.

"Well," he asked, glancing in the rearview mirror, "how did you like the sailing?"

"It was pleasant," I said deliberately, not wanting to sound overly eager.

"Pleasant?" he snorted. "Is that all?"

I laughed. "All right. I admit I loved it."

"So?" he asked expectantly.

"So what?"

He banged his head against the steering wheel in exasperation. "So when are we going?"

"Going?"

He clucked like a chicken and tried to shiver his jowls. "Still chicken, huh?"

"Now, be serious, Ludy," I said. "I did enjoy sailing this morning, and I am excited about working on the boat and planning a trip; but let's be realistic, Ludy. We haven't considered even half the problems yet."

"Like what?"

"Like how much is this going to cost. Like where are we going? Like for how long? I don't even know if your parents would let you go. School will be starting by the time the boat is seaworthy."

"I could quit school if they won't let me."

"No, you couldn't."

"Uh huh, at fourteen in Iowa—"

"No," I interrupted.

"Then it's off?"

"I didn't say that. I just think it's high time we looked at this venture seriously."

Ludy turned off the highway onto a gravel road, slowed the car to a stop, set the handbrake, and climbed out of the car. "What's the matter?" I asked.

"Just want to check the hitch." He knelt down behind the car. "Okay," he said as he slid back into the car. The trailer jerked twice as we started, then rolled smoothly and vanished in dust as we proceeded on. "You're the captain," he continued. "Tell me what to do, and I'll do it."

"But you make it all sound so simple, Ludy. You can't just clap your hands and have a genie bring us everything. Sure I had fun sailing today, but that was a dingy, not a thirty-foot sloop on the ocean. How do we even know it will float? I'm a farmer, not a boatbuilder."

"It will." He chewed the inside of his cheek.

"It may—I don't know, it *may* float. But we're talking about a homemade boat out of Leroy's head, and even though he could build anything he set his mind to, that's no guarantee we know what we're doing. I know it's the same principle of wind and vectors, but we had better investigate what we're undertaking a little more seriously. I'm not afraid. I just want to be cautious in doing the right thing."

Oh, dear Lord, I prayed silently, *let me know the right path. Lord, if only You were listed in the yellow pages, I could call You up and find out right now what we should do.* I promised myself to read the Bible more diligently that evening to see if anything forbade old women with their fourteen-year-old grandsons from sailing off the edge of the world.

"What should we do then?" Ludy's head dropped woefully.

"I don't know. This isn't something I embark on every year. Maybe it would be best to speak with your parents."

He was horrified. "Oh no! It'd be all over then."

"They've got to know sooner or later."

"How about later? You know, when the boat is almost done and we're better prepared. Okay? Okay?"

I could visualize David's face reddening as he worked his jaw over a resolute *no.*

"Well, we've got to talk to somebody who knows more than we do."

"How about this?" Ludy gradually slowed as we approached my driveway. Against the green stand of trees, the house looked like a lemon-drop box I had purchased as a girl. "How about if we go see this friend of Linda's in Cedar Falls. He runs the marina and boat shop and he goes fishing on the Mississippi all the time. Linda says he even used to race boats when he was in college because he's from a rich family in Massachusetts or someplace. And then he can tell us if the boat looks sturdy and anything else. Okay?"

"Okay," I said as we rocked to a stop. The dust we trailed caught up and languidly settled over us.

13 Mark Kenny, of Kenny Boat and Motors, had grown up in California instead of the East Coast, had crewed boats in college rather than sailed them, and had actually been on the Mississippi only once himself. But he did know boats, and his firm handshake attested to a quiet sincerity which I detected immediately. He also wore a small cross around his neck. I knew I would like him.

"I'm only twenty-four years old," Mark said, "but I grew my sea-legs when I was four, and I've been on water more often than land ever since."

"What about us sailing down the Mississippi?" I asked.

He puffed out his cheeks and exhaled. "Well, I don't see why not, just so long as you know how to sail, know where you're going, and have the proper navigational charts."

"And providing our boat is seaworthy," I added.

He smiled. "Well, yeah, that too."

"We were hoping maybe you could check out our boat and tell us what more we're going to need," Ludy said.

"Sure, where is it?"

Ludy jerked his head toward me. "On her farm about eight miles northwest of here, out the Janesville blacktop and then another mile and a half before you come to the river."

"Uh huh." There was a long pause as he scuffed a bare foot in the dirt. I suspected he was puzzled by Ludy's sketchy directions. "I don't know the area all that well," he said apologetically.

"Yeah, that's okay," Ludy said. "We'll draw you a good map." Just then a young woman in a pale blue tennis outfit called from the office that Mark was wanted on the phone.

"Yeah, yeah, just a minute," he waved to her. "Hey, listen, Ludy and . . ."

"Dorothy," I said.

"Yeah, Dorothy. Can you hang around just a minute or two longer? I really want to help you, but I gotta run inside and, you know . . ."

"Sure, sure, we understand." I smiled at him and nodded.

"Okay then, hang on and I'll be right back."

"Pretty nice guy," Ludy said, as Mark jogged to the office and bounded up the steps. "I hope he can help us."

We wandered around the fenced-in back lot examining a dozen cruisers and speedboats up on blocks. Ludy scrambled up the ladder of a pontoon houseboat and plopped down in a deck chair. "Boy, I bet this crackerbox is lousy to float."

"I'm not sure we should talk."

"Just wait," he protested. "I think plenty of folks are gonna sit up and watch when we hit the water."

"Most likely the Coast Guard rescue."

"Ehhhhh," Ludy groaned.

"Well, you've got the skipper sprawl down," Mark panted as he ran up to us.

"Think I look good, huh?" Ludy scrunched up one eye and mimicked a pipe-smoking old stalwart.

" 'Course, once you're on the river you won't have much time to laze around, what with tugs and commercial barges and the finicky river full of snags and wing dams and river monsters."

"What?" Ludy yipped.

"That's right," Mark winked at me. "Very few boats ever escape the fate of those huge channel cats that grow to over forty feet in length and can swallow a whole skiff just like that." He snapped his fingers.

Ludy scrutinized his face for a moment, unsure how to respond. Then he grinned and added, "Aw shucks, mate, we'll just take along a couple of forty-foot channel dogs to keep the cats in line."

"And maybe a couple of harpoons, too," I chuckled.

Mark stared at us, stroked his cheek, and then wagged his head. "Sounds like a great trip. Wish I were going along."

"You're invited," I offered.

He threw up his hands in dismay. "The world depends on me. Who will repair skis? Grease engines? Sell life jackets? But listen, I told Marci that I was going to lunch and to take a look at this legendary boat in some barn, so what say we go pick up a greasy burger and some fries and then I'll follow you out to the farm."

I looked at Ludy. "Why not?"

"Okay with me."

"I'm in the beat-up van with the canoe painted on the side." Mark pointed to a white truck that, indeed, did have the semblance of a canoe painted on it. "There's a great eatery three blocks north and then a block and a half west just past the Shell station," he grinned.

"We'll follow you," I said, remembering Ludy's directions.

"Nice guy!" Ludy fiddled with his hair in the rearview mirror as I tried to keep up with the van.

"I see you're a Christian." I pointed to Mark's silver cross as we waited for our food and for Ludy to come back from the restroom.

"Praise God, for three years now." He took the cross between his thumb and forefinger. "And my life just hasn't been the same since."

"What do you mean?"

"Sure you want to get me started? When I talk about God in my life I never shut up."

I nodded.

"When I was finishing college in San Diego, my roommate talked me into going to a little Bible study he and a couple of his friends had been having. The only reason I went was because this one girl I'd been trying to date was going to be there. I think I had only been to a church twice in my life before, and that was to be baptized and for my grandfather's funeral."

Ludy returned and slid into the booth next to me, listening as Mark continued.

"And the only thing I knew about the Bible was that it was a big, thick book written in old-fashioned language, and you put your hand on it and swore to tell the truth if you ever had to testify in court."

"Or it's used to keep track of family births and marriages," I said.

"I guess," he shrugged. "But my family never even had one for that. You see, my Dad is in real estate and his bible was the *Wall Street Journal,* and my mother considers herself fashionable, so for her the 'good news' was the latest issue of home decoration magazines. And of course, I was into surfing and sailing."

"Of course," I nodded.

"And you know, in southern California, religion isn't exactly the way to be popular with the beach and boat crowd."

Ludy sighed and looked over his shoulder for the waitress.

"But I went," he said. "And funny thing, the girl didn't show up. I'm sure if she had, I wouldn't have been able to take my eyes off her or concentrate on anything except what clever things I could say to her."

"God does have a way of arranging things, doesn't He?"

"So what happened then?" Ludy was disinterested.

"I remember the five in the group—a young married couple I didn't know, and three friends from school—were studying Paul's letter to the Galatians. They came to a part about circumcision, and I was trying to follow along in my copy and feign interest about something which sounded pretty weird to me, and then we ran across a verse in which Paul said he had been put to death with Christ on the cross, and that he no longer lived, but Christ lived in him, and then, 'I live by faith in the Son of God who loved me and gave his life for me,' and suddenly, as I read along I realized that Paul meant me, Mark Kenny, and I felt like somebody had plugged my foot into a wall socket because little sparks and tingles kept running up and down my skin, and I sat there for a long time repeating that phrase.''

"I know that feeling.'' I touched his arm lightly.

"All right!'' Ludy reached with overdone enthusiasm for his cheeseburger as the waitress returned. "And a large Coke,'' he told her.

"So then,'' Mark bit into his hamburger, "so then, when everybody left, I asked my friend to explain what the passage I couldn't get out of my head meant. And he said that some things can't be understood, but have to be experienced. And I thought, well, if he knows what this means, why isn't he going to tell me? So then I asked him about how strange I felt. He asked me if I was convicted. And then I thought he meant for a crime, so I said, 'Hey, you've known me for a couple of years, and I've never been in trouble with the law or school or anyone.' And then he laughed and said, 'Man, oh man, you're a million light years away, but the Lord is still tapping you on the head.' So I started to get mad because I thought he was making fun of me.'' He paused to wipe a spurt of ketchup off his cheek.

"You should have punched his street lights out,'' Ludy said as he gulped down his Coke.

"No,'' Mark continued. "Because he was on-the-stick dead right. I was in outer space and the Lord had searched me out. When He calls, you'd better listen, too.'' He looked directly at Ludy as he spoke. "I listened to my friend and then we got down on the floor and prayed, and when I stood up, I knew I was hooked into a billion watts of power. He said, 'Congratulations, you've just been born,' and I thought, I sure don't know what you mean, but boy do I feel great! There was no flash of lightning or burning bush, but when you meet God with your heart, you're never the same.''

"That's for sure.'' I thought back to my own encounter just a month earlier.

"My life isn't perfect, but problems don't seem as bad when you've got God on your side.''

"You should have punched him,'' Ludy said.

"You sound a lot like me when I was your age.'' Mark bit off a French fry. "Where do you fellowship?'' he asked me.

"I'm sorry . . . oh, you mean, go to church?''

"Uh huh. He's still the same Lord to all of us.''

"I've been going to church in Janesville for over thirty years. A small Presbyterian church with a fine pastor.''

"Is it a dead church, or are people committed to the Lord?"

"I'm not sure I know what you mean. They're all good people, and Pastor Bill is—"

"Spirit-filled?"

I shook my head. "You've lost me now."

"Spirit-filled Christians," Mark said, "lead their lives as if Christ were among us; actually He is, in the presence of the Holy Spirit. It's all scriptural and makes sense, but some churches are traditional, and —well, traditional isn't the right word, but it's all in the Bible."

"I guess I haven't gotten to that part yet."

Mark finished his iced tea. "If you're interested, I'd be happy to give yc ⸱ couple of books that explain it better than I can. I think you'd like t' ⸱m."

"Religion is dumb," said Ludy, who patiently crunched his ice and stared out the window. Mark appraised him a moment and then looked at his watch. "Time to buzz."

"Are we finally ready?" Ludy sighed.

Mark tousled his hair. "Lead on, commodore. I'm right behind you!"

Ludy was silent most of the way out to the farm, but I knew he liked Mark and was mulling over what Mark had said. I had a feeling that the hawk was circling over Ludy now, about to begin the swooping descent from which there was no place to hide. And with Mark around, Ludy would have all three of us to contend with.

"I think he is going to be a lot of help."

Ludy turned to look out the side window. "Yeah." Then he glanced in the rearview mirror. "Maybe."

"You're kidding me!" Mark gasped in astonishment as he walked around the boat. "He built all of this in the barn by himself?"

"We've been working on it too," Ludy said.

Mark smoothed the side with his hand. "You see," he explained, "the hull underneath is constructed of wood and then the fiberglass is built up in layers and smoothed. You're really only lacking a gel coat and then a coat of antifouling paint. Incredible!"

"Then it looks pretty good?" I asked.

"Considering the conditions of the barn and construction materials, you bet!"

"Then it will float?"

"Don't see why not. You've even got a well for an inboard/outboard motor."

Ludy pranced around the barn whooping.

119

"But don't get too excited," Mark cautioned. "This is just a rough hull. It may float, but you won't be going anywhere yet."

I was afraid to ask why, partly because I knew more money would be involved. But I was also realizing the fantasy was crossing into broad daylight. Did I really know what I was getting into? "What does that mean?" I asked tentatively.

"It means for one thing that you've got a solid frame to work with. It's like a house. You need proper wiring for electricity and then plumbing, not to mention basics like a galley set-up, an aluminum mast and boom, and heavy rigging if you plan on ocean sailing. Then you could add a radio receiver, a barometer, probably lifelines and harness, some kind of dingy—there's a hundred more things I'll have to help you prepare."

"I knew it would never work," Ludy said dejectedly.

"Don't get down now," Mark said. "The big job is done."

"You did say you would help us prepare?" I asked.

Mark gave me a thumbs up and nodded. "Wild river monsters couldn't keep me away!"

Ludy shuddered.

"Let's see what your basement looks like." Mark pulled himself up until he was sitting sideways on the boat, then swung his legs over and scrambled down into the cabin. Ludy followed him.

"See there, we put up that paneling," I heard Ludy say. "And I added two inches of housing insulation, and then I put tile under here, and that's indoor/outdoor carpeting in case we take on some water."

"Uh huh." I could see Mark appraising the size of the cabin. "And where did you plan the bunks?"

"Well, one forward there," Ludy added. "Right past the john, and then probably another back there."

"The aft berth might be kind of short."

"I don't mind. I always sleep doubled up anyway."

"Hmmm. Good head room."

"And then," Ludy continued, "a drop leaf table in the center with built-in shelves and storage cabinets, and maybe a portable Coleman camp stove set up there—"

Mark interrupted, "No, too dangerous. I've seen a new line of kerosene stoves that sit on detachable gimbal trays, you know what I mean?" Ludy shook his head. "So when the boat sways in the water, the stove still sits level." He rocked from side to side and demonstrated with his hands.

"What do you think?" I called in to them.

Mark stuck his head out a window. "Not bad, but you better let me draw up a list of supplies and materials. I can get them all at cost for you."

"If you're sure it's okay. We wouldn't want you to get in any trouble."

"Hey, no problem. Remember, this is my business, and I can help out my friends, okay?"

"Okay," I said with a smile. "Maybe we can even talk you into going along."

"Who knows? But first, have either of you contacted the regional Coast Guard Office? You should line up your nautical manuals and light lists, and you can probably get the navigational charts through them; also you'll have some locks to pass through, so you should check out procedures and permissions. I can teach you how to use a chronometer and a sextant, but really, I'd better get back to work now."

"You sure you want to get involved with us?" I glanced up at Ludy as I spoke.

"Listen," Mark swung his foot over the side and paused. "This is one launch I don't want to miss. You can count on my help."

"Yip! Yip! Yahoooo!" Ludy sprang from the boat and landed on a stack of bales.

Mark laughed at him, but then stared up into the loft, startled. "What on earth is that?" he said, pointing.

A familiar masked face poked out of the straw and peered down at the disturbance. "We must have wakened him from his nap," I said. "Mark Kenny, meet Hobo Raccoon." Hobo gibbered unintelligibly and then buried his face again.

"Is he your pet?"

I started to point to Ludy, but changed my mind and answered that more than likely we were his pets. "In fact, he has us so well trained that we usually jump at his beck and call."

"I see," Mark said with that mischievous sparkle about his eyes that made me think at any moment he could burst into uncontrollable laughter.

"You should see how smart he is," Ludy said as he sat up. "The first two nights we kept him in a cage, but he learned to lift the latch and even open the back door by himself."

"And he's made himself at home ever since."

"Probably couldn't get rid of him if you wanted to, huh?" Mark asked.

"That's Hobo," I grumbled good-naturedly. "Have you ever seen what a raccoon can do with a five-pound sack of flour?"

"I'm afraid to ask."

"Believe me, it takes a whole morning to clean five pounds of flour off a kitchen floor."

"Especially if you add a tin of honey," Ludy snickered.

"The honey didn't help, that's for sure," I said wryly, remembering the mess of a few days earlier.

"Don't think I want a pet raccoon," Mark answered.

"A wise decision."

"Okay." He changed to an all-business tone. "You two finish paneling the cabin, but leave the head open so we can work in it. I'll call you later for some measurements. Plan on my coming out for a couple of hours around noon each day so we can get this puppy in the water soon."

I began to protest.

"No, really it's okay. Let's just say that you're doing something I've always wanted to do. Every boat nut and armchair skipper has the same dream, only yours is taking shape, and I want to help."

"We can squeeze in an extra bunk," Ludy said. I was surprised at Ludy's offer, and even more surprised at how quickly we had become comfortable with Mark.

"You're good people." Mark's seriousness carried a full draft of sincerity. He turned over the cross around his neck again. "I'll ring you later."

He cranked and cranked and finally got his van to start, and as we stood in the barn door shadow and watched him spin a tire-full of gravel behind him, Ludy repeated softly, "We really are going. We really are going."

"God willing," I said.

Just then, an angry chattering filled the barn behind us. Up in the loft, Hobo shook his head and scolded as if to say, "Can't you let a guy get some sleep around here?"

"Okay, okay!" We both laughed and walked out into the sunny barnyard. A swarm of flies settled over our heads, and the pungent aroma of cut alfalfa and soybeans drifted up from the south pasture.

"Think I'll hop on my bike and drive in to the library to get those Coast Guard addresses."

"Oh, I forgot to tell you, Ludy. T.J. called this morning and said to tell you we've got eight books already a week overdue."

"That's right!" He smacked his head. "Well, I think I can straighten it out. I mentioned something about sanding and refinishing the library

122

door, so maybe they'll let me off with a light sentence."

"A stay of execution?"

"Yeah, I'll throw myself on their mercy." He grinned. I walked up to the back porch shade as he went for his bike. Watching him rev up the engine from where I sat on the stoop, I was the first to see David's green Plymouth turn up the lane. Two kittens dashed in front of the car and scattered from the horn's blast. Ludy, sitting patiently on his bike, reached down and clicked off the ignition.

I strolled toward Ludy as David parked in the shade and got out of his car. "Getting pretty muggy this afternoon, isn't it?" I tried to sound nonchalant, but my breathing was revving up, and I felt as if a flock of sparrows were battering against my chest wall.

David looked first at Ludy, then at the motorcycle, and finally to me. "Yeah, Mom, humid." He took out a folded green handkerchief from his back pocket and wiped his forehead. Ludy fidgeted nervously with a handgrip. I could think of nothing more to say. I realized a confrontation was inevitable, but for the past couple of weeks I had ignored the thought of my explaining the motorcycle to David. I recalled the disastrous supper when the subject first came up but quickly suppressed the memory. David carefully folded the handkerchief and stuffed it back into his pocket. "Well, that's a fine little motorbike," he said at last. Ludy wouldn't meet his eyes.

Oh Lord, bring peace to this situation, I prayed silently. I searched David's face for controlled anger, but his jaw was relaxed and his eyes indicated only a vague interest as he examined the bike.

"Yep, a real nice little bike."

"I earned it," Ludy blurted out. I could see Ludy begin to tighten up with agony, his hands clutching the handlebars.

"I know you did," David said calmly. "But you disobeyed me."

"David . . ." I began. He raised his eyebrows and looked at me. "Just a minute, Mom." The mild blue of his eyes made him appear old and sad, but I sensed there would be no explosion.

Ludy began to shiver and appeared on the verge of tears.

"You haven't fooled me about the motorcycle," David said. "I've known for some time. I'd be a pretty dumb father not to. But I'm not a mean old man, even though you may think so. You're my only son, and I just want to raise you right like my father did me."

"I'm sorry, I really am," Ludy whimpered.

David sighed, shook his head, and repeated softly, "You disobeyed me, Ludy."

"It was more my idea," I broke in.

"Mom," David gazed at me impassively. I rubbed my palms together, feeling awkward and anxious to carry the full blame. Yet I knew the matter was now as much in God's hands as anyone's.

David looked back at Ludy. "I'm going to let you keep it."

For the first time, Ludy glanced up at his father, his eyes glistening with tears.

"I know you've been helping your grandmother, and you have stayed out of trouble and that makes me and your mom feel real good. But nevertheless, you did disobey me, so I'm not going to let you ride it for a week. Understood?"

"I can really keep it?" Ludy caught his breath.

"Uh huh. And you can park it in our garage and not around the block at your friend's house any more."

I beamed at both of them and thanked God for his goodness and intervention. Ludy smeared dust across his eyebrows with his arm, but I could tell he too had felt a burden lift.

"Now go ahead and take that thing home, because I want to talk with your grandmother." David stepped back, a half smile on his face as Ludy switched on the ignition key and spun dirt up against our legs. We watched him vanish down the road and listened a while longer as the popcorn ping gradually faded.

"Come on in and have some iced tea," I said to David.

"All right, Mom. I hope you've got a gallon 'cause my well is dry."

I felt suddenly tender toward him, amazed that my own son had ever stirred up anxieties that frightened me. Now smiling, his eyes made him look like the fourteen-year-old he had so long ago been, ready to please and requiring only simple needs like food—lots of it—and drink, a gallon of cold liquid which was on the way.

"Come on in, David, and we'll fix you right up." I playfully cuffed his arm, then took him by the elbow and led him to the porch.

"I'm getting worried, Mom." David wiped his mouth and leaned back in the kitchen chair. I sat forward, resting my elbows on the sticky Formica.

"How come? I think Ludy has changed so much."

"I know. But it's not only Ludy."

"Well, what then?"

"Sheri got a call this morning from Dubuque."

"Uh huh?" I couldn't guess what he was leading up to.

"It was about four hundred and forty-six square feet of canvas sail. Do you know what that costs, Mom?"

124

"Roughly." I tried not to sound alarmed.

"Mom . . ." He searched for the right approach. "Mom, what is going on? I called Glenn and he said you were fixing up Dad's old boat."

"That's right."

"Oh, for heaven's sake, Mom." He stared at his calloused palms. "Don't get me wrong. I appreciate what you've done with Ludy. You've been able to get through to him. I don't especially like you going behind my back to get that motorbike, but there ain't too much I can do about it now. I can't understand just why you want to throw away money on that old boat. Why not upgrade the house some more? You could put on a screened porch. What is all this boat business?"

I rubbed my lips. The silence buzzed around us. I could hear the water pipes click and hum in the basement, and then David cleared his throat. *The truth shall set you free,* I remembered.

"We're going to sail around the world." I looked up at David. He was staring at my mouth, as if more words were visible and waiting at the end of my tongue. And then he broke into laughter, although I could tell it was forced.

"No, really, Mom, what's up?"

"That's it."

"You're kidding me?"

"No."

He fumbled in his chair. "You mean you . . . and Ludy . . . are . . . are . . . no . . . no, Mom, that's all too crazy."

"We're serious about this."

He exhaled. "I can see you are."

"It's all worked out on paper."

"What the hell does that mean!" he exploded. I stared at him until he relaxed and sat back, chagrined. "Sorry. Never was much good at controlling my temper, was I?"

"I know it sounds crazy," I began. "But lots of things in the world sound crazy until you look closely. Now I'll tell you honestly that I've had many doubts about this sailing venture myself, but ever since I started thinking hard about that empty hull out there, and the power of Leroy's vision, and my own empty and narrow life where I've never done anything or gone anywhere, I just . . . just get angry that I could have wasted myself so much."

"But you haven't, Mom. You and Dad built this farm and raised a family and now you're as much of a parent to Ludy as anybody."

I stared sullenly at him, wondering if he could ever understand what truly went on inside a woman, wondering if my efforts would be worth the trouble. "Do you know what a 'whole person' is, David?"

"What's a 'whole person'?" I detected an edge of sarcasm.

"You see, David," I searched for the right phrasing. "I'm your mother, and I know it's hard for you to think of me in any other way, but you have to know that there are other things going on inside of me than just being maternal."

"I'm not dumb, okay? Sheri and I have talked about this."

The sky through the window was bluer than any sea I could imagine, and streaks of clouds rippled across the view in an unseen breeze. *If only David would see the transparency and the depth of that blue, perhaps he would understand the allure.*

"I remember when you were a boy, oh, maybe twelve or thirteen years old. You told me one time that you were going to be a pitcher for the Chicago White Sox, remember? We drove in to Comisky Park one summer, and you saw all the fans and excitement and took in the smells, and when we came home, you swore to me that when you grew up you would be out on that mound hurling fastballs. Didn't you?"

"I was just a kid. It's natural to have dreams then."

"No matter how wild?"

"Sure."

"But when you grow up, you trade all your dreams for a real life, right? When you grow up you take on work and drudgery and raising kids and running a farm, and that's it, isn't it?"

"Now, Mom, don't go getting bitter."

"I'm not."

"Sure sounds like it to me." His voice softened. "Things have been difficult after Dad died, I know, but you're snapping out of depression now. Everybody knows you're getting over Dad's death. Maybe I haven't spent as much time with you as I should have, and I apologize if that's the case, but you know I'd rather just go hammer some boards together any time to work out my frustrations."

"We all have needs."

"I recognize that. But you don't *need* to go sailing around the world on some old patched up scow, do you?"

"It's more than that."

"Why don't you just get a job in town if you want fulfillment?"

"So that's what you think is wrong with me."

"Well, isn't it?"

"You think if I go to work from eight to five every day that I'll be fulfilled?"

126

"That's for you to decide, Mom. All I know is that if you want to go to work, I can talk to a friend of mine who runs a busy little real estate office about taking you on as a part-time secretary."

"Why would I want to be a secretary?" I said, exasperated.

"Okay, okay. Listen, Mom." He stared out the window, but his eyes were unfocused and faraway. "If you want to go around the world, I'll help you check into one of those three-month cruises. I hear you meet lots of retired people and have good food, though it is an expensive trip, but if you gotta get this out of your system then—"

"Get nothing out of my system," I broke in. "I'm not going to get mad at you, David, but obviously you don't have the least idea of what I want."

He sat back, flustered. "I guess I don't."

"All my life I've done for you and your brother and your father and when somebody said, 'Let's go fishing,' I said, 'Fine, I'll fix a picnic lunch,' and when somebody said, 'Boy, I could use a new sweater,' I made it. I didn't complain, and I'm not complaining now."

"So what is it you want?"

"Not to have to serve anybody. Except God."

"Fine. And I suppose He's telling you to make this boat and fill it with animals two by two because it's going to rain for forty days and nights."

"I resent that."

"I'm sorry, I'm sorry. I guess I just can't figure what is going on."

"For one thing, God has entered my life."

"We've always gone to church, Mom."

"I know that."

"I appreciate your bringing us up with religion, and I agree that man does not live by bread alone and all that."

"But God is a real presence now. He's inside me, alive." I tapped my chest and tried to gauge David's reaction. He sat, perplexed, and slowly shook his head.

"We don't want you to go get all flipped out on God, now. Not like the holyrollers going door to door and hearing voices."

"David." I tried to change my tone. "I'm happy now. I have peace in my heart. I know God is real."

"Well, of course He is."

"But you just can't know it in your head. You've got to feel Him inside."

"Okay, Mom, I'm not arguing. If you got God, fine. I'm glad for you. But this around-the-world thing has got to stop. I don't like you throwing

Dad's hard-saved money away, and I don't like you making too much of wild ideas, especially if Ludy's involved, because he's liable to do anything you say, no matter how unreasonable."

"David, your father is dead, and the money is not his any more."

"I'm sorry you see it that way."

"That's the way it is."

"Okay, Mom."

I looked at him intently, afraid he was patronizingly agreeable now.

"Perhaps you and I and Sheri should sit down some evening and discuss all of this. Glenn and Evelyn, too."

"I don't see any reason to. I agree the money is yours and if you want to build a spaceship in your barn, fine, go ahead. And if you want Ludy to help you build it, fine, he has my permission. But he isn't going anywhere on that boat, Mom, and I'll do everything I can to stop you from taking it any farther than the front yard."

"David . . ." I stopped myself. Further discussion was senseless. I couldn't convince him otherwise, and I doubted that Ludy could. Sheri might be more sympathetic. Maybe if David got to see Mark's involvement, things might be different, but for now I would have to be patient and expect God to work His ways.

"I gotta go, Mom. Thanks for the tea." He stood up and hesitated. "And thanks for . . . well, you know . . . Ludy." I nodded, but did not rise and follow him out as he left. I listened as his car receded in the distance and sat thoughtful and troubled, ignoring the scratch scratch behind me until the cookie cannister hit the floor. I leaped to my feet and turned to find Hobo cowering as if to beg forgiveness for the pile of broken cookies around him on the pantry floor. In spite of the knot in my stomach, Hobo's ludicrous posture caused me to laugh, and even Hobo chattered then as he scurried off to a dark corner under the shelves with his sweet treasure.

14 I was reading the twenty-second chapter of Luke that evening in bed when the twenty-seventh verse seemed to leap off the page and shake me by the throat. At the Last Supper, a dispute arose as to which apostle would be considered the greatest, and Jesus answered, "For which is the greater, one who sits at the table, or one who serves?" Jesus then went on to illustrate that even though He was at the table, He served His apostles.

I couldn't get past verse twenty-seven, as much as I tried to read on. My conversation with David kept coming back, and I felt God was trying to point out a principle I was reluctant to accept.

Why, I wondered, *was the servant greater than the one who enjoyed the feast? Haven't I been the servant for more than thirty years? I feel no freedom or joy or greatness in having given of myself for so long!* I could not reconcile how strong my impulse to live for myself and God was, against the idea of going back to waiting hand and foot on everyone around me. I was proud I never had once complained about the drudgery, the sheer terror of waking every morning to the same routine in an endless repetition of past days merging into thousands more of the same. But I should have been *happy* to serve? I wanted to understand.

Pastor Bill had spoken about the nature of the Jewish society in one of his sermons some time ago. I seemed to recall that women were valued only slightly higher than cattle, and a woman without children, even less. I wasn't complaining about my life, but it appeared that women hadn't really progressed much in the past couple of millennia. It was fine for a man to serve; didn't he have the choice if he wanted? But a woman didn't have the choice. She served. For that matter, where were the women gospel writers? Where were the women apostles? Was there a single Old Testament matriarch who led her people like Moses or Joseph or David had?

Heavenly Father, I prayed, *strike me down right now with a bolt of lightning, but why do I feel that your sacred Word is written more for a man than for me?*

Outside, crickets and frogs and nightbirds were tuning up, and a huge mosquito whined against the screen. I switched off my bedside lamp and went to the window. Trying to concentrate on the pattern of sounds, I could detect a call and an answer, an intelligible speech that was usually so easy to ignore. The Bible was a mystery to me. Just when I saw a glimmer of God's radiance break through, a tangle of doubts yanked me back to my own ignorance. Listening to the hub and patter beyond me, I felt that God did speak through nature, and for me right now, probably more clearly than through the Bible. What was that tree frog lamenting? And that owl? Was his plaintive cry not a hymn of praise or a heart-wrung psalm? Even the wind through the branches, the rasp of a limb against the eaves, the fluttering poplar leaves spoke God's love and glory.

Maybe David was right. At my age, traipsing around the world did appear irresponsible. How could I take care of Ludy when I barely could balance a checkbook, pump my own gas, or read a map? How could I jeopardize his life in the middle of an unpredictable ocean? How could I?

I would ask Mark the next day to level with me if I was being crazy. I knew the busy past month had strengthened both Ludy and me. I did have more confidence, and Ludy seemed less agitated, less bored with himself and his life. Mark could understand what we were undertaking, I hoped. He would also be sympathetic to my ignorance about Scripture. I didn't want my excitement for God to dissipate, but, staring out into the starless night, exhausted and sticky and my head abuzz with self-fears, I felt God receding; His warm arms no longer were close about me, and I blamed myself, though I didn't know for what.

"The Lord is my shepherd, I shall not want," drifted up from an evanescent past. Long ago, my mother had knelt in her dark room every night, whispering her prayers out across the moonlit prairies. I would lie silently at her side, watching her lips move ceaselessly until I fell asleep. She had taught me that beautiful opening from Psalm 23. It was one of her nighttime prayers, and so it was impossible for me to separate the psalm from the memory. And whenever the memory appeared, so did a wistful longing to once again touch the gentle hand and lay my cool cheeks against its warmth.

What thin wall held the past, now so near, back from the present iridescence of the room and the outer dark of the fields and scattered, faint houselights I could see as I too knelt at my mother's window. Was Leroy with her? I knew he was. Some inescapable knowledge was leading me. I did have an inner peace, even though the many doubts were hard to sort out. I couldn't tell anyone about this knowledge I felt so certainly inside me, but it was there, it was real, and I knew it was from God. I just couldn't turn it around so I could see it squarely in the light. Not yet, anyway. And breathing deeply the June night air, thinking of my mother and husband, hearing the chorus of life in the bushes and woodlot, feeling the rough textured cover of the Bible in my arms—everything did seem connected in a way that was beyond my grasp.

"I love . . . I love . . ." I whispered. I loved everything I could think of or smell or feel in the room about me, but to order and name every person and object that flitted past my sleepy eyes would have kept me up all night. I laid the Bible down on the pillow next to mine and slid the sheet up to my waist. *In a month, in two months, where will I be, God?* I drowsed. *Where, and what . . . what servant can I be for You?* And then I dreamed myself back to Mother's praying until I fell asleep again.

For the next two days, my argument with David kept coming back to distract my attention from helping Ludy and Mark apply a gel coat and then a sleek, high gloss white to our boat's hull. The entire barn smelled like a paint factory, and as I came from the house with a pitcher of lemonade, I could even detect the aroma wafting across the barnyard mixed with dried hay and compost and pig dander. I had to squint as I came back into the barn and stood next to Mark admiring his work.

"I think one more coat to the transom and we can start on the side decks. How's that side drying?" he called to Ludy.

Ludy poked out from underneath, his forehead and cheeks streaked with white. "Just great, but after painting Nana's house, I didn't think I could ever face another paintbrush."

"Hey, you're about to drip," Mark gestured at Ludy's brush. Ludy disappeared back under the boat. "We've even got more help aboard."

"What? Who's helping?" I asked.

"See for yourself," and he set up a small step ladder for my inspection. I climbed to the second rung and peered over the side, startling Hobo with my unannounced presence. He tilted his head back at me and flashed a mouthful of small teeth, as if grinning. Sprawled on an old boat cushion he had claimed as his own, he reminded me of the Cheshire cat.

"Makes a regal appearance, doesn't he?" Mark laughed.

"I thought you said he was helping?"

"As long as he keeps his little paws out of trouble, he's helping." I had to agree. More and more it was apparent that no door, window, latch, or lid was impervious to Hobo's curiosity. I had awakened abruptly the previous night to find a furry body curled next to mine. I shut him out of my room, only to find him that morning snoozing contentedly on a pile of bathroom towels he had pulled down.

"How about some lemonade, Ludy?" I called.

"In a minute."

The barn was hot and sticky, even though all the doors were thrown open as wide as possible. Mark struggled out of his sweat soaked shirt, sat back on an old crate, and gulped a glass of lemonade.

"Sure wish we had a breeze."

"I've got a fan in the house," I remembered. "Would that help?"

"I'll say. The paint will dry quicker too." He wiped his neck and chest. Deceivingly thin, with his shirt off his wiry muscles glistened and were well defined. Mark obviously had been out in the sun often.

"You've really got some tan."

"Well, it's more a year-round tan." He studied me and shook his head. "With your fair skin, the water and sun will fry you in no time. Remind me to give you a good sunscreen."

"No, now you stop giving us everything. You have a business to run and you should treat us like any other customers. Why, you must have brought out a half dozen gallons of paint that you won't even let me pay you for."

He waved off my protests. "Hey, don't worry about it. I've had those cans sitting in the stockroom for over a year. If I can't sell it, I may as well invest it in a venture I believe in."

"You really think we can do it then?"

He scratched his nose and gestured toward the boat. "When we get done with her, I'd trust my own mother afloat."

"Yeah, but she doesn't get seasick, does she?" Ludy yelled from the other side of the boat.

"I thought you were working, not eavesdropping," I chided.

"Go ahead, I can't hear a thing," he said.

I looked at Mark seriously. "I am a little worried, Mark. There's just too much to learn for . . ."

"For what?"

"Well, for an old lady."

He snorted. "You aren't old."

"Oh, I wish I wasn't, but some days I feel old," I sighed.

"Then don't feel old. Look at Grandma Moses. She didn't start painting until she was in her seventies."

"But there's nothing foolhardy about painting."

"Or sailing, if you know what you're doing."

"I don't, though."

"You'll learn. I'll teach you. I'll teach Ludy."

"But what happens when we get miles from nowhere and the thingamajig jams?"

"Then you unjam it."

"But what if I don't know how?"

"Then you learn. No one can be totally prepared. It's impossible to predict every thing that could happen. A good sailor knows his boat, is level-headed, and has an irrefutable resource.''

"What's that?''

"Jesus. Remember how He calmed the storm? Take Him on any voyage and you'll be in good company.''

"That's just what I was hoping to talk to you about. Can you come outside for a while?'' He followed me out across the barnyard to a shady oak behind the house. We sat on the grass as I finished explaining that sometimes I felt funny speaking about God with Ludy around because it made him feel uncomfortable.

"That's a good sign.'' Mark lay back and shaded his eyes. "He's just a typical fourteen-year-old kid who doesn't want to admit that maybe, just maybe, he needs Jesus, too. I was the same way.''

"But I shouldn't be embarrassed to talk about God around him?''

"Well . . .'' He paused and stretched his arms behind his head. "Well, yes and no.''

"What do you mean?'' I was feeling funny about asking Mark for advice, though I couldn't think of a single person who was more open.

"Believe it or not, it's a whole lot easier to talk to perfect strangers about God than our own family. You should never be embarrassed about Jesus. Remember He said, 'Whoever disowns me before men, him will I also disown before my Father who is in heaven.' But I can understand why you'd be uncomfortable, too. Not everyone is zealous or needs to be.''

"I guess I've just had some doubts lately.'' I hesitated.

"About the trip?''

"Yes, about the trip. And other things.''

"About God?''

"Oh no, not God, but . . . well . . . in a way. Now that I've got this boat and trip in my head, it all seems like a compulsion that I can't stop. Do you know what I mean? Just like that first domino in a whole line of dominos has fallen and now there's no stopping. I know that sounds crazy.''

"Not at all.''

"But you see,'' I continued. "I just want to do what God wants me to, and I don't know if this is His will.''

Ludy stuck his head around the corner of the barn door.

"Hey, is this a mutiny?''

"No, go ahead and finish my side,'' Mark shouted. "I'll be back as soon as I cool off.'' Ludy went back to work.

"I probably shouldn't have brought it up now,'' I said.

"No, I'm glad you did." He sat up on his elbows and blinked at me. "I do know just what you mean. I couldn't begin to list all the times when I've had the same thought."

"How do you tell if God wants you to do something?"

"Good question." He stretched, took a deep breath, and exhaled. "If I could answer that, I wouldn't make half the mistakes I do."

"I pray."

He nodded.

"I ask, 'Do I want to change my life so drastically, God, or do You approve, is this what You want too?' I'm too old for a mid-life crisis."

He started to laugh. "No, I'm sorry, I wasn't laughing at you. You just keep referring to yourself as old, and if you want to know the truth, when you came into the boatshop a couple of days ago, you struck me as being so vibrant and full of energy, I would have said you were probably twenty years younger than you are."

I brushed grass off my sundress.

"One thing I do know," he continued, tracing a vein down his forearm with his index finger, "is that if God doesn't want you to do something, He'll let you know. He probably won't appear out of the clouds with rolling thunder, but more than likely, He makes His desire known in a quiet, unobtrusive way."

I looked around at the handiwork of God flowering in every thing I saw, the lawn and trees and fields so vibrant with life. Mark's face glowed with a serenity that I longed for.

"Hey, I'm no expert, believe me," he spoke softly. "I just try to seek God in all things. Not just other people, or things I do, but also the desires of my heart and the dreams I want to accomplish."

"That's where I have trouble," I said. Trying to recall the gnarl of uncertainties that had so recently plagued me, I wondered if I could put into words what may have been only a woman's problem. "I don't want to offend you, Mark, but I can't stop feeling that a woman, well, I don't know, a woman is more complicated in her relationship with God."

"Oh no, I think just the opposite. A woman is more in tune with her feelings, more sensitive to others and their responses to her."

I fought back the frustration of not finding the right words. "But I feel so . . . so . . . tired of having been a servant all my life. I want to serve God, but all her life, a woman serves her husband, serves her children, and even though I want to serve God, I have this desire to live for myself just a little. This crack of freedom in my life is there, and I can't deny it. Is that selfish?"

"But serving doesn't mean servile. You can be a woman, a wife and mother, a domestic servant for that matter, and still have that liberation which God gives us. Do you know what I mean?"

"I don't know. Sometimes everything about my life seems so simple, but other times I feel like a Chinese roadmap."

"A what?" Mark burst into laughter. "A Chinese roadmap?"

"I don't know." His infectious laughter made me giggle. "It just came into my head. I don't even know what a Chinese roadmap looks like. But you understand, don't you?"

"Oh sure. Just because you're a Christian, doesn't mean you've got it made. Tell me a little about when you met the Lord face to face."

I launched into the events of the past year, beginning with Leroy's death, and then the emotional numbness of the winter and spring, and the culmination of frustrations and uncontrollable urges to experience deep and everlasting silence as a way to escape the life that had become grotesque and wearisome beyond endurance. I realized that I hadn't yet told anyone what had brought about the evident changes in me during the past two months, but Mark's wide-eyed and sympathetic face softened and nodded with interest as I detailed my failure to jump out the window. My encounter with God that evening came out in a rush of words and remembered emotions, though I felt oddly aware that the pain was gone. It was as if I were describing in sequence a movie I had seen, or a dream that was vivid but detached from the agony I felt at the time. "So you see," I concluded, "even though I had gone to church all my life, and would have classified myself as a Christian, it's only been for the past two months that I really have known Jesus Christ in a personal way."

"Whew! That's beautiful. What a testimony."

I realized I had been rocking back and forward holding my knees to my chest as I spoke. I relaxed and looked up at the spiral of green branches arching toward a lazy procession of cumulus clouds.

"You're really wrong about old then." Mark smiled. I looked at him questioningly. "Two months old, right? Just a baby Christian."

"I suppose so."

"Are you being fed properly?"

"You mean . . ."

"Spiritual food. Fellowship, prayer, Scripture."

"That's another problem. I love reading the Bible, but I don't always . . . I can't . . ."

"I know what you mean," he broke in. "That's why good fellowship is so important, because without supportive Christians who struggle and pray and learn with you, it is hard to grow in faith. You have definitely opened up to God, and like I always say, a Christian doesn't believe in blind coincidence. God has a reason for bringing people together. I think you told me you go to the church in Janesville."

"Uh huh, for a long time."

"And is the pastor good?"

"Oh yes, he's a gem. You'll have to meet him."

"I'd like to. You should come with me one Sunday to the Interfaith Center on campus. It's a very ecumenical group, you see, because I'm Lutheran, and there's Catholics and Protestants, and we all have an informal liturgy and then a Bible study and praise group with music and singing, and—hey, you've got company."

I glanced up to see a familiar car pulling into the lane. "Well, I sure won't believe in coincidence any more either," I said. "That's Pastor Bill there."

We stood to meet him. Bill got out of his car and came forward, his right hand outstretched.

"Pastor Bill Shaffer," he said to Mark. He then gave me a wink and a jovial half-hug with his right arm. "Enjoying this weather? Unmerciful, isn't it? But I complain just as loudly about the ice and snow of winter, so what do I know?"

"Mark runs the Kenny Marina in Cedar Falls," I said as we sat informally in the grass.

"Does he now?" Pastor said with a slight "oomph" as he stretched out his legs. "And what's a young, handsome, half-naked nautical man doing in the middle of these cornfields?" He added an expansive gesture with his arm. Mark shifted his eyes down uncomfortably.

"Don't embarrass him, Pastor," I chided. "He's helping Ludy and me. One thing I forgot to tell you, Mark, is not to let that clerical garb fool you. Underneath his religious disguise, he's one hundred percent tease. I can't remember all the times he's caused me to turn bright red. Right, Bill?"

"Ah, Dorothy. You are too harsh on me." He poked Mark's leg gently with his foot and whispered, "I'm really only eighty percent tease. The other twenty is out and out pure mischief."

Mark smiled back at him. "You're a good man, Pastor. I can tell."

"Uh huh. Do you see there?" He nudged me with the same foot. "A man with impeccable taste."

I shook my head.

"All right, all right, enough hot air from me. I'm curious to know what you are really up to. I see you've slapped a new coat of dandelions on the house. Did you do that, Mark?"

Mark held up his paint-flecked hands. "No, not the house."

"Ludy did that," I said.

"This is boat paint," Mark said, attempting to rub a dried glob off the back of his hand.

"Boat paint?" Pastor Bill scrunched up his eyes, perplexed. "Boat paint?"

"You didn't know I had a boat, did you?" I smacked my hands together. "You didn't even know I'm about ready to embark on a mission of exploration, did you?"

"Seriously?" He looked from me to Mark and back to me.

"Seriously," I said.

"Well now, you really do amaze me." He sat forward, interested. "Tell me more."

"Mark," I explained, "knows all about boats, especially sailing boats. He and Ludy and I are completing the work on Leroy's boat, the one he began a couple of years ago. Didn't I ever tell you about it?"

"No. Not unless my memory is worse than I thought."

"Come see it then." I crawled to my knees and stood up.

"Ugh. It's getting hotter than ever," Bill groaned, struggling to his feet. "Now where is this little boat of yours?" Mark and I looked at each other, both of us fighting to hide back laughter.

"It's not exactly a little boat," Mark said as we headed off toward the barn.

"I can't believe I never showed it to you," I said incredulously. "I thought sure you knew about Leroy's boat—that white elephant everybody was always referring to."

"No," Bill said. Mark led us into the barn. I watched Pastor's eyes flare wide as he took in the entire, freshly painted boat. "Jimminy-willikers," he whistled. "I am truly stunned. I thought you meant one of those tiny skiffs the sunbathers float around the county lake on. This is a . . . a . . . an ocean liner!"

Mark laughed heartily as Bill came closer to inspect the seeming apparition. Ludy's head popped up from the cabin.

"Hey, Pastor Wild Bill! What do you think?"

"Ludy!" Bill stared at him bewildered as he tried to grasp the incongruity of a thirty-foot sloop propped up in an old cow barn like a beached whale in the middle of Iowa. "Well, I know you didn't build this out of a hobby shop kit."

"Actually," Mark came forward and gingerly touched the hull paint to test its dryness. "Actually, it's patterned after a standard cruiser called a Catalina, a California design. You see the hull and deck are constructed of alternating layers of mat, cloth, and woven fiberglass. And then," he continued as he knelt down and peered underneath, "the keel is straight forward, the underbody has external lead ballast directly on the hull. She has a long waterline and a fairly wide beam. Ludy can explain the cabin fixtures and compartments to you."

Pastor Bill studied Mark. "I must admit that I am impressed."

"Come aboard," Ludy pleaded.

"In a minute." Bill looked at me, puffed up his cheeks, and exhaled slowly. "You're an amazing woman."

"Hard to believe, isn't it?" I squeezed his arm. "We're so excited."

"I can understand that."

"Gee, the paint is drying better than I thought it would," Mark said as he poured himself another glass of lemonade. He took a swallow but quickly spit it out on the ground. "Warm lemonade is awful."

"Let me go make some fresh," I volunteered. "Would you like some, too, Bill?"

"Yes, thank you."

"Got any cookies?" Ludy called after me as I left the barn.

"I'll see," I shouted over my shoulder.

The ice cubes in the freezer were only partly solid, but I dumped a trayful into the glass pitcher and then dug a plump lemon out from the vegetable drawer. Rather than drawing water from the tap, I went out to the well. Coming from over two hundred feet, even on hot days the water was always sparklingly cold.

As I pumped the cast iron handle I watched a cultivator dragging a loadful of dirt a half a mile away on the road that intersected my road. From the direction he was headed, I surmised he was either Dean Schwartz or his son Gunnar. Finally, a trickle and then a cascade of water gushed into and over the pitcher.

When I came back to the barn with the lemonade and a plate of raisin cookies, Mark was explaining to Pastor Bill and Ludy, who knelt on deck, about displacement and draft and then fluttering his hands to show wind angle and vectors.

"Can't you just picture," Ludy interrupted excitedly, "a towering, thirty-foot mast with these enormous, white sails straining against the wind?"

"I can, I certainly can," agreed Pastor Bill.

"And then this dazzling orange spinnaker, right up here." Ludy gestured with his arms. "You see, the rigging comes down across this way . . ."

"I'm afraid you've lost me," sighed Pastor Bill. "What's a spinnaker?"

"A type of sail." Mark took over the explanation as Ludy nodded in agreement. "It's a large, nylon, balloon-type sail used for downwind sailing. I'm sure you've seen them. They're usually more colorful than the mainsails."

"It all sounds rather complicated to me—all these different sails and rigs and changing winds. But I'm sure the three of you will manage."

"No, just the two of us, Pastor. Me and Nana. Mark's not going."

"Now I am a little worried," Bill said to me. "Where did you say you were going?"

"Where the wind blows." I chuckled.

"That's what worries me."

"It's probably safer than driving a car." Mark smirked as he took a raisin cookie and flipped another to Ludy.

"Oh, I wouldn't doubt that," Pastor said. He held out his glass for more lemonade. "Say, you wouldn't be going near Tahiti now, would you?" He brightened.

"Who knows?" I said. "Our itinerary isn't definite yet, but we plan to sail down the Mississippi to the Gulf and then either follow the Florida coast around to the Atlantic or head south by Texas and Mexico toward South America. But I expect we'll reach Tahiti eventually."

"Want to come?" Ludy asked.

"You really ought to." Mark grinned at him. "The Sailing Pastor—has a good ring to it, don't you think?"

"No, no." Bill shook his head. "The only water I'm getting in is in the privacy of my own bathtub."

"With your rubber duckie?"

"How did you know, Ludy?" He bent over to sniff the fresh paint. "Dear old duckie is supposed to be a secret. Seriously, though," he turned to me. "When is this adventure going to transpire?"

"Well, I don't know. What do you think, Mark: a month or so?"

"Oh, definitely by then. We should haul the boat out into the yard in the next couple of days, and then as soon as the mast and boom and rigging and shrouds arrive—well, I would say another week for fittings and adjustments. I'll probably install the motor at the marina, which will take two or three more days. We could predict launching in three weeks, providing all the details are worked out."

"I have a thousand loose ends to pull together."

"I should think so," Bill said. "What's the rest of your family feel about all this?"

"Well . . ." I searched for the appropriate words. "Let's just say their enthusiasm so far could fit into a Dixie cup. But we're going to convince them, aren't we, Ludy?"

"You bet!"

"Have you explained everything to your parents?" Pastor Bill asked Ludy.

"Not exactly. I've been waiting to get the boat finished first. It'll be harder for them to say no when they see how neat it is."

"And you expect to leave next month?"

"No sweat," Ludy said.

"Who's going to watch the house?" Bill asked me.

"We'll lock it up."

"How long do you plan to be gone?"

"Oh, I don't really know, Bill. I'm just taking one day at a time." I detected disapproval in his eyes. "I bet you think we're all insane, don't you? Everyone else seems to think so."

"It is rather . . . sudden."

"Bill . . . it's the first time in my life I've ever decided to do something without seeking permission from someone else or feeling guilty. I just wish people would stop expecting me to act like a widowed grandmother. I'm still alive. That's news to most people who know me. I'm alive. I didn't die when my husband did, even though . . . even though . . ."

"Dorothy, Dorothy, I'm not condemning you. I'm not even opposed to your trip." I could tell Ludy and Mark were uncomfortably trying to ignore my outburst. "If what you feel," Bill continued, "if that feeling in your heart is one of peace and confidence, then I share your excitement. I really do."

"Thank you, Bill. I knew you would." He smiled at me. I tried to catch Ludy's eye, but he had begun whistling as he finished the deck trim. Mark had gone over to a bucket of water and was cleaning a brush.

"Yipes! What's that?" Bill pointed to something behind me. A small paw had reached up to the cookie plate which sat on a wooden crate, and was carefully dragging the last cookie toward the edge. I leaned over and hauled Hobo up into the air by the scruff of his neck.

"Got you!" I scolded. "One cookie thief apprehended in the act." He squealed and pedaled his little legs in midair.

"And what is that?" Bill lowered himself off the boat and came over to inspect the masked bandit. "He surely does look like a criminal. But he's only a tyke. Give him to me."

Hobo curled his tail up between his legs as I handed him over. Pastor Bill stroked his underbelly. "Why, you're just a hungry little fellow, aren't you?"

"Hungry?" Ludy snorted. "He doesn't know what the word means."

Bill broke the last cookie in pieces and hand-fed Hobo a small chunk. Like an intelligent infant, Hobo stared up at Pastor Bill, with what I could have sworn was a gee-who-is-this-sucker gleam in his eyes.

"See what an attraction I have with wild animals," Bill said.

"Oh, right! A regular Marlin Perkins with the *wild animals,*" I teased. "This . . . this ferocious raccoon instinctively sensed your gentleness."

"You can tell then?" He smiled with aplomb.

"I hate to interrupt your act of mercy," Mark said as he toweled off his hands, "but I've got to get back to the shop."

Bill shifted Hobo to his left hand and then shook hands with Mark. "A pleasure to meet you, Mark. I'm sure we will see more of each other."

Mark nodded. "God bless you, Pastor."

"And you too."

"Remember to swing by the shop this afternoon and pick up the varnish for the galley," Mark instructed Ludy. "And Dorothy," he turned to me at the barn door, "God bless."

"He does." I smiled. "He really does."

"Gads," Bill dropped Hobo to the ground. "He devoured that cookie. And I think he was ready to start on my thumb."

Hobo tipped over my empty lemonade glass and began trundling it toward a hole in the wall which led to the tool shop.

"Hang on there." I chased after him and snatched it back.

"I wonder what kind of first mate a raccoon would make?" Bill said.

"Don't give him any ideas."

"They know how to catch fish."

"Hobo doesn't bother catching them," I said. "Not when he can snitch them out of my refrigerator."

"Well, I must move along myself." Bill brushed himself off. "You don't mind if I stop back periodically to follow your progress?"

"Heavens, no!" I said.

He held my hand thoughtfully for a moment and squeezed it. "I'm glad you're alive."

"Me too." I hadn't meant my voice to sound as husky as it had. I cleared my throat and repeated, "Me too."

"Ludy, my lad." Ludy looked up at Pastor Bill. "Heave ho!"

"You bet, Pastor. You can bring rubber duckie along if you change your mind."

"I don't think I will, but I'll tell him you said that." He winked at me, then turned and strode out of the barn.

I followed him for a couple of steps and called as an afterthought, "Let's get together for dinner before I leave. I'll cook." He grinned and saluted me.

I went back into the barn to watch Ludy for a few minutes as he finished stroking a brilliant red onto the cabin steps.

"It looks brand new, doesn't it?"

I blew on the hull. "It better for the fortune it's costing me."

"Good thing Mark is letting us have everything cheap."

Good thing, I thought. As I gathered up the glasses I realized I had lost track of expenses. For the first week, all the figures were in neat columns in a spiral notebook. But lately, we had been spending more time on the boat, some days from early morning until after supper, and we had picked up dozens of packages of screws and cleats and brushes and sheets of plywood and slats of tile and foam for cushions and so many other supplies, I couldn't remember to record them all. And then Mark wouldn't let me pay for some of the things he brought out. He would just silently unload his van and go to work attaching clamps and bits and things I didn't even know the names of.

I knew the motor, a small diesel with two blade props, would run almost a thousand dollars. Mark said the main sail and the genoa, along with the spinnaker, would total another thousand. But the more money that went into the boat, the less I was concerned.

I wasn't wealthy, but Leroy and I had saved about ten thousand dollars that we had planned to use for our retirement, which for Leroy meant not retirement, at least not from life, but disembarking toward a fantasy he had nurtured since boyhood. Had he been alive, he would still have arisen at five o'clock each morning to check the livestock and survey his crops. And each evening he would have disappeared toward the barn to, inch by inch, coax that fantasy a little closer to life, I was sure.

"Nana," Ludy interrupted my daydream.

I looked up at him. He had been working tirelessly, though his eyes seemed sleepy.

"You hungry?"

"No. I was just thinking . . ."

"Yes?"

"Well, I hoped that maybe, you might . . . you know . . . talk to Mom and Dad with me."

"Of course. I plan to. In fact, I spoke with your father just the other day when he was out here."

"Oh yeah?" Ludy's mouth drooped. "What'd he say?"

"We have to work on him, Ludy. You and I have to convince him."

"I know."

"And that means we need to pray. More than ever, Ludy, we might not be able to get through, but God can."

"I don't . . ."

"Are you willing to use every means, Ludy?"

"I'm not sure. I . . ."

I stared at him, aware that I had won a point for the Lord. At the same time, I knew Ludy could just as easily run scared from my pushing him toward God too quickly. I let up. "I want to talk to your mother, too."

"She kind of likes the idea."

"She does?" I was surprised.

"Oh yeah, she'd like to get rid of me for awhile."

"Oh you! You're as bad as Hobo."

He doubled his knees up to his chin and clicked his teeth. "What do you think of my imitation?" I just rolled my eyes and headed off to the house with the empty pitcher and glasses.

After rinsing off the dishes, I wandered into the living room and collapsed into an easy chair. The mid-afternoon heat was not as draining as the humidity. Switching on the television didn't help take my mind off the mugginess. I watched one soap opera for a couple of minutes, then flipped to another at the commercial. I found the plots tedious. If the characters were reflections of real people, then my world was better off without them. *Would a soap opera with average people,* I wondered, *struggling to do good, to raise children with traditional values, trying to make imperfect marriages work, based on Christian principles—would such a program be doomed to fail because of low ratings?* I was afraid so.

Just as I slumped back drowsily, the phone rang. I staggered over, hoisted it up, and mumbled hello.

"Mom, it's Sheri. Am I interrupting anything?"

"No, I was just snoozing in my chair. It's so sticky today that I feel like I'm moving underwater."

"I know. Have you got your fan on?"

"It doesn't help."

"You should invest in one of those small window air conditioners to at least cool your living room. You're welcome to come over here. I've just finished painting the kitchen, and the whole house smells like paint, but we're comfortable."

"No thanks. I'm expecting a special delivery package today, so I had better stay around."

"Well, if you change your mind . . ."

"I know. So you've been painting, too?"

"Finally. I'd been looking at those walls and grumbling for years. My canary yellow came out a little brighter than I had expected, but it still is an improvement. Is Ludy painting for you today?"

"Yes, out in the barn. I think he's finished now, though."

"In the barn? Is he painting that boat, Mom?"

"Why . . . yes." I hadn't discussed the boat or the trip with her yet, but I knew David and she had, and most likely Ludy, in his exuberance, had mentioned various ideas to Sheri.

"Mom, I would . . ." I waited for her to finish, already anticipating her objections. "I would like to talk this whole thing over. I really think we should. Soon, too. Are you busy this evening?"

She had caught me off guard. "Well no, not that I . . ."

"I called Evelyn this morning, and she suggested we have dinner together—just the three of us."

"That's something we haven't done in a long time. Should I meet you in town at the café?"

"We thought it might be nice to drive up to Waverly and eat at the Red Rooster. It's not that far, and the food is so much better. We can pick up Evelyn on the way. How does that sound?"

"That's fine with me. What time?"

"Is six too early?"

"Six is fine. See you then." It was three o'clock. I hoped a breeze would come up to bring some relief from the oppressive heat. I sat down in front of the revolving fan, but the air coming off the blades was more of the dense moisture that came from the cornfields. "Ghost steam" was the name we had given to swirling insect-like clouds hanging low in the air just above the tassels. From a distance it looked thick, but like a tremulous mirage, it dissipated the nearer we came. I could see ghost steam in the field across from the mailbox.

Ludy suddenly shot past on his motorcycle heading toward town. I was pleased that David had given his approval, but I sure didn't like the way Ludy drove it, especially on the loose gravel that bunched up in wheel ruts and made going any faster than a mule run a hazard. But what can you tell a fourteen-year-old?

15

I was rummaging through my closet for an old pair of brown pumps when I heard Sheri pull in the lane. Still perspiring from a too hot bath and clutching an open can of talcum powder in one hand and the shoes in the other, I hurried downstairs. She let herself in the back door as I put the shoes on the floor and slipped my feet into them. Then I stuffed a couple of tissues inside my purse and went to hook the front screened door.

"Boy, it hasn't cooled down any, has it?" I said as I dabbed powder on my neck.

"Your fan doesn't help much. Why don't you look into an air conditioner?" Sheri asked again.

I smiled, then followed her outside. "Maybe I will."

"Can you believe it's almost July Fourth?"

I slid into her car. The vinyl seat was so hot from the sun I could not lean back. "Are you celebrating this year?"

"Oh, just a barbecue and probably some volleyball in the backyard as usual. We expect you to come." She started the car and swung it around in the yard.

"I wouldn't miss it, so long as you let me bring a bowl of potato salad."

"You better! Nobody makes potato salad like you."

I eased back a little and relaxed. During the twenty-minute drive to Evelyn's, we chatted and gabbed about nothing in particular: the suntan T.J. was getting from hanging around the municipal pool, David's reaction to the painted kitchen, a new cake recipe Sheri had discovered that didn't call for eggs. When we drove up to Glenn and Evelyn's house, Jay climbed off the riding lawnmower and came over to the car. He held open the door as I struggled to my feet.

"Hey, Nana, Aunt Sheri."

"You've got a hot job," I puffed. "Is your mother ready?"

Glenn came out and sat on the porch steps as we waited for Evelyn to finish the hamburgers she was making for her family. Glenn tried to interest me in a story about one of our old neighbors whose tractor had tipped over and pinned him underneath, but I only half-listened. I knew the dinner that evening was only an excuse for Sheri and Evelyn to try to talk sense into my head about the boat trip. I tried to prepare my argument by rehearsing all the reasons for our voyage.

"He was just real lucky that the spring hitch was old, or his whole leg might have been snapped off," Glenn concluded.

"He's getting old anyway, isn't he?" Sheri asked.

"Probably eighty, but those old boys have to be dragged off their tractors. Why, you know Lafe Hermann. He's near ninety, and he's still going strong."

Evelyn came out in a whiff of honeysuckle.

"Whew! Did you douse yourself with bugspray?" Glenn ducked as Evelyn swatted playfully at his head.

"I'll bugspray you," she warned. "At twenty dollars an ounce, you better watch what you say."

"Twenty dollars an ounce? Why, for that amount I can go down to the Fleet Farm store and get you a fifty-gallon drum of repellent that has twice the smell of that."

"I'm sure you can."

"But you wouldn't want to get near her then," added Sheri.

"Oh, there's ice cream in the freezer," Evelyn said as she went down the steps. "And I've instructed Jason to do the dishes, so don't let him outside until he does."

"Yes, ma'am. Have a nice dinner, ladies," Glenn said, doffing his faded work cap.

Evelyn got into the back seat against my protests, and as we drove away, I could see her fiddling with her hair in the rearview mirror. She related how her trip to the dentist the day before had been disastrous because two teeth had to be pulled to make room for her incisors which were turning sideways. Sheri and I listened silently and added appropriate concern after she finished, but my thoughts were still on justifying what more and more seemed like a losing cause. With all of my family against me, I didn't know what I would do. I hadn't thought that far ahead.

The sky began turning a glassy crimson as we arrived at the restaurant. The parking lot was full, so we had to drive around the building twice before we found someone leaving.

"I made reservations," Sheri said as she led us through the door. From the outside, the restaurant looked like a weatherbeaten barn. But inside, once our eyes adjusted, the decor was elegant—what Leroy had called "Grant Wood Modern," since the designers only partly succeeded in capturing a folksy, midwestern style with the overstuffed leather and chrome.

Immediately after we were seated, the waitress came over and announced that the special of the day was Steak Diane.

"Is that with mushrooms?" I asked.

"Uh huh. Tenderloin and mushrooms."

She pointed at my menu with a teeth-marked pencil. "The baked potato and salad come with the dinner."

"All right, Steak Diane." I studied the waitress as Evelyn and Sheri scanned their menus. She was only mildly interested in taking our orders. I was certain she was barely twenty, if that, but too much eye make-up and a stiff hairdo under the dim lights made her appear older. I wondered what secret life was going on inside her, as she stared over the tops of our heads at an abstract painting on the wall entitled *Alfalfa*. Evelyn and Sheri agreed on Beef Stroganoff. The waitress mouthed a perfunctory thank you and sauntered off to the kitchen.

"Well," Sheri leaned forward on her elbows. "I haven't been here in ages."

"We were here for our last anniversary," Evelyn said.

"You're fortunate your husband believes in celebrating anniversaries."

"No, he takes a lot of wheedling to go out. But once we get somewhere, he enjoys himself and can't understand why we don't go out more often."

"Mom and I were talking about the barbecue on the Fourth. Will you still be able to come?" Sheri asked.

"That's right. Thursday is the Fourth already, isn't it? The kids have been after Glenn for the past week to dig out the sparklers and firecrackers he's had packed away. You're going to be there, aren't you, Mom?"

"She promised to bring potato salad."

"Why don't I bake a cake and a couple of pies then. What's David's favorite?"

"Any kind. T.J.'s is banana cream."

I sipped my water and thought about excusing myself to visit the ladies' room, but finally I had to blurt out, "Can we just get this matter over with now? I won't enjoy any of my dinner if we don't clear the air."

Sheri and Evelyn looked at each other. Had I breached the topic in the wrong way? "Sure, Mom," Sheri said. "We're not trying to keep anything back from you."

"You sound all tensed up," Evelyn said.

"Now, we all don't have to pretend what's on our minds. You might as well know that you aren't going to talk me out of going. I know you're concerned, you mean well, but I'm going." I sipped my water again and looked around the room.

Sheri smiled and touched my hand. "We're not going to talk you out of anything, Mom. We just want to find out a little more about what's going on. Information out of Ludy is impossible. You haven't really told us anything yet."

"I'm just curious, too," Evelyn added.

They were sincere. The fears I had concocted had just been exploded. I felt guilty for not having believed that my two daughters-in-law would stand behind me, supportive and loving. "I thought . . . I mean I expected . . ." They listened patiently. "I apologize to both of you. It's just that David, and I assumed everyone, knew about the trip and were opposed to my going."

"He just mentioned that you and Ludy were working on Dad's old boat, and that when you finished it you were going around the world."

"That's pretty ambitious," Evelyn said.

"You can imagine my surprise when a UPS truck delivered a package from a Chicago marine supply house." Sheri leaned toward me. "You're right, Mom, we are concerned about you, but we only want what you think is best. We aren't out to change your mind."

"It's a gorgeous boat," I continued. "We have an expert who runs a marina and boat shop helping us prepare it, and he's convinced that it's seaworthy. You both know how Leroy felt about that crazy boat. I started out wanting to fulfill his dream, but now it's become mine, my own. It's really quite safe, what with new technology. I just . . ."

"What, Mom?" Evelyn took off her glasses and rubbed her eyes.

"Well, I just one morning got tired of having to stand face to face with myself in the mirror. There's not much a woman my age can look forward to."

"Now that's not . . ." Sheri began, but I held up my hand to cut her off.

"I feel strongly about that. I wrestled many nights, sleepless nights, about my life after Leroy died. It's been a hard year. I hadn't known how much my life was invested in his. And when he was suddenly gone, well, so was most of what was important, you know, what gave shape to my life. If God hadn't come to meet me one night, why I don't know, I just really don't know what I . . ."

"Praise God, Momma. Praise God." Evelyn's eyes were teary.

"And you're as much to blame," I told her.

"You don't know how we prayed," she said. "Sheri and all of us, because we knew that God loved and loves you even more than we ever could. And He answered us."

My eyes became a little blurred. "I think that God planted this vision about the boat, too. I don't fully know what He wants of me, but it's going to give glory to God, I know that. I think . . . I think other women like me, women who are suddenly lost in mid-life need to find God, need to start over, no matter where they are, and if I can give some courage and inspiration to others, tell others what God has done for me, then that's what I want.''

"Like Saint Paul's missionary journeys?'' Sheri asked.

"Well, I'm no Paul.''

"By yourself,'' Evelyn said thoughtfully, "I don't think you could make it. But since God is with you . . .''

"I like the idea. I really do,'' Sheri said. "I've been a little afraid to talk with David about it, though. You know how unpredictable his temper is. I have to catch him in just the right mood, and then I'm never sure if the wrong word will trigger him off.''

"The first response from Glenn was, 'Why, I just might go along myself for a ways.' ''

"Glenn said that?'' I couldn't believe how quickly I could change from tripping on my lower lip to floating three feet above ground. And now Glenn wanted to go along. I had to ask the crucial question. "Sheri, what about Ludy going? I won't be able to sail the boat by myself. I need Ludy along.''

"Well,'' she sighed. "He does have his heart set on going. I'm so amazed at how he's changed in the last month. He really is pleasant with all of us. I'll say quite honestly that yesterday, after I talked with David—well, listened to David talk—I called school and spoke with Ludy's principal. At first he was silent—stunned silence, probably. But you know, after I explained just a little more, he got so excited and started rambling about what a great way to study geography and math and science and biology and even astronomy if Ludy was going to have to read his position by the stars—this is his principal, remember—and then it struck me as I listened, that here he was convincing me. Can you believe that? He even said we could work out Ludy's missing school by tailoring special lessons he could do independently and mail back. I was flabbergasted!''

Sheri had brought up ideas that hadn't even occurred to me. What an education Ludy could receive; how much the two of us had learned already. The local librarian had nearly fainted when Ludy began checking books out on boat construction and sailing. The principal was behind the idea. Glenn and Evelyn and Sheri weren't opposed. The problem still remained with David.

Something drastic would have to happen within a month, or all our work and plans and dreams would be for nothing. That's what it came down to. I would not become disheartened, not with a God who was willing to help me move a mountain if I had faith only the size of a mustard seed. *How big,* I wondered, *is a mustard seed?*

Our food arrived, and as I attacked it voraciously, I captivated Evelyn and Sheri with explanations of wind and vectors and what the cities I had always wanted to visit along the Mississippi were like.

When Sheri dropped me off at home, we got out of the car and stood on the lawn, both of us awed by the dazzling array of stars, never more magnificent than in the country, beyond the glare of city lights.

"This is the first time in a week that the sky has been clear at night," she said softly. "Can you believe all those stars? There must be trillions and trillions of them. And here we are."

"It's humbling, isn't it?"

"We are so minuscule!"

"And just think of each one of us," I added slowly. "Just think: each one of us is like a planet with worlds inside of us, like worlds within worlds moving through an immense, black space amidst all these vast stars and galaxies."

"It is humbling!"

"Yes, and comforting to know that God who made all of that, everything, should love us—us specks who exist for what? an instant in time?—that He should love us so much."

Sheri crossed her arms and sighed. "It's too much to think about." She shook her head. "I'd better scoot home. Thanks for coming with us tonight, Mom."

"Well, thanks for inviting me." I hugged her. "And thanks for the prayers when I was too pig-headed to listen to any of you."

"I'll see you on Thursday then?"

"You will, indeed. God bless and keep you."

As I watched her drive away, I couldn't help but feel that in dealing with my depression, had my family told me to "snap out of it" or had sent me to a counselor, without the healing power of God's love, I would, more than likely, have shriveled up inside my cocoon of stone and died. But thanks to Sheri and Evelyn, I was now, as Mark said, toddling forth at two months, joyfully toward my Father's open and loving arms.

16

The Frisbee just missed my head, but it didn't miss the overladen food table. It clattered into a half-full bottle of cola, caromed against a bowl of potato chips, and up-ended a ketchup bottle.

"Would you please aim in the other direction?" Sheri scowled at Ludy.

"T.J. threw it," he pleaded.

"But you missed it," T.J. called from where she stood thirty feet away.

"Can you throw it straight?" he shouted back.

"I did, but the wind took it."

"Listen, both of you," Sheri mediated. "Just move away from the table, or we'll be eating on our hands and knees off the grass, okay?"

Ludy backed up a dozen steps and flicked the orange disc out toward the house, but it dipped and arced gracefully right to T.J. She flung it back, though it wobbled and plopped at his feet.

"Whoever thought spinning pie tins back and forth would ever catch on?" I laughed. Sheri rearranged the table.

"I prefer horseshoes any time," she said.

Just then I noticed Glenn, Evelyn, and their family arriving in front of the house. A blast of their horn sent Ludy and T.J. around the house to greet them. Evelyn lugged a picnic basket toward us, and Glenn followed three steps behind, huffing and red in the face with a cooler, as the three boys whooped and slung a vivid maroon Frisbee across the path of Ludy and T.J.'s.

Glenn extracted a can of soda from under the ice and went over to talk with David, who was fanning the charcoal.

"Here's a fresh strawberry pie and a banana cream," Evelyn said, unpacking the basket. She handed one to Sheri. "You'd better refrigerate them."

"Oh, Mom! It looks like you made a ton of potato salad."

"About five pounds, I think. I remembered what appetites your boys have."

"Like starving hippos. Fortunately they're still growing up instead of out." She slapped her hips. "Wish I could say the same."

Sheri came back and sat with us as we talked and nibbled and watched the children switch from Frisbee to whiffle ball and then badminton. After two rackets broke, Ludy went to search for the volleyball, which he claimed was somewhere in the basement over T.J.'s insistence that it was up in the garage.

"July the Fourth doesn't seem to mean much any more," Evelyn said.

"I know," Sheri agreed. "When I was a kid, we always had a parade."

"And a band concert."

"That's right, a band concert. And a reunion."

"This is a reunion," I said.

"Well, my family," Evelyn explained, "brought in cousins and aunts and uncles from all over the state. We even had family come back from Wisconsin, the Dakotas, people I didn't ever know, but who were in some shirttail fashion related."

"Oh boy, did we eat and eat," Sheri said.

"That hasn't changed," I grinned. "And remember the fireworks? Glenn always loved the displays—every Fourth he would beg Leroy and me to take him and David to the stock car races so they could watch the fireworks. We only allowed them to have sparklers, but once in a while they would sneak in a cherry bomb they traded off a friend."

David came over to announce that the coals were ready, so Sheri dashed back into the house for hamburgers and hot dogs. A volleyball game was starting, but I declined Jason's offer to "even up the teams" by pretending my lumbago kept me from jumping like I used to.

"But it's three to two," he begged.

I pointed to Evelyn. "Ask your mother."

"You don't need my permission." She winked at me.

"You're taller than I am," I told her.

"Hey, we'll take Mark," Ludy shouted.

I spun around and caught sight of Mark loping down the street toward us. I had invited him the day before to stop by for lunch, and Ludy had even scrawled a rough map for him, but he had thought he would be canoeing with friends.

"Ah, the water was too low," he said to me before I had a chance to speak. I introduced him to Evelyn and then Glenn came over as the kids called to Mark impatiently, so he scratched his head, threw his hands up in dismay, and excused himself. He and T.J. and Jerry batted the ball back across the net to Jay and Jason who scurried around wildly to Ludy's instructions.

"Is that the young man you were telling me about?" Sheri asked, as she came back to the table with a plate of raw hamburgers.

"Uh huh. He's from California."

"I thought folks moved from Iowa *to* California," Glenn joked. "Not the other way around."

"He sure knows a lot about boats," I said.

"Are you taking him along on this voyage of yours?" Glenn asked.

"I wish he would come. Besides his sailing ability, we could use some of his effervescence."

"Effer— what, Mom?"

"Oh, Glenn, you know, sparkling personality."

"Athletic ability, too." He nodded toward Mark's diving save as the ball almost shot past him. Mark tumbled over and then sprang back to his feet. *We aren't the only ones admiring his skill,* I thought. T.J. appeared to be watching Mark with interest every time she thought he wasn't looking.

Sheri took the first hamburgers over to David who, by tradition, was conducting the chef's responsibilities. I explained to Glenn and Evelyn how the afternoon before, Mark had backed his friend's trailer and tow truck up to the boat, and with an ancient winch had gradually fit the trailer underneath the boat with Ludy knocking out the bracings one by one until the entire boat rested on the trailer. I had stood back nervously while they eased the boat out of the barn with less than an inch to spare on either side. Leroy knew what he was doing, I told them. I was afraid we would have to knock out a wall, but Leroy had measured perfectly.

"Can we come over and see it?" Evelyn asked.

"Of course. It looks twice as big in the barnyard."

"I would think out of place, too," Glenn added.

Sheri came back and tapped me on the shoulder. I looked up at her, sure that she was hiding a slight frown. "David would like to talk to you for a moment."

"What about?"

"Oh, you know him. If he can find something to complain about, he will."

Anxiety washed over me as I went around the rowdy volleyball game and ducked under the grill's smoke.

"Sheri said you wanted me?"

"Mom, who is that kid?"

"Mark?"

"Did you invite him today?"

"Well, yes, Ludy and I did."

He kept his eyes on the sputtering flames and flattened a hamburger with his spatula.

"I thought this picnic was just for family."

I knew what he was getting at. "He's a friend of ours."

"You didn't tell me he was coming."

"We didn't think he was. He was supposed to be canoeing today, but he said the water was too low. I don't know what you're upset about. We've got plenty of food."

"I'm not upset." He pressed down another burger. Grease dripped and crackled the fire.

"Then you don't mind if he has lunch with us?"

"He's the kid with the marina?"

"I resent your calling him a kid. He's a young man, very responsible, very generous, a Christian, and if you'll give him half a chance, you'll like him."

"You could have asked me first," he growled. I began to ruffle myself, but then I realized I was responding in anger to my son, to a son I had responded too often to in the past without asking God to carry the burdens that led to sharp words and resentment. *Jesus, love me and love David,* I prayed, *and open us to Your patience.*

"Do you mind if he stays?"

He paused for a moment. "I guess it's all right."

Thank You, Lord, I breathed. As I turned to head back to the picnic table I heard David mutter, "Thought it was just for family."

The volleyball game had broken up, and I had to fight my way around the pop cooler to get back to my seat. The kids were sweating; Glenn jokingly urged them to move downwind from us. I watched T.J. and Mark smile at each other. Ludy demonstrated how one "chugged" a can of root beer in one agonizing swallow. *They're just tuning up,* I thought. *Wait until after they eat!*

When the hamburgers were ready, Mark took one and sat down across from me between Glenn and T.J.

"So you're the fellow who talked Mom into taking this trip," Glenn said to him.

"Actually, she's almost convinced me to come along."

I smiled at Glenn. "Evelyn said *you* were interested in coming."

He bit into his hamburger. "I always wanted to go fishing in the Mississip. My neighbor has a cabin on the river up at Lansing, and he's offered to let me use it for the past ten years. I don't know. One of these years I'll probably take him up on it. Seems I get too busy in the summers."

"Me too," said Mark. "If everybody wanted to go boating in the winter," he winked at me, "I'd be with you in a minute. But if I don't do business in the summer, I don't do it."

"Are you selling a lot of boats now?" Glenn asked.

"Well, yeah. The boating season is almost over now, but people are still looking for runabouts, bass boats, a few cruisers and canoes."

"Sailboats?" Glenn asked.

"Some, but mostly the small hobie-cats and centerboard dinghies, occasionally a request for a racing design."

"Where'd you learn about boats?"

"California. I grew up on the water."

"All your family back there?"

Mark nodded.

"You miss them?" T.J. asked.

"Oh, sure, but I go home at Christmas, and they fly out here during the summer."

"You miss California?"

"In some ways. Not the freeways and smog. With all the oil spills, the ocean isn't as clean as when I was a kid."

"How about the weather?"

"I like to snow ski too, so I put up with Midwest winters. More than anything, though, I think people are more sensible here than in southern California. Not as many weirdos. I never feel as pressured, because life is slower here, and the values are more traditional and conservative —which is fine with me."

"I know lots of kids," T.J. said, "who can't wait to graduate so they can get an old, beat-up van, drive to California, and live on the beach."

"Believe me, I've been there, and it's not so great."

"It is when you've lived in Iowa all your life."

Mark looked to me for help, but I felt sympathetic to T.J.'s ideas. Having never been to California, I couldn't compare.

"Is that what you want to do when you graduate?" Mark asked her.

"No. I kinda want to live at home for another year and go to college. I'm interested in child psychology."

"So am I," I said. "All my life I've tried to figure out your father and his brother."

"She's just joking," Glenn told Mark. "We were model children." David called from the charcoal grill that more hamburgers were ready, and threatened to feed them to the dog if somebody didn't hurry over. Ludy swooped down from his perch in the lower branches of an ancient willow tree, followed by Jerry and Jason.

"Have some more potato salad," Evelyn insisted, making her way around the table.

"Oh, no, I couldn't," Mark moaned.

"You'll disappoint Nana if you don't." She scooped a huge spoonful and plopped it on Mark's plate, then did the same for T.J.

"How about me?" Glenn said, holding his plate out for her.

"You don't need seconds!" She pretended to scowl at him.

"There's no need to worry about my weight, too, is there?"

"Have some more lettuce salad."

"Well," he reasoned, "I'll just have to fill up on your pies."

"All right, all right, have more potato salad." She winced and handed him the bowl. "Just don't mention pies around me."

"Is she on a diet?" Mark asked, politely waiting until she left to fetch more hamburgers for the kids.

"Since she was twelve years old," Glenn said.

"Oh, you're exaggerating," I scolded.

"I am not! Ever since I've known her she's worried about her weight."

"She doesn't have much of a problem," T.J. said.

"It's my problem," Glenn whined. "She rarely lets us keep desserts in the house, and you know what a sweet tooth I've got."

"I know," I said. "No matter how many dozen I would make, cookies never lasted more than a day around our house."

"I guess families are the same all over," Mark said.

"How's that?" Glenn asked.

"Oh, somebody's always dieting, somebody's always pushing more food your way, somebody can't wait to move away from home and see the world . . . . You remind me of my family."

"Do you have a sister?" T.J. asked.

Mark held up two fingers. "Both older and married, a brother that's two, almost three years older than me. He's in real estate with my dad—a Porsche, a beach condo, chalet in the mountains—the whole affluent bit."

"You're not like him?"

"In some ways, but no, we're pretty different. I like to remind myself that it will all pass away, but God's love won't, you know what I mean?"

T.J. paused and looked at me. I raised my eyebrows, as if to tell her that I agreed.

"Game two is about to begin," Ludy called as he bounced the volleyball.

"Wish I had their energy," Glenn said.

Sheri got up to remove the plates. "Why don't you play with them for a while? We'll get cleaned up and then have desserts."

"Sure, why not?" Glenn said, still watching the game with a pained look. He finally turned to David. "How about it?"

They straggled over toward the net. "Okay, who's winning?" Glenn asked, holding his stomach as if the contents were highly explosive.

"They're mopping us," Jerry replied.

"Then they have to take me," Glenn exclaimed. "And the losers can have David."

"Thanks a lot!" Ludy joked.

"I was all-conference in high school," David told him.

"But that was basketball."

"Well, close enough."

Here we are, falling into old, familiar patterns, I thought. *The men get to wander away to play, and the women get stuck with the clean-up chores.* I wondered how the men would have reacted if Evelyn, Sheri, and I had jumped up to participate in the game and had instructed Glenn and David to handle the dirty plates and cups and spilled Kool-aid? Without protest, I carried a precarious stack of dishes into the kitchen.

When everyone was thoroughly exhausted, we sliced the pies and cake, David dragged out a watermelon, and the Frisbee toss resumed. As twilight approached, we began hearing distant pops and strings of firecrackers lit off.

"Can we get out our sky bombs now?" Jason asked his father.

"It's not even dark yet."

Mark told everyone how, as a child, he and his brothers had made a firecracker cannon with empty tin cans. They had put a two-foot hole in his parents' front door when the apparatus tipped on its side and fired a tennis ball in the wrong direction. David repeated his annual, gory retelling of his friend who dropped a lit stringer into his shoe and blew away all his toes. Finally giving in to his sons' persistence, Glenn brought out the fireworks. The aerial rockets sizzled up above the house and burst into thin strands of color that vanished just before they hit the treetops.

"Boy, those are duds," Jerry complained. "Give me a sparkler instead." After the two boxes of sparklers were twirled, waved, and flung into the sky in fading arcs of light, we sat on the grass, everyone except Ludy and his cousins, who climbed onto the roof to oooh and aaah at the drive-in theater's fireworks visible in the eastern sky.

"No, the Fourth of July just doesn't seem the same any more," Evelyn said.

"Maybe it's us who have changed," Sheri mused.

"You sure can't get off the ground like you used to." Glenn poked David.

"I'm thirty pounds heavier than when I was in high school, too. What's your excuse?"

"When I look at T.J. and realize she'll be graduating this year, I really

157

feel old," Sheri said. "Did you feel the same when David and Glenn graduated, Mom?"

"A little. Yes, maybe I did. I didn't ever really stop to think about it. Don't believe what you hear about age coming on you gracefully. No, sir. I can remember waking up one morning, and it had all happened. Maybe the body ages slowly, but some morning you wake up and boom! You're old. Of course, I don't feel that way any more."

"I reckon never to feel that way," Glenn said. "In my head I'm still twelve years old."

"That's for sure," Evelyn teased.

"No, seriously. Each day I step out into the fresh air, gaze across the rolling hills at the sunrise, and feel like I'm seeing the world for the first time, anew. Ever feel that way?"

"Don't get a factory job," David said. "You're like a mole going into the ground, into a dark smelly hole in the ground. I don't even have any windows near where I work."

"You should quit then—go on out and run the home farm. There's enough work there to keep you busy."

"The money's too good at the factory."

"No money could get me into a factory."

"You're never too old to do anything, right, Mom?" Evelyn grinned at me. "Life does start new each morning, doesn't it?"

"Grandma Moses didn't start painting until she was in her seventies," I remembered.

"Yeah, but most baseball players are washed up at thirty-five," Glenn said. "Football players even younger."

"The heck with all that age worry. Leroy always used to say, 'Dorothy, I can outwork any two teenagers without even trying.' I think his secret was enjoying whatever he did."

"No, his secret," Glenn said, "was that he was a workaholic. He never stopped long enough to be tired or think about aging."

"All I know," I emphasized, "is that I've never felt more energetic or happier, and I thank God every morning for a new chance, a new opportunity."

"Get a factory job, Mom," David said. "That'll change your mind."

"David!" Sheri laid her hand across his arm. "Any time you want to leave there, I'm entirely behind you."

"You know I can't leave because I've got seniority. That would be stupid after all these years."

"I could always get a job."

"Forget it. Just forget it. I'm sorry I brought it up."

Sheri sighed and changed the subject. "I'll make some iced tea if somebody would like any."

"I think we're going to pack up and head home," Evelyn told her. "The mosquitoes are beginning to eat me alive."

As Glenn shooed the children toward the car and Sheri and Evelyn went inside to divvy up the leftovers, Mark came over to thank David for the picnic.

"You really are great people," he said, shaking David's hand. I could sense that David had begun to warm up.

"Well, thanks. We're just glad that you've taken some of your time to help out Mom."

"It's my pleasure. If I can share some of God's goodness with others, that's all I ask."

"Uh huh. That's a good philosophy to have." David scratched his neck uncomfortably as he searched for something to say. "Uh huh. Well, you'll have to stop back."

After Mark left, T.J. came over to whisper to me that she and Mark had a date for the next Sunday. "If you can believe," she said wide-eyed, "we're going to his church together. He said there's lots of college students he wants me to meet. Isn't that something?"

"It's certainly not your usual first date, is it? But tell me, Mark doesn't hide the fact that he's a Christian. Does that make you uncomfortable?"

"Naw. Why should it? I'm a Christian, too."

"But you don't go to church regularly."

"I go in spurts."

"You aren't bothered by his talking about God then?" I asked.

"Heck no. He's a super neat guy. If he was some old preacher ranting like they do on television, I might feel different. But he's so confident, you know, runs his own business, and did you see that tan he's got?"

"But it will fade."

"No, he told me it was year around—his skin is just dark."

"But I mean, that's just something external."

"Oh, I know, I know. You don't need to give me a big lecture. But he's neat inside, too, isn't he?"

"Yes, I think so."

"Me too. I know what you're saying about church. If Mom and Dad made more about it, if they forced me to go . . ."

"They don't?"

"Not really. Sometimes they don't go; why should I? But I believe in

God. I'm not some whacky Hare Krishna—there's some of those at school, you know. I guess I just haven't needed God yet.''

"I have.''

"Well, that's what I mean. It seems that it's usually, well, you know, old people who . . .''

"Like me?''

"No, don't get mad. I should have said *older* people who start thinking they don't have much time to live, and they get worried and . . .''

"Mark's not old.''

"Yeah, that's true. I'm not arguing with you, Nana. It's just that I'm . . . I don't know . . . too busy for God. Adolescence is a difficult time.'' I could tell she was teasing me. "I'm a teenager, remember. I can't understand why everybody tells me this is the best time of my life. Just wait until I graduate; that will be the best time.''

I looked deeply into her eyes, sure that I had felt the same way once, but wishing she could avoid the empty depots I had passed along the way to discovering God's love. "Yes, I understand.''

She snapped her fingers. "Teenagers, Nana, are a race apart. No, I'm only kidding.''

"Maybe Ludy's a more representative example.''

"Huh?''

"Oh, I was just kidding too. You'll have to come over with him some morning and look at the work we've done on the boat.''

"I'm going to. Mark was telling me all about it. He said he was going to put a souped-up motor in it so you and Ludy could even waterski if you wanted to.''

"Ludy maybe. I'm not sure I want to go that fast.''

"Where is Ludy?'' she asked, looking around. I pointed up to the roof. "Oh. Well,'' she pushed her hands down into the pockets of her cut-offs, "this has been the best Fourth of July ever, don't you think?''

"I've seen a lot of Fourth of July's go past, but I agree. This was the best, for sure.''

"For sure,'' she repeated. "For sure!''

17 Ludy's hammering woke me the following morning. I rolled over and through glazed eyes saw the luminous dial on the clock inching toward 7:00. Vowing to be chipper, I sat up in bed for a few minutes reading Psalm 139, my recently discovered favorite of all the Psalms. But the meditation on God's knowledge permeating every fiber of my being was lost to the insistent pounding.

No, I said to myself, *I'm not going to be upset.* I admired Ludy's industriousness, even though it interrupted my sleep and quiet prayertime. Resigned to the fact that the morning had begun earlier than usual, I wobbled into the bathroom, swished a mouthful of water, patted my cheeks with moisturizer, and dragged a brush through my hair.

By the time I had gulped a lukewarm cup of coffee and pulled over my head a housedress with a number of makeshift pockets to hold nails, pliers, measuring tape, screwdrivers, and drill bits, two hammers were thumping in unison. I nearly tripped over a sprawl of fur as I went out the back door. Hobo, Molly, two unnamed kittens, and a moth-eaten squirrel stole which had disappeared from my closet weeks before were tangled in a drowsy heap. They complained briefly at being disturbed, but moved over two feet to the shade under a wicker chair.

"Don't you two know that decent folks are still in bed!" I rubbed my eyes convincingly enough to halt both hammers in midstroke.

"Sorry," Mark said. "We just wanted to get an early start."

"Yeah, the sun has been up almost two hours," Ludy said.

"All right. I deserve as much for being up late last night."

"Uh huh! You had a private celebration after you left our house, didn't you?" Ludy's eyes narrowed as he nodded understandingly.

"Not what you think. I plead the Fifth."

"Plead it—you probably drank it!"

"Why, Ludy, what a thing to accuse your dear grandmother of."

"I'm sure he's joking," Mark added.

"Heck no! Well, yeah . . . I guess I am," he said, grinning wickedly. "But come here and see why we started early." He pointed to an open horse trailer which sat propped against the barn. Inside were a miniature refrigerator and stove with assorted pipes and wires. "They work, too," Ludy explained. "I swapped them for my old go-cart and two washing machine motors at Ike's Junkyard. He salvaged them from a junked Winnebago travel trailer, and you know what? They measure out almost perfect."

"No kidding?"

"Fortunately," Mark said, "we can convert them from propane gas to electricity while you're dockside. We're doing panel wiring now so you can run them and your lights at 110 volts at a Marina or off your self-contained 12-volt battery. Convenient, huh?"

"I am impressed. What was that tray called you mentioned we would need for the stove?"

"A gimbal. I brought an extra one. That way you won't have Ludy's hot cocoa sloshing onto your feet when a wave washes underneath."

"We really will be able to live on the boat, then?"

"That's the idea."

"Boy, I should have picked up some doughnuts on the way." Ludy rubbed at his growling stomach. "You wouldn't have any?" he asked, looking up at me.

"Nope. Sorry." An idea struck me. "Ludy, I'm due for some fresh eggs today. Would you mind running over to the hen house for them?"

"We could have a batch of scrambled eggs then?"

"Sure, why not?"

He walked across the yard, bent down at the small door, and crawled into a furious greeting.

"Is there anything I can help you with?" I asked Mark, who was measuring a wood cabinet.

"Well," he stood back. "I'm going to fit these cabinets in the galley under the refrigerator. You could help me lift and steady them."

I climbed the ladder to the cockpit and waited for him to guide the cabinets over the side. He lifted them carefully, straining to keep the unfinished edges from scratching the gel coat. I took them, pivoted slowly, and let them down just at the cabin steps.

"Well done," he said as he climbed in next to me. Just when we were about to shuttle the cabinets the rest of the way, Ludy came back with a dozen eggs protruding out of his rolled-up shirt.

"I had to fight for my life to get these," he whined. "Your birds haven't heard about the right-to-life movement, have they?"

"No," I grinned. "But if the eggs sit too long the mommas do get possessive."

"Anyway, here's your eggs," Ludy said.

"Mark and I are just about to fit the cabinets in. Would you mind taking them up to the house and scrambling them?"

"Me?"

"Why not? Don't tell me you've never cooked scrambled eggs before. I'm expecting you to do lots of cooking when we get underway."

He looked up to Mark with a hopeless expression on his face. "I've cooked all kinds of stuff, but . . . well, it's been a long time since I made scrambled eggs."

"Let me refresh you then. Melt some butter in my skillet while you mix some milk and eggs together, and then just pour everything into the pan and stir until they're done. Easy, isn't it?"

"Oh yeah, I remember now." He gave us a smug toss of his head and went up to the house.

"That should be interesting," Mark said.

"It's pretty hard to goof up scrambled eggs."

"We'll see." He slid past me, and gradually we tilted the cabinets up and rocked them forward until they edged through the narrow opening of the cabin. They did fit perfectly as we pushed them back against the wall.

"Any snugger and you wouldn't have been able to open this porthole," he said.

"Now the refrigerator will sit on top?"

"Hopefully. We'll latch it on this side and then fasten it against the wall. The holes at the back of the cabinets here will allow the electrical connection and your propane hook-up."

I marveled at his planning.

"Well," he responded. "On a boat you have to use every available inch of space. The only problem is the water for your john."

"It won't be river or ocean water, will it?"

"Oh no. You have room for a twenty-five-gallon fresh water tank."

"Hey, Nana!" Ludy stood on the porch, hands on his hips. "Hey, I was gonna make some toast, but your toaster isn't working."

"I think the problem," I called back to him, "is that I usually leave it unplugged." He stared at me unbelieving and mumbled something as he turned to go back inside.

"Poor Ludy," Mark held his hand over his mouth to keep from guffawing.

"Poor Ludy? I'm the one who has to put up with him."

"I suggest you institute a course in basic cooking."

"I had better—at least the fundamentals of home appliances."

"Don't turn around, but I think we have a stowaway," Mark cautioned. "He's sneaking up the ladder now."

I turned my head slowly until I could see a masked face peeping over the side of the boat. "Hobo!" I startled him. "Shoo! Shoo!" He spun around and leaped frantically for the trailer wheel, missed, and scuttled around the corner of the barn. "I have to keep my eye on that rascal.

He's worse than a four-year-old child for poking his nose where it doesn't belong. He snitched an old fur stole in my closet and has been dragging it around for a security blanket.''

"And he's a notorious cookie thief, too, isn't he?''

"Cookies, bread, sugar cubes, or anything glittery that's not pegged down. He's impossible to keep out of the house.''

"You better teach him rudimentary knots for mooring.''

"No, I'd rather not take him along on the boat.''

"I thought you said he could get into your house. I'd hate to leave it in his care for long.''

"I see your point. You wouldn't like a pet raccoon, would you?''

"No. Felix my turtle is about all I can handle.''

"Felix?''

"After my uncle—he's bald.''

"Chow is ready!'' Ludy sang out. "Come and get it!''

"Well, let's hope for the best,'' I said. We went up and sat on the shady porch while Ludy bustled in and out with glasses of orange juice, a stack of toast on my cutting board, and finally, three bowls of scrambled eggs.

"Soup bowls?'' I asked him.

"I couldn't find the plates.''

"Now all we need is chop sticks,'' Mark laughed.

"Hey, I'm a novice, okay? I admit it.''

"They're good,'' I told him.

Mark chewed daintily and in an indistinct accent said, "Not bad, not bad at all.''

"Where are you from?'' Ludy asked.

"Outer Slobbovia. In making scrambled eggs, which are a rare delicacy, our chefs use wood chips.''

"Wood chips?''

"Oh, yes. For a real snap, crackle, and pop.''

"At least somebody likes them,'' Ludy said, holding out a forkful for one of the kittens. The kitten sniffed it and then pounced greedily before his companion could stick a wet nose close enough.

"Don't get excited, Ludy,'' I said. "I saw that kitten eating a dead mouse yesterday, too!''

"Yuk!'' He wiped off his fork and pushed the kittens away.

"You wouldn't have ketchup, would you?'' Mark asked.

"Ketchup?'' I stared at him.

"I always eat ketchup on my scrambled eggs.''

I shrugged. "If that's how you like them. There's a bottle in the refrigerator." He got to his feet and went inside.

"What about work today?" I asked when he returned.

"I said I'd be in by ten. Marci can open up and handle the first hour by herself. She does all the bookkeeping anyway."

"Leave when you have to. Ludy and I should make you a joint shareholder in the boat for all the work and parts you've contributed."

"That's no big deal, really. Oh, speaking of parts, remind me to get your help before I go today in unloading a fixture from my van."

"A fixture? What kind?"

"You'll see." A brown UPS truck pulled in the drive. The driver stuck his head out the window and asked, "Rural route four? Is this Morgan?"

"That's right!" Ludy sprang to his feet, and we followed him to the truck. The driver got out, went around to the back, and grunted as he slid a long package out of the truck.

"There's either your boom or your mast," Mark said.

Ludy helped the driver slide another package out. "And this," said the driver, puffing, "is yours, too." With his legs he pushed a flat, heavy box to the back. "Be careful. It's heavier than it looks."

Ludy deciphered the upside down label. "Hey, our sails!" Mark got on the other side of the box, and together they carried it onto the grass while I signed for the shipment. As the truck spun around and pulled away, Ludy was already tearing anxiously at the tubular canisters. "Look at that," he grinned as he yanked the end of a metal pole out. "Our mast!"

Mark and Ludy hauled the packages over to the boat while I carried the breakfast dishes inside, away from the pawing of the kittens. *Thank You, Lord,* I intoned softly. When I got back to the boat, Mark and Ludy were wrestling with a wooden box. After they set it on the ground, Mark grasped the tiny doorknob and pulled. Inside was a small but complete toilet and sink.

"Who is that for, munchkins?" Ludy smiled.

Mark stepped in front of me. "Now before you bawl me out for letting you have this john," he said, "you should know that I took it out of a boat that some guy dry-docked two years ago and never came back after. Legally, since it was in my possession, and according to our storage contracts, it has become my property. So it's only costing me the labor, and that I give willingly."

"What can I say?"

"That I snowed you, right?"

"You sure did, but thank you. Will it fit?"

"Trust me. Ludy," he said, "let me introduce you to another technical wonder. This is a chlorinator toilet which works on the same principle as a miniature sewage plant. This here," he touched a small drum, "is a holding tank so that you can pump everything overboard, which for ecological reasons is not recommended, or you can unload it at a pumping station. Most marinas have them. What do you think?"

"Great," Ludy said. "But how are we going to get it into the boat?"

"That may take some thought."

While they attacked the problem of hoisting the refrigerator into the boat, I moseyed out to the mailbox. Under the utilities bill were two large manila envelopes. The first, from the United States Coast Guard, St. Louis Office, contained a "Mississippi River Light List," a "Notice to Mariners Channel Report," and an "Aids to Navigation" pamphlet with additional printouts on regulations, advisory vessel traffic, and boating information.

The heftier of the two parcels was from the Mississippi River Commission's Army Corps of Engineers. I expected our navigational charts would be inside. They were, along with advisories on using locks and dams and updated sheets on repairs and constructions. I carried the armful to the back porch and tried to make sense of it all. The navigational charts, collected in a ring-bound volume, were imposing. Notations and markings indicated all manner of islands and chutes and wing dams and cable crossings and bridges with dimensions, feet and cubic feet and miles—my head reeled. I could never keep the boat on a straight course and read the complex charts.

"Oh no!" I heard Ludy scream. "Nana! Can you come here!" As I approached the boat, I could see Ludy staring glumly inside the boat from where he stood on the ladder. I climbed up next to him.

"What is that?"

"Paw prints, I think."

"Raccoon?"

I nodded. White paw prints tracked across the deck, over the cabinet top, on the carpet, zigzagging from one side of the cabin to the other. Hobo undoubtedly had explored the boat after all, and from what I could tell, had left a sticky imprint.

"Mark, what were those tubes of white gunk you brought and stacked in the barn?"

"In the corner?"

"Uh huh," Ludy grimaced.

"Calking for the seams. It's kind of messy to use."

"We know. Hobo just demonstrated."

I went to get a wet towel to wipe his prints up. Search as I could, he had hidden himself well, perhaps sensing that I would have gleefully throttled him because of his artwork. I caught Mark at his van as he prepared to leave. There were a couple of questions I had been meaning to ask.

"Tell me a little more about what *Spirit-filled* means."

"The Holy Spirit," he said as he loaded in his toolbox, "is the living embodiment of God which Jesus sent into the world at Pentecost."

"I'm not sure I understand."

"Well, most people think that when Jesus died and ascended into heaven that God took His hand off the world. Not so."

"And some Christians believe the Holy Spirit is alive today, for us?"

"Yes, that, and also He makes available to us the gifts of the Spirit. You should read First Corinthians, chapters twelve, thirteen, and fourteen, to understand more about them."

"It's about speaking in tongues and all that, isn't it?"

He sat down on the back bumper and watched Ludy's head bobbing inside the cabin. "It is, but don't let it trouble you. Most people are put off by speaking in tongues because they simply do not know what it is. It's scriptural, and there's nothing wrong with it, but there's so much more than just the one gift."

"Do you speak in tongues?"

He nodded. "That doesn't make me weird though."

"No, I hope I didn't imply that. Could you speak in tongues now?"

"Oh yeah. It's not some mystical language. It's a prayer language, and I could say it now, but I would rather you come to one of our services where praising is more natural."

"How do you get the gifts?" I studied the twinkle in his eyes. He was not at all uncomfortable about my persistent questions.

"You ask for them. God is willing to give them to whoever asks."

"To me?"

"Yes, if you ask."

"I will then."

"Good. Let me bring you a book or two that will shed more light on the gifts of the Holy Spirit."

I realized I was keeping him from work. "You better get going."

"I always have time to share the Lord."

"I know. I'm glad you've asked T.J. to go to church with you Sunday."

He grinned and nodded. "Call me if anything comes up. Ludy!" Ludy stuck his head out a porthole. "You better wait until I can come back tomorrow to struggle with the john. I'll try to bring some help. Why don't you get the stove in and wired for now."

Ludy saluted as Mark drove away. "Have you prayed to God for your father's permission yet?" I asked him.

He made a face at me. "No, but I'll put in a call before beddy-bye tonight."

"Let's do," I agreed. "I don't want to go down with the ship alone. I'd like your company."

"Ha ha," he smirked. "Very funny, Nana. Very funny."

18

The next few days I was bothered by a recurrent thought. I had come to appreciate solitude more and more, especially when I realized that only months before, being alone filled me with fear. Now, during quiet periods I was able to feel, beyond doubt, the near presence of the Lord. But I didn't really know how to pray. Prayer had to be more than reciting words. Prayer had to be more than just simple conversation. I thought I was certainly missing a fundamental, spiritual truth. I wanted God to direct me in His will so that whatever I did would be done in obedience. My plans in completing the boat and sailing forth to unknown destinations were blessed by God, I felt.

He had sent Mark, a person who glowed with God's love. Ludy was beginning to open up to the Lord. T.J. was going to church. And yet, when I prayed for David, I couldn't get past the thought that my prayers were all wrong. I felt selfish in asking God to touch David's heart so he would allow Ludy to sail with me. Shouldn't I ask for God to first meet David face to face as He had met me? Wasn't David's eternal soul more important than his consent for our trip?

I returned again to the sixth chapter of Matthew, where Jesus instructed His disciples about the birds of the air and the wild flowers, and how they were taken care of. "Seek first His kingdom and His righteousness, and all these things shall be added to you," answered part of my anxiety. But I still wasn't sure I was quite in line with God's designs. How could I know?

I wasn't surprised to see T.J. rapping at my back door the Monday morning after she had accompanied Mark to the campus Interfaith Center. I had asked her to tell me all about it.

"Isn't it a gorgeous day, Nana?" she bubbled. "Come on out and soak up the sun." Abandoning my stale coffee, I followed her down the steps to the yard and drew in a lungful of the summer morning's lush aromas.

"Fresh-cut grass," I said, breathing deeply.

"Ummm, smells like honey, doesn't it?"

"That's the clover."

"Heavenly." She knelt down and searched through the grass.

"Lose something?"

"No. I'm looking for a four-leaf clover. I always find them. See?" She held one up for me. "Have some luck!"

I glanced over to the boat. "It's unusually quiet today."

"It's Monday morning."

"I know, but I expected to see Ludy tinkering around with something. What do you think about the boat? It's changed some since you saw it last, hasn't it?"

"I'll say." She sat back on her heels and stared at it.

"Don't you want to see the inside?"

"In a while. Mark promised to give me the nickel tour."

"So, that's why you're here."

"Kind of. He mentioned that he was coming out about mid-morning."

"Uh huh." She handed me a dandelion. "How was church yesterday?"

"Okay," she said.

"Just 'okay'?"

"Well, you know."

"I don't know. Ooh! You young people." I pretended to be exasperated with her. "Ludy's the same way. You expect us to read minds."

"Nana," she smiled, "that's just how we talk."

"Economy of words?"

"Yep!"

"See what I mean? 'Yep.' Is that all?"

"No," she said with a laugh. "I was about to tell you. Why don't you try to read my thoughts instead?"

"Ooh!" I stuck the dandelion in her hair, and she retaliated by dumping a clump of grass over my toes.

"Now, calm down, Nana, and I'll tell you."

I sat down next to her.

"It was very informal," she said. "I thought everybody would be college students, but there were a lot of old, er . . . older people there. It wasn't really a church, more like a large utility room with plush carpet and sofas and folding chairs set up. And the pastor, well, he was kinda young and had a beard. He invited the Episcopalian minister to help him celebrate Communion."

"Really? Is that acceptable?"

"I don't know, but it was really neat. And instead of Mark's pastor blabbering on for an hour while everybody tries to doze off without looking too obvious about it, he just talked for about five minutes and then the other minister added a little more and then they sat back and opened up what they had said for discussion."

"You mean people just spoke right up?"

"Yeah, the whole group."

"That is different."

"But it was neat. Everybody participated instead of letting the ministers do it all. I really felt relaxed and close to the group. And when we sang, everybody sang and from the heart, too. You'll have to come."

"I'd like to. I wonder though, if the service was so relaxed, was it . . . solemn?"

"I think so. I got a lot out of it—more than usual."

"Hmmm."

"What's that 'hmmm' mean?"

"Just thinking."

"Well, I know what you're thinking, but Mark told me that if Jesus could preach from a fishing boat at the edge of a lake or on a mountain-side with sheep wandering around Him, then we could sit on the floor and participate with the minister."

"You sat on the floor?"

"There weren't enough chairs for everyone."

"I'm a little old-fashioned."

"There wasn't anything wrong with it. I met some of Mark's friends who were extra nice. Give it a chance."

"Maybe."

"You're welcome to go with us."

"You're going with Mark again?"

She smiled but refused to answer. A loud, sustained blast from what sounded like a tugboat came from in front of the house. By the time we jumped to our feet, Mark's van had turned in and was rolling toward us. Ludy hung out the side window and held a black cylinder up in the air. Again, a deep, brassy wail rang out across the still morning.

"You're going to scare Ev's cows," I told him when the van came to a stop. Mark got out first and came around to us, beaming.

"That's your new air horn."

"Everybody within five miles knows about it now, too."

"Ludy wanted to lay on it all the way out here, but I made him hold off until we were closer."

"Thank goodness."

"Hi, T.J. Can you do me a big favor?" Mark took her by the arm and led her away a couple of steps. I went around to the back of the van where Ludy was unloading a cardboard box with two twelve-volt batteries.

"One of these will run the horn and lights," he said.

"You certainly don't need both of them on the horn!"

"You should get one for your car." He grinned.

"Can I help out?"

"Yeah, here." He handed me a thin, sealed tube, weighted on one end.

"What's this?"

"A hydrometer," he said as he placed both batteries on the ground. "It's to check battery power."

"Oh." I watched him, aware that Mark was still intently giving directions about something to T. J. Satisfied that both batteries were charged, Ludy carried them over to the boat and came back with a small box in his hand.

"Did I show you this?" he asked. He withdrew a small clock and handed it to me.

"It's a little clock."

"Not just a clock," he emphasized. "It's a chronometer. It should be so accurate that it won't lose or gain more than a second a day."

"What's a couple of seconds?"

"A couple of seconds can be fifty miles when you're at sea."

"I don't understand."

"Well, it's real complicated, and I don't understand very well myself yet, but if you know the exact time, and you can measure the angle and height of the sun above the horizon with your sextant, then you should be able to tell where you are. Mark's going to teach us."

"Couldn't I just look at a map to tell where we are?"

He rolled back his eyes. "Like I said, you're in the middle of the ocean, and there just aren't many road signs."

"That's inconvenient," I teased. He shook his head and walked away.

T.J. climbed into Mark's van behind the steering wheel and ground the engine once as Mark shouted to put the clutch in all the way. The second time, she got it to catch. Mark came over as she backed out of the driveway to explain that he had remembered to bring out a VHF radio for the boat, but he neglected to put the extra crystals into the van that morning. The extra crystals, he went on, would allow us to call the Coast Guard and talk to the station masters at locks and even hail barge captains. More importantly, we would have access to weather information.

"You mean I don't have to learn Morse code?"

"Not unless you want to."

"What's SOS? Isn't it long dash, short dot, long dash?"

"Beats me."

I walked with him over to the boat as Ludy struggled with a wrench at the bottom of the mast. "It's looking like a real sailboat now," I said.

"The rigging does make a difference," Mark said. "Did you tighten the mast-step first?" He pointed at something to Ludy.

"Oh yeah," Ludy answered. "But I could use your help with the forestay." Mark stood on a sawhorse and lifted himself into the boat.

"What's a forestay?" I asked, trying not to sound too naive.

"It's also called a headstay," Mark said as he grasped the rigging, which extended from the top of the mast to the bow. "It's for support."

"I better learn the technical names for everything, hadn't I?"

"You will."

"Anything I can help with?"

"Just a minute." Mark pulled the rigging tight, tied it off at the bow, and then gave me his hand as I grunted and clambered over the side.

"I thought of something you can install." He took a pencil stub out of his pocket and began tracing a series of lines and triangles on a torn sheet of paper. "There's some plates and screws in a plastic package on top of the steps in the companionway. I'll show you where to attach them. That's your furling gear, and this is a diagram of how it works." He held the rough sketch and showed how the furling gear would enable us to raise or lower the genoa sail in seconds from the cockpit. "In rough weather, you'll appreciate that."

I took the paper with me and went off in search of the furling gear. Ludy and Mark took the rest of the morning to set up the mast and boom, adjust the rigging, and readjust what appeared to me to be yards and yards of lines shooting off in all directions. It was nearly noon when T.J. returned. I had dawdled longer than necessary over the half dozen screws on my task, so rather than stand around sheepishly, I volunteered to make sandwiches. In five minutes I was back outside, but my crew was nowhere to be seen. I called, but no one answered. As I carried the sandwich plate out to the boat, I thought I heard one of Ludy's faint whoops. Someone scuffled against the inside cabin wall. Just as I placed a foot on the first rung of the ladder, all three of them sprang up and shouted, "Surprise!"

"What's the occasion?" I asked, puzzled.

"Come on in," they insisted.

When all four of us were awkwardly crouched inside the cabin, T.J. opened the oven door and took out a small chocolate cake. "You didn't bake that in there," I said.

"No, I bought it on the way back. Mark suggested we have a party to celebrate."

"Celebrate what?"

"We've accomplished a lot," Mark said.

"Yeah, that's enough reason," Ludy added.

"Okay with me," I said, passing around the sandwiches. "I can tell now that entertaining in here will be interesting."

"Wait until I get our sound system hooked up," Ludy said.

"Sound system?"

"Stereo. Six speakers with boogie music blaring."

"Blaring?" I lamented. I had envisioned wind and sea spray and gulls flapping noiselessly overhead.

"Should I cut the cake now?" T.J. drew out a knife. As she sliced a piece, we heard a growl behind us. One of the farm cats raced in under our legs, chased by Hobo. He stopped at the companionway entrance, eyeing us while his nose twitched furiously as if to ask, "Did someone mention cake?"

"You may as well give him the first piece," I said with mock disgust.

19 Mark was gone the entire next week to a boat and equipment show in Minneapolis, but Ludy and I kept plugging away at the cabin. One day we laid in the fore and aft berths, the fold-down side berths which held our charts, pamphlets, sea compass, sextant, and first aid kit. The next day we attempted to complete the wiring for the stove, icebox, and water pump, but we were so inept that we had to call in an electrician. The following days we practiced fitting and hoisting the sails, adjusting the genoa tracks, and tightening the halyards and blocks. After a couple of tries, I was competent at securing the rigging with the proper locking half hitches, although my ability with knots was limited.

One time Ludy turned to me after successfully hoisting the sail in less than ten minutes, and predicted that we would undoubtedly pass inspection when Mark returned. I had to remind him and myself that sitting in my barnyard with chickens strutting around the boat and half-wild kittens constantly nosing through the cabin, miles from water, with a gentle breeze rustling the sails, was no test of our skill.

I had been sailing on a dingy once, Ludy twice. We would yet have to encounter river winds that were unpredictable, strong currents, stumps, creeping sand bars, snags, and blind reefs, not to mention wing dams, shoals, rock piles, enormous commercial barges, and the vagaries of the channel itself. And this was just in traversing the Mississippi! I couldn't conceive of what the ocean would be like.

There was no word about the laminated tiller Mark had ordered or the manual bilge pump, which was on back order. Ludy called the marina every day, but Marci had received no news. The boat, nearly complete, still lacked dozens of minor items like a fire extinguisher, a boat hook, flares, anchors, and mooring lines. We also needed to finish the wiring of the required searchlight and running and anchor lights.

"Let them wait until next week," Ludy said to me on Saturday morning. "I'm going to go trail bike through a friend's private woodland today. I think we could both use a day off."

I agreed, although after an hour of reading old newspapers, I found myself wandering listlessly through the house. Determinedly I headed back outside for the boat. I climbed into the cabin and took the pocket New Testament out which I had placed in one of the chart table drawers. Sitting on the carpet, I turned to the letter of James and began reading. God, I felt, had led me particularly to verses five and six: "If any of you lack wisdom, let him ask of God, that giveth to all men liberally, and upbraideth not; and it shall be given him. But let him ask in faith, nothing wavering. For he that wavereth is like a wave of the sea driven with the wind and tossed.''

The translation was not as easy to understand as my big Bible, but the sentiment was clear. I did want wisdom. I wanted to know what God expected of me so that if I stuck my foot forward in any direction, it would not end up in my mouth. I thought I had faith—at least my faith was growing—but the reference to ''wavering'' seemed to point a shaky finger at me. I had doubts; there was no denying them. The phrase ''wave of the sea driven with the wind and tossed'' embedded itself in my thoughts for the remainder of the day. Was I the wave? Was the wave, poised like a gigantic tidal wave, rushing toward me? I wanted wisdom, but was my faith sufficient? I telephoned Evelyn in late afternoon, but we merely chatted over small matters.

On Sunday morning I was pleasantly surprised to discover Ludy and T.J. with their mother two pews in front of me at church. Pastor Bill, eloquent and persuasive, emphasized the need for each individual Christian to say yes to Jesus. Were Pastor's homilies getting better, or was I more tuned in to what he said? I suspected the second reason, but when I left church I congratulated him on his message for that day. He took my hand and held it while he asked about our trip preparations. When he saw Ludy and T.J., he put an arm around their shoulders and went on as if they were the prodigal children returned home, embarrassing them both. In jest, he promised to stop out soon and place his reservation for the Scotland cruise since he had a week's vacation coming.

Ludy and I were back at work Monday morning, having resolved to connect the anchor and running lights. Mark arrived around noon to spend the afternoon with us, and shortly afterwards, Glenn and Jerry drove up. We ran up the sails and the spinnaker since the wind was coming from the west, as Glenn, dumbfounded by the full regalia, circled the boat in wide-eyed amazement. ''I can't believe it,'' he whistled. ''I just can't believe it. You have turned that old hulk into a real showboat. You should win a prize or something!''

''Come aboard!'' Ludy offered his hand. After Glenn and Jerry poked around the cabin, tried out the berths, and grinned through the portholes at Mark and me, they stood next to me, still eyeing the sails that were straining in a fairly brisk wind.

''That is truly magnificent,'' Glenn said.

''I like that big, flappy sail,'' Jerry said, pointing to the spinnaker. ''It's so colorful.'' It was indeed. Even I stared proudly at the vivid red, blue, and yellow sail.

''Hey, we brought you a present,'' Glenn said. ''We left it in the car.''

Jerry dashed off and came back with a book wraped in the funny pages of a newspaper. I unwrapped the parcel and held it up for Ludy and Mark to see.

"Chapman's *Piloting, Seamanship and Small Boat Handling,* " Ludy read.

Mark took it and thumbed through the pages. "This is a sensible gift. Chapman's book is considered the bible for boaters."

"Well," I said. "I'll consider it as a back-up to the real thing."

"A wise decision." Mark grinned.

"Thank you for the book. Can I get you something to drink?"

"No, no." Glenn shook his head, still gawking at the boat with his hands deep in his overalls. "You don't mind if we hang around and watch a bit, do you?"

"Heck no," Ludy said. "Hang around long enough and you're liable to have a hammer handed to you."

"I wouldn't mind. In fact, we were hoping that maybe we could help you out some. I took the afternoon off."

"Really?" I asked. "You came by to help?"

"Sure did!"

"Well, great," I said. "Mark? What can we put them on?"

Mark strapped on his carpenter's belt. "I could use a hand with the lights yet." He went around to the back of the boat with Glenn in tow. Jerry studied Ludy as he fiddled with a mariner's distress flag, while I went around to watch Mark and Glenn. Mark was explaining Coast Guard regulations.

"All boats of a certain length require a bell, a horn or whistle, flotation devices, fire extinguisher, but most importantly lights, so that these behemoth three-hundred-foot barges don't plow right over small cruisers. I've got the running lights to work, but somehow I've missed the connection with the anchor lights. They won't both run off the same battery."

"Let me see the terminals," Glenn said, taking his reading glasses from a hip pocket. He and Mark bent over a tangle of wires, obstructing my view, so I thought it best if I busied myself elsewhere. The horn still needed to be bolted to the interior cabin roof. I picked up a screwdriver, added a Phillips just in case, and climbed the ladder, vowing not to puncture a finger carelessly as I had with my last attempt with a screwdriver. I doublechecked the package of wood screws to see that my name was on none of them. Still, I drew blood inadvertently, but a hasty Kleenex tourniquet to my maimed index finger allowed me to continue as any ablebodied seaman would have done.

After a few trials, I managed to get one end of the horn to stay. As I attacked the other, Ludy yelled that the telephone was ringing. Sprinting as well as my slightly overweight, flat-footed frame could, I reached the phone just as it quit. I went down the back porch steps, and the phone rang again. This time the elusive caller didn't escape. It was Sheri.

"Momma, now don't panic, but I'm at the hospital in Cedar Falls. David's been in an accident."

"Oh, Sheri! When?"

"A little while ago at work."

I braced myself for the worst. "How bad?"

"Well, it was just his hand, thank God."

"What happened?"

"I don't know for sure, but one of the nurses said he got it caught in some machinery at work. They're X-raying it now."

"Will he lose it?"

"She said there was a possibility, but I hope not, Momma. I hope not."

"Okay." I tried to organize my thoughts. "Glenn's here. I'll have him drive Ludy and me over right away." She began to cry just as I started to hang up. "We'll be right there, Sheri," I said breathlessly.

I tore out to the yard. Everyone listened, shocked as I related what Sheri had said. Glenn led me to the car with Ludy right behind, while Mark volunteered to drive Jerry home. On the way to the hospital, I cautioned Glenn not to be reckless, but he shot past car after car on the highway. I was swamped with guilt. Try as I could, I knew the trip was definitely off. When I should have been feeling pity and concern for David, all I could muster was a dull anger that now he had really gone and shut down my chances for freedom. And if his hand should be amputated, well, I didn't want to bring about the worst by dwelling on it, but if he lost his hand, I knew he would be even more impossible to live with. I couldn't pray. My mind was too upset. Was it Psalm 34 that said, "I sought the Lord, and he heard me, and delivered me from all my fears"? I wished I had memorized more verses.

When we reached the outskirts of Cedar Falls, I began to calm down. I looked in the rearview mirror at Ludy. He was hunched forward tensely, staring out the window. *Please, Lord, bring peace into our hearts,* I managed to pray. *If anyone can take charge of the situation You can, and I ask You now in Jesus' name to do so.*

The hospital parking lot was full, so Glenn left his car in a bus zone as we hurried inside. Sheri was not in the lounge, but a nurse sent us up to the hallway outside the emergency room. T.J. and Sheri leaned against the wall. "How is he?" I asked.

Sheri came to me, her eyes red-rimmed. "I don't know. They just brought in some kind of specialist. We counted three doctors in there."

"It's going to be all right, Sheri. He's in God's care."

Glenn and Ludy shuffled their feet awkwardly and look around until a nurse came up to us and suggested we wait in a lounge down the corridor. No sooner were we seated than a bearded doctor with a stethoscope around his neck entered.

"Morgans?"

"Uh huh," Sheri said, biting her lower lip.

He straddled a chair backwards and faced us. "Let me say first that Mr. Morgan is all right. We ran a series of X-rays but found nothing damaged."

"He won't lose his hand?" T.J. asked.

He smiled and patted her knee. "No, definitely not. In fact, there is nothing broken. When the ambulance brought him in, and I saw the lacerations and heard his foreman describe what happened, I did expect to find serious structural damage. I even called down an orthopedist to make sure I wasn't overlooking something. But," he pushed his wire-framed glasses back on his nose, "he's very fortunate. We're putting in a half dozen stitches, and then he'll be ready to go with you. All right?"

"Thank you, Doctor," I murmured. He nodded and then left.

"Oooohhh, my gosh," Sheri sighed. "What a relief!"

"Well, that is good news," Glenn said. "I remember when Ernie Kepply lost an arm in his grain thrasher last year. I saw his mangled arm lying in the ditch before his brother-in-law took him away. He nearly died on the operating table 'cause of loss of blood. They tried to fit him for an artificial limb, but he refused. Stubborn old coot."

"Thank You, Lord, it wasn't anything serious," Sheri whispered, ignoring what Glenn had said.

Ludy wandered out to find a pop machine. In a couple of minutes he came back with his father. Sheri stood up and hugged him.

"We were so worried!"

"Sorry I got you all upset, and you had to drive down."

"We weren't going to sit home. Besides," I softened, "we *were* worried about you. How did it happen?"

"Let's go down to the cafeteria, and I'll tell you. I want some coffee to steady my nerves."

After we had found a booth and settled in, we all stared expectantly at David. He shook his head and began.

"You're not going to believe this, I know, because it sounds too unreal to me, even. But I was working one of the drill presses we have at the factory—they should be replaced they're so hazardous—and one of the cotter pins on the mechanism got hung up crooked, so I reached up to see what the snag was. I no sooner did that than the swing arm sheared off at the joint and the whole press shut down on my hand, trapping it like this.'' He demonstrated by bending back his fingers and forcing the wrist up.

"Did it hurt?" Ludy asked as he sipped a Coke.

"Hurt? Heck, that's three thousand pounds of concentrated pressure. I felt my fingers snap, and then white lightning roar up my arm. I thought my head was in a pressure cooker."

"How'd you get your hand out?" Sheri asked.

"Well," he turned his hand over and touched the gauze over the stitches. "This guy down the line heard me scream out, and he quick shut off the power. By the time he handcranked the press up high enough to lift my hand out, two others had run up. One of them went to call the factory nurse. The other made me lie down and told me not to look at my hand."

"Did you?" Ludy asked.

David smiled at him. "You know I did."

"And?"

"It was a mess. Ugliest thing I ever saw."

"Really?"

"Uh huh. I lifted my hand a little and shook it, and the fingers just jangled loosely like spaghetti. They flopped back all the way to my wrist and then forward to my wrist on the other side."

"Did they still hurt?" T.J. grimaced.

"Not then. They were numb. I knew for certain as I lay there waiting for the nurse, that they might as well just lop the whole hand off. Oh, it was ugly."

Sheri touched his arm. "You really were fortunate."

"Why's that?"

"No broken bones."

"I'm trying to tell you, they were all broken."

Sheri screwed up her face. "I don't understand."

"Okay now, that's what I was getting to." He took a deep breath. "So, there I am lying on the cement with a limp dishrag on the end of my arm and these guys crowding around me. I swear, half the plant came running over."

"Yeah?" T.J. leaned forward.

"And I know it sounds stupid—anybody would have done the same thing—but I started praying to myself, like, 'Please, God, don't let me lose my hand.' "

I caught Sheri's eyes.

"I must have blanked out then for a bit, but I remember thinking that if God can raise men from the dead, He sure can heal my hand. I know what you're thinking, right, Mom? I don't even go to church anymore, so why should God do me any favors?" There was strained emotion on David's face. Sheri continued to stroke his uninjured hand.

"This is pretty far out, right," he said, looking to Glenn. "Well, it happened just like I said. As I lay there thinking, *Is this really happening?* a warm glow starting spreading through my chest, and I thought—*Great, a heart attack to boot.* But then the thought, *God loves me too* started running through my head. And I know He doesn't owe me anything, but I wasn't scared because I knew—that funny warmth, you know—that there was absolutely nothing I could do about my hand or my life or anything else as I lay there—I was completely at God's mercy, except . . . "

Everyone sat silently, almost reverently, waiting for him to continue.

"I don't know. I was really out of it then, I guess. Two guys lifted me onto a stretcher, and as they carried me out I had the stupidest feeling as everybody stared down at me like I was on parade, you know, with the nurse leading us. One of the guys carrying me had on big fish-eye goggles."

"Did you pass out?" Ludy asked.

"No, but as they were sliding me into the ambulance, I remember looking down at my hand and you know, you're not going to believe this, but the fingers had sprung back up. They're still all bloody, but I can flex them." He made a fist, leaned back, and exhaled.

"I believe you," I said.

Sheri wiped her eyes. "I prayed. Boy, did I pray."

"I thought my hand was gone for sure," David repeated.

Ludy crunched his ice and stared at his father.

"Thank You, Heavenly Father, for always watching over your children," I prayed softly with my eyes closed. "Amen." I heard Sheri respond.

"Maybe I could use a good, strong dose of your religion, Mom," David said.

We sat quietly for a minute. Glenn cleared his throat. "Well, I better call Evelyn. She'll be worried."

We all went out to the lobby and waited until Glenn finished his telephone call. At the car, Ludy got in the backseat next to his father while Sheri went around to the driver's side. T.J. requested I send greetings to Mark as she slid into the passenger seat.

"I'll talk to you later." I bent over and peered in the car. "And God bless!" I thought I detected a wink from David as he slumped back, exhausted.

"Thanks for coming, Mom," Sheri said, relieved. As they drove away, I felt like falling to my knees in the parking lot and asking God to forgive my weak and wavering faith. I wanted to be as solid as rock. I wanted to be unshakable, yet I was still tottering along like an infant.

All the way home Glenn prattled on about the accidents he had known and loved, while I wanted to stomp my foot for his attention and shout, *What about the miracle of God's healing love that touched all of our lives today? We do have a God that loves us!* Instead, I looked out the window and ignored his analysis of what a baler would do to someone's body if they, through happenstance, should tumble in.

That evening, sitting on the porch as the sun fell through a net of gold strands, I was thoughtless. I sat and marveled and soaked in the coolness of the pines and the wet grass, but I thought of nothing. Silence glazed everything. The prow of the boat rose out from the shadows.

I resented the ringing telephone. I wanted my vista, my twilight undisturbed. David's voice was firm.

"I'll come right to the point, Mom. I've thought about it all afternoon, and my decision is to let Ludy go with you. I'm not sure why, but I know it's important to both of you. Besides, I have a selfish reason for allowing you to take him. Rather than shut up your house while you're gone, we're going to shut up in town here and come stay on the farm. I'm quitting my job."

"What? What about your seniority?"

"There are things more important than seniority. I'm not going back to the factory. I grew up a farm boy, and I suppose that's where I ought to stay; so I'll raise a herd of Holsteins. We would like Ludy back for next Christmas, but go for as long as you want, because your house will be taken care of."

Before I had a chance to reply, he hung up. I went back to the porch, but the magical glow had disappeared. Suddenly it was night. The chickens were cooing softly, a dog barked in the distance. I smacked a mosquito off my elbow, wanting at first to do handsprings, but then, I felt sadly disquieted as if my weeks of worrying over how to persuade David had been for naught. Mark was right. Try as I could, nothing of significance would ever get accomplished without the hand of God in one way or another.

How vast, I wondered, *will be the immensity of the oceans?* The Mississippi, the father of waters, seemed forbidding enough. *But we will sail,* I consoled myself, *in the name of the Lord.* That much was certain.

Part II

20

I shuddered when the semi thundered past. It seemed to miss the gunwale by inches. I glanced over to Mark, but his eyes were intent on the road. Since there was no radio in the cab of the truck, Ludy slouched on the other side of me with a small transistor radio clamped to his ear, oblivious to the narrow miss each time one of the enormous eighteen-wheelers went by, hardly slowing at all. I was sure the back draft from the trucks rocked the boat, even though we had strapped it securely that morning and had just rechecked it twenty miles back.

T.J. waved from her parents' car ahead of us, and both Mark and I smiled and waved back. In the seat in front of her, Sheri appeared to be reading a magazine and David hunched forward, probably with one eye on his speedometer and one eye in the rearview mirror to make sure he didn't spread out our slow-moving caravan too much. I knew that Glenn and his family were behind us, but I couldn't see them over the boat. A road sign indicated that we would be entering a divided highway.

"That's a relief," Mark said. "A four-lane road is sure going to make a difference after this narrow old highway."

"How far does the divided road go?" I asked.

Mark leaned forward to peer at Ludy, but Ludy stared at the fluttering orange caution sign on his father's car and kept thumping his left hand against the door panel.

"It's just a new extension that opened this spring. I think it goes all the way to Dyersville, and from there we have two lanes again for the last thirty miles into Dubuque."

"We're almost there, then." I sighed.

"Uh huh."

"What's that?" Ludy sat up, holding his hand to his ear as if they were attached.

"Turn off your radio and I'll tell you," I said.

"What?"

"Turn it off!" He clicked it off. "I said, we're almost to Dubuque."

"Oh yeah? What time is it?"

"Nearly noon," I said.

"Four hours? It's less than a hundred miles from home to Dubuque."

"Well, it takes longer when you have to go thirty miles an hour," Mark grunted.

"How's the trailer?"

Mark looked down at the instrument panel. "The trailer is fine, but our engine is beginning to heat up. I hope the radiator makes it all the way."

"Oh yeah, it will." Ludy slumped back against the seat and switched the radio on again. I tried to get comfortable, but the hump under the floor board made it impossible for me to do anything but straddle my legs and grasp the seat with both hands so I wouldn't tilt over against Mark or Ludy. Up ahead, T.J. was trying to spell a message in sign language. I wondered if Hobo had escaped his cage in the cabin yet. He had whined unhappily as we snapped him in that morning, especially after he had watched me stow food in the cabinets just above his head. But the cage was a new, sturdy one, and the lock would provide an unbeatable tussle for even the most dexterous fingers. Still, I had learned not to underestimate his determination.

"I can't wait to get out on the river after this hectic week," Mark said.

I wasn't sure I had quite his enthusiasm for the broad Mississippi, but I had to agree with him about the past week. Even though I hadn't actually installed the diesel inboard, for three days I had watched nearly every bolt go into place, and when someone was in need of the proper wrench, I was there to hand it over. What's more, scurrying about to buy food had turned into more of a job than I had anticipated, what with last-minute packing and trying to cram as many essential provisions as possible into our cabin. And then Ludy insisted that Hobo accompany us, so I had to dash out to buy a cage and try to lure him into it, which took me the better part of the afternoon. When I finally did get back to the marina, Mark was proudly revving up the engine and measuring rpm's, while Ludy took my hand and dragged me around to the front of the boat where he had neatly lettered the boat's name—*Ark II*—in honor, he grinned, of the menagerie which would soon be afloat. I liked the name, but I hoped it wouldn't be an omen of our impending weather.

"Are we there yet?" Ludy sat up abruptly.

"No, but we're just outside Dubuque."

"Whew," he continued. "I just started to doze off. I was dreaming about a huge whirlpool that was sucking us into a spin."

"You won't see any whirlpools," Mark countered. "Unless you get hung up in one of the pools under a dam, or worse yet, accidentally go over the spillway."

"How do we avoid those?" I winced.

"Watch your charts and know which bank of the river your lock is going to be on. You should have plenty of time to get positioned, since they have adequate markers upstream."

"I'm just glad you're going to be with us for the first stretch."

"Oh, it'll be great! I wish I was going farther than the Quad cities, though."

186

"You think we'll be able to handle the boat by ourselves from then on?" I asked him.

"Sure, sure. Right, Ludy?"

"No sweat. Hey, I think Dad is motioning for us to pull over."

Mark slowed the truck, and we came to a halt behind David's car. Immediately after we stopped, I heard Glenn pull up behind us. He appeared and followed Mark to a conference next to David's car. I stuck my head out the driver's window, but I was unable to pick up their conversation. Glenn gestured in one direction, and Mark pointed off in another, while David, still in his car, nodded and looked at a map and nodded to them again. When Mark jumped back into the cab, he was satisfied that the three of them had agreed on directions to the municipal harbor.

"We're getting close," he said as he waited to pull onto the highway. "Are you nervous?"

"Shaking," I said.

"Save it for tomorrow." His voice was calming. "We'll do little more than get the boat into the water today." By the time we got to the harbor and I caught my first glimpse of brown water beyond the floodwall, I was shivering uncontrollably. "Relax," Mark soothed. "Remember Psalm 34, 'I sought the Lord and he answered me and delivered me from all my fears.' "

"I know. I'm just excited. You want us to jump out and guide you down the ramp?"

"You might as well. I want to get as close to the marine lift as possible." He nodded towards the large crane that swung out over the water. Ludy helped me climb down as the whole entourage ambled up.

"Now we see if it floats." T.J. grinned.

"Oh, don't say that. I think I'd collapse right here if it didn't."

Glenn and David went into the marine office to see who operated the lift, as Mark parked the truck and trailer on the downslope, set the handbrake, and got down from the cab. Evelyn cautioned Jerry from getting too close to the water as he led his brothers in a rock-skipping onslaught.

"I wish I had left them at home," she groaned.

"Oh no," Sheri said. "This will be an event none of us should miss. You want your grandchildren here, don't you, Mom?"

"Of course. Maybe it's me that should have stayed home."

"Wet feet?"

"You might say that's what I'm afraid of."

Evelyn took my hand. "Calm down. Everything will go smoothly. It's really too bad that Leroy couldn't be here to see what he started." *Yes,* I thought, *wouldn't he have loved this day?* Completing the boat, and now

187

nearly launching it, were thrilling for me, but there was a tinge of sadness that Leroy, who more than anyone wanted to fulfill that crazy dream, wasn't with us.

"The operator will be out in a minute," David said, approaching us.

I watched Mark and T.J. walk along the levee as he compared the motorboats rocking in their slips. A young couple was sunning on the top deck of a double-decked cabin cruiser, and a little farther along the harbor curve, I could see a small brick building under a *U.S. Coast Guard* sign. It was comforting to know that if we should go down in the harbor, help would be near.

Sheri interrupted my thoughts. "Did you say Pastor Bill would be coming?" I studied my watch.

"Sometime this afternoon. He said he would get here before dinner."

"Oh. He could have ridden with us."

"No, he was going to stop somewhere along the way and visit a friend. He'll be here." I was glad Pastor Bill had promised to come. His presence always insured gaiety, but more than that, his inner strength was something I would need to get through the next few hours. In the last month I had slowly begun to work out my ambiguous feelings toward Pastor Bill. Had God not been guiding my steps through that precipitous darkness, I would have said, or worse, done something that could have irrevocably separated me from the one man who, next to Leroy, had been a beacon of warmth in my life. Everytime I tried to visualize Jesus as the man He must have been on the dusty roads between Galilee and Jerusalem, His eyes took on the ecstatic joy of Pastor Bill's.

"You the folks with the yacht?" a squat, bald-headed man asked.

"Yes," I stammered, unsure that we were referring to the same boat. No one had ever called it a yacht before.

"Okay," he said as he scratched a grizzled chin. "Why don't you unfasten it while I fit her up. What is she, six, eight ton?"

I shrugged. Mark came back and took over the negotiations with an assurance I had come to admire in him. He was self-possessed, but his confidence came from the Lord—that was evident. David and Glenn bent down to free the underhooks while Ludy scaled the trailer to the cockpit. I couldn't get over what a magnificent boat it had become. The couple from the double-decked cruiser strolled over to watch. The man, tall and angular, slid his sunglasses back onto his head. "Nice boat."

"Brand new," I said.

"No kidding? Inaugural voyage then?"

"Yes, I hope."

"Where you going?"

"To the Gulf."

"Of Mexico?" he asked in amazement. I nodded and watched from the corner of my eye as he looked at the woman with him. She was equally impressed. "You all going?"

"No, just two of us."

"That sounds great. The farthest south we've ever taken our boat is Davenport."

"We're heading for there tomorrow. How's the trip down?"

"Oh, gorgeous," the man continued. "It's really a lovely hundred miles of river, but around Davenport the water gets grungy."

"I'm sorry?"

"Polluted. Lots of factories and industry there, and they don't seem to have any qualms about dumping their sludge into the river."

"That's too bad."

"It is. It really is. You'll see for yourself." They sat down on the flood-wall and dangled their feet in the water.

"Okay, we ready to swing her free?" the lift operator asked.

"All clear." Mark motioned everyone back. I held my breath as the machinery gradually wheezed and cranked the boat up off the trailer. Sitting in midair, the hull caught the sun's reflection with a dazzling intensity that caused me to squint. I wondered what Hobo, still inside the cabin, was thinking about this unexpected ride. As the boat swung out over the water, I held my breath and prayed. I didn't want a single leak to mar the occasion. "Thank You, Lord, thank You," I prayed, eyes closed, "for Your hand of protection." I opened my eyes just as the boat hit with a splash. It jigged from side to side as it settled in, rocked again as a roll of waves collided against the hull, and then balanced, majestic and solid. A cheer went up around me, and before I could speak, tears were clouding my vision. It floated, as I knew it would.

Mark pulled it to the dock with a mooring line. One by one, we piled onto the boat and crowded into the cabin while Ludy added short blasts from the horn. I was surprised at how well it sat in the water, although seeing the murky waves slosh against the hull was something I would need to get used to. I had grown attached to the boat, but it didn't seem right for it to finally be afloat.

Glenn suggested we go purchase a bottle of champagne for the traditional christening on the following morning. Evelyn, anxious to get her three sons off the boat before one inadvertently tumbled into the harbor, was agreeable, so with everyone except Ludy and myself in tow, she marched off toward Dubuque's downtown two blocks away.

"Let's fire the engine and see how she handles," Mark suggested.

"Right now?" I said. "Shouldn't we check to see if there are leaks first?"

"We can do that later. I'm anxious to see if any major adjustments are needed before tomorrow. Okay?"

"Yeah, let's take her for a spin," Ludy said.

"Okay," I agreed. "*Ark II*, here we go!"

The motor kicked up immediately, and when Mark slid the reverse switch, the boat eased backwards. He pushed on the throttle and the engine responded, gliding the boat back into the middle of the harbor.

"Rest assured," Mark said. "It handles super. Let's take her forward." The boat lurched forward when Mark slid the switch. We were jarred off balance; Ludy banged his shin. "It will take some getting used to," Mark smiled, chagrined. "You want to take it, Dorothy?"

I switched places with him and took the tiller in my left hand and gripped the engine controls in my right. As I pressed the throttle, the boat shot confidently forward. Pushing the tiller away from me spun the boat to starboard, as I remembered from my experience on the dingy. We took turns piloting the boat around the harbor. Each sweep which took us near the breakwater cut where the river purled by, sent needles of fear through me.

"Tomorrow." Mark pointed to the river. "Tomorrow we'll hoist sail and challenge Old Man River himself."

"I'm just glad you're going to be with us," I said.

We nosed the boat into an unoccupied slip and unwound the new mooring lines. Mark showed us his favorite hitch, and Ludy demonstrated a bowline.

"We should check in with the Coast Guard to leave them a cruise plan." Mark went into the cabin, found the frequency for the Dubuque office, and called in a radio test. The reply blared back.

"Gee, no static at all," Ludy said.

"But we're only one hundred feet away from their transmitter. It will be different on the river, believe me. You'll find that out."

Mark snooped inside the bilge for a few minutes but found no water. Impatient to get out of his cramped cage, Hobo paced two steps, turned, and paced back to the other side.

"Let's take him for a walk," I suggested.

"Won't he run away?" Mark asked in horror.

"No. I'm prepared." I searched through the map table cabinets for the leash.

"A dog leash?" Mark asked when I dragged it forth.

"Why not? We used it when we first found him—for about a day. I'm sure he won't stroll far when we're on the river, but when we go ashore, the leash should keep him out of mischief." Hobo snarled as ferociously as he could when we slipped the noose around his neck, but that didn't deter us. We pulled it snug and sat back to watch him. He wrestled with it, tried to cram his head between his legs by rolling up in a ball, and then he lashed backwards, but the leash was secure. Finally he paused, looked up at our bemused faces as if to concede that we had won, and chattered angrily. Ludy tossed him a sugar cube, then led our hesitant raccoon off the boat and down the dock toward town. I accompanied Mark to the Coast Guard Office.

"Cruise plan? Yes, we advise you leave one with us," Captain Ayers said. "In fact, why don't you bring your charts in, and I'll go over them with you. There are troublesome spots on south of here you should know about."

I listened to the dapper, mustachioed captain's tale of a barge that had hit the Julian Dubuque Bridge pylons the previous week and nearly sunk midchannel, while Mark ran to bring the charts.

"Since you're going all the way to New Orleans," the captain instructed when Mark had returned, "you should keep some rules of thumb about the river. For instance, you only have locks to contend with until you reach Saint Louis."

"Well, that's good news," I said.

"But south of Saint Louis you'll have swifter currents and dozens of barges, some a thousand feet long. They'll crowd almost the entire channel, which is normally four hundred feet wide. Where the river bends, they can be hazardous."

"Our draft is only four feet," Mark added. "So if we have to veer out of channel—"

"You could," the captain interrupted. "But don't make a habit of it. There's thousands of wing dams that could tear out your hull in seconds."

"What's a 'wing dam'?" I asked.

"The Corps of Engineers, ma'am, built wing dams to divert the flow of water for a deeper channel. Many of them at this level of water are only six inches below the surface. They're like piers, you know? You'll find them on your charts." He pointed out dangerous islands and chutes, cable crossings, pilings to watch for, and shoals that had recently caused problems for boaters. "Don't be afraid to chat with other pilots, especially towboat skippers. It's their job to know the river."

"How fast is the current?" Mark asked.

"Two to three knots."

I looked at Mark, wondering how fast a knot was. "About two or three miles an hour," he whispered to me as the captain rummaged through a file cabinet for an updated light list.

"You shouldn't have any trouble with your mast," Captain Ayers added in parting. "Just toot for the drawbridges. And remember, the old gal can be fickle, so when in doubt, be safe."

We shook hands. "Thanks for your help, Captain."

"And have a good trip!" He winked.

"I thought," I asked Mark as we went back to the boat, "that it was 'Old Man River.' Why did he call it a 'fickle old gal'?"

"It probably depends on who you talk to." He grinned.

"Well, I prefer calling it a man." He stared at me quizzically but didn't press for an explanation.

When the family returned, they were laden with party horns, streamers, and crepe paper.

"For your departure in the morning," Sheri explained.

"I'm getting hungry, Mom," Jason grumbed to Evelyn.

"You just had an orange soda and a candy bar."

"Maybe we should take them all over to the motor lodge for a swim," Glenn offered.

"It has a pool?" Jerry shouted.

"You bet it does."

"Well, let's go, then!"

The three boys ran off the boat, nearly colliding with Ludy and T.J., who were trying to get Hobo to stand up on his hind legs for a gumdrop.

"We're still going to East Dubuque for dinner?" Sheri asked me.

"Yes. I think David called for reservations at six."

"That should give you a couple of hours yet to get arranged or whatever you have to do," Sheri said, clapping her hands together. "The kids can swim, and we'll come back around five-thirty. Is Pastor Bill going to meet you here?"

I nodded. "Any time now, I should think."

"You want to come too, T.J.?" Sheri asked. T.J., who was lifting a feisty Hobo back into his cage, paused to look at Mark.

"I've got a lot to check out yet," he responded.

"Need some help?"

"Sure. You can blow up the rubber raft for us."

She looked startled. "What?"

"No." Mark grinned sheepishly. "Just kidding."

I walked with David and Sheri to their car while Glenn rounded up his impish brood, who had taken to chasing each other in circles with a straggly clump of weeds.

"I owe you both a lot of thanks."

"Mom," Sheri took my hand, "we're with you in this all the way. Aren't we, David?"

"Uh huh." He sized up the boat. "And don't worry about the farm any."

"God love you both." I started back toward the dock, but Sheri called after me. "I almost forgot to give you these." She handed me a book satchel. "Ludy's lessons for the next three months."

I laughed as I took them. "He'll appreciate that, I'm sure."

T.J. and Mark touched up the inner seams below deck as Ludy fiddled with the radio. After surveying the jumble of foodstuff, I took out our untouched log and inscribed a favorite verse on the inside cover: "The Lord shall preserve thy going out and thy coming in from this time forth, and even for evermore." It was an appropriate verse for our seafaring.

Pastor Bill didn't arrive until we were leaving for the restaurant. "Well, I thought I'd gone and missed you."

"No, but you almost missed dinner."

"Let me chauffeur us then." He nodded toward his car.

Glenn's station wagon, packed to the seams, pulled up next to Bill's. "The entire family here?" Bill said gleefully. "That is splendid!"

Everyone gave Pastor a rousing greeting, and it was finally decided that Ludy, T.J., Mark, and I would ride with Pastor Bill.

"What's that?" Ludy pointed at a rectangular-shaped container on the back seat. A white sheet draped the mysterious package.

"That's a going away gift for you." He grinned. "Can you guess what it is?"

I reached out to touch it from the front seat. A shrill, rapid "Hello! Hello!" came from under the covering.

"I'm mystified. What is it?"

"It's alive, that's for sure," Ludy said as he pulled the sheet off.

"A bird? A talking bird?" T.J. said.

"A mynah bird," Bill corrected her. "Very intelligent birds too. Very clever."

"And it's for us?" I began to giggle. The bird cocked its head to the left and then to the right and repeated its initial "Hello! Hello!"

"Where did you get it?" I asked him.

"It was bequeathed to me."

We broke into laughter. Jay and Jerry climbed out the back window of their car for a closer look.

"An elderly woman acquaintance of mine recently passed on, and I was the fortunate recipient of her beloved Dinah," Bill explained. "So in lieu of a parrot, I give you Dinah."

"Dinah, the Mynah." Ludy thrust a finger in the cage at her. "What else do you say?" Dinah refused to speak. She blinked and ignored the finger.

"She does have quite a vocabulary," Bill said.

"Like what?" T.J. leaned down to the cage and cooed.

"You'll find out soon enough." Bill chuckled.

Everyone piled into their respective cars, and we backed out of the harbor parking lot. In a matter of minutes we had entered the evening flow of traffic which led up to the huge bridge spanning Iowa and Illinois.

"Can you believe how wide that river is?" Ludy bellowed as we were halfway across the bridge. "It must be two miles from shore to shore."

I glanced back at Dubuque. Old church spires rose against the steep limestone bluffs. Generally categorized a quaint, riverboat town, Bill said Dubuque not only retained most of her nineteenth-century buildings, but she actively was restoring much of the fading architecture, as I could see from the bridge. Looking down on the crisscross of streets, I saw scaffoldings attached to brick facades; the east half of the courthouse wore a coat of fresh paint. The enclosed harbor appeared to be a new addition, but as the sun caught the branches of oaks and elms on the river valley peaks and diffused the light over red and brown rooftops, the whole city took on the aura of another century. *I'd like to come back here,* I mused. I'd be sure to find hollyhocks sprouting against sagging porches and boys chasing dogs, and white picket fences, and the lazy riverboats churning upriver and wailing in the distance.

A piercing whistle interrupted my daydreams.

"Oh, yes." Bill smiled. "Dinah whistles rather well."

"They shall call His name Jesus," the bird quipped.

"Oh, my gosh! Did you hear that?" T.J. said in amazement. "She quotes the Bible."

"She speaks so distinctly," I added. "What else does she say?"

"Much, much more," Bill said. "And in her own good time, I'm certain she will repeat it all for you."

"Can I teach her to say things?" Ludy asked.

"That depends on her," Bill said. He slowed down as we came off the bridge, circled underneath the abutment, and came out on the main street of East Dubuque.

"Can you believe all the taverns?" I said. Looking down the three blocks of town, a series of one bar after another proclaimed their existence with a clutter of neon signs.

"That's all East Dubuque is," Bill explained. "The town sprang up during Prohibition."

"That one street must have fifty bars!"

"That one street," Bill smiled, "is called Sinsinawa Boulevard."

"They shall call His name Jesus," Dinah punctuated.

The Blufftop Supper Club was indeed located on the highest promontory in East Dubuque. As we pulled into the parking lot next to Glenn's car, we could see an expanse of river and the harbor, the buildings of Dubuque, and to our right upstream, a railroad bridge and Lock and Dam No. 11.

"I hear that the view inside is just as spectacular," Evelyn said as we all followed her.

"Just so the food is good," Glenn mumbled.

The food was good, and since we had arrived on smorgasbord night, the management must have cringed watching our gang of growing, Iowa farm boys return again and again to the entree tables. Ludy and Jerry had a contest to see who could devour the most Swedish meatballs, and Glenn had to be restrained by his watchful wife for attempting to smuggle an extra slice of cherry pie.

As twilight came on, the city across the river began to light up. In the water's reflection, the lights flickered like fireflies hovering in the summer dusk. My anxiety over departing in the morning was gone. I sank back and listened to everyone. Pastor Bill, as usual, was animated. T.J. and Mark were talking quietly to each other. Sheri sipped her coffee, her face changing each time Pastor Bill's expression changed.

During one lull in the conversation, Bill leaned over next to me and asked if there was room for a stowaway.

"There's always room for you, Bill." He took my hand and sighed deeply.

"I wish I could, but my responsibilities . . . and besides, it wouldn't look respectable for us unmarried folks to—"

"I thought you were married to the church."

"Yes, I've said that, but . . . I'm proud of you, Dorothy. You've grown so much—much more than I when my wife died. Maybe someday I'll feel different . . . " But he was off then, interrupted by Glenn, the air between us still resonant with his last words that faded away like unanswered questions.

Knights before battle, I remembered as everyone chatted on, *spent the eve in prayer. Would spending the night in prayer ensure our success?* God had already seen to it that the boat was intact and afloat with no leaks, no mechanical malfunctions; Ludy had his parents' approval, and what's more, God had touched David in a personal way. A funny thought struck me. *Was Mark an angel? If I pricked his arm, would it bleed?* He had so unexpectedly become a part of my life that his remaining in Davenport would leave a real emptiness. Ludy and I could probably muddle along with the boat, but Mark had the ability to put his finger on just the right word from God at the right time. Being with him was a blessing. Ludy's whole personality had altered because of Mark. I was pleased, too, that he had become a part of T.J.'s life now.

I thought back to the night of my accident when I had ended up in the hospital. Speeding down that dark road, I had nearly sailed off into the unknown. In the morning, I would resume that journey in a different way. A mile below me, sleek and black and silent, the river beckoned.

21

Gulls arguing under the dock and a slap, slap of waves from a catfish trawler leaving the harbor were the first sounds I heard. I sat up and peeked out the porthole. Mist hung over the water. From the looks of the early morning sky, an appearance by the sun was doubtful. I snuggled back down into my covers and looked around the cabin. Ludy was still snoring in the fore berth, and Mark hadn't stirred in his berth under the cockpit. I switched on the tiny burner closest to me to heat water for coffee. An acrid, fishy smell drifted through the open porthole and seemed to cling to everything. *It's an aroma,* I told myself, *that I'll eventually get used to.*

From my awkward position on the fold-down cushions, it was difficult to rummage through the bottom drawer where my New Testament was. I finally drew it forth. The binding was musty and reminded me of my attic.

"Praise the Lord," Dinah, her cage swinging from a bulkhead, muttered and tucked her head under a wing. "Hello, hello. Praise the Lord." Hobo, snug in his cage, was curled in a ball, asleep.

I turned to the Gospel of John and began reading, trying to catch as much light from the overcast sky as possible. Mark straggled out in wrinkled shorts, shirtless, when the kettle started to whistle.

"Morning," he croaked. "Boy, did I sleep great." He rubbed his eyes. "What time is it?" I pointed to the watch on his arm. "Oh, yeah. Six-fifteen." He turned around and crawled back into bed. It was nearly an hour later, after I had dressed, flecked water on my face, and had a cup of instant coffee, that Mark and Ludy resigned themselves to the new day.

I had to restrain Ludy from tearing open a box of crackers by reminding him that we were to meet everyone at a small café downtown for breakfast. He and Mark went out on the dock, both morose and sleepy.

When we got to the café and entered the bustle of working people, already about their breakfasts and morning papers and coffee, our grogginess slid away. Mark outlined instructions for manning the departure, assigning me to mooring lines and cabin maintenance. Ludy would handle the engine and guide us into midchannel, while Mark would prepare the mast and rigging so we could hoist sail as soon as possible, thus saving expense on fuel as often as we could.

Evelyn led the parade of Morgans into the café and stuffed all the children into the far back booth. Ludy, T.J., and Mark took over another booth from two fishermen just leaving, while I plopped down on the overstuffed cushions of a third booth and made room for Sheri and David.

"How was your first night sleeping on the boat, Mom?" Sheri asked after we had placed our orders with a harried waitress.

"Well, I was a little queasy this morning, but I expect I'll learn to like pitching from side to side."

"Enough room?" Glenn yawned.

"Plenty," I replied. "Room for a couple more."

"Are you nervous yet?"

"Scared."

"Just remember what the captain of the *Titanic* said." Glenn grinned. I held up my hand. "I don't want to hear it."

"Mom," David began, "have you got enough money?"

"I have traveler's checks to get us to New Orleans—providing, of course, that nothing major happens. I called the bank before I left to give you permission to get into the savings account."

"How long is it going to take you to get to New Orleans?"

"It's a good fifteen hundred miles. Mark predicts three weeks at least."

"And from there?" Sheri asked.

"I don't know. We haven't really decided yet. God will tell us which way then, I'm sure." My hotcakes and sausage arrived, but I could do little more than stare at them.

"Not hungry?" Glenn asked between mouthfuls.

"Nope. My stomach is going flip-flop now."

"You want to walk outside until everyone is finished?" Evelyn offered. "I'd like to look in some shop windows."

"So long as you just look," Glenn said as we got up. I noticed him pull my uneaten food across the table.

Outside, the air was cool but muggy. The sun had begun to burn off the haze as Evelyn and I wandered along the sidewalks.

"Tomorrow at this time you'll be in Davenport," she mused.

"Uh huh. And Mark will be leaving us."

"He's driving back up here?"

"A friend is bringing him up so he can drive the rented truck and trailer back to Cedar Falls."

"And then you and Ludy are on your own."

"Just the two of us."

"Any doubts?"

"Sure."

198

She put her arm through mine. "I envy you, Mom. I really do. I can't say that I would ever have the courage to strike out anew like you're doing."

"I wish I did have courage."

"Oh, but you do. You've changed so very much. I know that last winter your life had come to a standstill. You were alone and miserable. I know all that. I wanted you to come live with us."

"That wouldn't have really solved my problem, would it?"

"No."

"I love you and your family."

"I know," she smiled.

"But . . . well, we both know our heavenly Father loves you and me so much more than any person could. He got me through my struggles. That's why I can't think of myself as courageous. What is it Paul says? 'I'm glad I'm weak so Christ can be strong in me'?"

And right there Evelyn pulled me down next to her on a city bench and prayed for a safe trip. "You're going to make it, Mom. Wherever you go, you're going to get there. Come on. We'd better go collect everybody so you can get underway."

Walking back to the harbor, as my grandchildren chased ahead, all I could think of was what everyone would say if I decided to back out at the last moment. I couldn't find a suitable rationale. When we reached the boat, there was so much to do that I forgot about abandoning the voyage. Ludy freed Hobo so he could prowl around on deck. Dinah cackled and whistled but refused to talk. Colliding with everyone in the narrow cabin-way, I concluded that some preparations would just have to wait until the crowd vacated and we were on the river. Only Pastor Bill, who had had to say good-bye and return the previous evening, was absent.

After hugging everyone and untying the lines, we made a last check of provisions and equipment. A young man on a motorcycle sped around the road which circled the harbor and stopped at the dock's edge. He drew an expensive-looking camera from out of his backpack and approached the boat.

"Mrs. Morgan?" he asked Sheri.

"Yes, but you want Dorothy," she said, pointing to me.

He came over while everyone stopped to stare at him. "I'm from the *Dubuque Herald*," he explained with a smile. "Somebody called and said you would make a good story."

"Oh, I don't know about that." I shrugged, reluctant to be the center of attention.

"Mind if I take your picture next to the boat and then get a little information?"

"Hey, Nana. Can I get in the picture too, so when you're famous, I can prove to everyone I was there when it all started?"

I wanted to go below and hide, but everyone was insistent and proud of me, so I put my arm around T.J. and the young man clicked our picture.

"We're ready," Mark announced as I was finishing my interview.

"This is really it." I hugged everyone again as Ludy came out of the cabin to accept farewells from his parents. He stood stiffly as his mother and sister hugged him, and then received a rugged handshake from his father. T.J. climbed off the boat, kissed Mark to the hoots of her young male cousins, and then rushed past us and went up to the car. Finally, David spouted the champagne over our bow amid streamers and confetti.

As we backed from the slip and turned in the harbor, I heard Mark over the purring engine say, "It's going to be an immaculate sky, which means good sailing conditions." I knelt on the bow and waved, convinced that I wouldn't cry. I didn't. There was no time because the Mississippi yawned ahead. Nosing into the current, I caught my first full view of the panoramic sweep of river and green bluffs dwarfing the buildings of Dubuque. We headed directly downstream under the Julian Dubuque Bridge, the pilings of which arched up beside us, massive and defiant in the broad river.

It was the first of many bridges we would float under. I wondered if any of the cars whizzing overhead noticed us—*Ark II,* five minutes out of Dubuque Harbor, carrying a cargo of fifty-eight-year-old widow, grandson, friend, raccoon, and Bible-quoting mynah bird, bound for—where? Points south and beyond? Ludy cut the engine and we drifted.

By late morning, after having sailed placidly past wooded islands, the junction of the Menominee and Galena Rivers, miles of green sloping hills that tucked the river between them and few boats of any kind, we approached the markings which indicated that Lock and Dam No. 12 at Bellevue was ahead on the right.

"According to the charts," Ludy read, "the lock is 110 feet wide by 600 feet in length. We will descend 9 feet."

"Will all the locks drop our elevation?" I asked.

"Right," Mark said as he began to let the sails luff. "The series of locks and dams is like stairsteps that raise or lower you depending on which direction you're going. They control the level and flow of the river."

We tacked toward the right bank. "They even use stoplights," I said, pointing to the green, amber, and red lights just ahead.

"Start engines," Mark commanded, "and ease her ahead." We came up to the traffic signal and Mark reached out and pulled the signal cord on the guide wall for lockage. Immediately the green light flashed us forward. We crept into the lock and grasped the hanging mooring lines. Ludy shut off the engine, and we rocked up and down until the gate closed behind us. A shaggy, blond head appeared above.

"Morning, folks," the young man called down. His nose, covered with a white salve, stuck out on his sunburnt face like a circus clown's. "Where you headed?"

"Davenport," Ludy yelled back. "And then Africa!"

"Uh huh." The lockmaster grinned. "Have a good trip."

As the water level in the chamber dropped, so did the boat. I tried to measure the wall ascending beside us. When it looked like we had gone down about ten feet, the gates opened slowly, and a short toot echoed about us in the canal.

"Crank her up," Mark ordered. "That's our signal."

We putted out of the lock and into open river. I glanced back at the swirling pool on our left where water roared over the dam.

"I'd hate to get caught in that," I said.

"God willing, you never will." Mark smiled, and we were on our way again. "So far the winds seem to be prevailing from down river. The bluffs could cause strong crosswinds on a bad day, but right now, it's perfect for sailing. Want to take the helm, Dorothy?"

I switched places with Ludy, who went to sit on the foredeck in the sun and play cards with Mark. The wind gently buffeted our main and jib sails. I couldn't wait until we ran up the brilliant spinnaker. In the wide river, remaining inside the channel buoys was no problem. I occasionally had to tack and close haul to keep the red nuns on my left and the black buoys on my right to insure the nine-foot channel depth, but the boat rode high and sure.

Shading my eyes from the glare, I saw a profusion of birds and waterfowl swimming around the islets and sloughs or startled into flight from the numerous backwater marshes we passed. I kept my eyes on our telltale and steered a forward course.

"I wish I had gotten the sound system connected," I heard Ludy tell Mark. "Then we could have some music along the way. It's too quiet, isn't it?"

Mark glanced up at me. "No," he told Ludy. "You should get used to silence. It can be a beautiful prayer. Besides, just listen to the symphony of sounds. The gurgling water, those ducks over there, and the wind, the river maples rustling—you'll learn to appreciate the natural music around you. Your ears will become attuned to even the slightest sounds, ones you've probably never even heard before. I spent two weeks in the Rockies once, and believe me, your whole perception about the world changes when you merge with it.''

"Yeah, maybe, but I'd still like a little electric guitar and percussion.''

"Not me," Mark said emphatically.

"Anybody hungry?" I asked. From the looks I received, I knew the question was unnecessary. "All right, someone take the helm and I'll go make sandwiches." Ludy came back and relieved me. When I opened the cabinet where the bread was, I must have alerted Hobo. He crawled out from Ludy's berth where he had been napping, stretched and yawned, and began scratching his plump stomach vigorously. I tossed him a crust. Dinah was still quiet, but I imagined when she settled into a routine, we would hear more from her. As I dropped some seeds into her cage, I realized that now we would need a larger supply of newspapers. Dinah's cage would need to be cleaned every day, but also Hobo, who had never been a problem when he had free run on the farm, might retain his habits in the confines of the cabin. He would have to be paper-trained.

"I hope bologna and cheese is acceptable to you gentlemen," I said, producing a plate of sandwiches and three pint cartons of milk.

"Fine," Ludy warbled. "Got any chocolate milk?"

"Look, civilization," Mark pointed.

A small town clung to a sandy ridge on the west bank. "It must be Sabula," Ludy said.

Sabula was separated from the bluffs on the Iowa shore by a wide slough, across which embankments had been built to protect the town from invasion by floodwaters, I concluded. How many times that town must have tenaciously rebuilt itself after the spring thaws. A motorboat roared out from the slough toward us, towing a waterskier. The skier, a young girl in a red, two-piece swimsuit, drew near and cut across our wake. I watched Mark and Ludy's heads swivel after her.

"She skis pretty good," Ludy said as he gulped his second sandwich.

"Can you ski?" Mark asked him.

"Just on two skis. I can't slalom. Hey, you think we could get the boat going fast enough to pull a skier?"

"Maybe."

Mark turned to me. "Do you ski?"

202

"Ski? I don't even swim," I said as I tightened the drawstrings on my life jacket. "That's why I plan to sleep with my jacket on."

"You really don't swim?" he asked, amused.

"No, but I bet I'll learn."

"Yeah," he nodded. "It might be a good idea."

My eyes started to bother me. Mark suggested it was probably the glare off the water. I went below to rest, vowing that the next port we left would be minus one pair of sunglasses. It was pleasantly cool below deck. If I reached my arm through the open porthole I could dangle my hand in the cocoa brown water. "So we're really on our way," I whispered as I stretched out on the sofa and closed my eyes. "This is the day the Lord has made," I repeated, dozing off to the slap and roll of waves.

Three sharp blasts of our horn caused me to jump up in alarm. I stumbled up the companionway. "What's the matter?"

"Our first barge," Mark said calmly. Directly ahead of us in the channel was a series of flatboats being pushed by a snorting tug. What appeared to be open bins containing coal, followed by a half-dozen connected carriers with stacks of steel beams, slowly drew closer. "Why don't you try to call them," he told Ludy.

Ludy went below and tried all the frequencies, but he couldn't rouse the enormous craft that was bearing down on us.

"Let's start our engines, just in case," Mark said. We looped far toward the left bank to give the barge ample room to pass. When it drew along side of us, I could see two men up in the pilothouse, obviously not interested in us. They chugged past, kicking up a wake that almost swept over our bow and left us bobbing.

"You better get used to those," Mark said. "You'll be seeing lots of commercial traffic."

"Where are they going?" I asked.

"Probably the twin cities. Going upstream they'll haul gasoline and fuel oils from the refineries near the Gulf. In the other direction, it's mostly grains: corn, wheat, oats, and barley."

"They act like they own the river," Ludy said.

"You'd be surprised." Mark grinned. "They think they do own it." Suddenly a furious squawking from below deck diverted our attention. I rushed down the stairs and took in the whole scene.

"What happened?" Ludy panted right behind me.

Dinah's cage was swinging wildly, and underneath it Hobo stared up curiously, his ears twitching at each squawk.

"It appears that Hobo and Dinah have become acquainted." I took a rolled-up newspaper and threatened Hobo with it, warning him to leave our new companion alone. Dinah fluttered nervously and hopped back to her perch. "I hope her cage is high enough," I muttered.

We soon approached our second lock and dam, this time on the Illinois bank. "Lock and Dam Number 13," Ludy said as he searched through the charts. "Here it is. River mile 522 just above Clinton. Our drop is eleven feet. It says that right now we're in a four-mile-wide pool."

The distance between banks had increased, and as we slowed toward the lock, I counted four fishing boats anchored about fifty yards offshore. A thin peninsula reached out to meet us as we came up to the traffic signals. At the upstream end of the lock a crane dredged the river, and when we drew close, the boom stopped dipping water. I watched two fish struggle out of the side and flop back under the surface. There was a low retaining wall to our left, and when the gates shut and we began to drop, I gauged our descent by the roof of a farmhouse just past the lock station, until it disappeared and our vista was shut off by the brick wall.

"Hold her steady," Mark encouraged us, as the whoosh of water bubbled under us and the boat began to tilt. "In the future," he advised while pushing the boat away from the wall with his foot, "try not to let the hull bang the side."

"Well, how much farther?" I asked as we left the lock.

"To Davenport? Why don't you figure the mileage from the chart. Ludy said this was river mile 522."

I bent over the chart and traced the winding river with my finger until I came to Davenport, river mile 483. "It looks like thirty-nine miles."

"Anything we should know about the river between here and Davenport?"

"Well, right ahead is Beaver Slough, a recreation area. And then . . . oh, yes . . . right here there's a danger mark to indicate a submerged canal wall, the old LeClaire Canal that parallels the river channel. It says there's a government beacon."

"Do you know what a submerged canal wall would do to the hull?" Mark asked grimly.

"I'd hate to find out."

"That's why it's important to study your charts. How far to the submerged wall?"

"Near Lock 14, just above LeClaire."

"Okay, watch for it." We slipped past Clinton where the *Rhododendron,* an ancient paddlewheeler, rocked serenely in a small harbor. Ludy slept on the foredeck after I had lathered him with suntan lotion while I kept my eyes peeled for the government beacon. When I finally saw it, I imagined the submerged wall lying in wait like a river monster, ready to tear a gash in unsuspecting boats. We reached the traffic signals for the lock, and I leaned over and yanked the flaxen pullcord.

"Try the lockmaster on the radio," Mark told Ludy.

Ludy went below, and this time, a friendly voice blared over the radio. After exchanging chatty information, we went down another eleven feet, signed off with a "good luck," and caught the current in midchannel.

"Hey, pretty nice of the guy to talk with us, huh?" Ludy said as he came back on deck.

"If you sat in that little house for eight hours a day, wouldn't you be glad to talk to people?"

"I guess so. I should have asked him what the police patrol is called. River smokies?"

"Wrongo!" Mark playfully wrestled Ludy to the deck.

As we drew closer to the Quad cities and the last lock before Davenport, the lush scenery changed to industrial complexes squatting along the river. The buildings sent smoke into the sky and a brownish liquid into the river. I noticed more dead fish floating against the bow. We sailed under a succession of bridges: railroad bridges, old swing spans that pivoted on limestone piers, and the ultramodern four and six lane bridges that carried traffic, like on Interstate 80, from coast to coast.

"So this is where our tractors and farm implements come from," I said, pointing to a John Deere plant and the neat rows of green and yellow tractors.

The river traffic had also increased. We passed fewer fishermen but still dodged an occasional speedboat. A number of barges lined the banks, unloading and loading cargo bound for foreign ports. "Lock Number 15," Ludy warned us, "is a double lock which lets us down sixteen feet."

We slowed down as the approach to the lock became more congested. "It may take longer going through here," Mark said.

"Why don't they just move aside and let us through?" Ludy said as two fishing boats ahead of us tied up at the traffic signal.

"I was reading one of the pamphlets last night," Mark explained, "and we're low priority. Government boats, excursion boats, towboats, and commercial fishing boats have precedence over pleasure boats."

"Well, I wish I had a fishing pole." Ludy sat down on the foredeck and tried to attract Hobo's attention. Hobo was more interested in investigating a floppy sheet that wriggled like a snake.

I surmised from the interlocking levees and dikes that Davenport also encountered the full malevolence of spring floods.

Finally we idled forward into the lock with two couples in a speed cruiser behind us. In ten minutes we were through. An old black man and woman sat in folding chairs just beyond the lock. When we motored forward in the turbulent eddies from the dam, they reeled in their lines, waved, and shouted something we couldn't hear. I wondered how long they had been sitting there and if they had caught anything.

"Watch for Davenport Marina," Mark instructed. "They've got dockage and other facilities."

Less than a mile ahead, we saw the sign above a dock and gas pumps. Ludy jumped off like an experienced sailor, but he slipped and nearly tumbled off the slick dock. He fastened our mooring lines while Mark and I went in to see about an overnight slip. "This is just like pulling into a motel, isn't it?" I said as he opened the door for me.

"Except they don't have room service."

We registered for an unoccupied spot, got permission to hook our extension cord to an AC outlet and were told the procedures for dumping our waste-holding tank.

"I'm sure it doesn't need to be emptied yet," I assured the woman attendant.

Mark appraised my maneuvering of the boat into our slip and patted me on the shoulder with pride. "Great! Both of you should manage just fine."

"It won't be the same with you gone," Ludy sniveled.

"I have confidence in you and faith in God. Who knows? I may even show up for a rendezvous in the Caribbean when you get to New Orleans."

"We'll be disappointed if you don't," I admonished.

"Count on me. I'd better grab my duffel bag and hustle downtown to where my friend works so I can catch a ride." He disappeared below and returned with his gear. Hobo shook hands with him reluctantly, but when Mark proffered a piece of gum, Hobo snatched it and scampered under the slack sail. "And these are for you," he said, handing us two packages.

"What are they?"

"Going away presents. You know, tokens of friendship."

Both small boxes contained a gold cross and chain. On the back of the crosses were the words "*Pax Deus.*"

"That means 'God's Peace.' Wear them in health. And if you have any trouble with the boat, look for the nearest marina or boat club. If you get stuck on the river, use your radio. The Coast Guard is never far when you need them."

"And when all else fails," I said, "call on the Master Mechanic."

"Right. God bless!" He hugged both of us, hopped off our makeshift gangplank, and jogged up the hill toward town. He turned to wave, then disappeared in the evening traffic.

"Well." Ludy smacked his lips. "How about some chow?"

I pretended to cuff him. "Whatever you feel like cooking."

"Me?" he frowned.

"We take turns, remember?"

"Hey!" He brightened. "How about scrambled eggs?"

We all went below, exhausted after our first full day on the river and slightly melancholy with Mark gone. His absence, I knew, would be felt for a long time to come. Dinah, as if sensing our mood, awked and nibbled her bars and croaked for the first time, "The Lord is my shepherd, hello, hello."

"Hello, hello, yourself." I laughed.

22 Tragedy set in the next morning when we were preparing to cast off from the dock. We had agreed to store Hobo's cage in an out-of-the-way place, but rather than have him snoop all night, we put his collar and leash on and secured him to the galley table. I thought Ludy must have released Hobo and allowed our raccoon to sleep in the foreberth, since he was nowhere in sight when I crawled out. After a skimpy breakfast of toast and hot chocolate, we stowed everything in its place and went up into a warm drizzle.

"Visibility isn't going to be good," Ludy remarked.

"Maybe the sky will clear off by noon."

"We may as well get started, then. You want to crank the engine?" I sat on a wet seat and shivered as moisture seeped through my slacks. Ludy untied the lines.

"Did you feed Hobo?" I asked.

"Nope, haven't seen him."

"Didn't you take off his collar?"

"No, I thought . . ." He rewrapped the line around the dock post and jumped back on board. "Let me go check below." I waited, sure that the weather and Mark's absence would make today's sailing lousy. "I can't find him," Ludy called.

"Oh, no!" I moaned as I went down the steps. "It looks like we've lost another passenger."

Ludy, frustrated, rattled Dinah's cage. "Have you seen him?"

"Hobo!" I shouted. Ludy even opened and slammed the icebox a couple of times, but there was no response from our ever-hungry raccoon.

"He must have slipped the collar off last night and jumped ship."

"He wouldn't have jumped ship," I snapped. Ludy's face sank and he turned away. "I'm sorry. It wasn't your fault."

Ludy went dockside and called through the mist, but all we roused was a sleepy male voice that told us to "Keep the racket down!"

"Well," Ludy sighed, hands on his hips. "I don't know what to do. You think he'll come back?"

"Probably not. I think he preferred dry land."

"I hate to lose him like this. He was kind of cute."

I stuffed my hands in my pockets. "I guess we could wait around."

"It might . . ." he hesitated. "No. We'd better leave. He's gone . . . for good."

Unwillingly, I took my seat again and started the engine. It coughed and finally sputtered to life. I shoved the reverse switch and we glided back.

"That's good, you're clear now," Ludy yelled from the bow.

"Boy, what a gloomy day." I wanted to go back to bed and try starting over in a couple of hours. Maybe the sun would have burnt through by then and Hobo would have changed his mind and wandered back. The sky grumbled over the western horizon.

"Is it safe to be on the river in a storm?"

"I doubt it," he said. "The mast would probably act like a lightning rod."

"Oh, great," I wailed.

"Slow up, slow up." Ludy peered ahead. "It looks like a big trawler dead ahead. Can you swing to the starboard?"

I thought quickly, unable to recall which direction starboard was. I turned to the left.

"Starboard, sharp!"

I had chosen wrong. By the time I had corrected my error, the trawler was visible. It emitted a low, guttural blast and thundered by us with a foot to spare.

"Wake up, lady!" a contorted face called down from the bridge.

It took me a minute to recover. Meanwhile, in overcompensating for my abrupt turn, the bow was drifting into a concrete pier that jutted out between the harbor and the river. "Reverse engine! You want me to take over?" Ludy said sharply.

"I'm okay. I'm okay." I gripped the tiller and pulled it toward me. Wet hair began to droop over my eyes. I felt miserable.

"Hold it, hold it just a minute." Ludy stood up, excited about something under the pier.

"Would you make up your mind?"

He suddenly leaped off into the water, staggered to his feet about hip deep, and plowed onto shore. I tried to hold the boat steady. He crawled forward, grabbed at something, and then backed out, still on his knees. When he approached the water, I could see a familiar masked face sticking out above his cradled arms.

"He was eating a dead carp."

"Yuk! You want me to bring the boat in closer?"

"No, I'll wade out. Just take this gremlin and tie him up." Ludy came out slowly, testing his footing until he reached the boat. I took the wet and muddy raccoon while Ludy pulled himself over the side.

"Does he stink!" I thought of dunking him once or twice, but I knew Hobo would protest with his needle-like claws along my arm. Still, it seemed almost a fair trade-off considering his mangy countenance.

210

"Let me go change my jeans." Ludy went below and promised to clean Hobo with a paper towel.

When we finally disembarked, the rain had stopped. A sulphur smell mixed with the usual fishy aroma. As we caught midchannel I could see an ominous black smokestack spewing ash that waffled out toward us and settled on the wave crests. In all the excitement of the morning, I had neglected to thank God for the new day. It didn't take much mustering to breathe a prayer of relief that Hobo had returned. "And thank You, Lord, for speeding us safely on our way and blessing us with good weather." I also asked a special blessing on Mark and our families, who seemed so far away as we crept forward in the fog. By noon the sky had cleared, and we were headed toward Keokuk, our destination for that day.

We slipped past a long island with signs posted indicating government property. "Did you know there's a fine for landing on government islands?"

"No, I'm surprised. What about emergencies?" I wondered.

"They'd still probably fine you."

"Really?"

He shrugged. "They might have hidden missile installations."

"Here? Why would they?"

"Heck, don't you know the government has missiles hidden all over? Dad said that half the silos in Kansas are really missile sites."

"I think you're exaggerating."

"No, really."

"Okay." I smiled. "Just tell me where we are."

"According to the chart—" he mulled over a squiggle of blue lines. "What did that buoy say back there?"

"I don't know. I wasn't listening."

"Very funny," he groaned. "What was the mileage number on it?"

"I didn't see."

"Well, I would say we're approaching the Andalusia Chute, which is the slackwater pool above Lock Number 16."

"What city is that near?"

"Muscatine."

"I need to get a pair of sunglasses."

"What for? It'll probably rain if you do."

"Still, if there's a good place to tie up, I would like to stop." We didn't stop until we had gone through Locks 16, 17, and 18, and passed the confluence of the Iowa and Henderson Rivers and the picturesque burgs of

New Boston, Keithsburg, and Oquawka, all nestled on the Illinois shore. The approach to the Burlington Municipal Aquatic Park was through hazardous breakwater caused by an enormous dredging crane that periodically scooped bucketfuls of sediment across the path of incoming vessels. Ludy stood ready to pole us away from any rocks that jutted up in the cut. "We made it," he shouted jubilantly as I swung us broadside to the dock.

"You don't have confidence in me?"

"I was kind of squeamish when you just skimmed that shoal before the crane."

"What shoal?"

"You didn't see it?" he asked in alarm.

"No, where was it?"

"Never mind. Let's go get a cola."

I shut the hatch so Hobo wouldn't be tempted to escape again. Ludy was talking to an elderly man in a wheelchair next to the pop machine when I entered the shop.

"Yep, worked on the railroad for forty-two years. Chicago, Saint Louiee, Kansas City, Saint Joe—I know them all inside out. Every week I'd be on a new run."

"Is that right?" Ludy said politely as I came up.

"Yep." The man chomped down, toothless, and began talking to me. "I helped build this old bridge down river here. Seen it?"

"No." I shook my head. "We've come down from the north."

"The longest double track, double-deck swing span in the world," he continued. "Fort Madison Atchison, Topeka and Santa Fe. I helped build it." Ludy took a long swallow and committed the inexcusable.

"What happened to your legs?"

The man looked at him numbly and tilted his head as to hear the question better. "How's that?" I hoped Ludy would drop it there and walk away.

"What's wrong with your legs?" he asked louder.

With a faraway gleam, the man stared past us to some private vision on the wall. I took Ludy by the arm and dragged him away. "It's not polite to ask about someone's infirmity."

"I was just curious."

"You should have some compassion."

"I do. I feel sorry for him."

"But it's not the same as compassion. You don't want to upset him by prying into a personal matter."

Ludy drained his bottle and went to place it in the empties case next to the man, who now stared at his hands. At the sound of the bottle hitting the crate he looked up slowly, then grabbed Ludy by the elbow and pulled him close to his toothless mouth working over his gums.

"A boxcar run over 'em," he hissed with a grin, wild-eyed. Startled, Ludy pulled back until the man released his arm. Ludy hurried over to me and whispered, "That old guy is spooky. Let's get out of here." We went outside. "I thought he was going to take a bite out of my neck the way he looked at me."

"Jesus said when you treat the least of His brethren with kindness, then you treat Him with kindness."

"That old coot sure won the 'least brethren' award hands down," he shuddered.

"Now, that's not compassion."

"Easy for you to say."

"How can you be like that? Suppose he was your own father. Then maybe you'd feel different."

"Yeah, maybe," he admitted.

"It wouldn't hurt you to remember that poor man in your prayers tonight."

"Maybe." He spun around and hopped onto the deck.

He isn't far from You, Lord, I thought, pleased with the small success.

At the mouth of the Skunk River, just past Burlington's ten-mile island, the wind picked up, and we were able to shut off the engine for the first time that day. Not wanting to reveal my ineptitude, I cajoled Ludy into hoisting sail. He demonstrated his prowess at fitting the main and jib sails, and within ten minutes, we were under wind power.

"Gee, it's pretty gusty," I said, my eyes on our telltale.

"Hey, why don't I run up the spinnaker? It looks like the wind is holding true. What do you think?"

"Sure, try it."

In another five minutes the colorful geometric designs of our spinnaker arched out in front of us. I envisioned that, from the rolling bluffs on either side, we must have appeared spectacular. "Can I take the helm?" Ludy asked. I was only too glad to let him take over. The persistent pounding of the wind as we gained speed was a little scary.

"Whooooooeeeeeee!" Ludy screamed. "We're running now. Look at us fly."

"I think I'll go below for a while," I warbled.

Downstairs, Hobo had redecorated the cabin with shards from a demolished cracker box. A track of crumbs led to the darkness of Ludy's berth. I ducked under Dinah.

"Praise the Lord, what's your name?" she squawked.

Hobo, glassy-eyed and purring gluttonously, slunk back into the corner. "Come here, come here," I coaxed sweetly. He covered his eyes with his paws. "I can still see you." I snuck up on his tail. He rolled over but I had him. I shook him and pushed his nose into a pile of crumbs. He stared up sheepishly as if to disavow any knowledge of the crime. "Not this time, you rascal." He whined after the second swat of the newspaper and bristled back to his snuggery. For being only a handful of fur, his will was colossal.

Rounding a sharp bend near Fort Madison, we nearly got into trouble. A wide, flat-topped tanker was struggling upstream into a narrow drift that angled off the bank.

"Why don't we go around her to the left?" I suggested.

"Okay, but hang tight because she doesn't leave much room." As we sped to the pocket between the turning tanker and the Illinois shore, Ludy drew in the spinnaker to adjust our velocity. Before we knew what was happening, the tanker came to a stop and began reversing engines, its bow pointed in our direction.

"What is he doing?"

"I think we should slow down," I said.

Ludy shot three toots of our horn at the tanker. A deckhand appeared at the railing and waved us back.

"They do think they own the river, don't they?" Ludy huffed.

"We're going to collide, Ludy, if you don't stop!"

He furled the other two sails, but our momentum kept us drifting at a good clip. The tanker started its engines forward and gradually spun into midchannel. When we drew abreast, no more than ten feet away, the mate shouted angrily, "Don't you know which way to pass?"

I threw my hands up in apology. "Which way?"

He spat into the water. "Get off the river, you fools!"

After we were out of hearing Ludy trumpeted back, "Who do you think you are?"

"It's all right, Ludy." I tried to soothe him. "It probably was our fault."

"Naw, we got as much right to use the river as they do."

"Remember compassion." I was upset too, but I didn't want to show it. Ludy clenched his jaw and stared ahead.

Two towboats were locking through ahead of us at Keokuk. The lockmaster, a cheerful, sandy-haired fellow, invited us in to see the adjoining power plant. We climbed up the ladder and entered the visitors' room, where whirring turbines extended a hundred yards in front of us. Over the roar, I heard him point out that electricity for Saint Louis was generated around the clock and that the entire operation, including the lock, was owned by Union Electric, only one of two on the Mississippi not under government control. We followed him outside. The sun was vanishing through a crimson haze behind us.

"Did you know this lock," the lockmaster intoned, "is as wide as the Panama Canal?"

"Really?" I waited for him to continue his speech, which sounded well rehearsed.

"Yes. And when you leave the lock, you'll have descended thirty-eight feet."

"Amazing."

"And it only takes ten minutes."

"You enjoy your job?" I asked him.

"Wouldn't trade it for anything. I used to be a salesman. Baby furniture. Hated it. Wouldn't give up this job for anything. Well, I better go supervise my assistant. Have a nice trip, folks."

"Oh, by the way," Ludy called after him. "Is there a good place we can spend the night nearby?"

"Howard's Boat Dock, half a mile on your right." He nodded and went up the steps to his stationhouse.

We had to turn our lights on as we came into Howard's Boat Dock. All the slips were occupied, but Mr. Howard, a genial proprietor, let us tie up in front of his ice house for the night. "The only thing," he warned, "is that the dock topples over from time to time, so be careful how you climb up on her. I'd hate to fish you out in the morning."

"Don't worry," I assured him. "We won't breathe on it. I'm too tired to do anything except sleep."

"Join us for breakfast, won't you? My wife cooks up some good buttermilk flapjacks." His red cheeks rose over a smiling mouth like twin bulbs. *Add a white beard,* I imagined, *and he would make a great Santa Claus.*

23

Mrs. Howard knocked on our porthole at seven the next morning. I was in my bathrobe reading the Book of Romans, and Ludy was still snoozing.

"Did my husband tell you what time to come up?"

"No, he didn't." I stuck my head out the small opening.

"We'll breakfast in half an hour. Just come around to the back of the store and knock."

"Thank you." I watched her creep along the unstable dock. If her husband was an appropriate stand-in for Santa, then she fulfilled my expectations of what Mrs. Santa should look like. She was plump and seemed to have a bewitching smile and an eagerness in the way she spoke. I poked my head in Ludy's berth and tickled his foot.

"Awwwr," he grumbled. "Let me sleep."

"No. We have a breakfast engagement," I insisted.

He sat up, thunking his head on the low ceiling as he did.

"Ohhh. What time is it?"

"After seven. Rise and shine!"

"Do I have to?"

"Yes, now hurry up."

Mr. Howard was watching for us as we went past the window at the back of his combination grocery store and fishing supply shop. He stood at the door, beaming. "Good morning!" He ushered us into a small kitchen where his wife was testing the heat on a steaming griddle. "You hungry?" He slapped Ludy on the back.

"It's kind of you to invite us," I said.

"Glad to have you," he smiled. "We try to invite a traveler every morning. It's a good way to meet people, and I must say, we have met some interesting people. Right, Mother?"

"Oh, yes." She poured on the batter for her first flapjacks. "Have a seat, everyone. We'll be ready in a minute." While she built a stack of thick cakes, Mr. Howard regaled Ludy and me with stories about real river pirates who had lately begun to hijack sections of overladen barges that tied up just down river from his store. He speculated that they had connections with organized crime in Saint Louis.

"Oh, they don't want to hear about that," his wife scolded.

"I do," Ludy said.

After stuffing us with hot cakes and strawberries, then refusing our help with cleaning up the dishes, Mrs. Howard walked us down to their shaky dock. "Cross right in the middle," she advised, "and it won't be tippy."

217

I tried to catch a glimpse of the Howards as we guided the boat out past their store. "Nice people," I said, basking in the warmth of their generosity and the early morning sun.

The major cities before Hannibal—Canton and Quincy—both had locks that lowered us ten feet. Since we had left Dubuque, I had studied the birds, testing my knowledge against the pictures and descriptions in my pocket *Guide to American Wildlife*. It was during the morning stretch just before Canton, Missouri, that Ludy pointed to two shadows swooping effortlessly above us.

"Eagles," he said.

"Really? Your eyes are better than mine." One broke away and dipped toward the river, screeching as he leveled quickly, snatched a fish with his talons, and flapped off toward a stately oak. As we drifted under the branches where the eagle was feeding, I tried to spot him.

"Look." Ludy pointed to the base of the tree. The bole was blood-stained and dozens of fish heads and shredded entrails littered the ground. "Must be their feeding tree." Another eagle leaped from the branches and scudded out over the river.

"They are huge," I said. "What a shame that they're nearly extinct."

"I'd hate to tangle with one." He leaned back against the transom and followed them until they were out of sight.

Hannibal was a must on our itinerary. For years I had wanted to take an excursion to Mark Twain's boyhood home, and now I was about to arrive in style. As we drew nearer, I tried to picture the freckle-faced Tom and Huck poling past us on a raft. If any town had remained a symbol to me of unchanging, mid-America, it had been Hannibal. We docked on a busy wharf just a half block from the Twain monument. Two teenage boys departing in a motorboat whistled at our boat.

"That's a mighty fine sloop," the taller of the two said. "My cousin has one just like it."

"That's interesting," Ludy said. "Because we built this one."

Hannibal was a disappointment. Walking up the cobbled streets and peering in at the restored nineteenth century houses, we became aware how each attraction had been converted to touristy commercialism. Mark Twain mementos were everywhere: motels, restaurants, gift shops, museums, antique shops—Hannibal's favorite son was evident on everything. Even a laundromat capitalized on Twain's name. We had to wait in line for ten minutes to view Becky Thatcher's home, where life-sized, talking dummies related the popular legends surrounding the home. After deciding not to board a sightseeing bus that was loading weary passengers for a trip to the Mark Twain Cave a couple of miles outside town, we trudged down the hill to our boat. I did purchase a copy of *Life on the Mississippi* as a souvenir.

When we had caught the current and our sails filled with a western breeze, Ludy remarked that he suspected even Hitler's hometown had raised a hotdog stand to his memory.

"That's a grim joke, but it is depressing, isn't it, to see how national shrines spring up while dollar signs crowd out the real meaning."

"Personally," he said, stretching out on the foredeck, "I understand Huck Finn better right now than I ever would walking around back there."

He was right. I studied the forested bluffs of the Missouri shore. Hannibal meant little to Twain. It was the river, the same river that was carrying us inexorably through time, past many of the same trees that Twain would have viewed as saplings, that remained unchanged. The town had been tampered with, but the river didn't stand still long enough for anyone to clamp a dollar sign on it.

Debating whether to push on to a marina before the sky darkened further or to tie up in an inviting cove, we chose the cove. It would be our first night away from civilization. As I warmed a can of beef stew, Ludy splashed and cavorted in the shallows.

"Are you sure we're anchored?" I shouted through the porthole.

"Don't worry. I wrapped one anchor around a tree. We'll probably have to chop it down so we can leave in the morning. Come on in! The water's warm."

"Dinner will be ready in a few minutes."

"Hey!" He reached down and scooped something from the bottom. "How about crab legs?" He held up a wiggling rock crab.

"No thanks!"

"Ask Hobo if he wants it."

I glanced over at Hobo, sitting on the counter next to me, his eyes frozen on the chunky meat and vegetables in the pan. "Never mind. He has other plans for dinner."

24 We had less than one hundred miles to go before reaching Saint Louis the next day, so after sneaking out of the cove as the sun came out to a chorus of geese and bullfrogs, we headed toward Saverton, Missouri, in search of a gas dock. Our tanks had been nearly depleted from the past two foggy mornings when there was no wind, and it sounded as if the engine was beginning to act up. Instead of the familiar hum and stroke, the engine misfired and sputtered, dying twice before we were able to hoist sail.

"We should get it checked out in Saint Louis," Ludy suggested.

"I hope it's nothing serious. Our expense account doesn't allow for major repairs." I propped my feet on the gunwale and leaned against the mast while Ludy threaded us through a procession of wooded islands. On one island, a group of Boy Scouts was frying bacon over a camp stove. They waded out knee deep as we slid past and sang an off-key rendition of "Suwannee."

We passed through Lock and Dam 22 on the right bank, unimpeded by any other river traffic that morning. When we finally located fuel pumps, it was at the mouth of the DuPont Reservoir just outside of Ashburn. A chubby girl about ten years old managed to eat a large slab of red licorice while filling our tanks. Hobo sat fascinated on the foredeck and watched the girl tear at the licorice with one hand as she squeezed the gas nozzle with the other. She ripped off a strip and tossed it at him. He sniffed it, turned it over, and then gobbled it voraciously.

"I thought they was supposed to wash their food before they ate it?" she asked Ludy.

Ludy, who was unsuccessfully removing a knot from his wet shoelaces looked up and said, "This raccoon thinks he's human. Washing his food is too uncivilized."

"Does he do tricks?"

"Oh sure," Ludy bragged. "Card tricks, magic tricks . . ."

"Really?" Her eyes nearly popped out. "He's pretty smart, then?"

"Oh, not all that smart. I usually beat him at checkers." He watched for her reaction. I had become accustomed to Ludy's exaggerations, and now he had found a willing victim. The girl paused with her mouth full, obviously impressed.

"Does he talk?"

"Well," Ludy searched for an answer. Just then Dinah let out from the cabin a shrill, "Hello, hello! Praise the Lord!"

"Who's that?" she asked.

"Oh, that's his big sister." He grinned.

"Really? I never heard a raccoon talk before."

"This is your lucky day then." He bit the inside of his cheek to keep from laughing and looked over to me. I wagged my finger threateningly.

The girl's father came out to the dock, wiping his greasy hands on a rag, when Ludy started the engine. It coughed and shuddered. A new noise—of metal grinding—had appeared. "Sounds like you got a faulty piston," he said.

"Can you fix it?"

"Probably could, but it would take a day or so to get parts. Your best bet is try to limp on down to Saint Louis."

Lord, I pleaded as we swung out into the river, *You've gotten us this far. Please see us through today and any repair job. You know we're not prepared to handle any expensive breakdown.*

We continued on by the juncture of the Salt River, under the Wabash and Illinois Central Railroad bridges, and past a clutter of dilapidated houses at the edge of Louisiana, Missouri. A scraggly cat sat on a flood dike and tried to stare down Hobo, who was watching the cat with half-closed lids. The contest ended in a draw.

"This is strange," said Ludy, bending over the charts. "We went through Lock 22, and Lock 24 is up ahead at Clarksville, but there is no Lock 23."

"I wonder if it's like the thirteenth floor of a building," I said.

"Maybe the Corps of Engineers can't count." He stared at the chart, puzzled. "Oh, I bet I know. It says that Lock and Dam Number 23 is not constructed. They must have numbered it because they plan to build it eventually."

"How far to Saint Louis yet?"

"About eighty miles, give or take a few bends of the river."

"Let's pray, Ludy, that we don't have to use our engine too much. I'm not crazy about having to get out and walk."

Doubts began to nag me as the day went on. I found it difficult to concentrate on the scenery. Ludy pointed out a patch of emerald water that had an almost transparent sheen, but as I stared, it became muddy and clouded. I didn't want to dwell on negative thoughts, especially since I knew the Lord was guiding us, but each time we glided perilously close to an obstruction, I was afraid we would have to use the engine and it would refuse us.

When I went below to fix peanut butter sandwiches at noon, I realized we hadn't seen any town or houses along the shore in a couple of hours.

From the porthole, the territory seemed to move past us as if we were standing still. The region was untouched and primitive. I didn't need to stretch my imagination far to picture the area's original inhabitants perched on the ridges or paddling across the water in birchbark canoes. But then the fear I had been fighting back managed to distract my thoughts. I knew that God would watch over us; if only I could erase what my own weakness was conjuring.

We were again fortunate that Lock Number 25 was vacant. We sailed right up to the lock gate, signaled for passage, and drifted into the chamber without using the engine. Ludy called the lockmaster over the radio to ask about the river ahead. A squeaky voice came back that advised the water level was down where the Cuivre River flowed into the Mississippi, and that a number of mud flats had appeared. He suggested we proceed through with caution by hugging the left side of the channel. We never did see who the unusual voice originated from, but Ludy explained as we left the lock that the station had been taken over by aliens who could imitate Earthling speech.

"Why would they want to commandeer a lock and dam?" I asked.

"Don't you see?" I expected his nose to grow at any moment. "If they can control the Mississippi River, then they could back up the water for miles until they created a huge lake, and then suddenly release all the water and flood out everybody downstream."

"But why would they want to flood everybody?"

"To take over the country!"

"Wouldn't it be wiser to take over Washington first?"

His eyes flared wide in mock alarm. "You don't think they've already infiltrated the government?"

"Oh, go on!" I ruffled his hair and threatened to make him walk the plank. Sometimes I wondered what my fifty-year-old friends would think if they overheard Ludy and me. *Deranged* was too mild a word.

Something crashed in the cabin. "Oh, no. What has Hobo gotten into now?" I made Ludy go view the damage.

"He just knocked over your box of hair brushes," Ludy called.

"That's good news," I shouted back.

"The bad news, though, is that he knocked them into the toilet."

Fuming, I stared ahead at the river with murderous intent toward raccoons. God had certainly put masks on their faces for a reason.

By early afternoon we reached a point where the river seemed to divide, part of it curling off toward the east. "No," Ludy surmised, his finger on the chart. "That's the confluence of the Illinois River. You can follow the Illinois north until you come to Chicago and then cross the Great Lakes and the Saint Lawrence Seaway, all the way to the Atlantic seaboard.''

I hadn't known the Midwest was crisscrossed by such a network of waterways. After four days on the river, traveling by water struck me as preferable to overland highway. As the Illinois River mingled with the Mississippi, I thought I could detect a slightly bluer tinge to the Illinois. In watching the two streams gradually merge, I almost ran over a buoy.

''Look alive!'' Ludy screamed.

''It wasn't my fault.'' I tried to keep a straight face. ''Didn't you see the buoy attack our bow? It must be radio-controlled by aliens.''

''Right.'' He grinned in complicity and lay down on the deck. A brisk northwester carried the scent of pines off the bluffs beyond the man-made embankments. The number of islands increased, causing the channel to narrow. At one bend where a fallen tree caused a natural inlet, two middle-aged men stood in a bass boat casting toward shore.

''You hain't seen the *Delta Queen* go by, have ya?'' one of the men called.

''What's the 'Delta Queen'?'' I replied.

The man turned to his friend and repeated my question. ''She asks what the *Delta Queen* is.'' They both guffawed. ''Ma'am,'' he shouted back, ''if'n you don't know what the *Delta Queen* is, then you hain't seen it!'' They turned back to their casting.

Disgruntled, I asked Ludy what the ''Delta Queen'' was. He rolled over, shading his eyes from the sun. ''An old-fashioned paddlewheeler,'' he answered. ''It still carries people up and down the river. I read about it in some book about the Mississippi.''

''Then I sure haven't seen it.''

''I think Congress also declared it a national monument,'' he said and rolled over to his stomach again. I asked if he wanted to take the helm for a while, but he was asleep. I let him snore until I spotted Dam Number 26 spanning the river ahead at Alton, Illinois. A row of grain elevators lined the shore upstream from the lock. When I angled toward the gate signals, I could see cars bustling through town and curving up the ramp that led to a bridge. The cars seemed insignificant as they scurried with activity. From where I was, only the placid and south-flowing river seemed real. I had to start the engine to hold our position in the current as a towboat locked through ahead of us. In addition to the grinding metal, the engine began to heat up. Ludy went below to investigate smoke that was rising from the floor cover.

"You better shut it off," he called. "It's heating up."

We drifted against the lock wall and hit the side. I tried to balance the swells so we wouldn't wash against the brick wall again. Both of the double locks had jammed, so while the lockmaster inspected the stubborn mechanisms, we waited, now more concerned because of the smoke.

"I just hope," Ludy said, "that we don't have to dry dock to have her fixed."

"Can't we get at the engine from the cabin well enough?"

"I sure hope so."

We were almost an hour in locking through. Ludy bent over the side of the bow and examined the hull. "We scratched her some. I'm glad this is the next to last lock."

The final ten miles to Saint Louis were uneventful, with the exception of our confluence with the Missouri River. I remembered her nickname as the "Big Muddy" when I saw the brown current sweep into the Mississippi and travel alongside, still brown for almost a mile before its coloring began to take on the shades of its new mate.

From bank to bank, the two rivers created a lake nearly three miles in width. If the Illinois River had connected us with the Atlantic, then the Missouri linked us to the prairies and high plains and eventual mountain wilderness of Montana, half a continent in the other direction. I handed the tiller to Ludy as the river traffic increased.

Huge steel barges latched together in five-acre platforms were tied at the scattered docks of Saint Louis. Dodging tows and pleasure boats, we nearly rocketed past the Municipal Dock, one of only two on the Saint Louis riverfront that we could stop at. As we came from under the evening shadows of the Eads Bridge, the Gateway Arch jutted up against the skyline. Lowering our sails, we landed next to the *S.S. Admiral,* an excursion boat that was just departing for an evening cruise. I gasped at our paltriness next to its towering five decks. As it rumbled away, two other boats, both showboats from another era, lit up at their moorings.

The *Goldenrod,* with an elegant, red-trimmed forecastle, was deserted, but the *Becky Thatcher* had a stream of people entering its floating restaurant. The cacophony of cars and trucks, so luxuriously forgotten during the past week, was more than evident as freeways spilled a rush of traffic toward the suburbs. Ludy and I, famished and fatigued, resolved to walk over for dinner at the *Becky Thatcher.*

After we had wound our way up the latticed stairway and been seated in the plush dining room to the left of a Dixieland band that was tuning up, Captain Zachary Peters came over and introduced himself as skipper of the *Stonewall Jackson,* "the most powerful towboat plying river north of New Orleans." He was obviously proud.

"Mind if I join you? There's no sense in my sitting alone at the bar and you folks over here in the corner, is there?" He sat down before we had a chance to reply. "Please call me Zack."

The Captain, well over six feet tall and erect as a cedar, reminded me of a refined plantation owner. His sharp features were framed by gray, almost-silver hair that he smoothed back as he spoke. "I do hope you will forgive my directness, but you struck me as such generous and warm people that . . ."

"You really a riverboat captain?" Ludy interrupted.

Captain Peters smiled. "Yes, I am, son. Have you and your mother ever been aboard one?"

"Oh no," I said. "This is my grandson, Ludy, and I'm Dorothy Morgan. We're from Iowa."

"Iowa? I've hauled tons of produce from Iowa. Well, believe me, ma'am, this is a pleasure to meet you. Are you sure you don't mind my intrusion?"

"Not at all. We're alone, too."

"Well then," he smiled. "May I order you a drink?"

"No, thank you."

There was an authority to his voice that made me feel he was accustomed to receiving respect. "All right then, maybe later. Are you just visiting from Iowa, or do you live in Saint Louis now?"

"Just visiting." Ludy gawked at our short-skirted waitress who brought three glasses of water.

"Vacation?"

"Yes, sort of," I said.

"Hmmm. You make it sound mysterious." The Captain flashed his comfortable smile again.

"I don't mean to. We're also traveling by river, but we've had some engine trouble, so we may be forced to lay over for a day or two."

"By river? Is that a fact? And what nature of craft do you travel by, Mrs. Morgan?"

"A thirty-foot sloop that we built at home."

"By yourself? Why, ma'am, that's an impressive feat for such a delicate woman."

I didn't blush exactly, but my cheeks must have tipped Ludy that Captain Peters' flattery had found its mark. He looked the Captain in the eye and said, "We did it together."

"It takes a great deal of skill to build a boat that will withstand the Mississippi. It's not a backyard pond, you know. A thirty-footer? Does she handle well?"

"So far, excellent," I said. "But our engine has been acting up."

"I see. Serious trouble?"

"Something in the pistons."

"Uh huh. Where do you expect to have your boat repaired?"

"We don't know," Ludy replied. "We just docked tonight."

"And where are you docked?"

"Right next to the *Goldenrod*," I said.

"Do you have anyone else in Saint Louis who might be of assistance?"

"No, everyone is back in Iowa," I said.

"I see. Perhaps I could help then?"

"Oh, that's not necessary . . ."

He held up his hand to halt me. "If you would excuse me a minute, please." He walked stiffly over to the bartender, said something to him, and was handed a telephone from under the counter. In less than a minute, he was back at our table with his engaging smile focused on me. "I've just spoken with my chief engineer and he would be most pleased to repair your boat in the morning, and," he added in the same breath, "as long as you are unattached, then allow me to show you around the city tomorrow, agreed?"

"Captain Peters, we really couldn't expect . . ."

"Now, Mrs. Morgan," he broke in, "I do insist." He gazed firmly at us. "It would be my pleasure."

I looked at Ludy, who also seemed captivated by the Captain's politeness. He nodded. "Very well. We appreciate your kindness," I said.

"Ma'am," he winked and took my hand. "My distinct pleasure."

When our waitress returned, Captain Peters advised we order the Creole chicken with an avowal that he hoped someday to treat us to the authentic recipe of New Orleans. "Actually," he continued, "the best Creole restaurant in the country is located in Baton Rouge."

"You must know the cities along the river well," I said.

"For thirty-two years I've logged every foot of the lower Mississippi. I could tell you stories that no one would believe, but they're true; I witnessed them." He listed his favorite cities and the reasons why, and then began a long narrative about how the river had changed since he had grown up along its banks near Greenville, Mississippi. He continued through dinner, as I tried vainly to shuttle my chicken to Ludy, but we both found it too spicy. Captain Peters grinned and warned us away from Cajun cooking if the Creole was not to our liking.

After dinner, he wondered aloud if we would care to see the Gateway Park, which was a short walk away. Ludy and I had no objections, and after attempting unsuccessfully to wrestle our checks from him, we followed the Captain out into the city night. I revealed my naivete by spouting that I had never seen so much traffic at night before.

"You've never been to Saint Louis before?" he asked.

"I've hardly ever left my farm," I explained. "This is my first real trip to anywhere. Seeing the city all lit up makes me a little giddy."

Captain Peters pointed out that the 630-foot Gateway Arch was a symbol of westward expansion. He led us around the park, which was bordered on the west by modern buildings and the spires of the Old Cathedral. "And just past the columnar high-rise there," he said, pointing, "is Busch Memorial Stadium, and the dome just beyond is the Old Courthouse. Many more stately buildings in this vicinity have undergone complete restoration."

"There sure is a lot of activity," Ludy said. "I can't imagine how many people live here."

"Wait until our tour tomorrow," Captain Peters said. "If you're interested, I'll show you the world's largest brewery. The Anheuser-Busch plant covers over seventy city blocks."

"Hey, that would be great!" Ludy brightened. "Do they give samples?"

"Ludy," I cautioned.

"Just joking," he said.

"Where else would you like to go?" the Captain asked, clasping his hands together. "The zoo is marvelous, and there's Busch Gardens and Six Flags, the amusement park."

"Yeah, all of them," Ludy shouted.

The Captain looked to me and winked again. "I'm not sure we can manage all of them in one day, but we'll try."

He walked us back to our boat and left us with instructions to be ready at seven sharp. After Ludy had settled down in his bed, I thought about Captain Peters. He was at once formal and intimate; I felt immediately relaxed with him, and yet his doting concern and his charm, his apparent strength and assurance, made him something of an enigma. Perhaps Pastor Bill was the only other man I had known with similar complexities. Captain Peters was an attractive man, a stranger who had thrust himself into the midst of my life when the confidence that had carried me forth was faltering. Surely, the providence of my heavenly Father was at work.

25 At exactly seven, Captain Peters and his engineer, a barrel-chested, gruff ex-stevedore with forearms like steel cable (he answered to the name "Catfish") arrived in a Cadillac. Captain Peters assured us that Catfish, who could dismantle and rebuild any boat within twenty-four hours, would take *Ark II* down to their cargo dock a mile and a half farther down river, and have the engine repaired by that evening. As we drove away from our mooring, I felt a jolt of anxiety that maybe I wouldn't see our little boat again. But the Captain's easy manner pacified any doubts. He asked how we had slept.

"Terrible." I massaged my forehead. "Traffic noise all night."

"Me too," Ludy said. "Those trucks roared through without let-up."

"That's one thing I don't miss when I'm on the river," Captain Peters said. "My cabin is nearly soundproof. Remind me to show it to you. Well," he sighed, "if it's acceptable, I suggest we take in the zoo first. The animals are usually fed early."

We assented, and the Captain sped past the commuters heading to their offices and factories. On the way to the zoo, he gave us a concise history of how flatboats and keelboats in the 1800s were ousted by steamboats for hauling commerce until the steamboats gradually lost favor with the advent of extensive railroading. Ludy asked about the *Stonewall Jackson,* and Captain Peters, with a wry smile, invited us to dine aboard with him that evening when he would be happy to show us his tow.

Saint Louis Zoo, with its acres of naturalistic settings, was just beginning to wake up. Wildlife I had never seen before paced about waiting for breakfast. African wildebeests, giraffe, a slew of springbok, bears, two slumberous lions that refused to budge from their patch of sun when hunks of meat were tossed at them, kangaroos, elephants with mottled skin, an orangutan that reminded me of an elderly neighbor back in Iowa, a walrus floating on his back with one eye open watching me watch him—we strolled through the park fascinated at the array of God's creatures. I couldn't quite picture loading them two by two into a boat.

Ludy pointed out that the backgrounds to many American animal exhibits looked just like the palisades we had seen along the Mississippi. Spruce trees grew out of rocky, limestone formations, providing shade for foxes and badgers. A raccoon that could have been Hobo's big brother prowled above an artificial waterfall. I felt a twinge of guilt, remembering that our own masked menace was securely locked in his cage for the entire day.

I refused to go with Ludy to view the snakes, opting instead for the aquatic display where so many of the fish I had seen floating belly-up in the last couple days were identified. The carp and catfish I knew, but the drum, shad, buffalo, sturgeon, and spoonbill were unfamiliar.

Captain Peters and I rejoined Ludy and decided that we had covered enough of the zoo. Ludy's hunger pangs took us to another recognizable arch—the golden arches of America's hamburger giant. I was out-voted in choosing the next attraction. Ludy's pleading for the brewery tour won out, so we piled back into the Cadillac and headed for the Anheuser-Busch plant.

Our tour guide, a petite brunette, met us at the door of the brew house and announced that we were about to enter the plant where over five million barrels of beer were produced each year. As we followed, straining to hear her explanations, I became hypnotized by the technical wizardry propelling the line of bottles and cans—nearly ten million each day.

I entered the courtesy room with trepidation, but a hostess offered us our choice of the special brew or a sarsaparilla. Ludy and I picked the sarsaparilla, a sweet, non-alcoholic concoction as thick as maple syrup. The room was decorated in a splendrous Victorian rococo, our information booklet said, with bronze hop vines twining the length of ornate chandeliers, and gilt acanthus leaves wreathing the capitals of the interior columns. I told Captain Peters I felt out of place.

"Nonsense," he said. "You look right at home among this opulence. Had you lived a hundred years ago, I could see you descending that staircase in a gold brocade gown."

I stared at the marble steps. "No," I said. "A hundred years ago, I would have been a starving dirt farmer like my grandmother."

"Not as I see you." He smiled.

It was nearly too late in the afternoon to visit Six Flags, but Ludy insisted. On the way I watched silently as row after row of houses blurred past our concrete river.

"Do you drive your towboat like you drive a car?" I asked the Captain.

"Faster." He grinned. "I own the river." I caught Ludy's eye in the rearview mirror. He shook his head and made a disapproving face. At least the Captain was honest.

I was too exhausted from our day to get excited about rollercoasters and stomach-churning whirligigs, but as soon as we entered the gate, Ludy dashed off toward the most vicious-looking ride, aptly named the "Gut-Wrencher." Captain Peters and I trailed along and discussed the beauty of the Mississippi Valley, the enormous wealth the tows push, our

232

dissimilar backgrounds. I even began to talk a little about my family and the traumatic loss of Leroy—until Ludy grabbed my hand and dragged me off to a towering Ferris wheel. From the apex of our rotation, I could see miles of streets and houses and city center in the distance, just lighting up for the evening.

When Ludy vanished past the swinging door of the Haunted House, Captain Peters led me over to a bench. "Oh, my feet are swollen," I groaned.

"I doubt if I could walk another step either," he said.

The dazzling midway lights, the screams and aromas and incessant roulette of people made me dizzy. I leaned against him.

"Tired?"

"Uh huh," I sighed. "I've never done this much in one day."

"You've enjoyed yourself, then?"

"Oh, yes. Without you we would have never seen Saint Louis. We probably would still be sitting around a repair shop. Today was special."

"I'm glad." He put his arm around my shoulder.

"I just hope getting our boat fixed isn't going to cost much," I mused.

"Don't worry," he said. "We'll work something out."

"What do you mean?"

"Oh, no charge for my mechanic."

"Seriously?"

"I wouldn't do it for just anybody."

I sat up abruptly when I saw Ludy appear out of the Haunted House in his motorized car. He tried to stay in for another ride, but the attendant made him jump out.

"Was it scary?" I asked as he came up.

"Naw. It was all real fakey."

"That didn't stop you from wanting to go through again."

He shrugged. "What's next?"

"If you don't mind," I said, "I think we'll leave before you have to carry me out."

"Already?" he whined. "We haven't even seen half the park."

"Sorry." I turned to Captain Peters for help.

"Maybe I could talk you and your grandmother in to staying around Saint Louis another day? We could come back in the morning."

"Hey yeah, that would be great."

"I don't know," I said.

"Perhaps your boat won't be completed until tomorrow." The Captain grinned. "You would have no alternative."

"I thought you said your engineer would have it repaired by night-fall?"

He tried to be apologetic. "Well, I don't know for sure."

"Oh, all right," Ludy consented. "While you're deciding, I'm dying of hunger."

"My chef is preparing a special dinner," Captain Peters said as he ushered us toward the parking lot. "He's a remarkable chef."

During the drive I was oblivious to everything except my tired eyelids that drooped lower and lower until I gave in and dozed, my head tucked between the soft folds of the seat. When we reached the *Stonewall Jackson,* our *Ark II* was anchored like a toy boat next to the gargantuan tow. I stumbled from the car, unsure if I was awake or still dreaming.

Captain Peters led us up a winding staircase to the plate glass control room. A console of lights and knobs lined one wall like the cockpit of an airplane. He switched on a spotlight and swept the river, then turned it on *Ark II,* illuminating the boat in an uncanny glow.

"That's how she appears when we're bearing down," he said.

"You sound almost disdainful."

"Do I? I'm sorry, I didn't mean to be. But usually, the pleasure boats are a nuisance. Some boaters are on the river two or three days out of the year, and they just foul up our operations. Believe me, I wouldn't try to run you down."

"I hope not!"

"Come on," he said. "Let's go see about dinner."

His quarters were larger than I expected. The whole cabin of our boat would have fit neatly into his bathroom.

"One of the amenities of being a captain." He winked. He left Ludy and me alone while he went to check on dinner preparations.

"I can't believe this," Ludy said. He snooped in the closet. "He must be rich. There's about twenty pairs of shoes. And this carpet—it's like jungle grass, it's so thick."

"Well," I reasoned, "a Captain is responsible for millions of dollars worth of cargo every year. They're professional career people."

"I guess." He spread-eagled onto the sofa.

Captain Peters returned, exuberant since his chef had outdone himself that evening. We relaxed on the sofa while Maurice, an authentic French chef in a white suit, served us exotic dishes, which he described as being from the "Provinces."

"Thank God for sending you to us," I told Captain Peters after I could eat no more.

"Why thank Him?" he said brusquely. "I arranged this day."

"Captain Peters?" His response had startled me. I looked to Ludy, but he was staring absently at his second cola. "I believe God watches over us, don't you?"

"Why should I? I work hard. He hasn't done me any favors. Let me tell you, I worked myself haggard as a deckhand for two years before I got my mate's papers. It was another four years before I got my pilot's license. Do you know what that requires?"

Ludy perked up. "An examination?"

"Not just an examination," the Captain continued. "Coast Guard requires a map drawn from memory of whatever stretch of the river you plan to work. Between here and the Gulf, that requires every buoy, point, sandbar, and all the bank lights by name."

"It sounds difficult," I said.

"It is! Nobody watches over my life but me. God included."

"I'm sorry you feel that way."

He leaned back and closed his eyes. "I don't need pious moralism."

"I apologize for offending you."

For the first time he seemed weary, his face chiseled and rough. He shook his head. "I'm just tired."

"Ludy and I had better go, then."

"No, no—forgive me." He jumped to his feet. "I'd like Ludy to see the boat. You'd like that, wouldn't you?" he asked Ludy.

"Sure." Ludy set his plate down on the floor.

"Let me ring for a mate." He pressed an intercom switch and called for someone named Johnson. "These commercial tows," he told Ludy, "employ hydraulic steering, echo sounders, pneumatic hoists, radar, and fathometers."

"All that?"

"Oh, yes. We have nine thousand horsepower grinding away. We can't make any mistakes."

"Nine thousand horsepower?" Ludy asked, agog.

"I'll have Johnson show you." Johnson, a squat, thin-mustachioed young man knocked on the door. Ludy followed him out, stopping to ask if I wanted to go along.

"We're going to talk," Captain Peters answered for me. "You'll enjoy the engine room."

I slid hesitantly to the end of the sofa as Captain Peters sat down next to me. "Would you like an after-dinner drink?"

"No, thank you." He reached over to a storage cabinet next to him and removed a bottle of gin. I realized, as I watched him pour a half glass, that the strenuous day and rich food had made me slightly nauseous. I wanted to lie down on my own bed.

He took a drink, gargled it from cheek to cheek, and swallowed. His hand slid across to mine. "I'd like you to spend the night with me."

"What?" A flush of fear swept over me.

"Oh, come now," he said quickly. "You don't really think I'd go out of my way to waste a day and give your boat special consideration, not to mention a twenty-two dollar an hour mechanic, without expecting some gratitude from you."

"What?" I sat up, rigid. "I assumed you chose to help us because you liked us and because you were kind and compassionate."

He paused, his other hand stroking the hair at the nape of my neck. "You're lovely."

I sat paralyzed. "You're lonely, too, like me," he continued. "A lonely widow who needs affection." He bent over to kiss my neck. I pushed him back.

"You don't care about me, do you?" I glared at him.

"Oh, but I do. You're very attractive, and you want a man."

"I don't either."

"Your grandson can spend the night on your boat, and you can stay here with me."

"I will not!"

He pulled me close. Angry and scared, I resented his betrayal. I wanted to hurt him in some way, but he was too strong for my feeble resistance.

"I won't force you to spend the night if you don't want to, but I do like you," he whispered.

"Then let go of me!"

He kissed my ear. "Dorothy . . ."

Suddenly I went limp and began to cry. He stroked my cheek. "You said you enjoyed today. I wanted to make it special just for you. It's customary to thank someone when they've done something nice for you." His voice was lulling. "I think you do owe me your gratitude. That's all I ask."

My thoughts were in turmoil, but I managed a silent prayer. *Oh, Lord,* I pleaded, *help me out of here.* I was aware of someone's presence. Out of the corner of my eye, I could see Ludy standing in the doorway, perplexed. I pushed forward, away from Captain Peters's arms, and stood up. By the time I turned, Ludy was gone.

I pointed a shaky finger at the Captain and backed away. "You, sir, are not a gentleman. You have manhandled me. You have insulted me, and you demand me to go to bed with you. I resent your behavior, and I ask God to show you the mercy and forgiveness that I cannot." I grabbed up my purse and strode from the room.

When I got to our boat, Ludy was not there. Hobo, groggy and cramped, yawned and stared expectantly at me. I took him from the cage and held him to my shoulder, hugging him like an infant. Dinah was quiet, her bright eyes glistening in the dull light. *Where had Ludy gone?* I wondered. Still shaking, I slumped to my bed and sobbed.

I nodded off to sleep and tossed fitfully for over an hour. It was almost midnight when I sat up to read the clock. Too distraught to read Scripture, I nevertheless clutched my New Testament, worrying over Ludy. I thought of calling the police. On impulse, I put Hobo's leash around his neck and went onto the dock.

The *Stonewall Jackson* loomed next to us like a menacing evil presence. We were docked in an area of warehouses and freight yards, with a main thoroughfare just a block west. I pulled Hobo along the dock until we came to a gloomy alley where all the streetlights had been put out. Nervously, we trotted past boarded and iron-gated truck windows. Fire escapes rose into shadow above us. The main street was deserted except for an occasional car and a succession of traffic lights that continued from green to amber to red, then repeated the sequence.

We walked three blocks before we came to an all-night service station. An attendant sat in the office reading a newspaper as I came up the drive past the gas pumps. He wore a pistol in a shoulder holster over his stained tee shirt. A colorful tattoo of a snake curled around a flagpole flying the Stars and Stripes covered his left bicep. He stopped chewing a toothpick as we paused at the doorway.

"Have you got a telephone?" I asked.

He jerked his head toward the wall at my left. A black phone hung next to a pinup calendar. I took a dime out of my purse.

"Lady, those things get rabies," he said, nodding at Hobo.

"This one's healthy," I said.

"Tie him outside, will ya?" he snarled.

I led Hobo out front and attached him to a light pole with a half hitch. He sat on his haunches and watched me go back in to telephone.

A sleepy, distant hello crackled with static. "Sheri? Did I wake you?"

"Is that you, Mom?"

"I'm sorry if I woke you."

"No, that's all right. We were wondering just this evening how you and Ludy were doing. Where are you?"

"Saint Louis."

"Can you speak up, Mom? I can hardly hear. We must have a bad connection."

"Saint Louis," I repeated.

"In Saint Louis? Has everything gone well?"

I wanted to tell her that Ludy had apparently run away, at least he had witnessed a scene he didn't understand, and he hadn't come back, and I was upset, I didn't know what to do, we were alone in Saint Louis. . . . But I mumbled instead, "Yes, everything has been fine."

"That's great, Mom." I heard her say something to David. She came back on to tell me that they were moving out to the farm the next week and then she asked if she could talk to Ludy.

"He's not here," I said, my throat constricted.

"Oh sure, it's late, and he must be in bed."

"Sheri," I choked. "Something has happened."

"I'm sorry, Mom, I can't quite hear."

I glanced at the attendant, who continued to read his newspaper. It seemed that I was already talking too loudly. "Sheri, Sheri. . ." I couldn't formulate what I wanted to say, and I was uncomfortable that a stranger was listening.

"Before you go, Mom, I want to tell you that David and I have decided to come to New Orleans when you get there. Is that all right? Maybe even Glenn and Evelyn will come. We can spend a week cruising with you in the Gulf. Okay, Mom? I'm really excited."

"I'm so frightened, Sheri." I held the receiver against my mouth. "I'm frightened." The attendant paid no attention.

"Give Ludy a kiss for me, and we love you, Mom," and then silence. Either we were disconnected or she had hung up before I could tell her why I called. I went out to Hobo and looked back over my shoulder at the attendant, whose eyes followed my movements. His expressionless face was suspended in the reflection of streetlights on the window.

Hobo set a brisk pace for me to follow. At the second intersection I lagged behind and stopped, panting. A glossy green car turned in front of us, went on for half a block and then spun around and headed back, slowing as it approached.

A young black stuck his head out the window and called, "Hey, Momma, where ya goin'?" Two other men sat in the front seat beside him. I crossed the street and walked determinedly on. The car pulled up to the curb behind me, and I heard another voice taunt, "What y'all got there, Momma?" I ignored them. "You like coons?" he shouted amidst the raucous laughter of his companions.

I kept walking and tried to gauge how close the car was behind me as I watched for the side street that would lead back to our boat. When I recognized the street sign, I decided to walk to the corner, turn and run for the boat, hoping to lose the car if it followed. When I was abreast of the intersection, I darted down the alley, Hobo scampering at my side.

The car didn't follow immediately, but halfway down the darkened alley, I heard tires squeal and headlights swung into the alley behind me. I ran on and frantically pulled two garbage cans over, expecting them to slow down the car if they rolled in its path. As I neared the river, I could see a sweeplight patrolling the channel while a tow chugged upstream. My foot got tangled in Hobo's chain, and as I hopped forward to clear it, my other foot snagged on a pavement crack, and my ankle twisted.

Limping the last fifty feet to the dock, I prayed the men would give up their chase. I crouched down next to a mooring post and steadied Hobo, who also gasped for breath. The car must have halted, because the lights receded and then vanished. A forlorn horn wailed from across the river. Perspiration dripped along my neck, and I began to shiver as I went below, even though it was a stifling night. Ludy had still not returned.

"The Lord is my shepherd," Dinah greeted us. I gave Hobo a dish of water. He lapped it up greedily. There were only a couple of small ice cubes in the refrigerator to press against my discolored ankle. I hoped it wouldn't swell too badly.

When I thought about the events of the evening, I began to shake uncontrollably and sob. "If only Ludy would come back!" I moaned.

It was nearly two in the morning by the time I calmed down enough to think straight. At least I hadn't been harmed. Difficult as it was, I tried to force the worst imaginings about Ludy out of my mind. *Dear Lord,* I prayed, *You said, "Come to me, all you who are weary and find life burdensome, and I will refresh you."* A burden I could no longer bear had brought me to the point of despair. "I am weak and stupid and not worthy of anyone's love." I cried bitterly. I had caused Ludy to run away, and now he could be anywhere. I sat on the floor and then lay on my back with my knees bent. Tears and sobbing brought no relief. I prayed beseechingly for God's love, for His intervention. I had once experienced Jesus' touch, and now, more than I could express, I needed the Comforter He had promised.

A warmth began to creep up my legs. My breathing became regular and a stillness rose up inside. I listened to my exhalations and covered my eyes with my hand. Both arms began to tingle.

An unmistakable voice spoke to my spirit like a mother, whispering to her feverish child. "Be stilled, the storm is abated," it spoke. "You have loved Me well, and I have heard you call out in your distress. Know that I am with you now, near you now, and forever in you, even as you are in My thoughts. Be still and listen. You are My child, and I will not abandon you." I cried again in joy until I felt the pain drain away.

26

I didn't know how long I had been asleep, but when I opened my eyes, Ludy stood above me, staring anxiously at my prone figure.

"Are you all right?" He helped me sit up.

"Are *you* all right?" I asked him.

"I thought you'd had a heart attack and fallen on the floor. You scared me to death."

"I did? I was worried sick over you. It's almost five A.M. You don't know how I've cried." I dabbed my sore eyes.

"Well, I figured you would be busy with Captain Playboy," he sputtered.

"Don't say that, Ludy. I'm sorry you saw what you did, but you don't understand what was happening."

"It was pretty clear."

"But you're wrong, very wrong."

"So what were you mooning up to him for?"

"I wasn't. Believe me, he displayed how cruel and selfish he was last night. His behavior disgusted me."

"Oh yeah?"

"Yes. I'm sorry I gave him so much trust."

"You mean he put the moves on you?"

"That's one way to put it. I didn't encourage him, Ludy. In fact, I don't even want to think about him anymore. It makes me angry. Let's just drop it. I'm sorry, okay?" I put my arm around him. He looked down awkwardly and muttered, "Okay. I should have punched the guy."

"Don't feel that way. I'm okay. Now, where were you?"

"Walking."

"Just walking?"

"Uh huh."

"All night?"

"I said yes," he snapped. He shook his head, then rubbed his eyes. "I'm sorry. I just didn't know what to do. I don't know. I felt kind of . . . in the way, you know?" I nodded. "There wasn't any place to go. You and that crazy raccoon and our preacher bird there are the only ones that I've. . . ." He broke off, and his eyes teared up. I hugged him to me.

"I know, I know," I said.

He looked up at me bleary and woeful. "I even prayed. I didn't know where I was going, but I even prayed. You were all I had to come back to."

"I know. It's all right now." I stroked his forehead. "Would you like some milk?'' I stood up to reach for the refrigerator but nearly collapsed with pain.

"What's wrong?'' Ludy asked, alarmed.

I hobbled over to the counter and braced myself while I took down a glass. "I turned my ankle.''

"How?''

I remembered what the Holy Spirit had spoken to me. The fear was gone now. I poured a glass of milk and handed it to him.

"How did you turn your ankle?'' he repeated.

"Hobo and I went out jogging.'' I smiled wanly. "I was just . . . careless. You know me.''

He downed the glassful and wiped his mouth. "It's too late to try to sleep now. How about if we get out of here?''

"I'm all for that,'' I said.

Ludy started the engine. It sounded better than it ever had before. "It's fixed!'' he shouted down to me. As he backed us into the channel so we could come about with the current, I searched for something to wrap my ankle with. I located a pillowcase that Hobo had torn for his bedding, and when I began to wind it, he dashed out from under the table chattering, grabbed the other end, and tugged it away from me. "All right, all right,'' I conceded. "You have property rights, too.'' I crawled up on deck to watch us depart Saint Louis while the sun made a welcome appearance over the grim smokestacks.

We were two hours finally getting clear of the congested river traffic south of Saint Louis, but after the last dikes and embankments had faded away, the precipitous cliffs we had been accustomed to changed into sloping farmland where fields of alfalfa and corn and soybeans came right to the edge of the river.

Next to our log entry for departure time and river mileage, I scribbled the fourth verse of Psalm 34: "I sought the Lord, and he heard me, and delivered me from all my fears.'' I didn't know who the psalmist was that had written the verse, but he had taken the words right out of my mouth.

As we sailed along under full wind power, our spinnaker fluttering ahead of us like an indomitable banner past Saint Genevieve, Chester, Perryville, on our way to Cape Girardeau, Ludy and I sang all the songs we could remember at the tops of our voices. We sang roundelays of "Row, Row, Row Your Boat,'' choruses of Christmas songs, Mother Goose, spirituals from my childhood, refrains from television programs. We even attempted to make up lyrics, but I became tongue-tied, so we quit.

The sky was as clear as we had ever seen it, and the moon hovered above the western horizon like a porcelain teacup until noon. Ludy volunteered to fix sandwiches. He came up from the galley, spread three paper plates out in front of us, and placed a tuna fish sandwich on each plate. We took up our respective lunches, but Hobo, a recalcitrant flouter of good manners, stood on his plate and nibbled at the sandwich.

"Have you ever watched him chew?" Ludy asked.

"He's chewing on something most of the time."

"No, I mean, watch his mouth move."

As I studied Hobo's dainty bites disappearing under the coal-black snout, I could detect nothing unusual. "His whiskers twitch," I said.

"You can't tell," he said with a grin, "but he chews just like you!"

"What?" I croaked and flung my tennis shoe. It ricocheted past him and stopped right at the edge of the gunwale. Gingerly, Ludy leaned over and retrieved it.

"You almost lost a shoe," he scolded.

"I won't be able to wear it for a week anyway." I winced, looking down at the grapefruit that had grown from the side of my ankle.

We passed almost no one for most of the afternoon, though Saint Louis had left an indelible mark on the river. The water was more polluted. A brown scum stuck to the hull, and the number of dead fish that floated past seemed to increase. Ludy complained that all the industry and petrochemical factories and refineries were spoiling the river for everyone, perhaps irreversibly. I reminded him that *people* run the industries, and it is their disregard that causes damage.

"No," he fumed. "It's the big businesses always grabbing for that extra buck. All they want is free sewers for their waste." He spat in the river and went below. A while later he came up with a Corps of Engineers pamphlet in his hand.

"Did you know that the engineers pave the river?"

I didn't understand. "Pave the river?"

"Yeah. It's called *revetment*. They pave the underwater banks with a concrete mattress and then stone above the waterline called riprap, to keep the water from eroding and caving in the bank."

"That makes sense. But why don't they let the river take care of itself, except for the flood walls?"

"Because if the banks cave in too much," he explained, "then the sludge and sediment clog the channel, or pile up in bars, and the bars catch stumps and driftlogs, and you can see what would happen."

"I prefer not to see."

"You know," he said, "you sure are stubborn."

"And you," I replied, "are a chip off your grandmother's old block." He muttered something and went below again.

As we chugged into the Trail of Tears Park at Cape Girardeau, the billowy twilight clouds diffused the sun into scarlet and crimson pillars at the base of a heavenly throne. The still air nearly shuddered with silence, and the sounds of campers on the bank about their suppers were muted. After we tied up to the dock, we sat and watched the sunset, Hobo purring softly on my lap. Ludy brought Dinah up on deck and our makeshift family sat prayerfully until the final rays faded and merged into gray.

No one was attending the water and sewage disposal station, so we went below to tend to our hungers, weary from the hundred plus miles we had covered that day. Ludy insisted on toasted peanut butter sandwiches, and while I fought off Hobo for possession of the peanut butter jar, Ludy sprawled on the sofa with his arm across his eyes.

"You know, we're almost halfway to New Orleans now."

"I know," I said. "Mark would be proud of us."

"So would Mom and Dad."

"Say, I forgot to tell you that I talked with them last night."

"You called them?"

"Yes. When I was worried about you."

"What'd you tell them?" He sat up, alarmed.

"Oh, nothing about your being gone. In fact, I couldn't tell them much because of a poor connection."

"That's a relief!"

"But your mother did say they were moving out to the farm next week."

"Really?"

"Yes. And the big news," I paused, "is that your parents are going to join us in New Orleans."

"You're kidding?" he said.

"No, they are. They even want to spend a week sailing with us along the Florida coast. What do you think about that?"

"Terrific!" He grabbed Hobo and rolled onto the floor. "Oh no!" He stopped and sat up.

"Oh no, what?"

"I bet they're just coming to bring me more schoolwork," he brooded.

"Which reminds me. You had better dig out your books and get busy tonight."

"Aw, but...but..." he stammered.

"I insist, especially since you haven't even looked at them."

"But back home kids won't start school for another two weeks."

"All the better to get a head start on them."

"I'm too tired."

"No excuses."

"Oh, all right. But if I fall asleep with my eyes open, it's your fault."

"Very well." I grinned. "I'll take that responsibility."

He stood up stiffly, stared past me zombielike and walked toward his berth, banging into the wall as he went and caroming forward. He came to rest on his bed, moaning.

"You win," I said. "First thing in the morning, you get out those books or no breakfast."

"Gee whiz, that really hits below the belt."

Ludy's exhaustion didn't keep his mandibles from working over three toasted sandwiches, though. I listened to him snore for about an hour before I dropped off to a fitful sleep. I dreamed that Captain Peters was trying to run me down in his car, and when he forced me to to the edge of the dock and I tumbled into the water, he charged at me in a speedboat. Each time I ducked under the water and came up with fire in my lungs, he spun around and roared back at me. Finally, I sat up wide awake.

Waves lapped the hull, and I could hear the faint noise from a camper's television. I didn't know the camper, but I felt disgust for his or her inability to let nature seep in. I wondered how Jesus would react to all the gadgetry most people found indispensible. I wanted to go tell whoever was watching television to shut it off and listen to the voices of the night birds, the whispering trees, the hypnotic murmuring river. I wanted to say, "Listen to your heart pumping, to your chest rising and falling like the waves rise and fall and the wind rises and falls." But instead, I sat hating a nameless person and dozing intermittently until the sun whitewashed our cabin and Hobo crept up and sniffed my face.

After we refilled our fresh water tank and emptied our sewage, we headed out to mid-river, where the water was as blue and placid as the sky.

"What a great morning," Ludy said as he ran up our main and jib sails. "Don't you feel that we're the only people alive on the whole river?"

"Rejoice and be glad," I said. "This is the day the Lord has made."

Ludy finished cleating the halyard and looked up at me. "He made it just for us."

I smiled. "I don't care if we ever get to New Orleans. The beauty of the river and the trees and the warm air and the blue, blue sky just take my breath away."

"Don't get too carried away," Ludy said. "You're about to hit a channel buoy."

Just as I asked where, we thumped metal. "Can't see it," I said, arching my body out over the water on the starboard side.

"Other side," Ludy whined. "Crank it hard or we're going to scrape a thirty-foot gash."

I pulled the tiller and watched as the intruder bobbed past. Someone had scratched on the side that Harry loved Melba, and there was a phone number under "Melba." I thought of memorizing the number and then calling it at the next town to see what Harry or Melba sounded like, but before the buoy was out of sight, I had forgotten the phone number.

We drifted south all morning. Just before noon we slid into a gradual curve that brought us under the tower spans of the bridge at Cairo, Illinois. We watched the left bank excitedly, knowing that the confluence of the Ohio was just ahead. The river widened as we shot past an island and came suddenly into full view of the broad Ohio. The familiar tows and barges were pushing upstream, and a couple of ski boats cut wakes that rolled under us.

We gawked back at the juncture, speechless as two of the nation's mightiest watersheds met, though the Ohio's expansiveness from bank to bank dwarfed that of the Mississippi. "Hey, guess what," Ludy said.

"You're hungry?"

"Yeah, but guess what else?" I shook my head. "We just went," he continued, "from mile 1 on our charts to mile 975. Welcome to the lower Mississippi. Look out, New Orleans, here we come!" he shouted jubilantly.

"Just tell me," I smirked, "when we get to Memphis first."

27 That evening we stopped over in New Madrid Harbor, Missouri. There were no docking facilities, but Ludy lashed us onto an old fishing shack that protruded into the harbor on pontoons. I sat back and instructed Ludy step by step how to make spaghetti with canned sauce. At one point he turned to me and quipped, "Now I know why women love to cook."

"Why?" I asked.

" 'Cause it's so easy!"

"Watch it, Buster," I warned. "Tomorrow you can make homemade bread."

"Well, not all that easy," he amended.

My sleep that evening was even poorer than the previous night's. I didn't dream about Captain Peters, but I did have the sensation of being chased until I could do no more than fall on the pavement and gasp for breath. I woke myself up. Hobo slept on top of the refrigerator, doubtlessly to be close in case someone had the urge for a snack. With Dinah's head tucked under her wing, she looked like the headless mynah. Ludy's rhythmic breathing counterpointed the river slapping our hull. I listened. Each of them was peacefully sunk in their private dreams. I wondered if I was working up my experience of two nights earlier into something more traumatic than it actually was.

I scuffled over to the map table and took out my New Testament. Paging through the Gospels I landed on Jesus' declaration in John that, "Who soever sins ye remit, they are remitted unto them; and whose soever sins ye retain, they are retained." The message struck me like a jolt of electricity. I hadn't yet forgiven Captain Peters for winning my trust and then humiliating me in his cabin. By retaining my anger, I was retaining his sin. I had to give everything to the Lord, including the revulsion I felt welling up inside.

Dear Father, I prayed, *I am weak, but You are strong. You have searched me and known me, and You know what is troubling my heart. I do forgive Captain Peters and I ask that You take pity on him and touch his soul. I give You all of my possessions, my thoughts and prayers and work. Thank You for lifting this burden from me, and now, I commit to You my sleep also. In Jesus' name, amen.*

An unmistakable heaviness was lifted from my spirit. I realized that to solidify my agreement with the Lord, I should make a tangible gesture. The next morning I would write a note to the Captain thanking him for the splendid day he spent with us, and forgiving him for . . . no, I decided I would ask for his forgiveness. Yes, I could just imagine his surprised expression. And I resolved to add a one-hundred-dollar check for the boat repairs, so that all of his claims on me would be severed. I would hold nothing against him, even though I hoped never to see his *Stonewall Jackson* rumbling downriver at us. Then I climbed back into my bed and slept.

As we rounded the New Madrid Bend the next morning, we almost rammed the towboat *Ruby Lee*. She was turned sideways, laboring at the mouth of Sandy Hook Bayou to extract a partially submerged gravel barge. Ludy brought us alongside the *Ruby Lee* and asked if everything was all right. The skipper, a gray-bearded, skinny old coot, spat a wad of tobacco our way and told us to move along and mind our own business, thank you, he would mend his own problems just fine, thank you. He punctuated his last words with another rifle of tobacco juice.

Ludy saluted when we were downstream of them. "Yes, sir, thank you, sir, thank you right fine, sir."

"Don't make fun of him," I said.

"Well, I was only trying to be friendly."

"I know, but he's probably had a bad day, and we gave him the opportunity to unload some of his frustrations."

"But why on us?"

"Who knows? Jesus said to turn the other cheek, remember?"

"It's easy to say," he groaned.

"But hard to do, I know. I often feel the same way. Still, if you return anger with anger, you're no better than him. He might have a family at home that he's anxious to see, and maybe his problems are delaying him, or he might be responsible for losing his cargo, which will come out of his pocket. Who knows?"

"Yeah, I guess you're right."

I reminded him that it was his turn to change the paper in Dinah's cage. He grumbled but went below to do his chores. Hobo, whose regular custom was to patrol the river from his supine position on the foredeck, napped in the sun while I studied a primitive wildlife refuge on the west bank. We were now in Arkansas. I hugged the right channel to see if the profusion of long-beaked, leggy birds hopping along the slack pools were sandpipers or some other type of shore bird I was unfamiliar with.

Just then Ludy whooped from the cabin, and in a commotion of feathers and squawks, Dinah flapped by me and up into the air. We had always been careful in cleaning her cage to keep ahold of her talons, but Ludy rushed up and announced that she had slithered free this time. She circled the boat twice and then flew off to our right and landed in a tangle of pines. I tacked back upriver and aimed for the spot where we had seen her disappear.

"We'll never get her back now," Ludy whimpered. "I should have held her tighter."

"It wasn't your fault." I tried to console him and watch the river ahead as we neared the bank. "What's our depth?"

Ludy scrambled out to the bow and peered into the water. "I can't see bottom yet."

"What's that sticking up on the left?"

"A tree limb," he shouted. "Slow down and I'll jump out and walk us in." I let the sails luff while Ludy eased down into the water until he found bottom. The water just reached his shoulders. He pulled us ahead with a mooring line gritted between his teeth. "Don't step in a hole," I cautioned. The boat glided in under an overhang of branches. I had to duck while brushing a swarm of mayflies out of my face. We came to a stop and searched the branches above.

"Will she answer to her name?" Ludy asked.

"I don't know, but we may as well try." I cooed her name a couple of times and listened for her response. If she heard me, she wasn't answering. The foliage was too dense to spot her black form. Hobo, seemingly as distraught as Ludy and I, paced anxiously along the deck. Ludy tried to climb the bank, but the mud was slippery and the roots he grasped to pull himself up with tore away.

"This muck is up to my knees," he said. He called to Dinah four or five times in rapid succession, but with no better results. Then, like a voice calling out in the wilderness, we heard a faint, familiar cackle. We were upstream almost fifty yards from where the call originated. Ludy pushed the bow away from shore and splashed us through the brackish, waterbug-thick marsh. I detected a movement in a tamarack. "Hello, hello. Praise the Lord," she repeated. As we drew under her, she bent over and followed our movements forty feet below. Hobo stood up on his back legs and chattered.

"Come on down! Come on, Dinah," Ludy entreated. She stared back at us. "I'm gonna climb that tree," he said.

"No, she'll just fly away."

"How am I going to get her?"

"I don't know. Why don't I try to entice her with bird food?"

I dashed below and returned with her box. I shook it, held it over my head for her inspection, even poured a handful out on the deck, but she just watched and ruffled her wings.

"Maybe if I could just get halfway up the tree," Ludy suggested.

"Give it a try. My method sure isn't working."

He sloshed up the bank, clawing at the mud with his fingers until he had a handhold and could struggle to his knees. But when he tried to shinny up the wide trunk, he had nothing to grab. He jumped a couple of times, but finally gave up and looked at me helplessly. "Now what?"

"Let's pray."

"How's that going to get her down?"

"Well, what do you suggest?"

He shrugged and shook his head. "I just don't think anything is going to work."

"Scripture says," I recalled, "that when any two people ask for something in Jesus' name, it will be granted them."

"He doesn't care about a little bird."

"He does so, and He cares about us." Hobo raced in erratic circles and kept eyeing the bank like he wanted to leap the four or so feet from the boat. "Calm down, Hobo." I picked him up and stroked him.

"What if you bring her cage out? Maybe she'll see it and fly back in," Ludy offered. I went and got it but Dinah merely yawned and sidestepped farther out on the branch.

" 'No place like home' doesn't seem to appeal to her," I said.

"All right, all right," Ludy replied impatiently. "Go ahead and pray."

I closed my eyes and began our petition. In the midst of thanking Jesus for always hearing us, Dinah startled up and fluttered away downstream. We couldn't see where she came to rest. Ludy looked at me. "Boy, your prayers really worked, didn't they?" He waded out to the bow and lifted himself up. Just enough current caught the stern to propel us downriver. I tried to edge us along the bank so we wouldn't catch snags or tangle our mast, but in close enough to spot our flyaway mynah. "Yeah, real good prayers," Ludy whined. "Say good-bye to the Dinah bird."

"I'm sorry, okay?" I scanned the branches, but to no avail. Dinah had flown away or was hiding herself as we drifted past. When we were a half mile downstream, I had to restrain Ludy from casting her cage overboard. "Just simmer down, would you? She's probably better free than cooped up in a cage."

Ludy clenched his fists and stared sullenly at Hobo, who had resumed his pacing and was glancing back at the tree-lined shore.

Then from over the tree tops, we saw the graceful wingflaps of our returning Dinah. She veered low and came directly at us, cawing; then she seemed to backpedal, flapping more rapidly in her descent to the deck. She landed next to Hobo, perching on the mast thwart. Hobo slunk up to her like a contented feline and began to lick her face. She turned her head regally and allowed him to wash her red and white ruff. Ludy slipped behind them and clasped both of Dinah's talons in his right hand and then guided the cage toward her with his left. When she was again securely behind bars, he fastened a deck clamp to her cage so that she would be able from then on to survey the passing scenery with all of us.

Ludy sighed and took over the tiller. "I didn't know I could worry so much over a bird."

"Well, she's not just a bird anymore," I said. "She's fourth mate Dinah Mynah Morgan."

"How about Captain Beak?" Ludy laughed.

"How about don't shipwreck us, and I'll go fix chow."

"Great," he said. As I was going below, he chuckled and added, "Glad I suggested we pray."

"Right," I said to myself. "Glad you suggested it."

That evening we tied up at a ferry landing in Ashport, Tennessee, and went to bed shortly after dark. We had tried to sit on deck and watch the fading sun turn the river copper, but clouds of mosquitoes drove us below. We anticipated reaching Memphis the next day, so we talked before we went to sleep about spending a day sightseeing. Our guidebook implored us to visit Beale Street, the home of W.C. Handy and the "Memphis Blues." We agreed to rest over.

The next morning we wended south through rich bottomland where stands of hardwoods, particularly cherry-bark red oaks, rose 150 feet above the river. Ludy speculated that if the trees could talk, we might have heard some captivating stories about keelboats and river pirates and long-gone paddlewheelers. At precisely 2:00 P.M., we rode the breakwater in toward the Memphis Yacht Club. The building snuggled under the towering skyline on Chickasaw bluffs. A helpful couple in their early thirties caught our bow lines and were plying us with questions before we hopped off onto the dock. They invited us into the the club's air conditioned lounge and treated us to root beer floats.

"You must go see the old Front Street cotton market," the woman instructed. "It used to be the hub of the South."

Her husband warned us away from Beale Street. "It's pretty dilapidated," he said with a hint of Southern inflection.

Nevertheless, after agreeing to meet them for dinner at six, we trekked out into the bustling Memphis streets. Front Street was mostly closed down warehouses, and Beale Street a row of ramshackle clapboards wedged between hominy grits and chitterling cafés. Hobo quickly wore out in the mid-afternoon heat, and Ludy half-dragged, half-carried him back to the boat.

"It looks like any other city," Ludy said as he slumped down on the sofa.

"It must have been grand in its heyday."

"Think I'll take a nap." Ludy closed his eyes and soon dropped off. I sat down at our tiny table to write a postcard to Pastor Bill. My postcard multiplied to four cards, so I dug out an envelope and put the four different vistas of Memphis together. I could have rambled on further, but I promised to write him a more detailed account when we reached New Orleans. For a postscript, I reminded him that we were still reserving room for his passage to Tahiti. As I penned the words, I felt the idea had become less of a joke and more a possibility. *Why not?* I thought. Maybe sharing close quarters—discreetly—with Bill for a couple of weeks would result in our mutual cabin fever, though I doubted it.

That evening, we found out that our young hosts, Alan and Sue, had almost grown up on the riverfront. Sue's family had built and run the Yacht Club since she was a girl. We talked about the vanished antebellum South and listened, rapt with interest, as Alan retold the legends and romance of Memphis from the days when Davy Crockett was a Tennessee legislator. They led us on an after-dinner stroll along the brightly lit Riverside Drive, all the while pointing out the various buildings that loomed against the sky.

Sue offered to drive us around to additional city environs the next day, but one look at Ludy suggested that he was as anxious as I to push back out on the river. After thanking them and going below, I slid down in my bed with a warm glow from their graciousness. The fabled hospitality of the South had certainly not died out.

South of Memphis the river wove through cottonwood and pecan forests. At times the current was so swift we rocketed past interesting bayous and hollows where I would have preferred to linger and explore. We did tie up at a desolate island for lunch. While I cleaned up the dishes, Ludy ambled off for an hour and returned with reports of deer, wild turkey, lizards, doves, and a covey of quail that had leaped into his face and knocked him to the ground.

"You'd better keep an eye open for poisonous snakes from here on," I told him.

"And 'gators too," he mocked.

Continuing down the river, we didn't see any sign of alligators, but we did see where the capricious river had washed out the dying remains of Arkansas City. A wide swath of decimated sheds and buildings and telephone poles tottered on the bank.

"Sure must have been some flood," Ludy whistled.

The wild batture land turned into alluvial farmland which was fenced off by high dikes. Visible on both banks was a nearly unbroken levee and floodwall, which according to our charts stretched from south of Cairo to the Gulf. Ludy wondered if it was longer than the Great Wall of China.

"However long it is," I said, "an incredible labor must have gone into it."

The velocity of the river had seemed to increase the farther south we traveled, which meant more concentration by both of us. Time after time, only the grace of God kept us from running aground on shoals or charging over unmarked obstructions. Even though my confidence in handling the boat was daily increasing, my trepidation about dangers lurking around the next hairpin bend also grew. We were relieved to sail into Helena, Arkansas' tranquil harbor. I made Ludy march off to find a grocery store so we could have a special dinner. I wanted to make a chocolate cake in celebration of Dinah's return and for Ludy's forebearance with my countless mistakes of the past two weeks. And more than anything, I wanted to celebrate the Lord's goodness.

28 The cake came out looking like someone had stepped in the middle of it, but we didn't complain. As Ludy and I straightened the cabin after supper, faint sounds of a carnival wafted through the woods just north of us. We were anchored above the town, right at the edge of a dense timber plantation that was crisscrossed by narrow paths. Ludy suggested we walk over to the fair through the woods. I figured it would be one way to work off the calories from the cake.

Rather than take Hobo, we shut the hatch cover securely and entrusted him to Dinah's care. They had developed an affectionate friendship, which made me conscious of how humans seemed to be the only species out of whack with the sensible machinations of nature. The thought of a raccoon hunt, so popular in the territory we were passing through, appalled me. Hobo, without doubt, was the most intelligent animal I had ever known.

Ludy stuck a small flashlight in his pocket and we were off into the gloomy woods. I couldn't help but think, as we stumbled forward, that surely these were the same woods that Hansel and Gretel had wandered through. I wished I had dropped bread crumbs behind me to find our way back. But Ludy plunged ahead, pausing to listen at times and readjust our direction. After about fifteen minutes, I was ready to give up our position as hopeless, but we came out on a small rise, and below us stood a canvas circus tent.

Huffing down the hill, I could tell this was not a circus. We had come to an old-fashioned tent revival meeting, or as a crude sign said: *Revival Fires.* The service was already in progress with a rotund preacher thundering over the P.A. system in front of a couple hundred people in various stages of enthusiastic response. At the end of each sentence, someone called out an "Amen" or "Hallelujah." What we had heard through the woods must have been the electric organ, I decided. The preacher strutted and hammered his Bible and pointed a caustic finger at different people. Ludy and I stood at the back, just inside the dangling flaps, intrigued by the performance of the preacher and curious to see what was going to happen next.

Brother Calvin, as his faithful called him, leaped onto a makeshift stage and called for an outpouring of the Holy Spirit. A number of hands went up in the air, and two or three heads shuddered forward as people began to go under the power. I felt uncomfortable watching them. I knew my disquiet came from having never encountered this emotional Pentecostalism before, and I looked to Ludy, who only shook his head and stared, wide-eyed. The reserve of our Midwest Presbyterian up-bringing showed through, I feared.

At a signal that I missed, a dozen people rushed toward the altar and collapsed headlong at Brother Calvin's feet. He prayed over each one of them and then nodded to his assistants to lug the dazed anointed out through the back of the tent. I wondered about the fate of those being carried away.

Brother Calvin began praying in tongues and another half dozen folks sprawled backward in the dirt. A black woman began to play a small organ and led the congregation in a rousing "Spirit of Ages." I had never heard such ardor in hymn singing before. The intensity in the sweaty faces of those nearest me was fascinating. One old woman sang so hard, she rocked back and forth as if she might topple over at any moment. Ludy whispered that he wanted to leave before someone made him come up front and foam at the mouth, but I said I wanted to stay a little longer.

Next, the wild face of Brother Calvin bobbed through the crowd as he touched those who were unable to approach the altar. Friends of the fallen assisted those overcome with power back to their feet. I knew, watching a girl in a wheelchair being pushed toward the front, that the time for healing had come. Another woman struggled forward on crutches, and two men led a third man whose spastic body twitched uncontrollably to the weeping Brother Calvin.

He stroked the temples of the girl in the wheelchair and then urged her to stand. She shook her head frightened. He implored her to move her legs. Finally, exasperated, he yanked her hand so she would rise. Someone helped her up and then pushed the chair away so she was without anything to lean on. A stunned hush crackled over everyone's head as she wobbled forward unaided, and then shouts of "Hallelujah!" went up all around the group.

Moving quickly now, Brother Calvin wrestled the crutches away from the next woman, who also teetered, then began to walk stiffly. The man, when his friends let go of him, fell in a heap. He couldn't even lift his head. Brother Calvin called for the prayers of everyone to lift "the wretched, crippled man who Jesus loved so much." The man began to shake, his head and upper body convulsed with frenzied jerks. The zeal of the faithful gathered around him became louder. Finally he sat up, looked directly at Brother Calvin, and then slowly began to draw himself up to his feet. He held his arms out like a baby on the verge of his first steps and lunged forward. Brother Calvin caught and embraced him. The man then walked under his own volition and even started to leap and frolic around the altar. The entire group wept openly.

Ludy went outside, and I promised him I would follow shortly. A woman was brought forward on a stretcher. Brother Calvin bent down, then repeated what she whispered to him. She had been totally paralyzed from the neck down in an automobile accident ten years ago, he said. To demonstrate the deadness of her body, he extracted a silver lapel pin and thrust it into her arm to the gasps of the congregation. He prayed and prayed and cajoled and rebuked Satan, but the woman did not budge. He called a number of elders to join hands in a circle around her, and the organ started up again while everyone sang "Will the Circle Be Unbroken?" The heat was sweltering, for the surrounding trees cut off any breeze. I had begun to feel faint, so I went out to find Ludy. My head throbbed. The chorus went on as I walked around the tent, my eyes becoming accustomed to the dark. Ludy approached me from the back of the tent.

"Come here," he whispered, taking my arm. "I want you to see this." He led me to the back of the tent where one of Brother Calvin's assistants was arguing with the man cured of his spastic body. We stood in shadow and listened as the song ended and the drone of the praying group swelled again. The cured man was demanding ten dollars.

"I said five now and five more after the offering," Brother Calvin's assistant argued.

"You ain't gonna cheat me now, are you?" the man retorted. "I know what I got coming to me."

"Listen," the other insisted. "I but got only two fivers here, so you got to wait."

"Why don't you give me both?"

"I can't do that. You see me after the service and I'll even you up."

The cured man grumbled, but finally walked past us as if his legs had never in his life been the useless chunks of flesh they were minutes ago in the tent. I cautioned Ludy not to talk anymore until we were away from there.

When we reached the top of the hill and looked back, Ludy snorted and said he didn't care if he ever saw the inside of a church again.

"It bothers me, too," I responded, "but you can't lump all churches into one."

"That was so phony!" he said. "Don't you think they know that? It was as bad as that phony professional rassling on TV."

"I'm not arguing with you. I just think you've got to remember that

257

it's not the man, not the Brother Calvins that are important, but it's God."

"They got what they paid for," he said. He switched on his flashlight and led us back through the woods. Whoops and hollers from the tent drifted through the otherwise still night.

"Scripture even says that there are always going to be false prophets. Don't you know that Satan is called the father of lies and he can even masquerade as an angel?"

"I don't want to hear about it," he snapped.

I followed in silence for a ways. "You know what happened with your father's accident. You can't deny that."

He stopped and stared at me. "I'm just sick of all these people who pretend to be God's servants when all they want is somebody else's money in their pockets. Can you imagine what his take is going to be tonight?"

"I'm not defending Brother Calvin. Look at Pastor Bill. Do you think he would prance around like that? Do you think he's only interested in money? Ludy, don't put religion down because parts of it are false. Reject Brother Calvin, but don't reject Jesus. Brother Calvin doesn't love you, but Jesus does. That's what is important."

"Yeah, okay," he said. "All that stamping and hollering gave me a headache. Let's get back to the boat."

We retraced our paths exactly and within twenty minutes, we broke through to the river. Suddenly Ludy grabbed my arm and shushed me. Our boat was about thirty yards out into the river, and a shadowy form crouched at the tiller.

"Somebody is stealing our boat!" I hissed excitedly.

"Just keep quiet," Ludy said. "We shouldn't let them know that we're here."

"Shouldn't we call out and tell them to stop?"

"You think they will if we ask them? 'Course not." He began to remove his tennis shoes.

"What are you doing?"

"I'll swim out after them," he said.

"Oh, no you're not. What if they hit you over the head? Besides, they're going too fast now." The boat was still drifting. Whoever had stolen it was not using the engine.

We followed along the bank. "If they don't go far, we can always double back and get the police," whispered Ludy. I kept up with him as he stayed even with our drifting boat. There was no moon, or we might have been able to see who was on deck. The boat began a revolution in the current.

"Geez," Ludy said. "They sure don't know how to steer it." The boat swung all the way around so the bow was again heading downriver. I was panting by the time we drew abreast of the town, a half mile from where we had moored, but Ludy spurred me on. I raced to keep up.

"Why don't you go on ahead?"

"No," he insisted. "We've got to stick together."

"What if I fall down?"

But he didn't answer. He was loping ahead and trying to dodge pockets of muck and saw grass that lined the bank. As the reflection of lights from the town faded, the river became ebony, and I could barely see our boat. Ludy pushed through a thicket of vines and tripped. By the time I reached him, he was on his feet and tracing his way ahead past a gorge where a rowboat was upended. He went over to flip it on its hull, but it was chained to a tree. We sprinted to catch sight of the boat. It had vanished around a bend.

"I just hope they don't go to the other shore," he panted.

My lungs burned as I fought awkwardly through the grass, waving away mosquitoes. A bug flew into my open mouth and made me gag. We momentarily lost the river in a thick cluster of bushes, but Ludy swung fiercely at the drooping vines until we were free. When a rocky promontory barred further pursuit, Ludy hesitated a moment and then lowered himself into the river. I watched him wade along the outcropping. He slipped once and went all the way under, but he came up and swam forward until he found his foothold. Not wanting to remain alone, I jumped into the water. One of my shoes caught, stuck in the mud. I reached down and retrieved it, but my hair got wet in the process. I avoided the hole that Ludy had gone down in and after about five minutes of wobbling forward, we came to a low incline. The boat was out of sight. He drew me belly-flat onto the bank. We lay numb and out of breath, listening to the river purl at our feet.

"Now what?" I asked.

"Go back and see if that backwoods town has police," he said as he sat up. I lay silent, my foot sore from a rock I had stepped on.

"Listen," Ludy whispered. I tilted my head to hear out of the ear that had not taken in water. Through the trees ahead, a couple of men were talking quietly. We crept forward on our hands and knees and came to an inlet. Our boat was tied to a dock of floating gas drums. Beside the boat was a fishing shack, its door ajar. One man stood in the dim light of the doorway and spoke to another who knelt on our bow. We were unable to hear what they said because of the distance and also their garbled Southern accents.

"Do you want me to stay while you go fetch the police?" I asked Ludy.

"No way am I going back through that jungle," he whispered.

"Well, we can't just walk up and demand our boat back."

We watched them converse. I slapped at an insect that was boring into my neck. Both of us smelled like river slime, wet and uncomfortable. I wanted to pace right up to them, but I didn't know how they would react. My brazenness could result in another swim, only perhaps with my hands and feet corded together. I asked Ludy what he thought.

"Well, they may go to sleep soon and then we could sneak down and untie the boat. Or, if we wait too long, they may decide to go. I don't know yet."

"I feel like a pot roast being gnawed on by all these mosquitoes."

"Hey, they're both going inside," he breathed.

The man who was on the bow had climbed onto the drums and was crawling up to the shack. The other man lit up a cigarette and flicked the match into the water and went inside.

"Let's use stealth," I suggested. Ludy led me around the small cove, and then to get close to our boat, we had to crawl under the light which came through the broken panes of the shack's lone window. Ludy picked up a rock as we crept up to the cabin. We could hear their voices distinctly now, but I was still unable to understand what they were saying. Just as we were ready to dash for the dock, one of the men, a scrawny, shirtless man in his forties, came outside and heaved an empty whiskey bottle into the water. He guffawed at something the other said and staggered back inside.

Ludy poked me then, and we ran, crouching, for the boat. I clambered onto the deck first while Ludy unfastened the line. I heard him mutter as he tore at the knot. Suddenly the same man appeared at the door, grunting angrily about his companion's stupidity. Ludy slunk down into the water between the floating drums and the hull while I crouched in the companionway. The first man stumbled to the dock and nearly tumbled in as he set foot on the swaying drums. He yelled an obscenity at his partner. It was obvious they were both drunk. The man shuffled past Ludy and reached up to pull himself onto the deck. He belched as he climbed on and lay face down, chuckling to himself. When he sat up, I leaped out and demanded gruffly, "Who are you and what do you want!"

Startled, he jumped up and slipped off backwards into the water. Ludy sprang onto the boat and flung his rock at the shack as the man came up sputtering. The remains of the glass in the window shattered. The other man froze in the doorway.

"Police!" Ludy shouted in his best bass voice. The man in the shack cried out in alarm and ran into the woods. As I gunned the engine and backed us out of the inlet, the other man was still splashing drunkenly and attempting to pull himself onto an obstinate drum.

When we were clear of the cove, I swung the boat into the channel and drove us ahead. Both of us stank, my foot was cut, and Ludy's face was covered with scratches and streaks of mud like an escaped convict's. We continued on for almost an hour, too stunned to discuss what had happened. Finally I gave the helm to Ludy and went below to check on Hobo and Dinah. They peered up sleepily at me. "Sorry to disturb your dreams," I said, and went back on deck. Ludy glided us over to a private boat dock on the opposite shore while I unlooped our mooring lines. After we had secured ourselves, both of us took turns in the shallow water scrubbing off the remains of our hasty chase. Completely exhausted, I fell asleep instantly the minute I hit the pillow, even oblivious to my throbbing foot, the same one I had injured in Saint Louis. The next morning I discovered that Ludy had dropped off to sleep with a half dozen uninvited guests—mud-leeches on his back and legs that I had to salt off. We were anxious to push as far away as possible from Helena, Arkansas, so we skipped breakfast and departed for Greenville with only crackers to munch.

"Wait until I tell everybody back home about this," Ludy said as he rubbed his red eyes. "Nobody will believe me."

I nodded. "Whoever thought a little cruise would be so difficult."

"Difficult? That was fun!"

I stared at him, speechless. "My idea of fun is curling up in front of a fireplace with a good book."

He began to laugh. "Is that so humorous?" I asked him.

"No, it's not that. I was just remembering when you jumped up and scared that guy. You even scared me. You must have given him heart failure." As I thought about it, I realized how I must have appeared, suddenly popping out of the shadows, and then I too began to laugh. Hobo stared at us as if we were both mad.

"Oh no!" Ludy stopped himself. "I lost my flashlight." But he shrugged it off and laughed again until he nearly rolled into the river.

29 There was no place to tie up for the two days it took us to reach Greenville. We were still worn out from our stolen boat caper and ended up spending the first night moored to a Corps of Engineers dustpan dredge, one of the giant vacuum cleaners that suck tons of river mud out of the silting channels. The next night we anchored in an overhung bayou that could have been named the Kingdom of Frogs. We were just past the confluence of the Arkansas River, and rather than continue on in the dark, we motored into the bayou and nearly hung up on a submerged cable. Besides the incessant frogs, a twenty-foot steel tower with battery-powered blinker lights flashed at five-second intervals all night.

To cap the irritations, Hobo devoured a package of chocolate bars, which made havoc with his digestive system and left the cabin floor sticky and smeared. I couldn't wait to get off the boat when we sailed into Greenville's lazy slackwater port, past a huge tugboat fleet and barge-building yards to the Lake Ferguson Marina.

As I window-shopped around town, I discovered the meaning of the term *sea legs*. I had the strange sensation that the sidewalk was pitching under me, with waves sweeping and rolling the concrete. Ludy told me it was all in my head, but I was sure something inside me still responded to the constant shift of water under our boat. Ludy stopped to play catch with a couple of ten-year-old boys while I went to search the air-conditioned library for history books about the South and the landscape where we were sojourning.

We both benefitted from lazing for a day, and the next morning when we departed for Vicksburg, Ludy and I were robust and Hobo once again his frisky self. Dinah surprised us by imitating Hobo's excited chatter as we cruised past the flat farmland. I even caught a nostalgic glimpse of a Holstein herd browsing a meadow.

In the afternoon we drove aground to lunch on a sandbar and watch a black family wade out into the river with a dragnet and seine for fish. Ludy went over to help them haul in an abundance of driftwood and river scuttle, but only a few chubs, which were returned to the river. They cast the net out again, Ludy wading between a small girl and her husky, six foot brother, and when they lugged their harvest up onto the beach, they picked out two whiskered channel cats that each went over ten pounds, in addition to a slumberous turtle. They offered Ludy the turtle, but he declined. I invited them over for lemonade but they politely refused, all the while looking shyly at our boat. Finally, I persuaded the two little girls to come peek in the cabin, but their parents and brother never did climb aboard. They waved as we sailed away, and I wondered what kind of home they would return to along the meandering river.

From Greenville to Vicksburg we passed mostly unpopulated, tree-lined levees, though we came on to magnificent vistas of the wide flood-plain which extended forty or fifty miles from the west bank to the Yazoo River away on our east. We were in bayou country, as evidenced by the the black and yellow crowned herons high-stepping and calling, "Tell you what, tell you what?"—which convinced me they were gossipy birds.

I especially liked to see the muskrats and otters dive under our path. And we had to contend with colossal tows that squeezed by us in the chan-nel, their great diesel engines thrumming amidst a clangor of bells and horns and shrieking steel cables. Once an amicable tow skipper blared over our radio that we should watch out for shoaling and rockpiles at river mile 480 just ahead. But mostly, Ludy and I basked in the sun and watched the wind ease our sails. It was an idyllic stretch.

We slipped into a nine-mile-long canal, which connected the Yazoo tributary with an oxbow lake and Vicksburg on its lower end. Ludy car-ried Dinah below when she squawked in consternation at the gulls swoop-ing over us like beggars in search of a meal. Hobo sat up on his haunches ready to do battle if any should venture within range.

I tried to decipher the complex chart directions for crossing the busy harbor. Finally I spotted the Vicksburg City Wharf; next to it was the Marina where we planned to dock. After registering with the port authorities, we backtracked to the Yazoo Division Canal to inspect the streamboat *Sprague,* famous for its leading role in the movie *Showboat.* Re-stored, it housed the "River Hall of Fame Museum," a floating collec-tion of Mid-Americana.

"What's that?" Ludy asked the museum attendant about an elaborate gold mechanism.

"Would you believe," the guide said, "a fourteen-karat steam pump that actually was installed in a miniature boat. One of the city fathers had it built for his son. Tradition has it that the little boy set it in a pond where it promptly sank because of the weight."

"What a waste," I said.

"You want to see a real waste?" the young man said. "Look at that." He pointed to a picture on the wall behind us. The scene depicted a huge side-wheeler in flames. "That was the *Sultana,*" he continued. "In 1865, laden with fifteen hundred Union soldiers recently released, it burned to the waterline."

"How?" I asked.

"Boiler exploded."

"Everyone perish?"

"Almost. They were departing for home the next morning."

"Boy, that is sad," Ludy added.

"You haven't seen sad," the man said, "if you haven't yet visited the Union Cemetery at the battlefield."

"You're full of good cheer," I said grimly.

"That's my job." He smiled.

The hike up to the Civil War battlefield was an arduous one, up slopes, down ravines and meadows until we came to the crescent-shaped battlefield, which commanded a majestic view of the river. We stood respectfully in front of the stone memorials and read the story of the seventeen thousand Union and uncounted thousands of Confederate soldiers who died in combat.

"Weren't they all Americans?" Ludy asked me.

"Yes, brother against brother."

"Boy, that was dumb."

"It's not the first time men have done dumb things to each other," I reflected. "And probably not the last."

"There is no sense in that. I can maybe understand fighting communists or something, but men from Illinois fighting men from Mississippi? And only a hundred years ago? That's too crazy for me."

"Me too," I said as we trudged reverently across the lush green battlefield. We said a short prayer and headed back toward our boat. After a sumptuous dinner of fresh fish fillets, we sat and played cards, Hobo kibitzing from Ludy's shoulder and Dinah pondering like Poe's raven. We both admitted we were homesick, but the lure of New Orleans and the open sea drew us on.

"It will be great," Ludy said, "to have Mom and Dad sail with us."

"Too bad T.J. can't come along," I said. "But she has her last year of school to worry about."

"And Mark to fuss over."

"And Mark. I wonder how he's doing? He sure would be pleased with our helmsmanship. I should write him, too."

Ludy slapped down his cards. "You lose again," he chortled.

We had planned to spend another day sightseeing Vicksburg, but shortly before noon we held a hasty officers meeting and decided to push on for Natchez.

We labored through fast, strong river currents and irregular winds south of Vicksburg. The bleak countryside made me think of Humphrey Bogart poling cautiously through fog, but at one point we rode past an antebellum mansion visible through a frame of oak and cypress hung in Spanish moss. We also identified sycamore and sweet gums, but the velocity of the river and the fierce bends caused us to slacken our sails and proceed on engine power.

In late afternoon we started watching for a good tie-up. I spied a levee cutoff, so Ludy swung us into the backwater. No sooner had we reached the calms when I saw a rocky bottom rise up and scrape our hull as we came to an abrupt halt.

"We hung up?" Ludy asked, puzzled. "It looks a lot deeper."

I slid bravely into the water and limped around to the bow. Straining with determination, I shoved and lifted, but the boat did not budge. Ludy said, "Just a minute," and plunged in next to me. Together we got the bow to rock and then with effort, inched it back. I had to stop and rest. The water felt refreshing against my legs, and a pool just to our left looked inviting enough for a swim. We groaned against the hull again, and this time it slipped free and glided backwards. Ludy misjudged how hard we had pushed, because the boat had caught current and began to spin into an eddy. Hobo sat on deck staring forlornly at us while Ludy began to swim at an angle to intercept the free floating boat. He just caught the transom and pulled himself over the side, bruising his shin I was sure, before our runaway boat crunched a stone dike. Ludy maneuvered it back to where I stood, only this time he came in through the deeper pool. As I watched, I noticed a movement toward shore. A snake had slithered off the bank and vanished underwater. I yipped and ran for the boat. Ludy dragged me aboard, mystified.

"What's wrong?"

"A water snake dove in after me!"

"A moccasin?"

"I didn't have time to ask." I shivered and decided against an evening dip. Hobo and Ludy romped in the water though, and by sundown, I was recovered enough to dangle my feet in the cool eddies, but with a wary eye on sudden ripples.

Had we not been following the charts, we would have ripped past the massive bridge span and an indistinct line of buildings on loess bluffs two hundred feet above the east bank, and never seen Natchez. The city wharf was a minuscule dock festooned with barnacles. After we fastened ourselves to a rotted wood post, which threatened to tear loose at any time, we went scouting for a modest restaurant.

In our rambles, we were drawn into a procession of tourists ready to tromp through a palatial mansion that was supposed to have been the family home of Jefferson Davis's wife. Once inside, we were informed that Davis and his wife were married in the elegant foyer. Our tour booklet said the gala event of the year was the Natchez Pilgrimage, held in March. Colorful azaleas bedecked the balcony of a pictured mansion, but I found the contrast between the preserved and columned mansions, with the crumbling, run-down shanties just a block away, too much to rouse my enthusiasm. Only those who clung to the storybook grandeur of the South would fail to see the squalor that most of the poverty-ridden citizens of Natchez had endured.

I desired to visit a church, so while Ludy poked through gift shops for a souvenir, I wandered along a shady block to a red brick church and entered under the pigeon-laden porticoes. Inside, the air smelled a century old. I sat in a pew and inhaled the peace of the building. Two stained glass windows colored the air and illuminated dust motes suspended in the light beams. It was a holy place. I'd come to know that God didn't just dwell in churches, and during the past three weeks, I'd felt His presence more and more evident in the thriving landscape and river and ever-changing sky. I breathed in the stillness. *God has many ways of revealing Himself*, I reflected, and the old church bore a quietude that was unmistakably God's touch. The cross above the chancel seemed luminous in the shadows. I thought of praying, but instead sat silent, wordless, and let my presence be my prayer.

Ludy was munching an ice cream bar when I rejoined him. One of the Victorian movie houses in town was running a Marx Brothers film festival that evening, so we carried a package of cold cuts back to the boat, appeased Hobo's hunger, fed Dinah her daily ration of niblets, and strolled back through the August twilight.

We had been in the South since we departed Cairo, but it wasn't until that evening under a full canopy of stars with luscious oleander and verbena and orchids perfuming the night air, and the drawling conversation of the people lined to enter the theater ahead of us, that I was overpowered with an awareness that we had finally arrived in Dixie. The coalblack loam of my home farm was a thousand miles to the north, a thousand miles, and eons behind me.

30

The next morning we lolled in bed until ten, then I read Scripture for another hour while Ludy ran uptown to buy some fishing tackle. I dawdled over the first ten chapters from the Acts of the Apostles, mulling over how powerfully the apostles went forth in their mission. Even Peter, who always seemed so bumbling and thick-headed, had been transformed into a new, unassailable leader. The Spirit's presence was so evident in the early church that I wished I could have been part of those crucial days.

A squealing from on deck brought me up into the brilliant morning. Hobo was guarding our boat from the approach of a war-battered, gray tomcat. The tom coolly sat on the dock and watched Hobo pace and jabber menacingly. I tried to calm our raccoon, but he kept up his cant until the cat had moseyed off to inspect fish heads. No amount of scolding from me would change his protective caterwaul; so I left him sniffing the air for intruders while I went to prepare our departure.

Ten-mile-an-hour currents south of Natchez sent us across someone's trotline before we could steer clear. Ludy tried to untangle it, but it snapped and sank. I wondered if the fish I saw attached to it would be forced to swim still tied together, or would eventually die because of their predicament. It appeared their freedom would be brief.

We counted a number of pipes that jutted above the river, spilling a brown sewage into the water. The pollution was not only noticeable by the floating scum and increase of dead fish, but the river began to smell, particularly the brackish marsh pools along shore. The garbage saddened us, and the total disregard for river ecology by the polluters was bewildering.

"I wouldn't even swim in some of that gunk." Ludy scowled. "I hope no one drinks the water."

Near river mile 300, an extensive system of control gates diverted the river from meandering off into the Red Atchafalya River System. We marveled at the Morganza Floodway, the interconnecting canals and dikes and revetments, all of which preserved the surrounding countryside from the yearly inundations of spring floods. But the river controls seemed useless since so little was being done to stop the fouling from industrial pollution.

We nearly lost Hobo in the afternoon when his balancing to swipe at a gull caused him to slip overboard. Fortunately, I saw him bob up, and I was able to toss a flotation cushion in his direction. He clung to the cushion frantically until we turned around and grabbed him as he spun past. He gibbered and shook and went below for sympathy from Dinah. I tried to towel him off, but he had crawled into a bedding cabinet to sulk. When I came back up, Ludy pointed to a massive swirl of clouds that was pushing toward us from the south. "Could be a squall kicking up," he said.

"I'd better get on the radio and see if I can get any storm reports," I told him.

The waves grew choppy as I dialed for some response. Finally I cut into the conversation of two commercial fishermen who came back through heavy static and announced that I had better seek calm water and anchor, because sudden storms were frequently dangerous.

I came up to tell Ludy, but he was already motoring us toward a slough. We began to heel, even though our sails were down.

"Watch the depth," he shouted above the gusting wind. I clutched our charts so they wouldn't blow away. From the last mileage marker, it was apparent that we were somewhere above Saint Francisville, Louisiana. "How deep?" he shouted again.

Just as I crawled to the bow, pellets popped the water around us. "Too muddy to tell," I called back.

"Can you walk us in?"

"No," I screamed against the wind. I scrambled back to change places with him, and suddenly we were in the midst of a blinding rainstorm. The boom swung wildly and nearly toppled Ludy into the water. "Look out," I yelled, as he grasped for footing. He cut his hand on a deck clamp.

We had reached the slough entrance, but the wind tilted us so much that navigating forward was nearly impossible. Ludy sprang back to the helm and revved the engine. We drove ahead with only a few feet of visibility. I thought we had cleared the channel when abruptly the bow rose up and a vicious scraping along the hull rolled us to the deck. We had hit a submerged obstruction. Stunned, I sat holding the mast thwart, unable to comprehend the situation.

Ludy crawled below while we continued to pitch just outside the cove. One thought kept running through my mind. *Lord, you calmed the waves and storm,* I prayed. *You calmed the storm.* Ludy's head appeared in the companionway, and he waved me down. I struggled below. Water was seeping into the cabin, nearly knee deep, by the time I reached Ludy. He bent over the radio until he was able to bring in channel 16, the distress channel.

"Second Coast Guard District Natchez," a wavering voice came in.

"This is the *Ark II,* at river mile . . ." He stopped and looked at me. "Where are we?" His eyes were bright, his face unpanicked.

270

"280, 270, somewhere near there," I said.

He shouted the information into the microphone.

"Can you hold your position?" the voice replied.

Before we knew what happened, the entire boat lurched on its side and water swept in the companionway. The floor where Ludy had been standing ripped apart as the river swirled about us. I turned to catch Ludy's hand, but a wave banged me against the steps and lifted me out of the cabin. Ludy floundered behind me and then called out as the boat tipped again and began to sink. I realized that I was free of the boat, but in the rain I could not see the shore. I reached out and felt the tiller that was tearing loose in the current. It jounced against my chest, but I held on. Something jammed my leg against the boat, and for a moment, I thought I was pinned against the upturned hull, but I was able to wrench my leg out. The ferocity of the wind increased. I closed my eyes and prayed for the peace beyond all understanding.

Within minutes the rain shut down and the wind gradually decreased until the black cloud which had engulfed us swept upriver and left us rocking in an eerie glow. Though still overcast, the sky was radiant. We were caught up on something at the slough entrance. Ludy hung onto the mast, which floated perpendicular from the upended boat. He was dazed.

"You all right?" he called weakly.

I bobbed against the transom, still holding onto the broken tiller. "My leg is numb. Something wedged against it."

"Just hang on, and I'll swim over to you." He paddled around the mast and pulled himself along the hull which rose out a foot above water. "Can you swim to shore?" he asked when he reached me.

I shook my head.

"Wrap your arms around my neck then."

I reluctantly let go of the boat and grabbed Ludy's shoulders. He lunged toward the nearest bank, about thirty yards away, and began to swim, dragging me and trying to kick awkwardly without kicking me. He stopped once to cough water, but struggled ahead without protest.

When I felt bottom, I let go and crawled forward until I could collapse on the rain slick mud and catch my breath. Ludy panted beside me, face down. The storm had cooled the air so rapidly that I began to shiver. I rolled over and looked at the boat. All of it except part of the hull which bore a jagged gash, and the mast, was underwater. I sat up and grabbed Ludy. "Where's Hobo?"

He retched and spit out a mouthful of water. "I don't know," he groaned.

"Hobo?" I called.

A slight whimpering answered me. I could just see Hobo riding the wash on a piece of tattered sail at the base of the mast. His black snoot turned in our direction. Ludy swam out after him and returned with our raccoon on his head, his neck and shoulders scratched in the process.

"What about Dinah?" I asked with trepidation.

"No way," he said shaking his head. "Nothing we can do about her now." I nodded glumly, refusing to believe that so much had happened to us in the past half hour. The sun broke through for a minute, but it was on a downward swoop, and within minutes darkness had settled. I tried to dry myself, but everything was wet. Finally I took Hobo's small warmth against my stomach.

"What are we going to do?" I wondered aloud.

"Wait," Ludy responded.

"Wait for what?"

"Morning, I guess."

"And then what?"

He didn't answer. He rocked back and forth in his arms and stared out across the water where the remains of our boat slapped and battered the swells.

Two hours of silence must have passed when we heard a faint chugging upstream. A sweeplight prowled the river. Ludy shouted the boat over in our direction, and soon the light swung directly at us. A weather-worn scow drew up to shore, and an old fisherman demanded to know who we were. Ludy waded out into the shallow water and explained about the squall and our boat. The wizened old man turned his light on our boat, studied it for a minute and then cut his engine.

"What did you pull in there for?" he asked. "Ain't nothing but stumps and snags in there. Wonder is that you didn't go down with it."

"Have you got a warm blanket?" I interrupted.

He stared at me, his thin face bunched around a toothless mouth. "Come aboard then," he growled.

His cabin provided enough room for all of us to sit cramped. He avoided looking directly at us as he spoke, all the while staring at Hobo like Ludy and I were the strange bearers of the old man's dinner for that night. Hobo bared his teeth and gazed back. A bucket of fish bait sat next to me.

"You're a fisherman?" I asked.

"That's right," he said gruffly. "A damn pore fisherman, but I make my wages. 'Course this old tub would soon as gobble fuel as run, but it get me up river and back."

"Back where?" Ludy asked.

"New Roads. 'Bout forty minutes down river."

"Do you mind waiting until the Coast Guard comes?" I asked.

"What they coming for?"

"We put in a call on the distress channel," I said. "They'll be bound to search for us."

The old man sighed and scratched his cheeks.

"We'll be glad to pay you," I added, forgetting that my traveler's checks were probably soaking wet, along with my purse, still inside a cabinet on the boat.

He looked at Hobo and nodded, as if Hobo were the silent leader of our soggy band. The old man did offer us hunks of an acrid cheese and as we ate, Ludy suggested that we call the Coast Guard again and give them our coordinates.

"Call them on what, a telephone?" the old man glowered.

"You don't have a radio?"

"Hell, no," he said. "Wouldn't have one of them squawk boxes either."

We watched him scuffle with a dragnet, then withdraw from under it a bottle of whiskey. He handed the bottle to Ludy, but after one whiff of the contents he passed it on to me. I sniffed the whiskey and nearly fainted from nausea. It was the strongest smelling whiskey I had ever thrust under my nose, and while I was sure it would warm me and help wash down the cheese, I declined and handed it back to the old man. He looked at us ungratefully and took a long swallow.

"Got any family?" Ludy asked him.

"Nope."

"Live by yourself?"

"Nope. I got dogs."

Ludy leaned forward with interest. "Dogs? You raise them?"

"Yep."

"What kind?"

The old man paused and licked his lips. "Blue ticks," he said.

"What kind of dog is that?" Ludy asked.

"Blue ticks? Why, boy, them is coon dogs. You know, coon dogs," he said, nodding toward Hobo.

I suddenly understood his curiosity towards our pet raccoon. He had been picturing our impish third mate fried and skewered, I was sure. Ludy and I were so exhausted that we slumped against the dirty cabin walls and attempted to sleep. The old man sipped the bottle until it was empty, then retrieved another of the same. My head clunked back

273

against the wall and my fluttering eyelids finally shut and I slept. I woke once and through bleary eyes, saw our host snoring with his half-empty bottle cradled at his chest. Hobo was sniffing his hands cautiously, probably aware from instinctual scents that this man was no friend of raccoons. I dozed off again, and when Ludy shook me awake, the sun was just coming up. Stiff and bruised, I stretched on deck. The old fisherman lugged up a net and began to fling it out.

We watched for over an hour as he cursed, drew in his net, cursed again at the piddling catch and threw the net out in a new spot. The sound of the Coast Guard cutter awoke us to the full realization that our boat was wrecked, Dinah gone, and the three of us narrowly escaped from a similar unglorious end. When the cutter swung around the bend, we saw two crewmen scanning the river with binoculars. Ludy motioned them toward us. The Captain was the first one off the boat. He sank ankle deep in mud, but that did not deter him from striding forward and instantly taking in our bedraggled appearance and the torn hull of our boat behind us.

"Are you folks all right?"

"We're alive," was all I could muster.

He took command of the operations at once, instructing his crew to attach their chain and winch and try to right the boat. He sent another crew member for hot coffee. The old man meanwhile had loaded up his boat and was departing before we could thank him. I called a thank you, but he nodded brusquely and steamed away downriver.

"I don't even know what his name was," Ludy said to me.

In my heart I asked God to richly bless the generosity of the surly old man. He certainly proved that the Lord's help comes in all guises.

Our boat was righted in no time, covered with mud. *The Coast Guard works competently from much experience,* I thought. One of the crew climbed aboard to appraise the damage and to retrieve my purse. When he returned on deck, he held up Dinah's cage for us to see, and miracle beyond miracles—she was alive!

The Captain remarked that she had probably been caught up in an air pocket, which was not unusual for boats that go down quickly. When Dinah was ferried over to us, Ludy and I whooped with joy, a sight that brought a wide grin across the Captain's face. The crewman in charge of the winching came over to confer with the Captain, and then with us.

"The damage to your hull is not as serious as I had expected. With a hydraulic pump we can tow it for you."

"To Baton Rouge?"

"There will be some expense," the Captain answered.

"We can't just leave our boat here."

"Very well. But it will take us a day to get it there. Why don't I have the highway patrol pick you up at the next landing and you can catch a bus into Baton Rouge."

"Great!" Ludy responded. "Then we can get it fixed."

"Don't get your hopes too high," the Captain cautioned. "You probably can get your hull repaired, but it may run a couple of thousand dollars, not to mention your engine which is ruined and the damage to all appliances and provisions. You might want to forego the expense and just sell it for scrap wood."

The enormity of his words drove hard into my heart. Already we had invested almost all the savings that Leroy and I had. But what were our choices? I fretted, disconsolate, as the cutter slowly dragged the wobbling *Ark II* downriver.

A chubby highway patrolman waited, hands on hips, as we approached a vine-tangled boat landing. He introduced himself as Joshua D. Clemmens while helping us off the cutter. Ludy and I watched the Coast Guard tow our boat around a bend, both of us depressed by the sight of our wounded home on water.

Patrolman Clemmens did his best to cheer us, rambling on as he drove about our not being the most motley crew he'd helped out. "Why, once," he said, "I took a whole car load of nudists, you know, naked as the day they was born, folks, into Bogalusa for a hearing. Why, shucks, they were just plum crazee, but having no clothes on didn't bother them one shake. Ain't that something?"

"Didn't they have to wear clothes in the courtroom?" Ludy asked.

"Judge couldn't keep clothes on them. Funniest thing. Finally he up and said, 'Well, if the good Lord made you naked and you all don't mind catching cold, then my court ain't goint to stop you.' " He guffawed himself into a coughing fit. "Can I treat you folks to some breakfast? There's a fine little steak and grits place just ahead."

We pulled into the parking lot of the Gumbo Shack and elbowed our way through a group of truckers gassing up their rigs and swilling chicory coffee. Everybody greeted Joshua D. Clemmens.

As homey as the grits and eggs and ham hocks looked, I was unable to eat. Ludy polished off a full plate and then part of mine, but I was too upset to have much appetite. All I could think about was, *What had happened?* Was the boat really wrecked and our trip at an unexpected end? And now, what were we to do?

"Are you feeling all right, ma'am?" Patrolman Clemmens asked.

"Just fatigued," I answered.

"Well, I'll zip you into Baton Rouge and you can rest up in a motel. If you don't mind, my brother-in-law manages one on the south side—the Sleepy Hollow—a fine little place. I could take you all there."

"Why don't I save this for Hobo," Ludy said, holding up the remainder of my ham. "And we should pick up some seed for Dinah."

"I wonder if they're too hot in the back seat?" I said.

"I cracked the back windows, ma'am, but I could run out and check on them."

"No, that's not necessary. The smell of food is making me a little sick, so maybe I'll go outside and wait for you."

Because of the thunderstorm, the early morning air was heavy; by noon the mugginess would be oppressive. I left the back door of the patrol car open and sat on the edge of the seat next to Dinah's still dripping cage while Hobo pounced on a hapless beetle. A couple of fuel tankers idled in the drive, the diesel fumes suffocating me as I tried to clear my head.

What is God's plan? I wondered. *Has He failed us, or have I done something to bring on our troubles?* I could not sort out what to do. A two- or three-thousand-dollar repair bill and perhaps another thousand to replace our cabin would exhaust my savings. To just abandon the boat for scrap seemed impossible. The numerous early morning and late night hours, not to mention Mark's contributions and Ludy's singleminded determination made the boat more valuable than the financial investment. And Ludy had already indicated that he was all for repairing it. I felt a plain and direct reappraisal of our situation was necessary. Ludy would have to know we were nearly broke.

With the wind blowing against my face during the hour drive into Baton Rouge, I began to feel better. As we drove past miles and miles of enormous circular storage tanks and operating towers for oil refineries, Officer Clemmens pointed out that Baton Rouge embraced the largest petrochemical complexes in the world: gasoline, fuels, lubricants, waxes, kerosene—every refinable product passed through the industrial amalgam.

I rode in a daze through the congested city until we arrived at the Sleepy Hollow. When I was finally stretched out on a sag-in-the-middle bed, with Ludy and Officer Clemmens phoning the Coast Guard to locate which boat yard would repair *Ark II,* I shut my eyes and spun earthward, delirious with fatigue, until I hit and shattered into fragments and slept.

31

It wasn't until early evening that I dragged myself out of a nightmarish darkness to the dim room where Ludy, splayed on the carpet, stared up at gargoyles smacking and chasing each other. Gradually, as my eyes focused, the gargoyles became a Tom and Jerry cartoon. I sat up. My mouth felt like a gravel pit. I stumbled into the bathroom, but the water tasted horrible. I wobbled back to bed. "What time?" I croaked.

"Almost five."

Hobo crawled out from under the bed when he heard our voices. Dinah nibbled her cage bars in the corner.

"You sleep?"

He rose to his elbows, still intent on the television. "Yeah, a bit."

"Hungry?"

"Kind of. I bought some candy bars out of a machine."

I massaged my temples. "I feel like I have a hangover. Did the boat get in?" Ludy sat transfixed. "Did the Coast Guard call? Ludy?" I waited until the cartoon ended. "Did our boat get in?"

"Yeah, about 3:30. It's down at Red's Wharf."

"What'd you tell them?"

"What do you mean?" He rubbed his eyes and looked at me.

"Did you talk to Red's Wharf?"

"Uh huh."

"Well? What did you say?"

"I told them to fix it."

I stared down at my hands, away from the bright glow of the TV. I wanted to be angry, but I had known Ludy would be unbending. "I don't think you understand," I said. "Our plans are somewhat changed because of the accident."

"Why?"

"The expense, Ludy, the expense. I don't think I have enough money to build the boat all over again."

"Just repair it," he corrected me.

"But how much?"

"About twenty-seven hundred, they estimated."

"Oh, Ludy!" I buried my face in my hands. Finally I glanced up at him. He watched me, emotionless. "And what then? It takes money for fuel. It takes money for food. We won't even have enough money to get the boat back home."

"Does that mean that Mom and Dad won't be able to come down?"

"Probably."

"They'll be disappointed."

"I know, but what can we do?" I wanted to cry, but I felt empty inside.

"You could sell the farm," he suggested.

"No, I can't. Your family is living there now. I certainly can't ask them to move out."

"Well, if you don't fix the boat, you'll lose even more. At least fixed, you can sell it."

I tried to analyze the possibilities. "I'm all mixed up now."

"Why don't you pray?" Ludy said.

He surprised me. For the first time, he had stated what I had obviously overlooked. I tried to pray aloud, but I couldn't put my heart in it. Ludy listened patiently to my stutterings. Somewhere, I was afraid, I had misplaced my mustard seed of faith. I could see no way out of our dilemma, and God was offering no solutions.

"There's an ice cream shop down the street," he said when I was finished. "I saw that they have a new flavor called Rocky Raccoon. Don't you think we better try it?" He winked.

I stretched and puffed out my chest. "Okay. We'll worry later about what to do." The contents of my purse, which I had laid out to dry, smelled a little muddy, but at least our remaining cash was spared. I put some coins in my pocket and off we went.

From the honks and faces gawking after us, we made quite a promenade—Hobo trotting in front of me on his leash while Dinah rode placidly on Ludy's shoulder. I didn't think the ice cream shop would serve us the way we looked, but the startled girl handed over three ice cream cones—one for Hobo—that he demolished before we were halfway back to the motel. Off against the horizon, gray smoke and flames scoured the night sky. We rehashed our possibilities and finally agreed to fix the boat, proceed on to New Orleans, and put the boat up for sale there. Whatever money it brought would see us home.

"What happens when we go back home?" Ludy asked.

"I don't know. I hadn't planned on going back so soon. I guess life as usual." I fought down a faint stirring of rebellion. It seemed that being a lonely widow had overtaken me again. I had been unable to escape.

I sat in bed until past midnight watching vacuous shows on television, and then I groused about for another hour, unhappy because the room didn't even have a Bible. When I closed my eyes my head began to revolve. I tried to slow my breathing and then count my heartbeats, but I only succeeded in convincing myself that the palpitations I detected were the first stage of a heart attack from the strain of the last twenty-four hours. Finally I dropped into a pitiful sleep.

The next morning we took a taxi to the wharf and inspected the damaged hull. *Ark II,* winched six feet off the ground, was a mess. The interior was mucky and sandy: the gouged hull staves protruded and snapped off as two workers cut away a large undersection. I didn't want to think about how much effort would be necessary to recondition our cabin. We tried to stay out of the way, but one of the workers kept glowering at us. I whispered to Ludy that maybe we were pestering them.

We caught another taxi into town and scouted out a bank. I would need to wire a transfer of funds to cover our repair bill. The bank officer assured us that the money should come through within forty-eight hours. In my head I calculated that after the transaction went through, my account would be depleted. There was no alternative but to sell our boat.

In our wanderings we did happen on a small restaurant that had jambalaya. Ludy sniggered at first, but then he gobbled the concoction. Even better, the prices were moderate, a prime consideration since we were down to our last hundred dollars. I tried not to dwell on money, yet it seemed to be the denominator everything was coming to. For years, Leroy's hard work had made me oblivious to money. As our cash dwindled away now, the necessity of funds loomed larger.

We talked of calling Sheri and David but thought they would disapprove of my investing my last funds in the boat. They would hear the bad news soon enough. We walked around town listlessly, unable to appreciate the French influence of the area. The newness of the previous towns along the Mississippi had evaporated. We only wanted to get the next few days over with.

Ark II was ready for us the next afternoon, but the bank hadn't received the transfer, so we had to spend an additional night at the motel. The following morning the three thousand dollars had arrived. We glumly set about scrubbing out the cabin. Red's Wharf thought our engine would not need to be replaced after all, though it might run sluggish for a while. We chose to forego the replacement of our appliances even though it was apparent the wiring had shorted out. We would exist on peanut butter sandwiches for the day and a half voyage to New Orleans, and then worry about tuning the boat for any interested buyers.

We spent the night aboard on damp bedding, squishing with each step on the wet carpet. No matter how uncomfortable, we were home. The pages of my New Testament had inked together. Our charts were ruined. Shards of cracker boxes and packaged cocoa glumped the cabinet shelves. Only our radio miraculously lit up and sputtered to life.

The boat yard repaired our mast and patched the sails to speed us forward the next morning. We were a long time in leaving the industrial strips of Baton Rouge and not until noon did we see rice fields and moss-draped cypress bayous alternating with farms and occasional industrial smokestacks beyond the unbroken bankside levees. I detected the effect of ocean tides on the river, and we spotted oyster boats and shrimp trawlers. The boat handled well most of the day, and by sunset we had covered over half the 135 miles to New Orleans. There was no place to tie up for the evening, so we anchored against a levee as ocean-going tankers thundered by all night. I tried to decipher a page of Scripture, but the words were too faded. Ludy crawled out of his bunk and confessed that he couldn't sleep either.

We sat and reminisced about the past couple of months and the jumble of people and cities and wildlife and river vistas. Every face seemed to vividly reappear. I wanted to store each impression, each moment that flooded in front of me. Without warning, I began to sniffle, then tears began to trickle down my cheek. We had only touched a small part of the world, only the hem of our Lord's splendrous garment.

"I just wish there was some way we didn't have to quit now," Ludy said quietly. "If we just had some way . . ."

"God's thoughts are not our thoughts," I answered. "He must have other plans for us."

"The Lord is my shepherd," Dinah cackled, the first words she had spoken in the last four days.

"But we're so close to seeing the whole world, and to just go back home with nothing, you know, *defeated* . . ."

"But we aren't," I said, biting my lip. My throat knotted up as I tried to hold back sobs. Ludy was right. We were going back in defeat. Even a month and fifteen hundred miles worth of memories suddenly didn't seem important. A huge steamer ploughing upstream bellowed like a river god and faded away.

Exotic ocean vessels began to appear as we drew nearer to New Orleans. We spotted ships from Germany, Mexico, Peru, Sweden, Greece, Nigeria, Japan, and Yugoslavia lining the wharves, next to towering elevators that transferred the mid-continent grain ferried down on tow barges. When one of the tremendous tankers rumbled by us seaward, we dipped from crest to trough to crest on six foot swells. If I ever exerted will power over my unruly stomach, it was then.

Delta land spread out on either side of the mile-wide river. Oil derricks and rigs pumped ceaselessly amid a flotilla of tramp steamers and skiffs, boatels and docked tugs and commercial fishing scows. Finally we chose a pier where two boys were waxing a speedboat. I lowered our sails as Ludy guided us in, thumping hard against the dock.

"You should have come in leeward," one of the boys muttered.

"Sorry," I said, jumping onto the dock. I hitched our lines and then jumped back to help Hobo make the leap. When Ludy had followed us, we asked the boys if there was a telephone nearby. They pointed to a boat shop, the roof of which was just visible past a concrete retaining wall.

"They don't allow pets," one of the boys said, nodding at Hobo.

"Oh, yeah?" Ludy glared at them. "He goes with us everywhere, 'cause he's family."

Intimidated by Ludy's fierce tone, both boys looked away. Hobo scurried up the dock as if everything had been settled, as I loped after him. Ludy caught my arm from behind. "Can't we go have lunch first?"

"There's no sense in stalling now. We may as well get this over with."

"But, but, maybe. . ." He turned his back to me and stared toward our docked *Ark* while commerce boats of every sort clangored beyond. I wanted to delay the telephone call, too, but it had to be made. Ludy and Hobo waited outside while I went into the boat shop. A pudgy man directed me back outside to a telephone booth on the far side of the building. As I dialed the number of my farm, Ludy leaned against a nearby telephone pole and watched Hobo nose a garbage pile. The phone rang three, four times as I took a deep breath and exhaled. And then, distant but familiar, Sheri was saying hello.

"Sheri," I said weakly.

"Nana? Is that you, Mom?"

"It's us."

"My gosh, we've been trying to get ahold of you for the last week. Where are you?"

"New Orleans. We made it."

"You did! That's great. I'm going to have to make airline reservations right away, then. I hope you don't mind if Glenn and Evelyn come along, too."

My eyes clouded up. I looked at Ludy who was gazing at the river, his face expressionless. "Sheri? I've got some bad news." I paused, unsure how to begin.

"I've got some good news for you, Mom, some great news," she broke in. She was making everything difficult for me. I was ready to blurt out that she shouldn't come after all, when she repeated that they had tried for a week to locate us. "We found out from the Baton Rouge Coast

Guard that you had some boat trouble, but we must have just missed you.''

"What's happened?''

"Can you remember when you left Dubuque?''

I searched for the mental picture. "So much has happened since then—it's a little fuzzy . . .''

"Oh, Mom, let me tell you,'' she interrupted again. "You were standing beside T.J. and a photographer from the local newspaper came to take your picture. Do you remember?''

"Yes. What's happened?'' Irresistibly, I began to tingle all over because of Sheri's excitement.

"The paper ran the photo with a small article about how you were going to sail around the world on your homemade boat, and you're not going to believe this, Mom, but the wire services picked it up and have just reprinted it across the country. Even the New York bureau called us to get your itinerary, but we didn't know where you were.''

"I'm not sure I understand,'' I said, dazed. "You said it all so fast. We were in the newspapers?''

"All over the country, Mom!''

"Seriously?''

"Mom, just listen. A magazine reporter called with an offer of money to write your story, you know, follow you around. She thinks it's a great human interest story that will inspire other women to rebuild their lives, too. She wants to fly down and talk over a deal in New Orleans. Can you believe how good God is to us, Mom?''

I couldn't believe just then. I let the phone drop and sank to my knees. Uncontrollable tears, tears of contrition and joy and praise, poured down my face as I flung my arms toward heaven in the phone booth and cried even as I felt Ludy's hands take mine.

Acknowledgments

I would like to acknowledge the support of and faith in *Nana's Ark* of Thomas Nelson editors, Larry Stone, Larry Weeden, and especially Lisa Ferris, whose encouragement and fine tuning helped bring Nana's story to life. Also, I appreciate the writing grant from the Iowa Arts Council that assisted with manuscript preparation. And finally, I owe a great debt to many individuals who taught me about what it is to be a woman: my grandmothers, Mary, Rose, Clara, and Grace, the first Nana; to Dora and my mother, Dorothy, the second Nana; and of course, to my wife, Lynn, who salvaged the story time and again with her patience, faith, and love.

M.B.